I0544354

The Independent Bookworm

ABOUT THE BOOK

In 2002 ADR, the jewel of the southern empire is the city of Cryssigens, where life is an unending carnival of display, while intrigue brews beneath the surface. Nobles, guilds and House Cups scheme with and against each other, even in the best of times. But civil war stripped the city of its Overlord, and now factions emerge daring all in a bid to succeed to the throne.

Captain Justin seeks to win political favor in Tralmachia and return in time to tip the balance. But will the brave officer instead find doom for himself and his loyal men in the haunted hills ruled by the Baron of Blood? Feldspar the Stealthic threads through ancient streets and tunnels, past enemies villainous and monstrous, to locate a fabled artefact in the heart of abandoned Old Cryss. Peril only makes him smile: but how can he choose which of his many faces to honor when the danger bears down on those he loves? Preacher W'starrah Altieri, who loved the Captain and hired the Stealthic, sees too late the shape of the conspiracy threatening her city, her family. Will her unknown allies ever meet, now that she is helpless to halt the release of the Shard Demon?

As darkness and murder clutch Cryssigens by the throat, the flames of destruction reveal... *Shards of Light*.

"Shards of Light" is the last book in the Shards of Light saga set in the Lands of Hope. It is highly recommended that you read "The Ring and the Flag", "Fencing Reputation", and "Perilous Embraces" first.

ABOUT THE AUTHOR

Will Hahn has been in love with heroic tales since age four, when his father read him the Lays of Ancient Rome and the Tales of King Arthur. He taught Ancient-Medieval History for years, but the line between this world and others has always been thin. The far reaches of fantasy, like the distant past, still bring him face to face with people like us, who have choices to make.

Will has written about the Lands of Hope since his college days (which by now are also part of ancient history). He chronicled the adventures of Solmn Judgement dilligently in two tomes of over 1000 pages each (it's now being published as an eBook series and in print) and his Shards of Light series, a sword and sorcery story. He also chronicled stand alone stories like "The Plane of Dreams" or "Three Minutes to Midnight." More of Will's tales of Hope are available at several online retailers.

Find out more on his website: www.WilliamLHahn.com

SHARDS OF LIGHT

Shards of Light
Volume IV

William L. Hahn

Shards of Light, Shards of Light IV
published by the Independent Bookworm, USA und D
this book is also available as eBook at various retailers

If you find typos or formatting problems in the book, please contact
the publisher (www.IndependentBookworm.de).
printed On-Demand Publishing LLC, 100 Enterprise Way, Suite A200,
Scotts Valley, CA 95066, USA, www.createspace.com

ISBN-13 978-3-95681-097-8

Find more information on the publisher's website:
http://www.IndependentBookworm.de

From distant lands and varied ranks came a small band of the bravest and best. They combined courage, persistence, sacrifice and dedication to achieve a wonder unheard of in all the Alleged Real World.

They read the tale entire. And made it better.

For all the sense and humor and nearly everything good in this story, I thank the Writers Exreme and dedicate this book to them.

To Mary Baader Kelly, who got me started,
and by the end was asking for more.
To Antonio Diggs, who understands the epic style better than anyone I know, and makes the world wait for his tale until the fullness of time.
To Katharina Gerlach, who has read everything
and given so much of her knowledge and caring.

There would be no chronicle without all of you.
Ar Aralte!

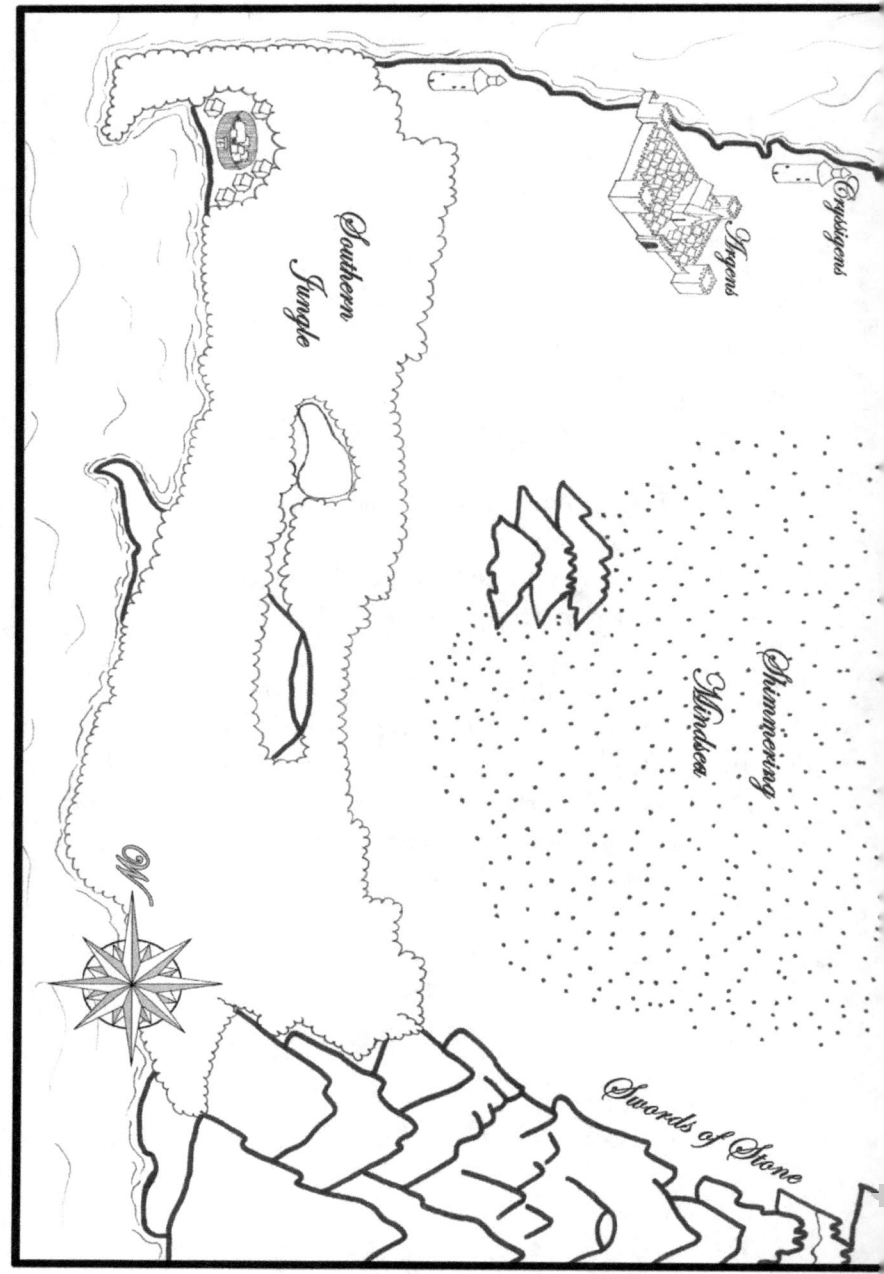

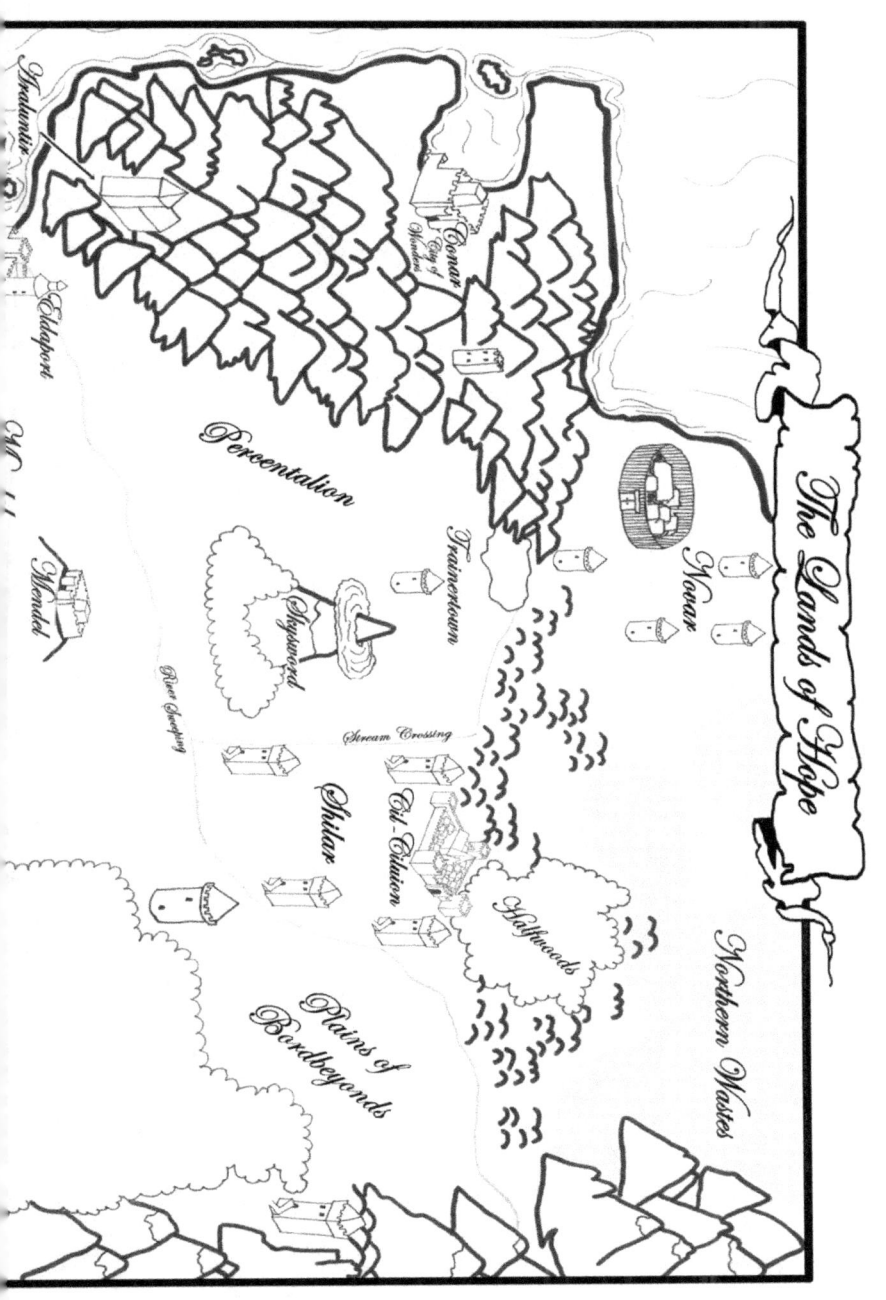

CAST OF CHARACTERS IN ORDER OF APPEARANCE

Shards of Light is set in the North Mark of the Argensian Empire, settled by Elves centuries ago and still dominated by that race. Every character is Elven unless otherwise noted.

W'starrah Altieri	also called Heaven's Eye, Myster, High Priestess, "Star", and Lavender Lady, prophetess and famed beauty of Cryssigens, Purple House leader
Chaktha	human, W'starrah's Nubian bodyguard
Welles	jeweler commissioned by W'starrah
Ellesmera	also called Elle, W'starrah's estranged daughter who has left the city
Myster Tanar'h	High Heart of the Stargazer church in Cryssigens, rival to W'starrah
Devout Teretheny	monk of Sinter
Curate Ekaterinye	also called Kat, Stargazer preacher, school-teacher, and W'starrah's friend
Et'run	young knight and devotee of the Red House, leads the city cavalry in battle
Vosur	Curate and Preacher of the Cryssian temple
Myster Cruryn	leader of the Cryssian temple
Minstrel Tambouri Shai	beautiful singer in Cryssigens
Cup Carnad Mias	head of Red House in Cryssigens
Captain Justin Thyme	Argensian officer on a mission to prevent war
Patriarch Z'kammet Hammer	leader of the church of Argens Hope-forger in Cryssigens
Emperor Yula	dwarf, also called the First or Usurper, ruler of the Argensian Empire
Fire Grip Gaspar Heugen	virtual regent and leading member of the Blue House in Cryssigens
Overlord D'stagnon Kreel	former Mark of the North, slain by Yula in 2001 ADR

Overlord Kreelon Kreel	son of Kreel, died soon after
Baron Pa'u Breret'n	Baron of Cesmir, allied to the Red House
Baron Soln Ge'para	Baron of Gaden, allied to the Blue House
Dekentar M'nesa Zetee	noble-son enrolled in the Imperial Army
Baron (of Blood) Voev T'yr	Baron of Tralmachia
Jal'i	Stargazer guard loyal to Tanar'h
Tamess	Stargazer guard loyal to Tanar'h
Eline	first wife of Tanar'h
Bereshutha	second wife of Tanar'h
May'stra	third wife of Tanar'h, baker for the temple
Qellen	armorer
Guildsman Farnh'y	glassblower partial to the Red House
Guildsman Trothfer	glassblower partial to the Red House
Sanhim	human, Bedou-uu tribesman, Guard of Devout Teretheny, taller
Elehar	human, Bedou-uu tribesman, Guard of Devout Teretheny, shorter
Oshuwen	mage working with Welles
Aumir'y	also called Mirry, noblewoman and friend of W'starrah, married to J'seff'n
J'seff'n	nobleman and friend of W'starrah, married to Aumir'y
Highforge Mart'l'n Ecclese	historic leader who crafted the Brow of the Ecclesiast
Myster Kama	human, also called Exemplar, Telholian preacher formerly with the Candidates
Step-Marchess Citari Kreel	widow of former Mark Kreel
Morinack	halfling, the Emperor's Hand and former member of the Candidates

THE VISION OF CRYSSIGENS' DOOM
(as seen by W'starrah Altieri in Perilous Embraces)

A hot swirling wind blows over Cryssigens by night, driven by a dragon's breath fanning flames and pushing the glow of reflected Red down every street, into many houses. The scaly beast clutches a treasure-hoard to its chest and settles atop it like a lover, heedless of the chaos its flame has caused. In the stars above, The Arbalest loads a deadly bolt into his crossbow and fires at once. From the whirlwind many-legged creatures begin to drop down.

> As the rule of men fails
> A woman's spirit rises to lead them
> Argens' Fire will not sear this soul
> Nor wound and ruin impede her path

SHARDS OF LIGHT

The Empire of Argens 2002 ADR

Justin's company crossed a small stream called the Machis just before sunset of the fourth day out from Cryssigens. Imperial soldiers had entered the Barony of Tralmachia nearly two days sooner than anyone expected, with the sole exception of their Captain. But as the men set up brush-barricades, firepits, latrines and tents for the evening camp, Justin looked north into the ever-rising range of dark hills and mountains ahead, and began to understand why no one else hurried to get here.

The deepening gloom fell unbroken by much talking; tired soldiers needed food and fire before they would find their tongues again, and knew their jobs by now. Justin saw to his mount Furta, briefly checked the gryphon still furious in its cage, then walked a short way beyond the limen of the camp, pacing to each side and assessing the terrain ahead. Nightfall did little to obscure his Elvish vision, but he almost wished to be mortal based on what he could see.

Only the banks of the stream held much grass or shrubbery. The pounded-earth road they followed began to wind and rise, seemingly a steady uphill track for uncounted leagues into the hills. Nowhere in his vision could Justin see a plot of land that looked capable of bearing crops. Most of the hilltops bubbled up bare of trees, yet the summits were sharper than such low heights should be; and more, they were deeply veined as if with channels, perhaps dry river beds though that made no sense so close to the peaks in view.

On a whim, he walked further than he intended along the banks of the watercourse behind him, trying to catch a glimpse of what lay around the staggered, rising hills. Since leaving Cryssigens, Justin had found precious little intelligence about the Baron's domain, and while he didn't give full credit to the horror that the beautiful priestess showed about Voev T'yr—a stab of pain at the thought of her, shoved aside—he felt an instinct to know all he could for their upcoming meeting. Or confrontation. Justin shook his head in anger, and reminded himself that what he sought here was a vote, not a fight. Just a few more steps to the side…

And there, darker against the darkness, beyond three layers of staggered peaks, a single tower thrusting through the horizon stars, remarkably high and perhaps slightly crumbling on one side. Justin felt certain that even by day the stones would be black.

"An imposing structure," someone said quietly to one side of him, and Justin jumped from his reverie with a cough. His chief subaltern, dekentar M'nesa Zetee ignored his captain's disquiet with the grace born of a noble heritage. "The men have made good time."

"I knew they would," Justin responded, returning the salute, "Your force march to the city last week told me all I needed to know."

"Gaspar Heugen estimated more than a week, you said sir?"

Justin grinned. "He is no worse than most of us nobles, without training. Thinks horses are faster than foot, yet probably goes to war with loaded wagons and ten attendants for every three fighters. We march light, and steadily. With luck and the favor of Argens, we'll be back so quickly his jaw will hit the table."

"And the conspirators, whoever they are, will also be surprised." M'nesa observed. "Or so we hope." Justin watched him staring at the distant tower, one corner of the castle housing an Elf the peasants called Baron of Blood. Get his vote, or no point coming back.

"Did you see something move, on that hill over there?"

M'nesa looked, shook his head, but kept looking. "Hard to imagine much of anything lives in his barren country."

"Something has to. He's a feudal lord, by Argens."

"Those merchants we met on the way were hardly forthcoming, sir."

"Your usual talent for understatement, dekentar Zetee. They were hostile."

"They were petrified."

"Even so. We saw one coming and one going and still know nothing about the trade of this barony."

M'nesa nodded in agreement. "That trader we overtook heading north, already looking unhappy with half her journey to go. She had food, cloth, pottery, bright trinkets—a little of everything, it seemed. And money to spare; when we searched her accounts—she seemed almost of two minds."

"Yes, protested she needed the coin to complete her trade, so all that wealth in the wagons was only partial barter." Justin rubbed his face and stared out at the tower, now catching a slant of the rising lower moon behind it to the north. "On the other hand, she looked askance at us before we turned the money back over. As if... if we confiscated it, she could turn back. And preferred to."

His officer continued. "But the fellow we met coming south, yesterday. Faces of ash, his handlers and assistants, even his animals were quivering with fear and haste, though already five leagues and more south of this stream. And what did he carry away?"

"Some wood," Justin admitted, "not a coin to his account, unless he hid it. And his old containers, barrels and pots and casks, empty except for a few inches of earth in the bottom."

"Ballast," M'nesa replied, "as on a ship, to prevent too much jostling. But not enough in wood to be worthwhile, if the merchants are at all similar."

"An entire barony that must import the simple necessities of life," Justin mused aloud, "and exports something even less valuable? Who would pay into such a trade?"

M'nesa shrugged. "If the Baron robs them, why do they come?"

No point picking at the knot further, Justin thought. The breeze of nightfall bought a sharper chill than normal for the southlands, more like the tales he had heard of the frozen northern kingdoms. He stood closer to them now than ever before in his life. Even the tallest mountains here seemed free of snow, but Justin sensed it was a lack of rainfall, not a matter of temperature.

He turned back, to behold a camp sprung into being as if by magic. Small cookfires cast light down a grid of paths between straight-staked tents, the sides of the little fortress lined with tangles of brush and decked with corners that bulged a bit, allowing the guards within a wide field of vision and fire. Less than an hour, without orders or prompting, and not enough noise to disturb his conversation. Justin felt a swell of pride to know this much power was at his command. Just above eighty men, working as one and never questioning the march-pace nor knowing spit about the mission. They had already faced a monster of the unknown, and caged it. These soldiers would not fail him.

Which hardly meant, of course, that the reverse was true.

The strapping bulk of his mortal subaltern approached to join them, the former gladiator whistling off-key as usual, so badly it was impossible to tell what tune if any was intended. Together the three officers surveyed their camp as the men settled in for sleep.

"Did you ever hear about Tralmachia from your companions in the arena, Tass?"

The muscular human shook his head at once. "It's amazing, really Captain. These nobles controlled our lives and deaths; bought us, cheered us, bet on us, threw us jewels and coins and gifts... but I never thought about them, not for four seconds in a week." He squatted down and rubbed some earth between his hands, as if readying for another bout. "Never heard of a fighter owned by the northern barony, though."

"They may have had other entertainments here," M'nesa suggested with his gentle smile.

"And now?" Justin prompted.

M'nesa broke into a full grin. "I have no doubt, Captain, they will provide interest and amusement for all." So his subaltern was feeling the tension too.

Tass laughed, then dusted his hands with a grimace. "Balls of Argens, even the earth here smells like blood."

Justin reflected how easy it was to make something of nothing. A few steps to spot a tower, a finger-snap of time to create a camp.

16

Less than that, perhaps, to start a fight when all he wanted was to avoid war. But no, he admitted, not always something from nothing. Justin recalled again her image, standing there across the sands in the brilliant sun of noon; the preacher who saw the future, beautiful and spirited woman high in Argens' favor. She had tried to hold him back, convinced he would not survive this expedition.

And what could he offer her; no wealth or land since rebellion had put the current Emperor on the throne, no reputation because of the secret mission he had adopted. Justin knew in his heart that he held truly nothing, except what he wanted, what he lacked, which felt to him much closer to everything. Anytime he wished, he could bring her face, her flashing eyes, the dance motion of her every move to his mind. Anytime he could stand the pain of separation, he did. Justin had done so less and less while the march lengthened. Thus he dismissed the ache, or dulled it, though it made the entire world dimmer and less interesting.

And that too was an illusion, making something of nothing. Whatever this dusty, dark, deforested barony showed to first glance, Justin could sense there was surely danger here; his body prickled with the premonition of his death—or worse, death for these good men. Tomorrow they would march straight to its center and Justin silently swore to find a way, to end one pain or the other.

The men were up early, and just after sunup the camp was empty of life. Fires out and covered, cold breakfast buried, gear stripped away and packed tightly into the company's two wagons, the manmade fort stood there with its brush-gate gaping open behind the marchers, as if astonished it could be abandoned so easily. Tonight they'd build another: and each man knew, if they had to fall back in the face of superior foes, their former friend would be there ready to forgive them, just a day's march away. Justin admired these aspects of Hansen's training most of all. Not a battle-maneuver, no clever trick to work once in a campaign, but an order in things, a routine of discipline that taken together supported victory. His father had never known such ideas, nor any of his generation. But the new emperor was changing the world, and Justin felt a thrill to know he was playing a small part in it.

The march this day was normal pace. No double-time, no subtle races to keep up, no extra hours on foot for the cavalry. For the first time since any of the men had soldiered under the "bought-badge", they kept to the prescribed pace and took every break the manual indicated. By mid-morning, the men knew why without asking. The rock-hard earthen road delivered on its threat to steadily, steadily rise as it wound around higher hills and toward the true Tralmach Mountains. Never steep, yet never ceasing, it ate the thighs and calves like rot on wet wood, until spear-ends dragged in dust and a man's pack felt loaded with rocks.

Tass paid no attention to such details, loudly calling upon men to sing the time away. No man there would admit that it did help, nor Tass deny how dreadful his pitch or rhythm were when he took his own turn. Whenever a man wasn't singing, he much preferred cursing his neighbor's voice to clenching his teeth against the pain.

"Great news men!" Tass bellowed, "Every league up on the way in is a nice downhill trip on the way back. We'll roll all the way to Cryssigens."

That actually brought a small cheer. But everything quieted at the sight of the first abandoned village.

Justin felt a charge as he had before that hamlet south of the Mark, where his men saw their first action. He signaled a halt and they waited for a quarter-hour without the slightest sign or sound of life.

"M'nesa, two dekents by the western side, and two more with me around the east. Tass, enter with the rest and stay on your guard."

Justin eased his men around the perimeter, looking up at the hills while to his left Kein Trador scanned down the spaces between buildings.

"Small birds," Justin remarked, "some rabbits, signs of something like goats or pigs perhaps."

"Far more than I'm seeing, sir," Trador replied.

Justin turned his troop to enter the village directly, and men dismounted to search buildings in groups of two, calling out.

Within ten minutes, it was quite clear that not so much as a cat remained inside. The threescore buildings had begun to warp and fall in, but there were no signs of wrack or burning. The three columns met and reformed in the center. Someone had boarded up the small

18

tavern here, and signs told of wagons and hoofed traffic all around. A small cistern behind the inn also showed activity.

"The merchants," M'nesa observed, "probably use this as a waystation to and from their destination."

"It's insane," Trador rejoined, "who are they selling to? Where are all the people? No one's lived in this village for thirty years."

"Will we bivouac here Captain?"

Justin looked at the double-layer of boards across the windows and a part of him prompted. But not the part where his courage lay.

"Half our daylight left. Move on."

The next turn in the rising road brought them in view of a low hill directly ahead. The road snaked to one side of it as usual, but that wasn't why Justin called a halt. It was the humanoid figure atop that hill, nearly naked and holding either a short spear or thin club, who threw out one arm dramatically in a gesture of forbiddance.

Justin sensed in an instant, no man acted so confidently unless he was not alone.

"M'nesa, flank the cavalry. Tass, two-arms formation for the foot."

He sat his horse at the van, while his men spread out behind him in wider formation. The distant figure well beyond bowshot raised his arms in an angry gesture, as a farmer shooing children from his garden, then a few swipe-and-cut passes that meant nothing to Justin. Dimly he could make out syllables but no words.

"Kein Trador, with me. Stand ready everyone."

Justin rode slowly forward with one subaltern to his side. The distant figure—a man certainly, but not much else yet—shook his head and made the stopping gesture again. When Justin continued, the interloper turned about and walked directly away.

"Hold!" Justin cried, reining in and raising his hands to show no weapons. The figure turned back but folded his arms. Justin motioned him forward with no success. "We wish only to pass," he cried out, producing a set of rapid rolling gestures from both arms and more syllabic cries.

"He doesn't speak our language, sir," Trador said, "perhaps not any language."

"He's not alone, I can sense it. But what does he want? How did the merchants—?"

"The wagons!" Trador cried, "He wants to see the wagons."

Justin looked over and nodded. "Surely that's it." They sat their mounts and watched him on the hilltop gesturing madly, driven by impatience, or perhaps panic. The cold wind whistling between the hills was frosty; Justin thought he had never felt such chill through the darkest day of winter back home in the Domain. Where was spring in this blasted country?

"Well we are not merchants, and I won't let him poke through our wagons to prove it." Justin signaled the troop to advance in line, and they slowly came on, weapons at the ready.

The hill-man shouted, waved, and fairly jumped with annoyance, his syllables and gestures collapsing into a jumble of incoherence. Suddenly he drew up something tied around his neck and blew a whistle-tone that carried off rocks in all directions. In three hand-claps of time, the hills to every side were lined with figures, waving clubs and storming down to the road-vale where the company advanced.

Justin held his arm up to signal the wedge, and in a trice the infantry formed a V, with the back open where the horsemen could ride out at need. Still in two-arms formation, there were twenty bowmen in the second rank: as the ragged horde screamed downhill, he could see no missile weapons of any kind among them.

"Archers aim… and loose!" The sudden accuracy of the volley brought down a dozen attackers, tripped scores more, and slapped the charge to a halt like a lightning-strike of dismay. Howling and grunting they turned to flee, and this was the time to exploit their losses with more arrows and then the cavalry. But Justin bellowed "Hold!" and let them go. In less than a minute, they were all out of sight again. Nothing from something.

"Certainly unusual," M'nesa observed as if seeing a rare flower. For a few moments the only movement came from the chill wind, blowing over eight or ten cloth-draped bodies on the hillsides. Justin signaled to reform and continue the march, and the men needed no orders to keep their shields and bows limbered.

Incredibly, the gryphon in its wagon at the center of the wedge slept through it all.

The sun was still two palms above the horizon on their left when the winding road brought another village in sight. This one was larger, and walled, at a crossroads nestled between the rolling hills. The way still led slightly up, as if the road owed these intruders a grudge. The low fencepost stockade obscured most of the buildings within, and again nothing stirred except the occasional form lurking on a surrounding height; the hill-men were keeping watch and Argens only knew how many more there were. Justin signaled the men in by the southern gate, which was closed but not barred. The men muttered encouraging words: no need to build a camp tonight.

Two dekents of bowmen ascended to prowl the ramparts, and occasionally called down to report spotting a head here, someone running between hills there. But there was no repeat of their reckless assault as the rest of the men combed the empty streets and buildings. Without knowing how, Justin felt a sense of recency about the abandonment. Buildings were still intact, and the grocer's shop had dried seeds and other edibles not yet spoiled.

With M'nesa he ascended the northwestern corner of the stockade and there to the north beheld the castle tower, not as distant, larger, black in the sunlight and showing part of the outer curtain wall in a much larger keep. It was more than a day's march off still; Justin could not make out any sign of life there either, though the upper stories were peppered with windows. Neither man said a word; the wind had stopped, yet M'nesa suddenly shivered with a chill.

A lone shout from several streets away brought them down the ladder on the double. A cavalry dekent searching the area held position, while Kein Trador rode slowly further ahead, looking intently at a crevice in the wood between buildings. He gestured to hold his captain back a moment, and called gently to the blank wall.

"No one will hurt you. Come out."

At first there was no response, but when he dismounted, stepped forward a few paces and crouched down, a face appeared at a crack in the wood. It wasn't wide enough for a child's body, but a child emerged anyway, her dress horribly loose and barefoot, staring fearfully over the man's shoulder at his horse.

And behind her, three more children even smaller.

Justin whispered to M'nesa, "Food from the wagon." He came quietly down the street to overhear, but allowed his officer to work with the children.

"We thought you a monster," the bigger girl whispered, pointing to Kein's horse. "But then you… broke apart." The others nodded sincerely, despite the fantastical depth of this assertion.

"Oh Mellick here, he's no trouble," Kein said with a grin. "Come and pet him if you like."

At first only the lead girl approached, and she was most hesitant until Kein took off his gauntlet and stroked his stallion bare-handed. Then she stepped up and did the same. A little light came into her eyes then. She turned to the others and spoke matter-of-factly.

"It is a horse."

Immediately the other three rose and came over, whispering excitedly. Justin thought how normal it all seemed, except for the stone-cold silence and the empty buildings all around.

When M'nesa came back with some hard rolls and a few apples in hand, the children all stopped and faced him. He held them up, saying "I bet you are hungry."

No one could have guessed what happened next.

Almost as one, the four children ran to M'nesa, dropped to the dust and pressed the hem of his cloak to their foreheads.

"Please! Please, kind master." "You will take us slaves now?" "Please!"

M'nesa and Kein looked in astonishment, then over to their captain with dismay. Justin took some of the food and bent down to detach one of the children, firmly placing it in his hands.

"Never mind who is master. You must eat, all of you."

The children looked agape at him, almost on a level with his eyes while he knelt. They began to whisper as if he were out of earshot.

"He was a monster before too, I saw him on the patchy horse-monster."

"He is their master."

"We should eat, or else he will be displeased."

Without further word, the foursome fell upon the food and devoured it as a gale through dry leaves. Justin felt slightly ill, to think of their plight. Why would they wish to be slaves? Had Baron T'yr defied the emperor's decree? Or had the children here been without human contact since the slaves were freed, more than eight months ago? Justin could not decide which was worse.

"Where are your parents? What has happened to them?"

"Gone," the taller girl replied, "the hill-men took them."

"How long ago was the battle?"

"Battle? No fighting, master, the hill-men come and take them."

"When? Where?"

"When they are needed. To the Baron."

The littlest boy spoke. "Or when they die, the hill-men take them then too."

"To the Baron?"

"To the ground. Over there." The boy stood up and pointed west.

Justin rose and looked to his officers, who shrugged.

"They have been alone a long time, Captain. Perhaps their stories grow to fit their fears."

Justin nodded, then looked at the girl. "The hill-men come into town?"

"Not much anymore. Everyone is dead now."

"Except those who went to the Baron."

"Them too. By now."

Justin looked in their eyes, calm and trusting and completely without hope.

"Where is the chapel, children?" Not a hint of comprehension from any of them.

"The church, where you revere Argens."

Nothing.

"Perhaps they only have an outdoor shrine," Trador offered. "Children, the place with a statue?"

"Statue?" the oldest girl sounded doubtful. "Well, the alderman had one in his office."

"Good, perhaps some records too. Children, take us there."

Just a few streets away as it happened, and when they arrived all the children stopped, only pointing to the door.

"Stay with them M'nesa." Justin and Trador entered.

The offices within were dusty and all the shutters closed. The two men let in the last of the afternoon light and searched. Justin came across rather extensive records of births and deaths, and saw at a glance the latter outpacing the former in recent decades. Brief references to an "escape collection" were noted after each rare birth, lacking in details as whenever a custom is well known. And after each death, the inscription denoted "to the western ground" with a date. Finally even those trickled down to just a few a year.

There were also references to an irregular "census" and "levy", words which here seemed to have no meaning. No trade records, no mention of war with the hill-men, the only thing that concerned this leader was how many were left.

No word, of course, about the author's fate: toward the end, the changes of handwriting were practically one per entry.

"Captain, in here."

Justin joined Trador in a clean quiet inner room, lit only by a sconce the dekentar had found. In one corner, on a pedestal stood a forearm-tall statue of an aquiline nobleman wearing the elegant style of several centuries ago. He seemed nearly heroic by bearing, weaponry and dress, yet his posture was strikingly dark, standing with hands behind his back and head down with the gaze of his eyes boring ahead, almost as if he had demanded to know and waited with little patience for the viewer's answer.

"Perhaps this is our noble baron," Justin ventured.

"Notice this, Captain." Trador raised the sconce to shed more light, bringing into view a spread of something wing-like incised into the wooden wall behind him. At first it seemed a part of the statue, but on close examination Justin could see it was simply carved, with expert skill, to appear attached. This revelation came as a sudden shock through Justin's knees to his groin. The hair on his nape stood up as he recalled again the exquisite, delicate face of the woman he loved, filled with horror at the prospect of this mission.

Justin found himself earnestly hoping the hill-men would attack.

And he shouted with fierce joy, when the calls outside indicated he was getting his wish.

The hill-men charge was absurd in every way. Almost all of them massed against the west wall, no ladders or equipment of any sort, and aside from a few thrown rocks no way to affect Justin's men at all except through the ears. And this they did with gusto, shouting incoherently and urgently, half-hatred, half-warning.

Tass wanted to sally out.

"Stay within, hold your arrows."

"I'll go by myself," the ex-gladiator pleaded. "I'll fight without my sword. I promise to try not to kill them!"

"Don't doubt you will have your fill of fighting," Justin replied, gesturing beyond the teeming scores at the base of the wall, to the nearby hill where stood a figure in cloak and armor.

Justin stared into the westering light, and admitted the resemblance to the statue was not perfect, but unmistakable. The way he observed the scene, laughed at the futility, his scorn at the company's intrusion, was just a bit too obvious, almost young. Justin reflected that if the tales were true, Voev T'yr had fathered a dozen sons; this "youth" could easily be two centuries old.

On an impulse he saluted the hilltop figure, and when that brought no response he ordered the mission flag brought up and waved. To the west, the noble was harder to see, but in sunset he could not have missed this symbol. Yet it brought no change to his demeanor; as the sun touched the horizon he turned and walked away, dipping out of sight. There was no sign how he had come through the ranks of the hostiles to this place, nor how he planned to return, nor that such matters concerned him in the least.

But the hill-men: their reaction to dusk was decidedly unambiguous. At a howl from their leaders, they looked to the skies and shrieked in chorus, fleeing upslope in every direction. Justin could see some of them leaping into the rock-veins and out of sight, using them like roads to traverse the otherwise exposed peaks of the hills. His tactical instinct prompted—could all that scraping be the work of men, who seemed to wield no metal? How much labor…

In the last echoes of light following Solar's final setting, Justin made out high, tinny cries unlike any he had heard before. Looking all about, he spotted on the distant castle tower a winged form gyring up and around into the night sky. Another, then another joined this far-off, enormous bird as they circled wider and away from the center, perhaps hunting.

"Captain, look!"

Following M'nesa's arm Justin saw a similar form to the west, already hundreds of feet off the earth and heading further away. The lazy flip of its wings belied the size of the four-limbed body they held in the air.

The men were unnerved to see all this, none of the expected jokes or curses from them. The children, on the other hand, became frantic: Kein Trador and his men had to corral and hold them off the ground or they would have fled to another inaccessible covert. They begged for a hiding place and were immune to reassurance even in the company of armed men. The dekentar brought them to the wagons, and they crawled under the storage tarps to huddle. Their voices emerged from out of sight.

"Please master, keep us as your slaves."

"The collection was taken, our parents promised you would keep us."

"But the merchants, master, they do not come anymore. Only you."

Trador talked to a wagon in seeming. "Do you mean, the merchants do not stop here?"

"Not at night! No, never at night!"

"Why is that?"

A long silence, and then one said quietly, "Our parents will come. The grown-ups will all come now."

And after a pause, another spoke. "From the west. From the ground."

"Wait, hold, do you say your parents are still alive?"

No answer from the wagon. Trador looked back to his captain with a face etched in confusion. Justin felt a deep kick of the need to decide, here and now. And though he had no idea which course was best, he knew he must sound certain. Bivouac here offered shelter and cover; the road ahead was dark, the skies held monsters. But he hated sitting still.

"Form up to move out. Cavalry to flanks, wagons in the center. We march at moonrise."

The men snapped to it, even their fears yielding for a moment to the habit of following orders. Justin tried not to over-estimate any well-being he felt to see men about and doing at his command: he had made plenty of mistakes in his young career. But there was no denying he had a bias for acting, and while keeping his eyes and ears open to a change of course, he could hope that his choice pushed something in his favor. Maybe Argens would be pleased at his initiative.

Besides, this company also had a flying monster.

"Gird the beast for flight," he ordered, loud enough for the assembling troop to hear. "I shall oversee our progress." This brought a cheer and something like their normal banter again.

Aral was off the northern horizon ahead of them within the hour, half-full and dousing the road in moonlight when the company pushed open the gate and marched out at double-time pace. Several men with some experience at handling the beast helped equip and offload the gryphon. Justin sat his mount equipped with helm and crop and waited, scanning the sky to spot distant wings in the moonlight. The handlers limbered up the cage-wagon and set out, leaving him completely alone in the walled town. The gryphon sat tensely, waiting for any sign of weakness to renew the death-struggle against its rider. But Justin was determined not to cow that fierce spirit through beatings. Risking his grip he reached forward to stroke its neck and wings, before giving just a gentle kick and the command to go "Hai!"

He could tell the gryphon loved to fly as much as it hated captivity. With a scream it launched into the air and he felt again what a foolish risk this was, a chance of death by falling or his mount's treachery, and for what? To encourage the men, of course; his head caught up to his instinct as he gained height and banked to fly over the march-route. A commander needed to supply his men with faith, more than weapons or food. They had seen horror in the skies, and heard of worse to all sides. Now it was time they felt strong again. The dekents cheered as he flew overhead. The monster between his legs followed even subtle signals from the reins, almost willingly as long as it could fly. Once it looked back at him, neck craning like an owl to snap its beak in his direction, a reminder. Justin held up the crop half in threat, and it turned back to scream and search ahead.

From this height he could see down all four roads leading away from the village and into the twisting hills. To the west, his eye caught sight of a group of men walking toward the town. They seemed somehow unlike hill-men, not crouching or running but barely trudging it seemed. Perhaps they were exhausted refugees, survivors of this hellish place. He circled closer and as the group emerged into moonlight he noted two things in quick succession.

The nobleman spotted on the hill before sunset was behind them.

And the group, dozens in all, wore the tatters of civilized clothing and moved far too slowly to be natural.

They would reach the village in under an hour. Justin banked to pass over the marching column again, and signaled the force-march pace before flying ahead over the turns of the snaking road to scout the land for a defensible spot.

Hauling in the reins, he urged his mount up and higher, ever higher to see as much of the surrounding terrain as possible. Both moons were risen now, nearly as good as daylight for the broad-brush picture.

The scope of this northern land was instantly breath-taking—he reflected that no one among the Children of Hope had ever been at this vantage point before. He must be a quarter-league above the earth, and looking straight down definitely would not do. The hills grew quickly steeper, the wind alarmingly cold and the stars above seemed closer. There to his right, the Arbalest almost fully above the horizon now, crossbow at the ready and to Justin's mind, only one target in all the world.

He crested a true mountain peak, sweeping in faster than a horse could gallop and passing within an easy drop of the summit. The stab in his groin nearly unseated him as the backside revealed a cliff drop into the shadowed vale below, and Justin beheld the dark castle in its entirety. Ringed by mountains, the final approach road reinforced with stone met a land-bridge across a deep chasm to the outer gate. Two full baileys with curtain walls of solid stone; even at night Justin could make out the darkest shades of granite, enormous blocks that beggared his mind to imagine moving. Now crumbling in several places, it was still the most imposing fortress he had ever seen: a garrison of seven hundred would hardly feel crowded in there.

Scores of windows, arrow-slits, open trapdoors and even a few spots where ceilings had fallen in, but there were no lights, no signs of life except some dim flickers near the central keep. Itself the size of a palace, yet this was a war-building, rising higher than all but the outer towers and massive, round, wedged into the inner bailey, seemingly off-center yet clearly the linchpin of the place.

Justin gaped and briefly wondered if he had already given cause for offence, by taking advantage of his beast to reconnoiter a lord's castle. But then, that sort of thought was appropriate only among chivalrous peers, and only in war.

As he turned back along the approach road, the gryphon snorted and snapped its neck in both directions, smelling or seeing something it hated. Justin checked his reverie and saw two of the horrid winged forms racing back to the castle, screeching in that high, tin-edged call but clearly giving this new intruder a wide berth. Far off to the east, Justin caught sight of a third, dropping like a hawk toward the ground where a small party of hill-men ran across a vale. There was a vein-channel behind them and they headed for another, but the hintermost was not in time and the raptor fell on him as his screams echoed all too human from the dark carved cliffs. Slowly the attacker rose into the air, plunging with its head and ravening on the victim, until his struggles and cries finally ceased. One reason for a shortage of the living suggested itself. Shortly after, the attacker dropped the remains to fall a score of fathoms to the rocky earth, and joined its brothers in flight to the rear towers of the massive keep.

Shivering from the cold, surely, Justin scouted the land rolling beneath him and saw at least part of what he wanted. Urging his mount to greater speed, he bolted back toward the troop, who stopped their march when he descended to land with a thunderous impact, nearly tumbling head over heels out of the high saddle. Must work on landing-form.

As soon as the men had the gryphon restrained and back in the wagon, Justin summoned his dekents.

"Those winged creatures have left the sky. Two hours' march ahead, we will camp. There are no trees or brush, but the rocks provide some cover and there is a creek to water the horses. Tomorrow, we shall arrive at the castle in the forenoon, Argens willing."

"And then, Captain?" Tass asked with a straight face.

"And then, dekentar, we shall take the Baron of Tralmachia at whatever welcome he chooses to accord us. Double the guard when we encamp."

"No shortage of volunteers there, I'll wager!" Tass cried, with a meaty laugh, then turned away muttering "I might stand a turn myself."

The remainder of that dark march was hard and eerily quiet. No hill-men, no night animals larger than insects, and the flying creatures did not return. Take the good with the bad, Justin thought as they reached the half-camp he had spotted from the air. The road was steeper than before but the ascents to either side were sharper still; they were truly in mountain country now, higher than those which bordered the North Mark and the Domain. Bare, rocky faces loomed above the road, sometimes leaving less than a hundred yards across where anything with wheels could pass. Sections of the way were paved, perhaps to stop erosion from runoff, but overall there were few signs of maintenance or regular traffic. Side-turnings were few and small.

Near the road's peak was a spot where the slopes became nearly cliffs and looked cut into a box-corner shape, as if with a saw. Encamping against those hills, the men planted shields and used the wagons lengthwise in a perimeter to the remaining sides. No tents or fires, but the men laid down their blankets in rows with room between to reach weapons and deploy.

"All in all," Justin remarked for public consumption, "a terrible place to have to defend."

"One of the worst you could have chosen, Captain," replied Tass, causing the camp to hold its collective breath. "Except, of course, for all the others we saw." Some men chuckled at Tass' wit, others whistled low at his pluck. The mortal ex-slave had never batted an eye at any of his commander's orders, yet seemed at all times to ignore giving respect, though woe betide any man who refused to give it to him. The six survivors of his original dekent had spread the word to all of his prowess and murderous temper, and Justin was sure the tales had grown a bit like those of the children.

On the other hand, perhaps they had not exaggerated.

He saw Kein Trador sitting with them by the end of a wagon, sharing food and listening with patient interest. He motioned M'nesa over and walked a bit to one side of the camp. Quietly, he told his subaltern what he had seen in the air.

Zetee was clearly moved, and recited the Elvish meme of patience before responding with his usual calm wit. "Well Captain, from the moment we saw them it was too much to hope they were plant-eaters." He stared into the night a while. "But in truth, it's not good news.

They came from the castle and returned there. The Baron is at least complicit in attacks on his own people."

"Unless he is in permanent war with these hill-folk. Could they be rustics, descendants of those who predated the coming of Argens?"

"I think it likely, sir. We saw them up close during both attacks, they are not Elves certainly. Not like these children."

"But then, there are citizens in this barony," Justin snapped, "or there were! What kind of lord—what has happened to the Children of Hope in Tralmachia?"

M'nesa took nothing personally, and Justin reined in his emotion as they both thought on the matter.

"The barony is surely wide, sir, and we've seen roads leading east and west. Perhaps this center path, leading to the castle is… afflicted in some way."

Justin smiled. "You do credit to our former caste, dekentar. But we must look at this as soldiers now. Voev T'ry could not have stood by while his villages were drained of life. Any goodly folk left alive in this barony, and I pray Argens there are, must wait on our progress with him. But will he treat with us?"

M'nesa shrugged. "We don't know the origin of these flying beasts. Could they be the cause of all the death? Perhaps they afflict him in like manner, it could even be that he is dead. Or in part besieged, and needing our help."

"Aye, that could be. Tomorrow we will arrive, by day praise the heroes, and hopefully without those things overhead."

"Yes sir."

M'nesa saluted and moved off, leaving Justin to watch Kein Trador snugging a blanket around all four children as they lay in the wagon, before checking on his own dekent. The terrain ahead was another slaughter-chute: steep rocky slopes to both sides and almost bereft of trees, worse than the time he had led the men against Skeer Two-Eye (was it only a week ago?).

But Justin felt reasonably sure there was no attack coming, at least not on the march. In fact, why should he be expecting a fight at all? M'nesa could be right, the Baron besieged by these monsters and in need of help. Had this curse or disease, which emptied the villages, come on slowly or of a sudden? Were the hill-men enemies

31

or not? He decided to tell no one yet, about the van of slow-moving men behind them. Too many variables to parse, how should he plan?

Justin stood alone under the moons, not in the least tired, and remembered the early days of training, when Commander Hansen addressed the entire cadre for the first time, on the parade ground back in Argens.

"There will come a day, if you survive," he had said, "when you will be faced with what seems like too many obstacles. Unknown enemies, short supplies, wounded men, foreign terrain: there are many other examples. At that time, I want you to remember the following rules for determining a friend from a foe."

Hansen had waited for the last echo to die, and Justin fancied he could hear it now, bouncing off these tall cliffs and through the clear night.

"Ask yourself two questions. *Is he armed? Does he do as I say?*' The rest, you can ignore. But if the answers are Yes and No in that order, you are facing an enemy."

Justin grinned wider than an idiot, and the men failing to sleep could relax a bit, to hear their commander chuckling as he strode by.

Tass always deputed one dekent to forage before the day's march began, as per the manual. Justin decided on impulse to join them, while the rest of the company packed up camp. The group scattered in a loose line and ascended the western slope, scouring for anything edible or interesting. The men saw signs of deer and smaller animals, but no track of human activity. Justin felt his body respond to the challenge of the climb and without much thought found himself above and beyond the group, nearing the tree-bald summit of the mountain as the eastern sky lightened.

The rugged country in all directions was startling and wondrous, and he could see for leagues as the light grew. Justin faced directly south and allowed himself, once more, to think of her. They met for the first time five days ago, though it seemed a year since he left W'starrah there in the arena. Alone among enemies, her hand scarred by some uncouth assassin, and nearly slain by the gryphon too, truth to tell. All Justin had wanted, since that fateful interview in her chambers, was to protect her; but duty called, and so he had left to interview the Firegrip of the city and afterwards march here.

He strained to make out the southern border of this land, and counted the hours it would take to return if he headed back now. W'starrah's beauty had stung him as it would any man with blood in his veins. But she saw the future with him, she committed her cause to his, and understood why he had to leave. How could he love her better? No use to think of returning until he fulfilled his mission. Get the vote, or die trying: Cryssigens would not survive otherwise. And she would die before losing her city. Justin knew he would do no less, for her, though she had given him no reason to hope.

Tass far below shouted the recall, signaling readiness. In a small stand of wind-battered brush nearby, Justin spotted a single sprig of jasmine flowers. Perhaps a sign: he broke it off and breathed deep the scent of her as his throat tightened and his heart dropped within him. He affixed it to his uniform coat like a medal. None of the men saw fit to comment on it when he strode back into camp, mounted up and led them out.

The march was quiet, just the creak of wheels and clop of hooves rebounding from the stones, a dirge with lyrics as strange as the hill-men's speech. No signs of human life, still very few trees, a land cleared of ambiguity, not bothering to hide its threat. Peaks overhead held back the light and cast shadows at all hours, an eternal dusk even on a clear day.

When one of the horses kicked loose a stone, the commotion slapped around the cliffs and a bowman accidentally loosed his half-drawn arrow. Whispered curses ran through the formation, crested by Tass' boisterous laughter as he ordered the errant archer to recover his shaft from the crevice where it lodged. "You'll likely wish you hadn't left it, Bullseye!" he crooned, awarding another of his dreaded nicknames to the brief general amusement. But the tension closed back in like water over a drowning man as the march resumed.

Justin let his horse fall back through the ranks, until he was level with M'nesa.

"Wish we still had that trumpeter."

"He fell in the first charge, I understand sir, under Valin's command."

Justin glanced over at the two drovers guiding the supply wagons, then the young man from Cryssigens who seemed to know about handling large animals and had begged to come along. He was riding on the gryphon's cart now, looking at the four children from the village dangling their legs off the wagon ahead of him and staring back the way they came. Unarmed, they would do whatever he said, the opposite of enemies by Hansen's rule. Innocents, even as the trumpeter had been: just like Valin to have exposed him to needless risk. Yet here he dragged these peasants ever-closer to that castle where all his instincts screamed lay peril.

"M'nesa, be sure to keep these civilians safe, in the event of any unpleasantness." His subaltern looked at him in mild surprise and nodded. "I'm serious, whatever we can do, even if I…" M'nesa saluted him soberly and Justin rode up front again as the path ahead opened into the cliff-walled valley.

Signaling the halt, Justin rode across the front of the column and addressed the waiting men, already blown from the endless climb-hike.

"Our destination lies ahead, and you men will have an opportunity to show why we have come. The curse that lies upon this land may not be in our power to lift. Those we come to treat with may be friendly, or not. Our success or failure will very likely matter more to the people of this Mark than they would ever admit to lackeys of their hated Emperor. Those things are beyond our view, and thus unimportant. Whether we rest and wait, or fight and die, I expect each one of you to carry himself as befits a soldier of the Empire, and a true son of Argens." Justin flicked a glance to Tass, the sole mortal human among the men he commanded, who grinned back wide enough to show his missing teeth. He signaled the advance and they emerged from the road within sight of Castle T'yr.

Dekentars growled at soldiers to stop cursing, keep step, eyes front. Justin sat straight-backed on Furta, listening to the sound of boots and hooves behind him and briefly wondered if this vale had ever known such an intrusion. The castle across the land-bridge showed no reaction, gates still shut, not a flicker of movement anywhere. But listening, it seemed, taking the measure of these Fire Ants who crawled so near its base and tried to scratch out a home for themselves.

Justin pointed to the left, the area he had scouted from his pass-over the previous night. The ground rose slightly and leveled off again, backed up against a slope nearly steep as a wall.

"A camp sir?" M'nesa asked. Justin nodded; it risked a hostile look, but better prepared, they all had that drilled into them. Brush was scarce, but Tass' dekent began rolling rocks for a barricade, and the men dug a trench outside that low wall to increase its effective height.

It was two hours' work and not a sign of life from the castle throughout. The men moved all the more quickly to finish, the silence driving them to haste. There was no water, and Kein Trador rode with his men to find some on the opposite side of the vale. A few small kegs at a time came back, but that would be a concern if they commenced hostilities and could not hold this ground.

Justin cursed himself to catch his thoughts drifting back to battle. But he could not fight the habits of his training. In his heart he recalled how drills and tests felt like a return of something he had always wanted. To study the situation, seize advantage, to constantly think ahead about what one could do, what the opponent was capable of. He told himself it was only prudent, to be ready. Then he summoned the dekentars to his tent for a briefing.

"We may assume for the moment, as our host has not yet greeted us, that he is either unprepared, unable to respond, or less than entirely happy to see us." Grins all around at this, the men were feeling better.

"Or possibly," M'nesa gently intervened, "that he feels no loss of advantage letting us entrench on his front door." That tempered the room immediately, and Justin nodded in agreement.

"If it came to a fight, we have no engine for those gates. Tass, can we storm the outer walls?"

"Certainly sir, against such opposition as we can see. Assuming he puts ten or twenty men on those battlements," Tass waggled his hand in ambivalence, "no ladders, only hook-and-ropes, but I'll wager our bowmen, including young Bullseye there, can lay cover enough to win through. I might lose three or four."

Some of the other officers swallowed at his frank assessment, but no one disagreed.

"Yet there are those flying things," one put in.

"Which could be the real enemy," M'nesa replied.

"Opinions?" Justin surveyed the room, and finally Kein Trador raised a hand.

"Fearful to be sure, sir. But the hill-men showed no bows. We might wager these things would get a nasty surprise, from men who do not flee their approach and who can fight back." Nods and affirmations all around, not from certainty so much as desire, but Justin knew a gift when he heard it. The young dekentar was proving his worth.

"And what shall we do, gentlemen, when I am gone?" This brought exclamations from all the officers, except M'nesa and Tass who had been with him long enough to know better.

"Captain! You will leave us again? I mean, sir," one fellow stammered into muttering, but the damage was done. The "bought-badge" had left his company twice before, no matter it had worked to their benefit both times. Justin had a reputation for mystery, which cut both ways, and this needed to be hashed out or they'd panic when the time came.

"He simply means," M'nesa replied gently in the silence, "that the Baron will likely summon him."

No one moved at that, faces frozen in thought and dismay. Without question, the youngest Zetee was perceptive beyond his years: Justin nodded his thanks before taking up the conversation.

"We must expect so, whether he means us well or ill it would be the same. Either to treat with me seriously, or pull me from you before attacking. And do not mistake me, gentlemen; when the Baron invites me, I shall go."

That settled in. Finally a young dekentar asked "What are your orders, sir?"

"Remain vigilant. Keep everything in perfect order, give the Baron's men no excuse to indict us. Defend if attacked. For the rest, wait. Dekentar Zetee will command in my absence."

"Captain, if I may be permitted to accompany you." M'nesa's request was echoed around the room. Justin held up a hand at once.

"Even if the good Baron offered to accommodate the company, I would refuse. I was thinking of taking young Trador with me as adjutant."

He locked eyes with his newest dekentar, who smiled broadly and saluted back. "The honor of a lifetime sir."

36

"Let us see it doesn't come to that. Dismissed."

The officers with Justin emerged from the tent, and the company remained alert while they waited. The rest of the day.

The hours crawled with the long valley-shadows and there was no sign of life from the massive piles of built stone across from their camp. Dekents practiced maneuvers in pairs to one side, just to keep from boredom and to make a little sound. Justin wished again he had the trumpeter, to announce them and perhaps force a response. He thought about advancing to the gate, but no, that would be foolish with too few men, a mistake with too many. What if the Baron intended to ignore them until they starved? Their supplies were adequate for a few days, but foraging had been scanty even on the lower slopes.

Kein Trador returned from exercising his dekent with a face unaccustomed stony; he signaled with his head for Justin's attention, and together they rode back beyond the camp and out of earshot.

"Over there, sir," he gestured around a stand of rock and brush several furlongs away on this side of the chasm. Then he whispered "A *kemetaria*."

Justin snapped to look him in the eye. "You're certain?"

The young man lifted the air with his hand. "I only know what I've heard in tales, sir. Stone markers in the ground. And sir," he looked as serious as Justin had ever seen him. "turned earth, sir."

Justin looked back at Kein a long moment, then nodded him to continue. They rode casually, as if taking in the terrain or exercising the horses. Furta shied a bit under him as they came around the stand; she sensed it too, or else his knees had tightened involuntarily. But Justin could see, and it removed all doubt.

Here, in lands controlled by Hope, a burial ground. Bodies beneath the earth, as if these were the Children of Despair. He had to force himself to dismount and approach on foot. Behind him, Trador choked with surprise, but did the same and caught up with his lips drawn thinner than a knife-cut.

The ground was a gentle slope, grassy in most places and without any wall or gate. Rectangles of turned earth hinted at plots, headed by dark stone markers and some of them, closer to view, very worn and rounded with extreme age.

Trador read some of them, with comments. "*Perishune, fifth son*—no date, or here just *Fourth wife*, not even the courtesy of a name? *Bel't, Al'yris; Makdal a good hunter*—is this a hound?"

There were some threescore markers all told, and Justin's mind reeled at the thought of family members, castle staff, or even animals interred here for all time. Who could countenance such savagery? But perhaps there was yet some explanation.

"Let us return, dekentar. No word of this for now."

"Yes, sir."

When the portcullis creaked up the company jumped to its feet at the sound, weapons in hand. The gate swung open and after a pause several figures emerged, led by one of the tallest, brawniest Elves Justin had ever seen. His armor was polished and dark, bearing the emblem of a pair of disembodied wings, heraldry of a kind Justin had never seen before. The half-dozen retainers also had fine armor, helm and chain with halberds that seemed little encumbrance to them, yet moving slowly and without much discipline. Their leader could not seem to stop smiling, and on the whole Justin felt he should be insulted before they even arrived at the entrance to his camp. The brush-gate was pulled back and the men stood at attention in rows to let the party through, but he stopped and waited for Justin to come out.

Signaling to Trador, he marched up and saluted, determined to behave in perfect decorum whatever the reception.

"Captain Justin Thyme, formerly of Argens and now on a mission to Baron Voev T'yr with a message from the office of the North Mark."

Grin turned to smirk as the strapping nobleman took in this address. "What does the boy want from us, I wonder?"

Justin hesitated, wondering a moment if they believed Kreelon still ruled in his father's absence, and had not heard of the vacant throne. Or did this insolent fellow think Gaspar Heugen, or even dead Kreel himself, were children? It was time to turn the tables.

"You have me there, sir, I gather time passes more slowly in Tralmachia. The world outside has fought several battles since the day we saw her knights on the field."

A puff of air escaped the other's lips, curling toward a snarl. "My father greets you and requests your presence at dinner, now served in the audience hall within."

"I am at the Baron's disposal, sir, if that is to whom you refer." A calculated risk, this fellow's favor was already a dim prospect, and he needed to learn the amenities.

Recovering his grin, the tall warrior sketched a bow and replied, "I am indeed the Baron's fifth son. He is ready to receive you now."

Justin turned away and motioned M'nesa in for a final word.

"Guard the flank. There was a cadre pursuing us from the western road at the village. Perhaps tonight."

"Perhaps the reason for the delay," M'nesa replied quietly, saluting. No flies on this one; Justin grinned and turned away knowing he left the company in good hands. "Argens with you, sir," M'nesa said at his back.

Though the Baron's deputy had taken no notice of Trador at Justin's side, he turned again when they both began to follow. Kein stepped up smoothly and intercepted the raised arm with his own, transforming forbiddance into greeting.

"Dekentar Kein Trador, the Captain's adjutant." Even as he spoke, Kein's face dropped into shock, and he released the arm-grip abruptly.

Now the semblance of courtesy was unavoidable. "I am Perishune," he snapped and turned to lead the pair between the honor guard and back into the castle.

Justin looked askance at his subaltern, who fidgeted with his cloak as an excuse to lean in.

"That name, Captain."

"On the marker?"

Kein nodded. "And his flesh, so cold I felt it through my sleeve."

A fog of unreality settled over Justin at those words, with the shadow of the fortress they entered. No explanations made sense anymore, he could not believe where he was or what he did. The dark walls loomed as he stepped into the under-gate chamber. Even in the shadows of late afternoon, he could make out the blacker-on-black shapes of the murder-holes above and to the sides here, slits where the first to make it past the iron grating would be peppered with arrows by the garrison. Not war, he reminded himself, but the idea brought no comfort. Here was death, on all sides; irrelevantly, he thought of his direction, deeper into the fortress now with every step. Further north. Further from her.

Beyond the gatehouse a tunnel-hallway led through the outer bailey. Justin's mind churned furiously: attackers who pierced the portcullis and rammed through the gate would not control the bailey. The hall was lit only by four torches its entire length, but he made out two seams overhead, where perhaps a secondary wall, or hot oil or some other horror, could be lowered on invaders. Yet where was the access to let horses and men out of the castle? The sheer depth of this defence staggered the mind. A sudden thought that he might already have seen his last of the open sky jolted him, and Justin clamped down on any further gloomy thoughts as they strode to the second portal, as deep and buttressed as the first. He was in Argens' hand now.

As the inner door moved ponderously back, they beheld another tall, more slender figure, decked in the house livery and bearing himself with straight shoulders and a serious face. Perishune pulled up short at the sight, not evidently pleased.

"I have guests, castellan, clear the way."

"I shall escort them to the Baron, brother," the other returned without fear despite his lack of arms and what he gave away in breadth. "I have his instructions on this, and you are ordered back to the gatehouse in his name."

At these last words, Perishune flinched and scowled, but spun away. Sparing only a single hungry glance for Justin, he took his retainers back down the entry hall.

This chamber was broad, domed and gorgeously decorated with carvings, inscribed pillars, pedimented arches to both sides and a grand curving stair inset with dark wood leading up from the opposite wall. Servants here closed and barred the portal behind the visitors, and their new host bowed, speaking courteously.

"I offer apologies for my elder brother, who thinks only of battle and is no doubt disappointed. I am Sordinay T'yr, seventh son of Baron Voev T'yr and in service to him as a kind of butler."

Justin felt the warm manly grip with a flush of relief, and immediately took a liking to this fellow, who did not seem to bear the weight of much age. "Justin Thyme, your lordship, and my adjutant Kein Trador. We are most impressed at the strength of this fortress."

40

A quaver flicked across their host's lips, either amusement or pain. "I should be most pleased, Sir Thyme—"

"Captain, only, your lordship."

"Please, call me Sord. If you would fancy a tour of the inner chambers, I can assure you will come to appreciate its more civilized aspects." Sord held his hands behind his back, but his brows indicated a touch too much eagerness, to fulfill this offer.

"Perhaps in time, many thanks," Justin replied, "but since we have been summoned and our matter is somewhat urgent—"

"No doubt, but surely you are tired. We have rest chambers prepared down this hall."

"The invitation was to dinner."

Again a flicker of something, some doubt perhaps on his face. "As to that, the Baron is quite old, and takes less note of the passage of time than most. He would no doubt look upon you with just as much favor at breakfast as now."

Justin realized something was amiss and applied the training of his father, to seek the lie. Sordinay had a noble face, and was trained as they all were to conceal emotion. Cracks in this kind of armor, therefore, were even more significant. He showed nothing but kindness in his voice, yet had pitched his words not to carry as far as the edges of the great room, where servants trudged about their chores and only occasionally glanced at the strangers.

"You did not, in fact, have your father's direct word to escort us," Justin said, gambling it would not go worse for him. "You are here on your own, and wish us to wait before meeting the baron."

Now something much more formal closed down over their host's demeanor. "I wish to help you of course, all I can, as I would any ally of this Mark. Please believe that, sir."

"I do, and I thank you for your kindness. But it puts me in mind of my obligation, not only to those who sent me, but to our new friendship, that I not place you at risk of any displeasure in this matter."

Sordinay sighed then and nodded. "Rest assured, sir, I fear no diminution of my... condition from tonight's events. But remember what I said."

He led the way to the stairs and up. Men could march a dekent abreast on these treads, much wider and broader than those in

W'starrah's tower. Justin remembered how nervous he was then, how agitated he became later in her presence, and found it strangely calming.

At the top of the stairs' curve a straight hall led to the right, perhaps along the back wall of the inner bailey toward a more brightly lit chamber beyond. Tapestries here were rich and dark, with scenes Justin could not make out well, and the carpet underfoot completely muffled their steps. When the slight jangling of his sword in its belt came to the fore, he started and clapped his hand to cover it. He and Kein looked discreetly about for a stall to quarter them, but Sordinay noticed.

"Have no fear, gentlemen, of bringing weapons before my father. He likes military men better than courtiers, and will take no insult." His face showed a little remorse at that last.

Coming from the chamber was an Elven lady, richly dressed, small with a delicate face. Justin thought of W'starrah's friend, the elderly teacher: this woman, though as slight, held her years as yet, and she smiled when the party approached extending her hands to Sordinay.

"Mother," he exclaimed taking her in his arms, "how good to see you well."

"My son, he is in good humor now, and I go to walk the battlements before it is full dark." She stepped away to regard the strangers; Justin bowed low and took her offered hand to his forehead. As he rose he saw in her face a strange sadness, and noted her other hand was still protectively placed on Sordinay's arm.

"A great privilege to meet you, Lady T'yr. I hope this will be but the first of many such encounters."

Her lips smiled without the rest of her at this.

Kein Trador impulsively stepped forward to bow as well. "Perhaps, milady, I might escort you on the outer walls. There may be dangers—"

"Oh no, kind officer, no, I shall be quite safe within this castle. And the Baron no doubt will wish to speak with you both. My thanks for your concern." With a small backward glance, she moved on to descend the stairs: Justin guessed that the chamber ahead had no other exit, if the main reception hall were truly the shortest path to the battlements. Everywhere divisions. Or perhaps he made something of nothing again.

He stepped into the audience hall, and it was all he could do not to gawk.

Visually it was a barrage of mahogany, thick tapestry, polished dark brass, crystal and a score of high hanging lamps that left shadows across the massive space. Wider than a ship and twice as long, the first half of the chamber was bereft of furniture and large enough for a joust. Crossed weapons on the walls and the prevalence of rich red in the carpet underfoot reinforced the notion that men fought to the death in here. The table at the far end was three paces wide and could easily seat a score of diners. The Baron sat facing the newcomers on a deep-set throne of cushioned basalt, whose wings flanked his sides and shaded his face despite the chandelier. He was tall and aquiline, draped in velvet and without question the model for the statue in the village. Justin had only seen sculptures of persons from the age of heroes twenty centuries ago, and his nape-hair tried to jump off his back at the thought. He forced himself forward, noting Kein Trador from his peripheral vision as they silently strode the absurd distance, thirty steps down the hall to bow before their host.

Two figures stood guard behind the throne on the raised end of the room, nobly dressed and bearing the unmistakable mark of House T'yr about their dark eyes, sallow skin and arrogant smiles. Passages led from the room on this side, but narrow and draped, not large enough for this massive table that put nearly two fathoms between them.

Licking his lips, Justin spoke first. "Milord Baron, I bring you word from the rulers of Cryssigens and a request to know your mind regarding the succession to the North Mark." He drew a sealed parchment inscribed with authorization from the Fire Grip out of his jacket and laid it on the table.

The Baron's hand on the goblet as he drank had three jeweled rings; his other hand toyed with a golden amulet nearly the size of a dinner plate on his chest. The silence stretched on as he set the goblet back: Justin realized the Baron's end of the table, like his throne, was raised above the rest.

"You have come far, knight of the emperor, and brought many men to deliver this message."

Nothing in particular made his voice stand out, yet every syllable no matter how gentle gave an echo in this room.

"If you please, milord, not knight but simply Captain, on a mission from Argens until last week, and now seeking my fortune. My company and I are quite indivisible."

"An interesting choice of words, Captain. You take responsibility, then, for their actions here?"

Justin cocked his head slightly as if the question were a puzzle. "They are under my command, milord. I will make account for any actions taken, as I ordered them."

Baron T'yr smiled then as if the answer pleased him. "Indeed so. Let us come then to the business of your message. But first, who is this with you?"

Justin gestured as Kein snapped off a salute and bow, introducing him. "My adjutant Kein Trador, dekentar of the Imperial Army."

The Baron regarded him without turning his head, then gestured lightly with one hand to the sides of this throne. "Bel't and Zogith, my tenth and eleventh sons."

"Such a blessing, milord has so many sons as to need few soldiers, it seems."

"I have come to value trust above all other qualities." The Baron went still after that statement, as if deep in thought. Justin exchanged a glance with Kein and waited at ease while his mind whirred with possibilities. The corners of the room whispered *"trust... above all...",* and behind it his imagination populated the silence with the scrape of metal on stone, the meaty flap of a huge featherless wing, the last echo of a woman's cry of terror uttered a century ago. He had to swallow hard before trying to speak.

"Milord Baron, if you are tired?"

The figure in the throne stirred to regard him again. "It is as I told Toll'k'r," he snapped with impatience, "I brook no interference in my rule of the Barony, and offer none to his over the Mark."

"Milord, Overlord Toll'k'r ruled some four centuries ago—"

"And the merchants who come," he sailed on, "they adhere to the agreements I made with their Cups in the beginning." He glared at Justin, who felt the floor underfoot rolling like the deck of a ship.

44

"We come not to discuss trade, milord, but the succession. Gaspar Heugen has ordered—"

"Heugen!" The Baron seemed determined to lose his temper. "Warn that puppy not to let greed govern his thoughts. Gold for the earths, the precious Colors may continue as the turnings continue. Stray not beyond your kennel, dog of the Overlord."

Justin looked to Kein Trador a moment, just to be sure they were hearing the same thing. His subaltern was biting his lip and his hand on the hilt was white-knuckled. Justin doubted the Baron was still in his right mind, mixing centuries, titles and juxtaposing nonsense with such anger. Not war, he reminded himself again. Do not make something of nothing.

"Baron T'yr, clearly I have given offence for which I apologize." Justin saw that he had the Baron's attention, and his gaze seemed clear and rational again. "We are not here to interfere with the manner in which you protect your citizens, nor to restrict your trade, or to lever out any, ahm, secrets you may wish kept from view. With Argens as my witness, we wish only to know your vote for the new Mark, and perhaps to offer what aid we may, in light of your current situation."

"Argens?" The Baron's word ran from corner to corner, and Justin bitterly regretted the error, here in the North Mark when men no doubt swore by Cryss Altair. "I told him, I warned him as he tried to build the place. All the heroes as one, yes, but not in stone. Devotion, triumph, immortality: these come from the turning earth alone. He knew, the Cups knew from the earliest days of Color. But Toll'k'r would build the chapel, such a fool." He trailed off, seemingly living half a millennia ago and making little sense.

A distant high tinny cry snapped his head up again, vital and clear-gazed, aiming at Justin as if he held a crossbow. "You are quite correct, Captain, when you state that you will not interfere. I am curious, however; what aid do you think I might require?"

Justin took a deep breath and felt balanced on a narrow beam. "Not the hill-men certainly. They lack the means to threaten you here, with weapons as you possess." The Baron's gaze did not alter, so he continued. "We thought instead about these flying monsters, who seem to roost in your rear towers, perhaps unoccupied? We could, that is, my men would follow me with your permission to see them slain."

45

The Baron smiled gently then, and closed his eyes as if seeing someone of whom he was fond. A few moments passed, and Justin began to think he could relax and breathe, when a door behind the throne opened. In stepped a thin, grey-skinned abomination with hooks for hands, protruding fangs, and giant wings that barely let it through the lintel. Yet the eyes, the toothy grin were of a horribly familiar kind.

"And why, mortal Captain, would I wish to slay any of my sons? Here is Vol'tun, my eldest and first to turn the earth. Death holds little terror for him, you see, and I trust him. He is as loyal to me as he is ugly to behold. Spies and thieves from Argens, on the other hand…"

"We are your guests!" Kein Trador cried out, drawing his sword. "Only a craven would break the customs when offered no insult."

But the Baron had lost interest, raising his goblet again: belatedly, Justin noted the enormous table had only been set for one. He leaped upon the wood with sword in hand, better able to dodge the spears of the guard-sons as he sprinted up the center and hopped the final step to thrust directly into the Baron's chest. The point of his blade punctured the cushion behind his host and thunked into the stone of the chair. Smiling, the Baron looked down at the lethal blade embedded in his sternum, then rose with such power that Justin's feet left the ground while he clung to the hilt. One hand on his neck and a wave of cold overtook him, drowning out the light of the chandeliers, the reek of death at close range, an anguished protest from the far end of the room, the clatter of another sword against the side wall, monstrous chittering and Kein Trador crying out in agony.

⊕ ⊕ ⊕

I left the Stargazer temple with my feet barely touching the ground. Twenty thousand silver! And five thousand right now, whenever I wished it; suddenly I thought of that as expense money, and for the mission I had just accepted it might be. Recover the Brow of the Ecclesiast or die trying. Find a way among the most desperate band of murderers a city never knew it had, snatch a priceless artefact from the hands of some diseased monster, and bring it back to the Lavender Lady within days. Deep inside me Feldspar was cackling with delight.

46

I was in such good spirits I nearly forgot how I was dressed. Walking through center city, the bravo drew the usual challenges to his sword, his colors, his arrogant manner. But while normally he would fence for pride, for money, or just for amusement, this night I waved off all proffered gloves and let them call coward to my back. The bravo's reputation was only a means to an end, I could recover it at need with a single duel. Right now I was after the approbation of the most beautiful and worthy lady in Cryssigens. And the favor of Astor, no doubt in my mind.

I located the small shed almost in the center of the new city, looked both ways on the back street, and worked the latch-lock I had installed when I bought it. Barely large enough to shadow-box inside, it held several changes of clothing for my most popular persona, plus an extra set of Feldspar's black gear, in a small chest set into the floor. When the workers were just completing the nearby building I had bought this structure from them along with the deed to what was probably the smallest plot of land in the North Mark. No one ever noticed it sitting in the shadow of a tavern; no one could decipher the trick to opening the latch I had designed and installed myself. I could always change here, then use the spyholes to be sure I was not observed as I left.

Jonn Simith emerged and walked with his usual deferent step in the direction of The Boards. I had some ideas about how to accomplish my mission and the equipment I needed was there. The night was not far advanced and the streets were quiet as neighbors took their supper. I wondered what I might do for food. Probably go hungry: Feldspar was very impatient of any mortal weaknesses when I was on a mission.

As I closed the front door to my home I froze to overhear something metal dropped in the kitchen. A mild child-curse relaxed my battle nerves but heightened my curiosity. Wasn't I just imagining the smell of bread and stew?

"Oh good you're home. I made dinner, sit."

It was indeed Keilee, whom I had seen at the temple marched off to the prison of school registration. My change-stop couldn't have taken a half-hour: was I slowing down that much?

"Well good evening mistress cook, and look at this feast!" In truth, Simith wasn't really exaggerating: every utensil in the drawers looked as if it had been taken out, rubbed in something and thrown in a corner. But there were two large bowls of thick soup on the table and a loaf of bread that must have been baked from scratch between them. Even Feldspar was too surprised to object, and I was very hungry.

As I sat and reached for the bread, my wrist got a sharp swat from the last clean wooden spoon in my house. "Citizen Simith, we have to give thanks first."

"Ah yes. Of course. Forgive me, mistress cook, but I so often eat alone…" I could see from her face that this was only getting me into more trouble. When was the last time I had heard a prayer over food? "Perhaps, ahm, perhaps you would favor us, since you are the guest as well as the source of this bounty?"

Keilee folded her hands and I did the same: hungry as I felt I was also curious what she would say.

"Argens, thank you for watching over us this day and for Mister Simith our new neighbor who got me off the docks. Twice. And I didn't burn the bread."

I raised my brows as she opened her eyes, and she nodded happily, her chin barely above table-level. We dug in.

I was sure that my hunger would carry me beyond the imperfections of any meal prepared by an eleven year-old girl, and I tore into the thick soup and bread with gusto. Only when I heard someone making grunting sounds of appreciation, and realized that person was me, did I understand the food was actually quite good. Solid, earthy fare, not complicated or delicately spiced or gorgeously presented but the kind you could eat a second helping of, and above all fresh. I thought of the finest dishes I'd sometimes treated myself to in the inns, posing as the bravo or as Simith's employer Chay. I'd sample the food—admittedly marvelous, the fare of the nobility—plunk down a gold piece and use the occasion to make an impression, study a mark, listen for news. But here, the taste of salted potatoes and chunks of plain meat in broth, hot bread with butter, everything except ale (bless the little one, no one would sell that to her): and nothing to do but eat and enjoy it in silence. Or else speak to a little girl.

48

I ate and enjoyed it in silence. Two helpings, and so did she.

Keilee filled any gap in my conversation though, telling me first where she got all the food and then about any little thing she saw or heard along the way. No mention of her visit to the temple, she seemed eager to think about other matters. It just needed an occasional nod and perhaps an "Em, yes?" to keep her talking.

I could eat no more: indeed I don't think I ate so much most entire days. But then I'd had an interesting visit and a lot ahead of me so I was certainly keyed up. I helped Keilee clear, but she body-blocked me from the sink and insisted on cleaning up. I gathered the various utensils from wherever she had dropped them (or thrown it seemed at times) and piled them at her side.

"Well madam, I must say I am most, er, most impressed at your abilities. A splendid meal, simply marvelous."

She shrugged with her back to me. "Mother is the best cook in the city."

"Indeed. And you must, ah, watch her then?"

Nod.

"Well but how do you know there are no better?" I was just teasing to pass the time, but evidently I had made a silly mistake. Keilee turned and stared at me as if I were a moron.

"You have seen my father. He's the biggest man in the neighborhood!"

Well of course, that was that, and I laughed and nodded. "It is certainly settled then. I would be delighted to have you shop and cook for me. Once in a while, that is. We shall have to arrange… and I do not believe, that is, we should not look on this as a chore. But a, rather as a job."

I deliberately used the same word she had at the temple, and it produced the desired effect. Keilee whirled around and shouted "Yes! Then I was not a liar!"

I had to laugh, as any grown-up would to hear such a statement. But as the bravo I had heard her claim as much, and like many, Keilee probably believed that anyone who lied in a temple risked having their tongue burn to ashes in their mouth. My mind was working now, and I had to be careful how to handle this little problem.

"Yes, well then, I propose... let me think. I propose to leave a message at your house each day that I would care to eat a supper at home. It won't be very often, mind you, but I should hope it would prove convenient, mistress, for you to come and cook that evening. And to keep the kitchen stocked and clean, as you have so far." I cocked my head as she willingly nodded, to compose the rest of my plan. "Now as you can hardly be expected to do this job without funds, the shopping and cooking and all, I shall leave the sum of six silver pieces right here on this table, each week." I matched the action to the deed, counting out a stack of one silver for each day.

She gawked in surprise—escaping from school was her only thought of reward. "I'll leave you whatever I don't spend."

"You will keep it. I shall need you irregularly, and having you on retainer, if you will, is quite worthwhile to me. Does this seem acceptable?"

She nodded with a crafty look in her eyes, and shyly reached for the coins.

"Best of all," I casually remarked, "you will still have your mornings free each day."

Keilee pulled her hands back from the coins as if they had turned into a viper. "But why? Don't you want breakfast, I mean—"

"Not necessary, mistress. I sometimes keep out until late and skip the first meal altogether. Or I will take a trip, as I'm afraid I must tomorrow. It could be two or three days until you hear from me again."

"But, but I need to work in the morning!"

I affected puzzlement. "Why in the world—"

She sighed in utter defeat. "I have school now."

"Ah!" I said eagerly, "You have been enrolled, I see. At one of the temples, perhaps?"

"The Stargazers. And the teacher there is seven hundred years old."

"Come, Keilee, it cannot be as bad as, ehm, as all that. Why I recall my school days with fondness. And the teacher is not as old as that, she's the kindest soul in the world. You will learn a great deal from her, as I did—ahm, as I did in my youth."

I felt a bit alarmed to have said so much, but Keilee only thought I was assuring her as any adult would. I must guard my tongue better: talking to this incredible child was too much like work.

50

"So you see you won't need to come—"

My mind froze as I recalled the simple fact that Keilee had been here, in my kitchen, when I came home. I sat back in my chair and drew a deep breath.

"Keilee, may I ask, how did you get into my house to prepare this fine meal?"

She looked at her feet a moment and mumbled a bit. "I used the window. I did not break it! I only need a little room."

I walked out to the living room to inspect the sill, then back into the kitchen while she waited in misery. "Well that won't do at all, mistress, not at all."

I held my face in a mien of impending punishment while I frantically thought about how to secure my secret life against this wily urchin. Feldspar lazily asked me why I even bothered, and opined it would have been best to leave her in the Bug-tunnels. The greatest Stealthic in the city was not a warm heart, certainly. Keilee stood there in misery, and I let her; she needed to respect the boundaries here, at least until I could secure my home against prying. But in the meantime, compromise; I let Simith handle this, not Feldspar.

Reaching into my sash pouch I produced a key to the door and laid it carefully on the table next to the coins. Keilee's face lit up but I held a forestalling finger.

"Come in only when delivering food or preparing a meal. If I am not at home, do not tarry here and please respect my privacy."

She nodded happily, forgetting for the moment that she would still have time for school and lessons.

"Except for when I need to use the privy."

I was rising to go and stopped cold. There was no garderobe on the first floor, and as much as I wanted to keep her off the second floor altogether, it would appear another compromise was needed. Feldspar inside me chuckled at my discomfiture.

"Ah yes, of course that. But be aware never to use it—"

"Midnight of the full lower moon, of course, we have one in our house too."

I laughed then and nodded. "At any rate, if you are here at that time, we'll probably have a bigger problem to address! Very well then, mistress, you are hired." I watched as she took up the key and coins, then shook her hand very gravely and saw her out.

"Remember, now, nothing tomorrow and certainly not the next night either. I shall be out the whole time, most likely. Good night and thank you again for a marvelous meal, my compliments to your mother."

I closed the door and realized I was sweating. Dealing with that child was greater exertion than I was prepared to handle, always it seemed. I spent an hour working on the house, installing another hatch and almost finishing a secret compartment beneath the master bed. Then I changed into my Feldspar garb and stole out through an upper window to the roof and off to the river. Tonight I was for the Old City again, to study a bandit-king and look for an opportunity to separate him from the lethal artefact he possessed. Good thing my stomach was full.

I slipped over the neighborhood, leaping to the next roof and taking in the view no one ever had of their fellow citizens. A few folks out this late, some noise over by *The Grog's Lees*; not sure what they could be arguing about now but it was getting pretty loud. I could hear the voice of Giurid the brick-hauler, and several others—the curses were getting rather earthy and I caught the sound of broken pottery. Ah, there was Beirill with his men drifting toward the door, always alert for justice. I could rest assured on that score; with a chuckle I continued over the rooftops of the close-set streets, heading north parallel to the River Tepid until I was beyond The Boards district and not far from the eastern city walls.

This was another precinct dedicated mainly to shipping and storage, with very few residences. The warehouses held little of great interest, lumber and foodstuff and such; guards here were practically paid to sleep and most did their jobs quite well. I slid past them using the shadows and making less sound than the lapping river, not because I needed to but because I'm a professional. At the shore I cast about for what I sought, namely a place to cross.

The tunnel I had used on my first trip to Old Cryss was a happy accident, and would either be blocked up or rigorously guarded now. I had no idea how long it would take me to scout out the bandits in their ruined temple and decipher a way in and out with the Brow. But

I would certainly need to get back and forth several times, and for that I required a narrow, quiet space without too much current. That last was not a problem: the Tepid earned its name and hardly ever turned a whitecap on its lazy way to the Western Sea. I had seen ships fully loaded make their way to dock upstream with just the foresail unfurled. But few came this high upriver anymore.

Almost immediately I found a place where the dock pilings stood up eight or ten feet into the air; the river level had certainly been higher in ancient times. I gauged that I had enough cord with me. Taking it from my pack I attached one end securely to a piling and waded into the flow. There are definitely advantages to being a swimmer, though that could not be the long-term plan. Whatever disguise I chose to infiltrate the gang, I doubted whether "soaking wet" would pass muster. After tonight, I intended to ride.

I held the nether end of the cord in my teeth and swam steadily out and across. The current's tug was gentle if persistent, I was sure my mechanism would handle it. The water was chilly beyond words, but the danger I was heading into fired my spirit and I reached the opposite dock in what seemed a few moments. On the Old Cryss side, nearly everything was made of stone. I sank into the water and fixed the cord around an iron dock stanchion about three feet beneath the surface, knotting it tightly and by feel in the night-dark waters. I surfaced quietly and emerged with a smooth slow kip that brought me onto the granite docks without splash or grunt. I need not have bothered; everything around me was as still as ice.

Which was also as cold as I felt: hugging myself I bent low and jogged off the dock into the lee of a building. There, I stripped naked, wrung my outfit and laid it over a stone rail to dry in the ceaseless frigid breeze that pressed through the streets.

This would be a bad time to meet an armed patrol of killers, drugged assassins and former gladiators, led by a plague-ridden king of crime who thought nothing of sending children off to be eaten by Bugs. Standing there naked except for my mask, I held the *noun-chakas* and shook my head, grinning with the absurdity of the peril. But I was ten blocks north of the place where I had come in last time, and there was no sound through the long minutes I waited until my clothing was dry. Feldspar was disappointed at not facing combat naked, but I assured him there would be richer challenges soon.

One more week and the start of Swan would mean spring to most folks. Yet I could swear on this side, in Old Cryss, there was a chill among these valleys of solid stone that spoke of mid-winter, or even the frozen north. Of course, not wearing a stitch of cloth from my soles to my scalp hardly helped. But the menace of this precinct was unmistakable, quite aside from the sights I'd seen in my first foray.

My clothing dry at last, I donned shirt, head-wrap, breeks and boots and set out toward the piazzo. The fabric was the temperature of granite and still a bit crisp; but decorum must be observed.

I stuck to the street level here, though I knew that once I started scouting there would be no substitute for altitude. I thought about all the tales men told of the disaster that overtook this side of the city; I would likely have to find out which, if any, were true. And I needed to know about Salivaar's mysterious patron, though I had my guess already and I hoped I wasn't right about that. Carnad Mias was already too close to W'starrah Altieri for my comfort; if he dealt with such murderers he wouldn't hesitate to take the life of the most beautiful woman in Cryssigens. I thought about the Brow of the Ecclesiast I was hoping to obtain for her, and what it had done to Farlo. Perhaps if she died, it would be my fault. So then, I needed to know more about the Brow as well. Perhaps I should write this all down.

I made no noise as I walked, but absorbed in my thoughts I forgot to check at each corner. Turning onto Salva Way, I saw a group of armed men walking my direction not a spear's throw ahead.

Without stopping or turning I reversed my step back around the corner. I might have been in sight a full second, maybe two, without sound, a black shape in the black shadows. Lucky enough?

"What was that?"

No, not this time. I ran, taking turns on impulse to evade the group, who were arguing and trotting over to check the first corner where I had been. Feldspar smoothly suggested this was good luck after all, and I parried the thought while hugging the buildings and checking each corner briefly before crossing. Old Cryss is not the place to be stupid twice in the same hour. I had missed which direction I was taking: but the sounds of pursuit died and I was betting the group would argue no one had been there. Still, it seemed Salivaar was risking nothing after the intrusion, and sent patrols out now which would make my immediate task more difficult.

Ten minutes later I was sure I had distanced my pursuers. I felt confident I wasn't going to underestimate the dangers again. And as always, I had no doubt Feldspar's pluck and talent could see me through the unknown. What I didn't have was the faintest idea where I was right now. Trying to gauge my position from the moons only brought me up against the fact that I had lost track of time. It was past midnight, for certain, and I seemed to be east of the piazzo somewhere. But the enormous stone buildings only changed flavor in ways I could not decipher: still no homes, no markets or open space or smaller streets. Just massive piles of municipal ambition, all intended for some kind of public business in the light of day, now abandoned for centuries whatever had been their original purpose. I was assailed by the loneliness and alienation of the waste inherent in deserting the Old City. What stroke of calamity could have sufficed…

I came out into an oval space where a carriage-path surrounded a lovely fountain, and across from it wide steps led up to a high, broad building that stood out against the moonlight almost as if it had lights on within its windows. And I had never seen it before, but I knew it like an old schoolmate. *The Eye of the World*, spoken of in hushed tones by all my former peers at the *Flames of Hope Hall* in center-city. The theater of Old Cryss, and my heart leaped with joy, for here would be everything I needed to secure an extended spying expedition, including my conveyance across the Tepid River. Nothing could keep me from entering this place tonight, at once.

The enormous doors were still open, as if there had been a performance on whichever night the catastrophe struck, and everyone within had fled. So much the better, I thought, no salvager before me. I paused in the outer lobby, where shreds of moonlight through the upper story windows showed me a space as large as three houses back on Simith's street. I saw the winding stairs looming up into shadows, the heavy-curtained archways leading into the auditorium. And I could sense them, the massive crowds in glittering array passing through and chattering with the excitement, the anticipation, and even the disappointment that was the stuff of life for me more than a decade ago. *The Eye of the World* was no commoner's hall, where the acting had to convince and guffaws or boos told you where you stood with them; here the audience arrived already half-believing, they earnestly wished to be fooled, and a geared contraption or some puffs of smoke did the trick. They came away sighing, because for three hours they had breathed in another place and time, been a braver or more beautiful person.

Everyone wants to believe they can be someone else, live another life; who knew that better than me?

I pushed through the arch curtains and lit my bullseye lantern. The auditorium was clearly enormous, the darkness felt almost the size of the arena, and the air was utterly still. The smell of musty cloth was strong, and something else too, something so faint and sickly sweet I tingled with a sense of danger. Groping down an aisle, I lost count of the steps until I came to the stage, level with my chest: this house must be three thousand persons, which got me thinking about the acoustics. And I knew it was stupid but I couldn't resist. I pushed up onstage, found the curtain, turned around to face the hundred-score empty seats, and declaimed.

Were we not bound by blood I would whisper to thee of such horrors as I have seen,

That nary a mortal could avoid the impending Moment of their death.

Let none of mine family know a like fear, pay any price to protect thy beloved,

And when comes the test pray ye can unsee the grewsome vision whose like I forbear to sully thy sanity withal!

The Ghost-speech of the Overlord's dead father, from a play long ago. A perfect ring-echo in the darkness, once and done, carrying to every corner with clarity. The ceiling must be domed like a seashell, and more clever tricks besides, to achieve this miracle. How I longed to light every bracket, hoist the chandelier no doubt hanging over center-house, and take in the gold-plated plaster and deep wooden frames, the frescos on each wall.

Feldspar grumbled that perhaps I would prefer to stay here and relive the glory of Perion Toll'k'r to a vacant hall forever. I suggested that the city's greatest Stealthic was just one of many roles I played, and he was so insulted he actually shut up awhile. I explored the backstage area, certain I could find everything I needed.

One solid yank on the curtain-rope snapped it in my hand, hundreds of years later it was of course rotted out. But I wanted the pulleys at top and bottom, perfect for my needs. Another half-hour's search brought me everything else I wished—wood planks and nails, metal brackets and in a locked storage room, stored coils of rope kept dry and still in good condition. I shed my pack to take out the gearing-crank I had put together in my home. But needing more light, I went back to the wings to find a full-sized lantern.

Astor smiled on me, as just before I lit it I heard voices in the lobby.

"Well met, holy sir. I am honored to host you in my humble kingdom."

"Never mind the feeble courtesies, churl. Tell me why I had to come here to transact our business."

The second voice was not familiar to me. But the host could only be Salivaar. I slid back up the aisle in total darkness to listen at the archway curtain.

"I shall be candid with you, Devout: we have no basis for this business you speak of. Or rather, we have half a business: I have something you want indeed, and when my patron instructed me I supplied it to you, even risking a trip across the river for the privilege of your acquaintance."

"And your elixir was everything I hoped for. Well, then?"

A nasty chuckle in response. "Well then, sir, we come to the question of what it is that you can offer me, if you wish to excise our mutual contact from the equation."

In the pause that followed, I inserted one finger to the side of the thick velvet and pushed it far enough off the wall to allow one eye to see. There stood Salivaar, if you could call anything with that bent a back standing, with three of his pock-skinned toughs behind him, rubbing his hands a bit as he awaited an answer.

Across from him was a monk, the tall thin fellow in brown robes I had seen in the arena at the Ides voting. From the holy place at Sinter, I think it was. Behind his glaring eyes and rigid arms stood two mismatched fellows, occupying the spot normally blocked out for bodyguards, but hardly looking the equivalent of their opposite numbers in this particular drama. The shorter one had all he could do not to fall asleep, evidently, with his fellow holding him up and looking miserable.

"I can give you a place in the new order of your precious Mark," the cowled monk hissed. He seemed not in the least concerned for his safety here in the haunted city surrounded by murderers and so poorly protected.

"But with respect, holy sir," Salivaar replied with a smile, "I am already promised that by my patron."

"And what place will you have should your patron not survive?"

Salivaar's face showed his shock at this. "You! You think your magic tricks will hold you up against the most powerful Cup in the city?"

He snapped his fingers and his guards drew their blades. The monk did not move but fixed his gaze on Salivaar, who shook his head in pain, then cringed back a pace, and cried out "Take them!"

As the first guard stepped in, the brown-robed mystic shifted his gaze to him. The raised arm never brought down its sword, he stopped in place with his face in shock. The monk produced a short wooden rod with a length of rope on its end and slapped his opponent with it across the shoulder. It was a toy-strike, like a glove to the face, but produced a howl of fear and a dropped weapon. The monk stowed the whip-baton in his sleeve and glanced to the other two swordsmen, who stopped and looked to their leader.

Salivaar snarled in disgust and waved them back. "My patron will not take kindly to the release of elixir before its time. What assurance can you offer—"

"A guarantee?" bellowed the monk, his hidden face only emphasizing the threat. "I tell you, churl, there is a storm coming to uproot everything you know, to level buildings, customs and all previous agreements such as you wish to wrap yourself in. Cold comfort, to have an assurance hovering over your dead body! Fear not the Red Cup, nor the Blue, nor all the guards and miracles and spells that lie marshalled across the river in all the city. The One Wind comes, to unite those who believe and char the rest, making room for a better world. What are you, to stand against the One Wind?"

"What am I?" Salivaar replied as quiet as a slow-drawn sword. "Who am I indeed, great holy sir. Perhaps you should know, before we conclude our business." And with that, Salivaar stepped closer to the monk, out to where the moonlight shone on the lobby floor. He stopped, and smiled, and began to change.

I felt a tingle and put my hand on the *noun-chakas*. Hair, everywhere across his swarthy face and along his arms, ending now in claws. I would have said a face such as his could not possibly become more pointed. But then I was thinking of a human being, not a long-toothed rat who reared on two legs and laughed like a choking man.

The monk at last took a step back, one arm warding the sight before him.

"Abomination!"

"And your humble servant, holy sir," the giant vermin responded. Stepping back into the shadow, Salivaar's features disappeared a moment, and when I could make them out again, he looked almost handsome by comparison.

"You impress me, holy sir, with your sermon. I shall bring more elixir to you in a week's time."

"Tomorrow. And five times as much as before."

Salivaar held up his hands. "Impossible. The B--, my source of supply cannot work so quickly. Perhaps in three days, two canteens, or perhaps sooner, but I cannot promise."

"As quickly as you can. Shall it be here again?"

"Let us be more cautious. My agents shall convey the word to you as before, at the Stargazer temple. I will select another location. And now, my man will guide you back to a safe crossing."

The monk spun on his heel and left, his bodyguards lagging behind and one of Salivaar's guards jogging to catch up. Salivaar watched them go from the edge of the door, then muttered a curse and gestured to the remaining pair who followed him out.

My spirit nudged me, and as soon as the man I had come to find was out of hearing I left the theater and followed the monk. The Brow was with Salivaar, and Feldspar shouted that we needed to track him, learn his routine and find a way to beat him or take his place. But this deadly fanatic who could cow a lycanthrope was quartered at the temple of the Stargazers, where my patron lived perhaps unaware of the threat.

And Kat, her life might also be in danger.

I jogged along silently behind the group, easily catching them up and avoiding another patrol they saluted in passing. Salivaar was really looking for me; I was flattered by the attention. A bit tougher to get to the temple, Feldspar admitted, but easier to move around once inside. I agreed. When the group turned down a narrow alley off the main street, I knew they were headed back to the tunnel. That would never do for me, and I didn't want to risk the pilings-hop I had taken with Keilee the other day, with more eyes on this side watching. I broke into a sprint back to the pier where I had come across. No way around it; I was going to be wet for a while.

The water seemed even colder on the way back; I didn't bother with stealth on this end but shot out of the shallows to the dock, leaving wet tracks behind me as I ran on. If I took time to strip and dry I would lose him. This next hour was going to test my endurance.

I knew the alley where the tunnel came out and took up station across the street, rubbing and hopping as I waited for the monk to emerge. Detour, swim and all, I knew I was ahead of him. More than a quarter-hour later and I was shivering before I heard the sounds of argument and frantic shushing, which caught the attention of the thug detailed to keep watch from the warehouse window overhead. The monk emerged with his two guards and Salivaar's man still trying to keep him quiet. The former waved off the escort now and moved on with that odd-shaped pair behind him; the thugs for their part were glad to be rid of him with gestures behind his back. I looped around the rear of my block and kept their forms in sight at the cross-streets.

I knew their destination of course, but my instincts told me this man needed careful watching. He was essentially masked, like me, and I wondered if that made others curious in the same way. His guards, as I looked them over, were Bedou-uu, the desert dwelling rustics who seldom came among the Children of Hope except to make trade or war. The short one seemed wounded, clutching his arm where a torc was wrapped tight, while the taller split his concern between master and mate. At times I could hear the brown-robed mystic muttering something to himself, evidently a steady stream of words but I didn't dare get close enough to overhear the private sermon. No question, he was impatient to the point of rage. Every time he looked my way I could have sworn he saw me though I huddled in shadow.

Center city was too brightly lit to allow an easy track, so I reluctantly split from him and ran about the darker perimeter, past homes, closed up shops and even taverns now shaded in the lee of morning. There were two main entrances to the Stargazer compound, and I gambled he would not take the one closer to W'starrah's tower, or else I'd have seen him on one of my scouting missions. I almost wished I could run full-out and steadily, it might have dried my clothing faster. I felt as chilled and soaked as if still on the dock. Perhaps the gate-guards wouldn't mind a black-robed masked man standing there a spell to warm himself at the brazier. Yes, and perhaps the Stargazers were all chaste.

Here came the monk up the darkened side street directly behind me. I couldn't approach the compound now or I'd be seen—I needed time to gauge the wall-walk guards. With a long slow breath I squeezed back between the lintels of a deep-set doorway and stood completely still.

The monk passed by, then stopped at the end of the block where I had stood a moment ago. His guards behind him were close enough to my doorway that I could almost pluck the torc off the shorter one's arm. Their leader took a look both ways from the edge of the shadows, then closed his eyes, for what seemed to me the first time.

His image began to fade and flicker, clothing first and then the features beneath. Around his neck I caught sight of a gaudy, golden, jewel encrusted choker, with many limbs clutching around to the back. It shimmered and moved, legs in exact imitation of an insect as the sorcery worked. My skin crawled and I felt a chill even deeper than the river. Before me stood a man nearly as tall, more muscular, bald and handsome, wearing white silk pantaloons and above the waist a pair of leather straps crossed on his chest. The ornate crawling thing on his neck was gone, replaced by a single golden band. The monk was the high priest of Argens Stargazer, the same who had accosted the bravo in the temple earlier this night. But how was that possible?

I was so surprised I forgot not to sneeze.

The priest turned angrily back to stare at his guards, who were bewildered by the sound.

"I swear to you, holy sir, Elehar is ill, you heard him."

"Take care of your friend, Sanhim, I have need of him yet."

61

"Master, may we not take off the—"

"Never. Come with me."

He headed toward the gate and I knew time was short. I could not afford to lose him, I had to risk it. Looking across the wall for the head of a passing guard and seeing none, I sprinted out and leaped up; grabbing the low edge, I kipped completely over and into a stand of mulberry on the inside. Not much sound, and no outcry followed. There came the priest down the path to the rectory and I resumed my pursuit. I tingled with the threat this man posed; my mind could make no sense of the miracle I had just seen.

And it made even less, when the door to the preacher's quarters opened and the same bald handsome priest stepped out to confront his twin.

The first mystic stopped short and looked both ways, as the other seized him by the shoulders and bodily dragged him to one side, into the shadows. The precinct was deserted, except for the two guards and me. Sheltered behind a bench I could hear every hiss and whisper perfectly.

"What did I tell you!" the newcomer growled, furious and shoving the other one loose against the wall. "Never to take my form again."

"I was in a hurry, brother, and the guards—"

"I said *never!*" To my eye the only difference between the men was the plain gold circlet around the monk's neck, while the preacher from inside the building was clear of any jewelry. "Ever since you accosted the Heaven's Eye, tried to wring from her the secret of the new Mark, I have forbidden you this."

"Stop mooning, brother," the other scoffed, "there is more at stake here than another bride for your bed. The One Wind is coming."

"To all the hells with your wind!" This preacher was clearly the original—what was his name, Tanar'h I think—and knew how to carry himself around the monk. Sloughing off his stare, Tanar'h seized the imposter again, while his alleged guards just stood by as if in shock. "Don't try your gaze tricks on me, Teretheny, I have been immune since our childhood."

Shrugging, the choker-wearing preacher stood back a pace, and again his flesh and clothing flowed the way the surface of a pool ripples around a stone. Just a brief glimpse of the metallic band growing

62

its gem-studded legs, settling upon his neck, and then the brown-robed monk was back, taller and thinner than the High Heart of the Stargazers, masked to the eyes and clearly as angry as the original.

"You fail as always to see the larger picture," Teretheny sneered. "The day my father foresaw is upon us. You did not spend enough time with him to learn your part."

"He threw me away!" Tanar'h cried. "What part was I supposed to take, brother, sold to the Rom and sent to the settled lands?"

"He needed you here, ascending in the ranks to prepare the way for my coming. You knew that."

"We were children. I did not climb among the Stargazers for love of my father, any more than I remained a slave among the Gypsies. They freed me at once, settled me with good family, and when I found my vocation here, it was Argens who guided my steps. Not the line of a Bedou-uu shaman, crazed with hatred for all civilization and bent on destruction."

"Nonsense," Teretheny replied, "you are exactly where our father needed you to be, and now it only remains that you stand back, take shelter from the coming storm, and be there to gather into the fold those worthy of survival."

"Madness! You think you will slay thousands, just to secure the primacy of the Stargazer."

"Of Argens! Never, nor any of the other fantasy tales by which you discern the heroes." Teretheny stood proud as Tanar'h gasped, fell back and laid his hand on a dagger at his waist. "The One Wind sweeps all such lies before it into the flame, leaving only one virtue, one path, one leader to follow."

"You?" Tanar'h choked. The masked man merely shrugged, but his eyes still stared unblinking as if at something sun-bright a league away. "I cannot believe you are even half my brother; sorrow to both our mothers, that they might look down on what has become of us." He shook his head and sagged back against the wall. "What kind of viper have I let inside these walls?"

"We are bound by blood," Teretheny spat back, "and you will not deny the vows of family which you swore as a child. I am here. You are my host."

"I am bound, indeed. But mark you, 'brother'; offer no insult to W'starrah, nor to any of my wives, do not even speak to them as you value what you call life. Keep to your quarters." He pointed to the door with authority, but Teretheny grunted as one unimpressed before breezing past. When he was alone, Tanar'h knelt in place right on the walkway stone and clasped his hands in silent appeal to his hero.

I left him to search for his answers. I needed plenty of my own. I took a moment to time the passing guards, vaulted the low wall at a point practically in the shade of a cross-alley, and sauntered through the quiet streets with the light that comes before dawn providing an easy path back to my warehouse hideaway. I had to know more about the cataclysm that left Old Cryss to a man like Salivaar; about how the Brow of the Ecclesiast could have fallen into the hands of Carnad Mias who passed it along to the bandit-king; and about its connection to the desert and Sinter, which had sent us Teretheny.

In short I needed a sage, a lettered Elf of the noble class with nothing better to do than read and remember. And Feldspar didn't know anyone like that.

But Jonn Simith's employer did.

⊕ ⊕ ⊕

"Zetee, I don't like it."

"So you have said, Tass, several times."

Justin's two closest officers stood in the light of dawn at the edge of their encampment, scouring the castle ahead for any sign they might have missed. Scouts reported the skies overhead had been clear of those winged horrors, and the hill-men did not evidently come this close under any circumstances.

"Send me. I'll take my dekent right up to the gate and get that overstuffed air-sack to tell us where the Captain is."

"We know where he is." M'nesa was as gentle and measured in his words as ever. "We need to know how he is. And on that score they cannot reassure us."

"Demand to see him!" Tass was unaccustomed urgent now—such concern did not fit his usual habit. "Make them tell us something."

"To see him? On what basis? We will look weak."

"Cark it! Let them underestimate us, all the better!"

"And we would make the Captain look weak." M'nesa saw Tass stop with his jaw open on that. "Let us get our commander back before we try to play mind-games with the enemy."

"At least you admit that much," Tass grumbled before stomping off to awaken his dekent for a pre-breakfast drill. M'nesa Zetee was left alone with the burden of command, and it made him want to stay just like this, closer to the castle than any of the men so no one could see his face.

Give them no cause to complain of us, those were the Captain's orders. Whichever way his mind turned, he found he could argue himself against it. Tass was typically direct in his thinking, and it wasn't the worst of all ideas, to try and force a response. Based on what they had seen so far, the company might outnumber the garrison ten to one. But if not... M'nesa thought about leading five men across the chasm far from the gates, to see if they could infiltrate the place. They might confirm the defences, perhaps find some clue to the Captain's fate, and possibly get out undetected.

But if the castle was fully manned, they would be caught in an act of war.

Fourteen hours now, and M'nesa's best friend missing with his commander. It made part of him rankle close to frenzy, but he knew that anything would feel better than nothing, and that this was just a form of panic.

Calling to the veteran dekentar, M'nesa took him aside for a private chat.

"Take your men to the stream for water. See if there's a spot to dam it, and roll some stones into place."

The veteran's eyebrow went up. "In sight of the fortress, yes? So they get the idea we might cut them off soon. Aye, sir, well done." He limped away whistling for his dekent.

M'nesa quietly asked two more men to scale the mountain behind them. "Take your time, stop and look back at the castle whenever you see a good perch from which to do so."

"Unseen, sir?"

"Not necessary, don't mind if you are spotted, just find out what you can about the inside. I want a full report before this evening."

The men both grinned and saluted before heading up. M'nesa strode out of the camp and turned right, up the slated road to its narrow apex, out of sight of the castle where his volunteer was sitting on a rock to one side.

"How are you doing, young fellow, tired? Do you need food or a replacement?"

"I am well sir, no need."

The gryphon-handler was surely less than twenty years, his manner betrayed him as he snapped to alert and saluted. M'nesa had noticed his desire to help, to belong, and he remembered what Justin said about those following. He had asked the youth to stand lookout here, with the old trumpet from Valin's day, and blow it on first sight of anyone approaching.

"You have been a big help to us. But come back to camp when you are tired, or need water, something. You're no good to us falling asleep."

"I'm not sleeping sir, I swear! And I have plenty of food."

M'nesa nodded, thanked him again, and returned to camp. It would come tonight, his instincts shouted to him. The men were prepared as he could make them, and he ordered mandatory rest following the mid-day meal.

It came that night.

The creak of the gates brought every man to alert and running to their positions without need of orders. As a cadre of armed men stomped over the bridge, the moonlit sky showed their Captain and Kein Trador were not among them. M'nesa stood by his mount with his dekent, one of only two saddled and ready for use as cavalry. The other men lined the perimeter behind the low rock-wall and the dry ditch they had prepared to deepen it. Tass grinned and held up a fist as he stood with his men at the brush-gate, the only place without a ditch and thus the best avenue for an attack. Twenty men were detailed for bows, at the camp corner and behind the spearmen. Six men under the veteran dekentar stood by the wagons, a tiny reserve and also to protect the children huddled beneath.

The force coming to them was only twenty strong, yet each one armored like a foot knight and bearing a halberd with reach and cutting power to command respect. The large plate-visored commander behind them could only be Perishune, hefting a two-handed axe with a shield slung over his back.

At two hundred paces, the Tralmachians stopped and waited.

"Hold your bows, men, we've had no hostile sign yet."

At this, Tass laughed and spat. "No worries, Zetee. He's waiting on his reinforcements."

"Ho there," M'nesa called out in what he hoped was a confident tone. "In what way may we be of service to you, milord T'yr?"

Perishune lifted his visor far enough to spit. "You can all lay down your weapons and take shelter in the inner bailey."

M'nesa smiled and made a show of searching the sky. "Shelter, milord? You are most kind but it does not seem like rain." The men jeered and hooted at this; but Perishune joined in the laughter.

"Keep watching, little one. You'll beg for shelter soon enough."

"Perhaps," Tass shouted, "if you come a bit closer, air-sack, you and I can see which one is quickest to start begging."

Almost on cue, the sound of high tinny screeching echoed through the vale. The men all gasped and looked up in every direction.

"Steady, men," M'nesa put in quietly, "bowmen, stay sharp." He recalled what Kein had said about the winged monsters, and earnestly prayed his friend was right. Or for that matter, still alive.

The first attack was too sudden. One of the flying things had maneuvered low to the ground until it was behind the camp. Diving nearly vertical down the mountainside, it stooped into the center and snatched up a bowman from behind before its first scream of triumph. Men cried out and some hit the ground, no one dared assist the poor fellow as the monster bit and tore him in the moonlit sky. An unmoving body fell three full counts through the air to slam horridly into the earth between the two troops.

"Bowmen form a ring!" M'nesa cried. Three shapes were visible at various angles, and the men called out sightings and cursed their inattention.

Perishune ordered his retinue to resume the advance, and shouted "Last chance, Emperor's men, surrender now and we will protect you."

Tass came to stand behind the center of the brush-gate and gestured to the baron's son. "Worry about your own protection, you flabby carker."

Another cheer from the men was cut off by the sound of a trumpet, blown both loudly and poorly, from up the road to the right. M'nesa's heart dropped as he saw the youth clambering along the slopes above, waving and gesturing down into the vale he had been guarding.

As Perishune's troop approached he ordered some of them into the ditch and up the other side. M'nesa thought they were admirably steady, if a bit slow. The first few to enter the ditch regained their balance, stepped across, and then swung their ponderous heavy halberds with power and menace, if not deadly aim. Shields blocked, and spears counter-thrust down into visors, necks, repeatedly stabbing to find a crevice in their armor. M'nesa felt a clutch of fear—no one planned on facing foot soldiers armored as well as royal retainers.

The screams from above signaled that the flying monsters were coming in for a group attack. They were fast but did not much maneuver, and M'nesa saw signs they expected an easy kill. With a dropped arm he signaled the first volley, and the bowstrings thrummed in unison. At least half a dozen hit, and everyone heard the tenor of the monsters screaming in outrage and pain. They veered off, one a bit wobbly in flight with a fold of its leathery wings pinioned like the hem of a too-long sleeve. The gryphon in the cage rose up and screamed its ear-blasting din, which seemed to add to their speed a moment. But they all circled around, calling to each other and gesturing in a horribly human way.

Perishune and his remaining men approached the brush-gate over level ground. Tass and his dekent stood in, dodging the massive halberds and trying to counter with their spears through the hedge. Tass awaited his foe with sword and shield, barely taller and broader than the Elf who whirled his axe through half the barrier in a single blow.

Waiting until he chose to step through the wrack, Tass engaged the foe and had him in some difficulty at once with snapping branches underfoot. Ducking under the first swing he countered with a strong sword thrust directly into the chest. Plate and chain were excellent protection from such blows, but Tass was larger and stronger than anyone M'nesa had ever seen. The crunch and rasp of penetration were audible over the melee, and Tass shouted with triumph as four inches of his blade sank into Perishune's body.

The baron's son snarled in anger, but not much pain it seemed. Striking a back-blow with the ax, he sent Tass hurtling bodily down with the sword plucked out and skittering to one side. Only a trickle of blood indicated there was any wound. Tass rolled to his feet and slapped on his cestus, grinning like a cat and shuffling back in. Perishune hesitated, then swung again; Tass took the blow on his shield, then countered with a punch under the jaw that knocked his foe's helm clean from his head. The baron's son staggered back but closed again with a great sweep that made Tass give ground. Other men approached the flanks, but the ax blade endured no invasion and Perishune swung it like a letter-opener in a weave of steel.

The men were crying out all along the line now, as their work was having so little effect. None of the attackers had crested the ditch, but numerous stabs and blows on them seemed to have no effect either. The halberds did not always miss, and wounded men fell back to have their places filled. The flying things circled and called, but kept from bowshot.

M'nesa saw to the right, a slow-moving band of figures trudging into the vale and toward the camp. It might have been eighty or a hundred forms in the darkness, and behind them glinted the armor of the nobleman they had seen from the village walls. With hardly any weapons or armor, they looked very much like a peasant levy marched laboriously here to do war-service as in the olden days.

Except they also moved so slowly. And some had horrible wounds, or clods of dirt in their hair.

M'nesa looked out to the ditch where one enemy soldier had taken an arrow through the eye-slit buried in his socket to the feathers, and fought on unaffected. No longer any doubt, then.

"Hack the limbs! Aim for the head!" M'nesa ordered half the bowmen to take up spear and sword, and sent them to reinforce Tass at the gate where the brush was already cut to kindling: he directed the others to stay trained on the skies.

Now the village gaunts had reached the camp and the sounds of shouting, clashing metal, and the stifled curses of the wounded rose to a clamor that echoed around the vale and off the black castle walls. With no tactics, speed or subtlety, the enemy clambered in a wave of flesh down into the ditch and up the other side, stepping over dislodged rocks, the men of Perishune's troop, and each other in an effort to reach the top and seize the living opposite. Hacks and shoves generally worked to stave them off: stabs did very little, and a few who grappled were overcome by clusters of hands, pulling them screaming over the wall and down.

The desperate work continued for what seemed an hour. Tass strove with Perishune at the brush entrance, his men slowly pushing back their foes beyond the level of the ditch. M'nesa led his bowmen into the gap, and from there took the foe in flank. With a sudden shout and strange full-armed gesture, the nobleman ordered a retreat.

As the foes broke contact and pulled away, M'nesa felt a surge of elation and ran back to his horsemen. They mounted and rode out; now was the moment to exploit the victory. Tass' men were already in pursuit on foot, and had hewed down several of the undead. M'nesa led the horsemen past on the right side, hacking down at bodies as they cantered by. This seemed well done indeed.

The high screeching cries overhead froze his blood, even as his horse startled beneath him. They had come beyond the cover of his bowmen, without orders. "Assemble! Back to the camp and mind your heads!"

The men began to gather, but it was too late. Screaming down from the sky came nightmare forms, seizing bodies and turning up again as blood spattered down behind them. Three men, two on foot and one snatched from his horse's back, rose up trailing choking screams behind them. By the time the flying things had slain, dropped and returned, the foot dekent was inside the camp. M'nesa let all the others past and was close enough to see the first horror gliding down, as it took an arrow in the shoulder, screamed and veered off. Then they were all back behind the flimsy wall of rock.

"Seven lost, sir."

"I make out twenty-three of the enemy down as well."

M'nesa took in the reports, his eyes fixed on the enemy across the vale. Both contingents had reformed now, stopped and faced the camp again with a score of bodies between them. One riderless horse galloped back and forth whinnying in confusion and panic. The flying creatures flew off to the castle walls, this time on the near side, where they stooped and also waited, some bad dream of gargoyles come to life.

M'nesa tried to catch his breath and wondered what could be next. He had enough time to give up hope that his friend and his Captain could still be alive. Should he try to march the men out at first light? What else the point of remaining here, except that he had no orders to retreat. That would have to be enough.

From the direction of the gate came a deep, sonorous voice calling out in a language M'nesa had never heard. The shout was not strained nor did it start out loud, yet echoes of its syllables seemed to kick between the rock faces repeatedly like the clangor of church bells. Slowly at first, so that he doubted his eyes, M'nesa made out the forms of the slain starting to move. The dead of both sides rose again, turned and shuffled toward the camp, as the nobleman signaled the other two cadres to return to the attack.

Tass called over from his post by the now-stripped gateway. "I'm just an ignorant arena man, Zetee. But the math here is not very hard to do."

M'nesa smiled grimly at his dekentar, then looked to the skies where the creatures had returned to wheel and cry. Moons headed down now, perhaps two hours until dawn. Pay as few lives as possible then, for each hour.

No more pursuits, for one thing.

$$\oplus \oplus \oplus$$

When I investigated the report of a tavern brawl, milord, descriptions of the assailants matched these two. I saw them a few blocks away, hailed, and they fled immediately. I thought it best to pursue."

Beirill's account was crisp and clean, just the way Gaspar Heugen liked it. No extraneous titles of address, the deeds minus all subjective coloring. This dekentar felt ambition and lacked humor; the acting regent of Cryssigens understood both tendencies quite well.

The Fire Grip took in his officer's words while gazing to the accused, two grungy toughs standing at the head of a pack of other plaintiffs and suspects, here for the day of Common Pleas. Citizens willing to risk the penalty of costs could bring suit against rivals, neighbors and family one day a month, and the Mark Guards emptied their holding cells of those accused in crimes, for summary judgment. Here was one of the latter such cases, two men arrested on suspicion of assaulting a minstrel in the dock quarter.

Attending to the cases of the common citizens was part of what kept Heugen so busy; his reputation for sleeplessness was legend, not myth. Keeping the city running, personally attending to the innumerable details of North Mark administration in the absence of so many officials and minor posts, unfilled since the death of the Overlord and his son a year ago; Gaspar Heugen was willing to appear ruthless and haughty, to be thought scheming after the throne he served. With non-stop work, he could avoid blaming himself for the calamity that had overtaken his city, and deny responsibility for the storm he suspected would threaten it soon.

"The victim, then, is still incapacitated?" Heugen asked, fixing the arrested pair with his eyes.

"We took her to the healer, sir, he's a walking miracle." Beirill's voice and rare hyperbole drew a glance from his commander. "She'll recover, but must rest another day. Both legs broken." At this the audience gasped and muttered.

Heugen knew the woman, Shai, was quite popular with the tavern folk, a reputation for gentle humor and of excellent voice. Concerts were a rare occurrence for him, taverns even rarer. But he did not require emotion to do his job, a rule that had guided his life for several decades and now was more vital than ever.

"Bring the accused forward. You there, tell us your story."

"With great respect, Fire Grip and beloved of Cryss Altair, hope of all the city," the first stammered, and already Heugen began to feel unclean just from the sound of him. "We are innocent men, Jangs and me both. Weren't either of us in that tavern, lordship, we stay together all the time."

"Testimony from those in *The Grog's Lees*, sir," Beirill interjected, laying a sheaf of reports on the bench. "Descriptions match both suspects."

"Heard the racket," blurted the second man, "went to help, found her, that's the truth, found her lying in the alley all beat hollow."

"Signed statement from the victim, milord," Beirill laid another sheet atop the pile, "attesting to the presence of the two in the tavern, becoming drunk, starting an argument, and accosting her as soon as she left."

"It weren't us, great Fire Grip milord your honor!" the first man shouted and blathered on, his face showing fear at the presence of so much paper he could not read. His companion stood silent but as tense as a pulled bowstring: without his friend, Jangs would have confessed already. Heugen cared nothing for the accused's state of mind, nor even much for his guilt or innocence. This was the job of the hour. Let the laws and precedents make your decision, bang the gavel, and move on to the next case. Plenty to keep busy, no need to feel anything about it.

There were only a few left in the queue, behind those gawking onlookers. A woman with children, no doubt to complain of spoiled flour at the market or some injury to her garden. Two tradesmen standing shoulder to shoulder, unwilling to let each other out of sight until the court had heard every detail of their trivial disputation. He wondered why that old man in the back was already bound, what trouble he could have caused to draw a personal guard. But this was not to the purpose. Do justice here first. No hurry, the longer the work the less need to think about the future.

"Descriptions!" the first thug cried, "No doubt, very accurate descriptions, great Fire Grip exalted lord and judge of mercy. What do they say, eh? These descriptions, scribbled on those papers there? Two men, innit? Look, there's two back there—" he pointed to the tradesmen. "Or that we were dirty, perhaps? Who wouldn't have some dirt after a long day's work, as are half those here today!" His sweeping gesture brought him a step closer to the bench, and Heugen's nose confirmed what his intuition had earlier guessed.

"The victim identifies the two men." Beirill growled.

"And where is she!" Jangs shouted, "To say it was us who attacked her. We were helping her I vow great lord, just as my friend here said."

"As you lie under suspicion," Heugen announced, "and unless someone stands surety for your freedom, you must be bound over until the victim can return to testify."

"With respect, milord," Beirill said, "we have had too many sureties posted of late, with suspects not honoring their obligation. These two are guilty, I tell you."

"We are not!" the first thug shouted, feeling his oats now and sensing victory. "Where do our names appear in those paper records before today, tell me that. Any previous crimes? No witnesses to any misdeeds, I'll swear."

"None that lived, you mean!" The clear voice broke through the room from the back bringing gasps and a parting crowd. The grey-haired old man lurched forward in his guard's grasp, eyes blazing with a vigor that belied such age.

"Quiet you!" Beirill shouted. "Your case is coming."

"Dekentar, hold a moment." Heugen was looking at the accused and saw Jangs' face blanch at the sight of the older man. Laying aside the ancient gavel a moment, he gestured the speaker forward, and his guard brought him hobbling up by the elbow, wrists bound in front and upper arms also tied behind his back. It was a mortal Man, dressed all in grey and looking almost a warrior. Beneath his thick court robes Heugen felt a chill at the sight of him; something about his eyes.

"Who is this fellow, what is his case?"

"A northerner milord, gives his name as Solemn Judgement. There have been many reports of him around the city, citizens upset and afraid of his, well, his manner and I ordered him brought in to answer for his business here. But he gave no satisfaction and claimed a need to leave." Beirill hesitated, and Heugen sensed he was not entirely happy to have this one here. "I ordered him to remain, and that's when he instigated a fight. With soldiers of the Mark, a clear felony and worth a whipping by the law."

The stranger stood straight and returned Heugen's gaze as if the discussion concerned someone else. There was something about his manner that spoke of youth, he had only shuffled because of the binding ropes.

"We will not muddle the current case with that discussion just yet," he announced. "Mortal, Judgement, what is your testimony as regards the actions of these two? Are you a witness to this assault?"

The grey man turned to look at the others and his face hardened even more than before. "Of that one, nay milord, but three nights previous with another woman. Aye, these men would rape and kill, if they could."

"It's a lie great lord!" Jangs shouted and his partner proceeded to elaborate while Heugen ignored them to study the Man. No—the youth, he realized, perhaps twenty years but uncommonly reserved and controlled, even under arrest and with hostile fellows accusing him.

"We've seen this one, yes your honor, but he assaulted us—"

Heugen watched carefully and saw the grey mortal quietly strain against his bonded biceps. Not an attack, no attempt to strike or seize his adversaries. He seemed to be trying to touch his odd-shaped holy symbol, large and silver with a bottom arm long enough to grasp.

"And we fled, great lord, of course, what could we do him armed with that magic staff and all. And the lady, who knows what became of her the poor thing—"

And Gaspar Heugen, despite his best efforts and decades of practice, had an emotional reaction to a situation. Instead of doing his job, he became curious.

As the two thugs poured out their story, he gestured to the guard, saying "Release his bonds."

The guardsman looked up shocked, and briefly to Beirill who grimaced in disapproval. Then he obeyed the orders of the virtual regent of Cryssigens, and pulled open the bonds around the grey man's wrists and arms.

As the accused were still talking, the strange youth took up his holy symbol in one hand and gestured with the other, crying "I call upon Areghel to detect the lie!"

The two men stopped in mid-word, and the entire court gasped and rose to see the crimson aura spring into life around the pair. Heugen noted as Beirill stepped back with a curse, that a faint reddish glow clung to him a moment as well. But enough time for that later. Now the court had dissolved into chaos: onlookers among the commoner's gallery were shouting in fear at the miracle, some guards had drawn blades. Up above, Heugen spotted in the balcony reserved for nobility a slight figure sat forward, robed and veiled in the black silk of mourning; only her white hair peeking out gave away Citari Kreel the former Overlord's widow.

And at this Gaspar Heugen felt another wave of emotion. And again it was curiosity.

He slammed the sacred gavel twice and the room calmed immediately. The two accused men still glowed as the Man in Grey stared them down, and now the mortal spoke with anger.

"Scum of villainy! It lays against mine conscience that I treated not more vigorously with thee when I did apprehend thy first attempt. Even thy filthy words in that hour were enough to occasion punishment. Had I bethought me the chance ye would repeat such unspeakable transgression, and I'd have remonstrated with thee both in such wise as would have kept you from this court for all thy days!" The targets of his words cowered back and spoke no more, seeing their own red aura with terror.

"Save us, great lord! He attacks us again in open court!"

"Milord," Beirill spoke low with urgency, "This churl used sorcery in the court, expressly forbidden! And called upon a northern hero, totally against the custom. Let me put him back in irons, I beg you."

Heugen forestalled him with one hand, yet Beirill was right. All the common sense of it lay against the stranger: post bond for the two thugs, sentence this one to a whipping for multiple transgressions. Preserve the precedents of Argensian law. Keep busy. Instead he lay the gavel down and spoke to the mortal.

"You say they attacked another woman, some nights hence? Where, and who?"

"In the area below the docks, nearby this court, milord. A fair lady, a preacher methinks, of golden hair and dressed all in purple."

"The Lavender Lady!" Heugen could not help exclaiming. "What was she doing with you in the under-docks?"

"With me, sir nothing. I came by as these two accosted her, and of her business I know naught."

Heugen reflected that he had indeed seen W'starrah Altieri at the palace three nights past. He glanced up to the balcony where the widow Kreel still sat and watched the proceedings. Alongside his burning curiosity, which threatened to unseat his habits of control and calm, there now arose a second emotion inside Gaspar Heugen. Looking up to the noble box and back to the grim, righteous youth, the Fire Grip of Cryssigens realized he wanted to do justice here. To hold his head a little higher than merely keeping the law required. To earn, perhaps, the respect of the Lady Kreel for once and for no reason.

76

"You say the Heaven's Eye of the Stargazers was assaulted in the poorest quarter of the city. Where is she now, that she might affirm your story?"

The Man in Grey spread his hands, but Beirill spoke up. "She is reported to be in her tower, milord, answering to no one, perhaps in prayer or else…" he shrugged to indicate the rumors ran thick and fast.

Heugen took up his gavel again and rapped it once. "You two stand accused of the most serious of crimes. And your defence is proven a lie by the miracle of this fellow here, who has had dealings with you. Neither victim can appear to seal your fate with their testimony, but that too may lie against your account." The accused were white with fear, and it gave Heugen pleasure to be the cause. "You are bound over until such time as we can have testimony. Should either victim affirm you were not, in fact, the malefactors, I will release you pending trial in the other case. If not, then your penalty shall be death by hanging. Bailiff, take them away."

"And this one, milord?" Beirill's eyes were hungry for another prisoner, but Heugen remembered the slight red aura and smiled; the guardsman's tale was no doubt stretched a bit in his own favor, driven by his pride he had exaggerated the hostility's source, vigor, or both.

"Return his effects to him at once, and let him go." He looked down to the youth, who bowed low over a straightened knee. "I want you to seek the High Priestess of the Stargazers and request her testimony in this case. Do not rest until you find her, I charge you."

"Milord, it shall be done, and I swear it."

Murmurs ran through the courtroom as Heugen gaveled the session closed. The mother and merchants would have to wait, his guard inspection was nearly overdue. Must keep busy, Heugen reminded himself as he shed his robe and carefully placed the sacred gavel back in its strongbox, locking the changing room and ascending to the upper halls which connected with the rest of the Crystal Palace.

In the hall his progress was arrested by a cloud of the usual courtiers, pressing forward with documents to sign and requests for instruction. Normally there would have been a tier of officials for these functionaries to consult, but the rebellion cost many lives especially among the noble classes. Rather than break precedent and appoint them, Heugen had chosen to await the new Overlord, and in the meantime handle them personally. Keep busy. But today, he waved them all off with the once-swept arm that meant "no business now" and the civil staff reeled back, to better reveal what he glimpsed over their heads; Citari Kreel, still veiled and clearly waiting to speak with him.

This in itself was not so unusual; in the first months after her son was slain and the empire changed hands, she besieged him at the head of mobs such as this one, bitterly complaining about his every move, each decree or refusal to act alike. But in recent weeks she had quieted, absenting herself from the chosen position of gadfly to his efforts, and staying within her chambers (where the servants whispered she kept a shrine to Argens Demonbender in defiance of the Emperor's decree) or walking by the steep cliffs at night (where rumor insisted she was tempted to leap to her death).

Now she stood there, as the pool of busy attendants and adjutants drained away leaving them alone in the hall. And Gaspar Heugen felt another thrill of emotion, one he could not name at all but blending two parts fear with a dram of excitement and the dregs of that leftover curiosity which had begun to plague him.

"Step-Marchess", he addressed her with a stiffly correct, bow-between-peers, to which she nodded.

"Fire Grip, you took liberties with the customs today."

"And this interests you, milady?"

She shrugged as they turned to walk together toward the palace which housed them both and little else. "Hanging or a death-flog for the two who assailed a priestess."

"On just the word of a common mortal? We need more evidence."

"You saw the miracle! And certainly a strapping on that impudent fellow for so insulting our dignity."

Heugen raised an eyebrow at her words and considered carefully his own for a few quiet steps.

"We differ here, Step-Marchess. I cannot agree that the truth insults the dignity of anyone who deserves to govern. He is indeed quite proud, as are both of us. But this only shows how easily that quality may be attained. How proud he was indeed, and only a youth, did you mark that? We must aspire to something higher, I believe, than the defence of our imagined dignity."

78

The widow Kreel flapped a hand in disgust. "You waste time in such merciful distinctions, Fire Grip. Death for two who threatened a noble lady, and a whipping for a commoner who broke the customs. Why pause a moment for any other ruling?"

Heugen stopped and smiled at her, knowing full well she might take offence. "We have so many years before us, milady. Would another day, or a week in the pursuit of justice seem to you a price we should scruple to complain of?"

Citari Kreel stared back at him through the veil of widowhood, and Heugen thought he saw something flare up then, either anger or a kind of horrid determination. Touched a nerve, most likely. But what drove this clenched, unyielding woman? And why should he have cared?

Heugen could not tell as he stood there taking in her fiery eyes, nor had he any notion what drove him next.

"Milady," he said, bowing again and extending his arm, "will you walk the battlements with me? May I have the privilege?"

A long moment passed in which Gaspar Heugen was quite certain he would be refused. This woman was his superior in rank, at least by her former marriage; she worshiped a different sect now outlawed, and if any Color won her support it would have had to be the Red, opposed to his Blue House these centuries. Two small stones rattling about in this enormous palace, who by random chance might never have crossed each other's path, and until now Heugen believed his adversary wished it that way. Yet he held his arm and waited, as the blaze in her eyes gradually dimmed back to the temperature where courtesy could survive. Without a word, she laid her hand on his and they ascended to the walls, two backs as straight as spears and with heads as sharp.

The afternoon was clouded but fine with a sea-breeze that whispered of spring, not now but soon. As they emerged Heugen delicately turned so that he would be closer to the battlements, and her glance told him she was aware of his precaution. They strode without speaking for several long minutes, a dance of patience the Elven nobility all knew well. The first to speak gave away a point. Heugen considered her with flash-glances and thought about her devotion to the outlawed sect, her strong words in council (usually opposed to his), her avidity for the arena games now also forbidden by imperial decree. None of the slaves assigned her suite had left despite their free condition. No doubt she had the ear of Carnad Mias, Heugen's chief rival who sat at the center of a web of guilds, and who according to Heugen's agents was close to the support he needed to name the next Mark.

Why, he wondered again, should he care? No doubt he would be dismissed, perhaps with some mark of disgrace or a manufactured scandal; retirement to his manor in center city held no terror for him. Let them try to run the Mark without him and good riddance. But then, why had he asked Citari Kreel to walk with him? Heugen considered how best to begin, to lose the point and still gain in the game.

They were at the extreme northwest corner now, overlooking the cliffs and the bay that led to the Western Ocean. The breeze kicked hardest here and the surf far below required one to speak up, dispense with subtlety. Gaspar Heugen searched his heart, thought about pride and risk and justice, and decided the conditions against him were but a delicious trimming to a meal long forgotten.

"Milady," he began, then paused to show he was in no hurry. "Several days ago you sent me the silversteel Token of Fire without instruction or restriction." His conversant continued gazing over the cliffs and sea, and the only sign she had heard his words was by removing her hand from his arm. "I do not stoop to ask why. But would you hear how I disposed of it?"

A moment of puzzlement crossed her brow, and Heugen knew he had scored back the point. She assumed he would use it himself, or perhaps had already done so. He looked out over the sea with her awhile, and then continued.

"I sent it by unliveried messenger to the Emperor's Captain, with instructions to approach the Stargazer temple and open as many doors as he could with it."

He could tell she was calculating, which meant he scored another point. It was only a moment, in which the line of her mouth was tight and closed, but as good as words. Citari Kreel did not know his reasons, which meant she might be guiltless of the suspicion he had formerly held of her. Heugen ached to ask, but that would lose the game completely.

She turned a moment to regard him, and nodded. "You thought to throw his support under the enchantment of the Heaven's Eye, and thus to draw that vote away from the Red. She only cozened up to Carnad Mias recently, after her feud with Hammer."

Heugen rejoiced inside but let none of it show. So close! Yet Citari missed the mark, and lost face with him to have guessed wrong. So much revealed, and now the right play was to return her gaze with only a hint of approval, say no more, and withdraw to contemplate his new advantage.

But he thought of that lovely child, alone and threatened in the under-docks despite his efforts, and it cut him to the core. And Heugen decided to double-down instead, to put his advantage back on the table to see what else the wheel of fortune might bring him.

"No man could resist the beauty of W'starrah Altieri," he admitted, "but in truth, milady, I was trying to protect her life."

This brought Citari's face around again a moment, with a look that seemed too angry for this news. Heugen continued.

"W'starrah Altieri and her confidante were nearly assassinated, less than two weeks ago. Just two days after we met at the arena."

"But why!" Citari's tone was truly angry now. "What debt did you owe this precious little mystic with her tangled visions and smooth skin? Why do you care who lives or dies, or when?"

She still stared out to sea now, and something in her tone made Heugen move to take her arm in his grip. She looked back to him furious, and he willingly sacrificed all the points he had won in the game, to make a final one.

"Why, milady? Do you seriously argue that you do not see?"

"I see nothing, milord, from your words." The widow Kreel tried to take a step back but Heugen retained her arm, the act of a commoner. Or someone risking too much.

"Not my words, milady, but your view." He gestured to the sea and cliff before them. "Your face is ever to the unchanging prospect of the water, the fall, the end." She gasped in shock to hear him hint of suicide, but he turned her with both arms in his hands now, a familiarity that would have merited a slap, had there been a witness

81

to it. "Listen not to me, your enemy by church and Cup, but look, milady, look for yourself in a better direction."

And he turned her then to face back over the inner bailey toward the rest of Cryssigens glittering in the late flash of the setting sun peeking between clouds behind them.

Citari's voice was filled with ashes. "I see my ruined temple."

"Yes milady. But beyond that. Between our feet and the Emperor who ruined our lives, what is there? A city full of people. Young like W'starrah Altieri, who risks her life with no debt to repay. Proud like you and me, and that young mortal Man who thinks his honor worth protecting, as we do, but despite his common birth and the paltry years left to him. Wealthy men like Carnad Mias, who will do as he pleases to suit his ambitious plans for ever more of anything. Thousands of them, milady, who laugh and need and lose; who deserve justice more than custom, and who will not gain it without help."

He had released her arms but the widow remained to hear his unaccustomed speech, staring at the city of Cryssigens with a face bereft of recognition. Heugen wondered if he would have to deny having said such things. Or if he would want to. Something inside him was changed by the events of this day and he knew not where his soul traveled anymore.

Her cry was sudden and sharp like fractured glass. "I would have the dragon!"

Heugen was so surprised he stepped back a half-pace. His thoughts raced, struggling to assemble the clue. "You asked... you requested the Overlord your husband to show the beast, in the arena. These many years ago."

"No more children," she spat back, "no real part to play in governance. I had my church and my amusements. And I wished to see something novel, and more! To gain my way with my husband, who offered me so little else, ever since... So I sat there as the handler pleaded his case, and you were there as always making sense, but I argued he should be allowed."

Heugen rubbed his face and considered this confession. Both of them, it seemed, were determined to lose the game as it had been usually played. "And the creature had fire, as it happened, and many died." Including W'starrah's parents. He had never thought Citari bore any blame for that day. But when the Heaven's Eye had visited with her—he saw from the battlements as she returned—that must have been an intensely painful interview for the widow. The poor girl, probably had no idea; Heugen suspected she might afterwards have gone looking for the way down to the prison of the Shard Demon. And thus fell afoul of those villains.

"So you favor such rough justice, for those who threatened that girl, or failed to protect her." Now Heugen saw Citari Kreel meet his gaze, level and unfazed, awaiting judgment and ready to return scorn.

"Milady," he said gently, "I have found it will not do to forget my station. Neither of us ruled, on that day you referred to. We give advice, but it is for the ruler to decide. You and I have seldom agreed on matters of policy, but I will say without hesitation your judgment stands above that of others in all matters. Excepting, perhaps, questions of mercy before the law."

He waited a moment to see if the jibe would reach her. Her lips beneath the lace veil flicked and the gaze softened a touch. "I have no patience for court pleas and precedents," she muttered in the closest she had come to good grace in a year.

"Milady, as Fire Grip of the city I have no authority to order you about, and I trust you have not found my presence here too confining. But in the absence of any right, I would still advise the heart you rule, as you advised your husband and son, to cease looking for lost sources of happiness. The current day has taken them from you, I do not deny it. But there can still be work, and worth, perhaps a kind of contentment. I would gladly partner with you in this if you wish it."

Now the lady stepped back a pace, staring with wider eyes and a hand to her chest. Heugen feared she might call the guards to witness a complaint, but instead she gasped and whispered.

"Her very words... contentment and partnership..."

Suddenly the widow Kreel turned and moved off to the battlement stairs, never looking back at him and neither making any move to leap into the sea. Through his worry that he had offended her, Heugen noted that she seemed to move with some idea in mind now, though what it could be eluded him. As he walked briskly back to his chambers to prepare for the troop inspection, he tried to pull in the fragments of old habits, his usual countenance and attitude which had swum far away from him on a sea of strange emotions.

He had only just finished changing into his evening uniform, pulling on dress gloves before the mirror, when he heard a light rap on his window. There on the third story of the gate tower that was his home stood a figure draped all in black, by a ledge too narrow to perch on, yet comfortable as a man on the ground.

⊕ ⊕ ⊕

He awoke to complete blindness, and agony in his left wrist. No amount of blinking could create a flicker of vision in the wall of black before his eyes. He called out and heard a slight echo, stone all around most likely as it was beneath his body. The stench of dank and rot was suffocating, and a gorge of panic began to rise inside him. Moving his left arm brought a sting to make him hiss; when he reached to feel the spot it was curiously numb but horribly swollen between forearm and hand. His fingers touched something hard, wet and sharp protruding from the skin and he cried out in fear.

But then he had a thought to drown all terror and pain; his Captain might be nearby and able to hear how he comported himself. Kein Trador remembered then that he was a soldier of the Empire.

Sitting up, he struggled to aid himself and recall what he could. The audience hall—that monster, it seemed his sword did it no harm, and the grip that broke his wrist like kindling: the young dekentar took a shot of pain just to remember the awful strength of that thing. Feeling with his good hand, Trador undid his belt and held the empty scabbard across his lap, picking at the leather straps and painstakingly arranging them around his injured wrist. His memory showed him glimpses: a dim-lit stair leading down to blackness, a small room to one side where the guards tossed their weapons, onto a pile of others. The clang of his cell door after they shoved him inside (the pain of that fall, he must have passed out from the agony of landing on his wrist). How long since he had lost consciousness?

As he worked, Trador called out to his captain and heard nothing but the single echo of his voice. Think, he ordered himself, learn what you can. The chamber sounded larger than needed for a single cell, but surely smaller than the great halls of the castle above. He must be below ground, from the smell and utter quiet. Trador thought of buried bodies, how he was now entombed, of a horrid unlife beyond death, and had to master his breathing before he could continue with the splint. Looping the knots with one hand, he grasped the other end in his teeth, drew a deep breath and pulled hard to tighten them. The clench of his jaw muffled the scream somewhat, and when he spat out the string he let loose with another; maybe no one to hear it anyway, no loss of pride in that. He redid his belt with great effort, and then tied off the long ends of the leather straps to hold the splinted wrist against his buckle.

Was he alone? Did he see the Captain with him when dragged to this place? Trador could not remember. The seeping cold of the stones was taking all feeling from his legs, so Trador struggled to stand using only one arm and then shuffled slowly with his good hand before him in every direction. Stone walls, blocks so massive he seldom touched a crevice between them. Above his head, a ceiling of native rock not two inches past his hair; it made him stoop to know it. No drafts, following the walls he felt stone, stone, then bars, solid, prickly with corrosion but nearly as thick as his arms. He called through them again and again.

"Captain? Captain Thyme, are you there, are you well sir?"

Only his own voice came back through the stifling darkness, and Trador's spirits began to sink. He slid slowly down the bars to his knees and wondered what death would bring. Had it already been an hour? Three? Perhaps his adversaries in the castle above were undead creatures, as horrid as the thought appeared. He felt drained of Hope, and wondered if that was part of the preparation. The next time he saw M'nesa, he might reach out to rip the throat of a friend...

From his knees, Trador remembered to pray, and he did not hesitate to speak aloud.

"Great Argens, let your fire bring light to the darkness in which I find myself. Help me with courage, give me strength to strike a blow for Hope even from this hole of Hell. Flame of the First, watch over the Captain wherever he is. I pray he is not dead, nor turned to some foul purpose by our enemies now revealed, and that you would aid him. Free him, great Son of the Sun, if it be your will to leave me here, only bring my Captain out of whatever straits he is in and put him back in command, where no doubt he will win the victory."

No energy left after that, Trador knelt where he was and felt the growing pain of stone on his knees without caring.

"My thanks… for your good… opinion, dekentar." The voice was weak, its owner sounded prone and groggy, but Trador felt a bucket of energy wash over him at the sound.

"Captain! You're alive!"

"Apparently. Perhaps an oversight on our enemy's part?"

"Assuredly, sir."

The Captain's voice sounded broken and hoarse to Trador, but no matter now. "Can you reach the bars of your cell, sir? Let us see if we can grasp hands."

The two aligned themselves by directions and reached through the gap, waving their hands in inky nothing without result. Justin cursed a couple times from pacing his cell, a bit taller than Trador and grazing the uneven ceiling.

"So then," the Captain muttered. "If my cell matches yours, a chamber here nearly ten paces across including this hall between us."

"Impossible to tell how long it might be," Trador replied, "I can find nothing in my cell to throw."

"Are you injured, dekentar?"

"A little bother on my wrist, sir, I've splinted and tied it off." Trador cursed inwardly that he could not keep that slight quaver from his tone.

"I see. For myself, I might not be shouting for a couple of days, but otherwise I seem to have been left intact."

They compared notes then, finding nothing of interest to a plan of escape. Kein tried to budge his bars, and heard the Captain grunting with the effort on his side.

"Nothing. Of course."

"They are very old, sir, by the feel of them."

"Yes and thick. But not set into mortar, by what I can feel, drilled right into the native rock." There was a pause before the Captain spoke again, and all pauses seemed to last forever. "I don't even feel a door or a lock on mine."

"We are like those tiny ships inside glass jugs, then."

A grunt of approval from across the way. "We are like deer in a trap, rather. I touch no bones in my cell, Trador. They will not leave us here to stare and rot. Much as we might wish it."

"When they come, sir, we must be ready."

Now the grunt was more negative. "Separate and disoriented, weaponless and injured. I agree we will try what we can, dekentar, but let us have no illusions here. If only I could get some idea of the situation outside."

They discussed the possibilities, none of them very appealing. Trador excused himself to pray, more quietly this time. The Captain also prayed, and Trador tried not to listen. Over the endless stretches of time with nothing in them, he attempted to respond always as a good soldier should, direct answers, no hint of despair. When he heard nothing from across the way he tried to sleep; when he heard a sigh he thought of whatever quick joke he could, or even sang.

Boredom was the mother of insanity, and he spent the time rehearsing tactical drills from the manual or fondly daydreaming of M'nesa leading the men in a rescue. Whenever he slept he invariably dreamed of that face, his opponent of those last seconds in the light, not at all human yet sneering and somehow drenched in noble training. The hardened cruelty that he saw there, without mercy or concern, stayed with him as he rose up shivering and sweating, then returned to prayer.

As endless time weighed down he became unable to ignore the rising pain in his wrist. The swelling became no worse, but very little better, and it was often wet when he felt the area, as if steadily bleeding. The aches became a drumbeat that kept him from sleep, pounding him with every pulse and painting a grim vision behind his sightless eyes of something gangrenous and ruined, a target for amputation. The end of service and the end of life started to merge; Trador found it increasingly hard to respond when the Captain spoke.

The clatch of a key in metal lock was so loud when it came that Trador shouted in alarm. He tried to rise and failed, stunned at his weakness, but managed to stagger up on the second attempt with a lurch into the bars.

"Stand ready, dekentar," Justin said, in that tone which always steadied him. Trador nodded for no one's benefit, and thought about using his head to butt, since he doubted he had strength or balance to kick.

Light from the single torch was more painful than being stabbed in the eyes. Trador cursed and squinted toward the edges of its advancing radius, through his tears making out the stone cut hall, levers in the wall, and one pair of boots.

"I was sent to check on your condition."

Trador still could not bring his eyes to look so close to the blinding light of the torch, but the voice had the ring of someone living.

"You are Sordinay," he said, "the seventh son."

"I am so very sorry, dekentar, captain," the nobleman checked his words as if speaking against his will, "I tried, that is I could not, you must understand—"

"You have no need to explain yourself, milord Baron," Justin said quietly from the shadows of his own cell.

"Why do you address me thus, sir, in mockery? I tell you I had no choice."

"No mockery, milord. Am I correct, that of all your brothers only you have been left alive?"

Trador could make out a form now, but few features, as the slender Elf nodded. He saw the Captain as well, stepping forward into the light and thankfully uninjured. He was shocked at the sallow and sunken frame of his leader, and only thought then to glance down at his aching wrist. Red, blue and swollen, and the jutting bone only a finger-width but ivory stained with dark crimson. Finally viewing the extent of his injury dispelled the nightmares of his imagination and Trador felt his spirits rally a bit on that, as well as the mystery of his Captain's claim.

"This is true, sir; Perishune and the younger six excepting me are all gaunts, their hearts removed and completely enslaved to my father. The elder four… with them he has practiced an even darker art, and I know not the proper word nor even if there should be one for such abominations. But they can fly, no longer taking human form as my father still insists on for his vanity. And they consume life from others, I cannot fathom how."

"And of course your father is one of these creatures."

"The first, to my knowledge, and I sincerely hope the only one in all the Lands."

Justin took in the statement, nodding and returning a steady gaze to Sordinay.

"Thus you see the point, milord. You are indeed the only surviving issue of House T'yr and as such, the Baron."

"Harder to fathom!" Sordinay's laughter cracked with hysteria, "He speaks to me every day, you see. He commands, he drinks and eats as if, he looks... sometimes he looks at my mother." Trador could see the tears start now, though he gave no other sign. "I am his seventh, you know. There was never a day, I do not remember..." his voice trailed off into nothing and he stood there slightly quaking.

Trador felt weak himself, and wondered briefly how long they had been held here. But now was not the moment for trivialities. "Why does he, that is, why did—"

"I have not been turned, alone among my brothers. No. It must be the prophecy."

"A prophecy?" The Captain's face as he spoke shone with its own light, the word meant something to him. "Whose, and when?"

"Before I was born. My eldest brother, Vol'tun told me the story once, to mock me with my weakness. A Rom seer from before... when my father was still warm in body, she cried it out in full court and he slew her with his bare hands. I've often thought on it in my bitterness." And he recited from rote:

The Blood makes spite of years and death
Unto all its generations
Beware only the seventh
Neither before nor after it shall resist the turning
But that which loves the light and warmth of Argens
Shall make the Baron anew

"But what does it mean?" Trador asked.

"I have never deciphered it, and I hope in my heart that he has not either. Perhaps it is only uncertainty that stays his hand. I cannot tarry here. He sent me to determine your condition. My father intends you for his ritual, Captain. Your mention of Argens, he believes, means your life's blood can restore his youth and vigor."

Trador never felt his knees give way, only knew he was prone from the stone's cold on his arm and shoulder. The torch's flare came close enough for the heat to touch his forehead, and he felt something small pressed into his hand.

"Your weakness is advancing as expected. The Baron needs you close to death before he dares the ritual, he will take no chances with any of us. This is a tonic, drink half now and wait as long as you can before the rest. I don't know if I will be allowed to return."

"We must escape and destroy him," the Captain's voice was not loud but firm.

"He is immune to blows, fire, age, disease," Sordinay spoke now into the other cell. "A magic blade, perhaps, but of those we have none, at least that I know of. I must leave now."

"No weapon at all? No aid you can give us?"

"None, sir. Or rather, none in my reach. I heard the hill-rustics speak years ago of blades made from a stone, abrasor, but I have never seen it. And it is hopeless in any event, much to my sorrow. I will not aid you against my father."

Sordinay backed up the hallway and Trador was too weak and dismayed to count the steps. He looked at the levers on the wall as the shadows grew, but was too weak to rise again and gauge their height or distance.

"You must help us!" the Captain cried. "That monster, your father must be destroyed!"

"No. Never."

Trador shouted as the door began to shut, "He is already dead!"

A short pause, and he heard the son's doleful voice. "But my mother is still alive."

The crash of metal in the jamb was final.

⊕ ⊕ ⊕

"A theatrical production, you say?" The Elvish nobleman poured tea for his guest and sat back, at home and relaxed. "How novel, I don't suppose there has been a truly new play written in, why I'm not sure how long."

"Just an idea, you understand, Sage J'seff'n, yes. One of several, but I have high hopes yes, rather high hopes."

"Sage? You honor me, sir. Merely a student of history."

Surely, but I could see he was pleased. The idea of letting Chay sponsor a new drama was inspired. It gave me every excuse to consult with this scholar of the noble class, a man who would have yelled for the guards if he saw Feldspar at his window. Chay was already known to his fellows in the Stone Guild as one who loved entertainment. Anyone who heard about this plan of his wouldn't bat an eye. And for the theater, I didn't even have to fake enthusiasm: indeed, the more we discussed the notion, the more brilliant it sounded.

"The life of Mart'l'n Ecclese," J'seff'n mused, "a worthy subject for dramatization. Have you thought about a theme?"

"Oh yes, well that is, I had given a few moments' consideration," I temporized, coming around to it gently and trying not to arouse suspicion. "I thought of course, that his effort in avoiding a war, yes, that this would be of interest as it were."

"And particularly now."

"Yes? Oh, that is yes! Of course now of all times." I must not let him suspect Chay was drawing that deep an inference, so I patted my ample stomach, took another sip of his marvelous tea and pretended to reflect. "It is simply that, well yes, that we need to be sure of the spectacle, yes? As it were? I believe there was some notion in the legends, some story of a great diadem or other, that he created?"

J'seff'n nodded patiently, "The Brow of the Ecclesiast, of course. And you would like a description, I'm sure so that you can recreate it onstage."

"Paste and foil, I assure you sir! Yes, the properties of the theater are of a decidedly humbler stamp. And then too, we must consider the distance, perhaps a larger size... ah yes, well, leave that to me, or rather to those I shall hire for the purpose." I took another sip and tried to appear unconscious of any meaning as I rambled on. "And then too, yes, any details about its crafting, as it were, the moment of creation, other persons there, other... things, yes, as it were, that sort."

At first, I thought despite my efforts I had bungled the matter, for the sage looked at me steadily with a wondering face. I blinked a couple of times and waited, while inside me Feldspar grumbled that we should have done with this farce and just break in later to read whatever we wanted. Nonsense, I assured him; we had already seen the shelves on our way in, more books than walls. It would take me a year to find what I needed.

"So strange," J'seff'n said after a long pause, "that two persons would ask about the same things in less than a week."

"Oh? Oh yes? Do you mean, the Potters Guild are also writing a play!"

"What? Oh no, sir, nothing of the sort. I mean another person, a dear friend of mine, asked about the creation of the Brow just the other day. Interesting tale, actually and you are quite correct to express an interest. The great preacher Ecclese partnered with both a northern dwarf and a shaman of the Bedou-uu."

"Indeed? Oh splendid, marvelous, yes. My, who shall we hire to play a dwarf I wonder. And such a shortage of great actors these days, with the, as it were, yes, the great tragedy of the Glass Parade." I was getting carried away by my own idea. In the old days I know the part of the dwarf would have been mine, and I would need to figure a way to appear five inches shorter.

"Certainly a rich acting opportunity. The three men worked together for several weeks, the histories say, and our great preacher came away with the Brow."

"Yes," I said, coming to it at last, "and, em, yes, and the others?"

"The dwarf took no such reward," J'seff'n replied, "just a block of the magic metal back to his homeland for what purpose no book says. And the Bedou-uu shaman created another jeweled item, a kind of tight necklace or choker called the Throat of the Spider."

Feldspar's rejoicing could not be fully contained, and I cried out with good humor. "Oh marvelous, yes! Yes, that is, another prop to create as it were. And shaped somewhat like a Bug, I should think? Horrible, the ladies will scream."

J'seff'n laughed and agreed, while I wondered how I could have suspected the truth. When I had seen Teretheny with that horrid crawling necklace, something about it reminded me of the Brow. That must have been it, some style of the craftsmanship, and of course both were set with gems though the neck-piece was simply studded with them. Was he aware of the existence of the Brow, and scheming

92

to get it as W'starrah was? Or did the artefacts call to each other over the years and leagues, pulling their human couriers into ever-closer orbit... with a small start I realized I was beginning to script a play already. Feldspar huffed that it was unnecessary, and I agreed.

"So then, Sage J'seff'n, are there any tales, as it were, concerning the sorcery instilled, yes, or enchanted I suppose, into this necklace?"

"I am not aware of any," J'seff'n said slowly, "but I will look into it."

"Many thanks, noble sir, and of course I am prepared to pay whatever you think reasonable—" I rose and could see him dismiss the notion with an elegant wave. But that was the way of it with the nobility. Only a commoner such as myself could suggest direct pay, and with it the implied insult of employment. He would research only driven by his interests, of course; and within a sentence or two from now he would lightly mention some charitable interest, or a cause of some kind that could use an infusion of capital. And there of course would stand any chance I might have of gaining another audience.

J'seff'n had fixed his gaze to a rare spot on his wall that was bare of books. He reached for an elaborate pipe and drew on it as he thought; he might have forgotten to dismiss me but I had nothing more I could say in courtesy, so I waited and watched. The aroma of the smoke was tinged with something I could not quite name, but familiar to me nonetheless. Somewhere recently, in another place...

"You know," J'seff'n said in a decisive tone, "I believe I shall ask about this very subject, tomorrow night, at the Red Cup's gala."

"Oh yes? Why yes!" I said encouragingly, giving up on any effort to recall what event in the crowded social calendar they would be observing.

"There are a few others of my set who might know something. And then that holy monk from Sinter will be there, I gather, the Red Cup's guest. The legends say the shaman long ago passed through Sinter on his way back to the desert lands."

I gasped slightly as the chill shot down my spine, struggling to maintain Chay's genial, rotund posture and conceal my urgency hearing this plan. I lurched into a bow, and said "I congratulate you, milord, for no doubt that will be an excellent plan."

Turning to go, I heard him call into the inner chambers to his wife.

"Drat it, Miry, I need a good smoke to think, but I'm out of that love-leaf you bought. Perhaps you had better fetch some more from the under-docks, or I could break free of the enchantment you've cast upon me."

As the noblewoman laughed within I stumbled out the apartment door and grabbed the stair rail like a drunken man. That aroma, of course! Even masked by tobacco I could not mistake it, a bit like the sea... the assassins at the temple, that night when a pair of ex-Vipers tried to kill W'starrah and Kat. Vipers wearing belt buckles so Blue they practically shone with it. I walked the streets of the center city with my hands behind my back (they barely fit around the paunch Chay had) and thought about as hard as I had in a year.

Whoever was behind this conspiracy had access to drugs that could enslave the will, or perhaps cause desire, or both. I had never kept up with the various kinds, somewhat relieved when the Emperor had forbidden them by decree. But enforcement, of course, was trickier. And the hands behind the attempted assassination of a seer who might know the next Mark's name also spread this drug more widely, probably sprinkling a light amount into all manner of things consumed.

But who? Feldspar ripped out a curse in my mind and ordered me not to outthink myself. House Blue on the buckles, the assassins must have been hired by the Blue Cup, whose chief representative and highest ranked nobleman was Gaspar Heugen. It fit well, I had to admit: Heugen had left the meeting at the Hopeforger temple before either Carnad Mias or W'starrah Altieri, and of course their host Z'kammet Hammer could hardly have set his own church on fire just to... no.

No, something was wrong, the theory was too pat. If Heugen wanted to hire assassins, why dress them in House color at all? A ruse, a plant to throw suspicion: expensive, to steal or hire out a rival Color, probably even dangerous.

I knew the rat-king of Old Cryss had a patron. I knew that powerful mystery man was also in league with Teretheny, or thought he was: the monk was plotting to sidestep him and get some substance from Salivaar, and soon. Assuming it was not my current employer W'starrah, that left only Carnad Mias. And yes, I answered Feldspar's thought before he could voice it in my head—I know, he's hateful and I feel jealous of the attention he's getting from the most beautiful woman in the city. And he's fat.

But he also makes sense. He has the wealth to suborn items of a rival Color, he wants to control who becomes the next North Mark. And tomorrow night House Red will throw a party where no doubt he and Teretheny will meet.

Sunset. I changed to my work clothes and headed for the Crystal Palace.

He opened when I tapped at his window and strode away to give me room. I could tell the Fire Grip of Cryssigens was tense, or perhaps angry, at any rate different than usual. He certainly had no idea why Feldspar was calling on him again. I wasn't sure myself, but it was time to try.

"Feldspar, I must admit you have the advantage of me. I thought our business concluded."

I stood still and waited.

"Your payment, I assume, came through properly? All in order?"

A nod sufficed instead of words, and I let it.

"Well then? If you would forgive me, I am somewhat occupied."

I continued to wait him out. No chance he would say yes if I begged.

"My guard captain Beirill has been seeking you in every spare hour. Are you perhaps, come to turn yourself in?"

I barked a laugh, then produced the message I had composed, laying it on the table and whispering "Favor".

"A favor!" He reached for the paper, unfolding it and reading quickly.

Astor's son requires a suit of Red livery,
As will serve unsuspected at tomorrow's gala.
Great good may come of what he learns there
Further danger to the Mark if he is absent
Only the Fire Grip can manage this discreetly.

Heugen took time to read the message twice, then walked around his desk to sit, carefully burning it in the lamp before steepling his hands.

"You wish to sneak among the Red Cup's servants, at his celebration less than a day from now. You are asking me to secure you a suit of Red, the cloth and cut prohibitively expensive and inimitable of course, thus requiring that one of the genuine servants be rendered, ahm, indisposed. And you wish no one to suspect that this has occurred."

A nod did just as much for me as it did the first time.

Heugen's turn to laugh now. I reached inside my sash.

"I think you have the current of our relationship reversed, sirrah. I hire men such as you, at need, not the other way around. Quite aside from the cost, for what earthly reason should I—"

The sound of something metallic hitting his desk cut off the speech, and Heugen looked down to see a bright Blue belt buckle. He stared without comprehension, then looked up to me, where I showed him its twin.

I waited. Heugen was a proud noble, and a very smart man; I knew my chances were better if he figured this out for himself.

"The dead assassins at the Hopeforger temple," he said slowly. "Her Nubian claimed he saw a dark spirit before he dragged the Heaven's Eye out like a rag-doll. So that was you."

Waiting and not talking was working for me tonight, so I kept at it.

"We investigated, of course, and wondered about the missing belt buckles. You took them, why?"

I crossed my arms and leaned against a wall.

"You don't think I ordered the attack. Or else you would never have given me one of these." He stood and walked behind his desk with hands at his back. "And thus you reason, if not the Blue, then a plot by Blue's enemy. Who else could afford it?"

I made a palms-out gesture to encourage him, but truth to tell holding up my end of the conversation was becoming exhausting. Heugen knew how to take his time, and the temptation to spoil it by saying something was bringing my teeth too far into my lip for comfort.

He waited again, damn him, with a pursed mouth to show he was hesitating to tell me. He shrugged and said, "Were you aware that others have been trying to kill the Heaven's Eye?"

I stood away from the wall. Dedication to work, it appeared, had its drawbacks.

"She was at the Glass Parade, poor thing; saved by Carnad Mias or so everyone says. And earlier, a poisoned fruit of purest Yellow. Items of Color are not supposed to be worn or used by anyone outside their Houses. With the Blue, I know the penalty is death: Carnad Mias may have something worse in mind. Before this month I would have said such theft was impossible. But someone clearly stole these." He paced some more, before dropping in a casual finish. "Just the other night, here in the under-docks, Myster Altieri wandered from her bodyguard and was nearly raped or killed. Those two worthies, at least, we have in custody. But for the rest..."

Under the leather mask I swam in sweat, but put my arms akimbo and tried to convey readiness and indifference. He was masking the issue, or temporizing for some reason.

"Whatever quest she has you on now—naturally, I know it is she who has hired you—the smartest course might be to keep an eye on her. W'starrah Altieri could be the only noble in the city not under suspicion. And someone feels she knows too much to live."

I saw it then, and made a dismissive wave to indicate my mind was made up.

"Very well, you suspect the Red Cup. So do I, whatever that may be worth. But still, why should I do this thing? You may imagine it will be no mean feat to accomplish, and what do I gain from it, tell me that sirrah."

I let him finish, paused a moment, and then silently held up the other buckle.

"You, you would accuse me? Put these items into evidence?" Heugen's tone was not angry or shocked, just a bit wondering, as if he hadn't thought me capable. I wasn't sure I disagreed with him, but I held my pose.

"You do not think I hired the assassins, but you would let me suffer the accusation rather than not get what you want?"

I shrugged slightly, as if to say it was no great thing.

"I had not thought you to have any noble blood, Feldspar, with this penchant for masking your face and hopping over rooftops. But you certainly show some of the requisite ruthlessness."

He sat, smiled, and tossed me the buckle from his desk. "Let us keep the set together." Brave, on top of all; I bowed to him and put the pair away.

Heugen began to write out a message, then stopped to look up at me with just his piercing eyes. "I hardly think this will become a habit, young Stealthic."

When I nodded he returned to writing. "In the hollow of a large elder in the Demonbender compound you will find what you requested, no earlier than sunset tomorrow. Leave the buckles behind."

I turned to the window and he added another word. "Of course it will be easier to simply kill the servant." He wanted to know what sort of man I was. I turned back and did not shrug, but instead cocked my head to the side to hint at disbelief. Heugen's eyes sparkled and he nodded goodbye.

"Very good talking with you Feldspar. Whatever you are up to, I think it in my best interests to wish you good luck." He addressed himself to the message again, saying, "Don't come back."

The cool night air outside his high tower window acquainted me with how much I had been sweating. Before I got to the bottom I had sneezed two more times: this was getting to be a nuisance. Probably the gala would be dry and warm. Feldspar chuckled inside me; make that hot as hell, knowing him.

⊕ ⊕ ⊕

Y̨ou have forgotten me, as I had foreseen you would. Not completely of course, not at the level of your knees and clasped hands and the life-giving rituals you attend to regularly. My name is on your lips as much as ever, indeed more so. A high priestess of the Stargazer does not forget habits formed as a child so easily. But the desire of your heart has moved from me, cherished one, and you come to me less in thanks, more to ask. As it should be, for there is so much you need.

You pray for your people, there in your room after you send the Stallion away. You urge me to save them, promise to let me use you as an instrument of that purpose. Of course, that is already set in the stars, cherished one. You cannot change them, neither can the heroes themselves; we read them together, and that is all. But you no longer come to the roof among the stars, too busy in your efforts to unmask the Dragon's plans, and dodge his clutches.

You beg safety for your friend the teacher, whose love of you brings her so close to peril. You cannot know she is already as safe as anyone in your city: the Dragon and Arbalest now believe that Ekaterinye can be of no further use to you, and focus their plots on your containment or death. It was always the Heaven's Eye they sought to blind.

And sometimes, when that driving energy flags and spirits touch their lowest point, you murmur a wish to find release from the grip of the Insectir's fevered visions, the haunting hunted sense it inflicts on you to make you panic.

And there your prayer must go unanswered. This is the hour of your passion, cherished one. I send you the visions again, the prophecy of the burning crown and your leadership over men. You were willing to pay the price before, years ago, when I showed it for the asking. Nothing has changed, except you begin to suspect that the way to your destiny lies through dark foetid tunnels past the ratcheting chorus of clicks and scratching. Take your thoughts elsewhere, these can only affright you and blunt your purpose.

So of course, you think of him. More and ever more, since that day less than a moon ago when he first came to you—but always I saw him—the Captain of the Empire comes back to your mind. And you think yourself miserable, and deprived that he is not nearby. You little know how this separation creates the needful moment that, if your twinned courage be not found wanting, may save this city from ruin.

The thought of your Captain is the only antidote to this pressing fear, the isolation you feel in a world of violent men. He too will fight of course, blood will spill on your own temple grounds, in this very tower. At his command dozens will die, but you never doubt the Fire Ant's tireless and steadfast will. He is unlike these other monstrosities, swarming beneath your city and scrabbling closer to seize you.

You see new visions now, the Ferret healed by the Turtle and entering the lair of monsters where he and the Serpent make war in various forms before your hireling flees with the Brow in hand. Your Captain and his Fire Ants fight sore pressed and close to annihilation, in the ebon hills where bloodshed drains life from some, sustains it

99

in others. The Dragon moves to free the Fly, as the Arbalest aims his quarrel to unleash destruction. To a mortal still breathing this foretells ruin and failure; you little suspect how much your actions have unsettled them to the point of panic and haste.

The Raccoon knocks at your door and speaks of plans; the request to contact your Captain, he knows well how much you share the need of him. You warn him of the Arbalest and Dragon, recommend that he seek the Stone Oak for shelter and aid. Well done, my cherished one, this too is needful though you see it not yet. Time passes without your will, more than you believe but far too little to prepare for the ordeal ahead. The Stallion has not returned; you cannot see what dread discovery he has made, will not know more than that crazed letter told you.

This, then, is the proper state, the correct moment. The miracles of Argens do not form at a whim. The mortals who gain my aid must be deserving, in need, and connected by more than their own intent. For Hope springs most forcefully when none of us expect it. Now the ring, now the speaking-spell. Now to bring the severed splinters of heroes together. Through you, my cherished one, and at the cost of you it comes.

Would I could not already see what happens next.

⊕ ⊕ ⊕

I slipped into the Demonbender compound, found the hollow tree and scooped up my package, leaving the Blue buckles in their place. It never occurred to me, all the way across the city, that I should try to double-cross Gaspar Heugen. Not until I reached my changing booth and saw the servant's outfit he had given me to dress up in.

It was, in fact, a dress.

I stood in the booth and looked the lovely cut and frills up and down, until I started giggling. First a suppressed running gasp, then louder and higher until verging into hysteria. Not that I was out of control, though this was certainly a funny situation. No, I was practicing. I can play a woman near as easy as a man, or at least that's my opinion. That girlish giggle was my most convincing feature. And after all, I had not specified. I dove into preparation, starting with the make-up.

Putting on the finishing touches in the mirror, I had a sudden thought. Did Gaspar Heugen suspect me of going about in disguise? Was he trying to expose me to his agents (who could be among the guests) by giving me a tougher role to play?

Not likely, I decided. He was one of the smartest men I knew, but even the Fire Grip did not suspect the truth of me, or indeed of anyone. People in this city bent their every effort, their last silver bit, and all their waking hours to showing that one true self to the world. With House Color and rank, for mastery of a craft or of noble style, in physical beauty or from famous deeds done however long ago: the full time job of every inhabitant of Cryssigens was to stand up and shout "Here I am, see me". Even my fellow actors, in mid-production, would turn aside between lines to wink at a mistress or bow to a patron. Ridiculous. For all his wit and foresight, Gaspar Heugen probably thought I wore the black mask day and night.

I shrugged into the wonderful livery-dress and thought about disguises as I arranged the folds and admired the fitted shape of it. Near the Red palace, some serving woman sleeping off a goblet spiced with *somnos* was a buxom lass indeed. Fortunately, so was I, and it would be an experienced groper of butt or breast who could tell the difference. Even if I slipped up in what I said or how I acted, my enemies would only suspect that a female agent of the mysterious Stealthic had made a mistake.

But on second thought I realized it wasn't quite true, to claim everyone in the city was ignorant of disguise. Carnad Mias used no rouge, never changed his stripes; but he was surely pretending one thing and intending another with W'starrah Altieri. And with the city as well, I was betting. The Red Cup was the one I had to get close to tonight, and he was certainly the sort who might suspect what I was doing.

I ran to the palace just east of center-city without concealing my haste; late servants all look the same, whether real or pretending. Even the streets of the precinct were set with red mosaic tile, much less the walls, gates and lampposts to every side. A ruby haze reflecting off every surface made me feel I was trotting through blood.

Around to the back, I joined with two others carrying in wood for the dozens of small fireplaces set around the mansion's five floors.

Inside, more of the same, crimson and scarlet on the most mundane items and in all the guests' attire. Red, the real thing, in shades so dazzling you almost didn't need the chandeliers to light the way: and if you cut open or broke anything, the cloth or wood or stone would be Red through the grain.

I had never had the pleasure of entering Mias' city home before. While I gained the lay of the land I did some actual work, as chores gave me an excellent cover to go places with an excuse, and to get lost when convenient. The butler never looked up as he read tasks off his list and we filed by to receive them. Carrying trays of food to the upper levels, I naturally reviewed the guests; the more famous faces I counted the worse I felt about anyone's chances of reversing the vote. Preachers, guild leaders, nobles, crafters, all were here in abundance.

"Where, I wonder, is the Lavender Lady?" one knight mused aloud to his group.

"Probably sleeping, poor dear," a noblewoman replied, "I see her nearly every night, on our host's arm. He's been rather hard on her."

The others roared as she sipped her wine, completely oblivious to her own wit; I curtsied and slipped past them, wending up to the top floor.

I spent a moment trying to recall if tonight's holiday was a general one: neutral parties and even a few rivals might attend such a celebration if the Red House sponsored something related to city history. But with the vote ahead I had to admit, most folks here were probably supporters. The mansion seemed smaller for the crowd in every gallery, admiring artwork, dancing, or withdrawing to alcoves for a little rest and accidental touching.

There was J'seff'n in splendid garb, expertly sporting tiny Red accents without clashing the style of his Purple suit. He was deep in conversation with two other nobles, and I bet I knew the subject. I skirted them, seeking the evening's quarry while carrying drinks and parrying drunken hands. But despite the giggling, dodging and half-promising, my ears picked up fragments of things I longed to hear.

"My theory, just as the Brow served to convince the hearer's mind, the Throat could alter the wearer's form."

"Indeed? But why for should a man wish to change his appearance?"

"Oh no doubt for nefarious purposes only, to escape the law or perhaps ruin a rival. A very cheap, low purpose in my view, nothing at all like the high destiny of the Brow!"

"Still, to think of it. Don the jewel—"

"Ugh! A Bug on my neck, not for a baron's ransom."

"—and then just think of another man's look."

"Like the Glamor spell of the wizards?"

"Aye, but without end or limit."

"Truly, the work of a rustic villain. Praise the heroes we see it no more."

There on cue was Teretheny, knifing between the partygoers without touching a sleeve, while his two Bedou-uu guards knocked into nearly everyone within arm's reach. The short one was already drunk, lurching in random directions and looking pale as a settled Elf. His taller companion had one arm clutching a sleeve at all times, making a tottering inseparable pair virtually certain to collide with anyone not facing their way.

There was nothing about the two of them with Teretheny that made the slightest sense. I'd have found a way to follow the trio if this had been my first time seeing them.

Conversation quieted wherever the monk went and he took an arrow-straight path through the galleries, wasting no time and speaking to no one. I risked a guess about his destination and sashayed quickly down a parallel hall, hoping the floor plan here was the same as it had been on the levels below.

Without sight of them I agonized and tried not to hurry. But Astor's luck was with me, and at the end of the gallery there was Teretheny, passing into a private room where I caught just a glimpse within, of Carnad Mias before the crimson mahogany portal closed. Teretheny's guards lurched to a halt outside.

This was the conversation I had to catch, and Astor had put it a single wooden wall away. Time to take some real risks, I thought, approaching the guards with three glasses left on my tray. As I spoke to the tall one, I caught snatches of Carnad Mias arguing with Devout Teretheny through the door.

"Thirsty, brave sir? Your comrade looks as if he's had enough."

"—*foolish to stand in the path of the holy gale.*"

"*Blast you, preacher, enough about your One Wind, I won't—*"

The first guard looked at me with a face that made me gasp. Still clinging to his partner, he snared a glass with his free hand and downed the wine in a gulp. As he reached for the second, I could see desperation oozing from the hollows of his eyes, a face almost torn with fear and frenzy. We exchanged a long glance, bereft of desire or banter or hope, and I nearly cried, despite myself, from the aftershock of such suffering.

"*You must tell the vermin… much more, at once.*"

"*At once? No, Teretheny, we move in a week, no sooner, or else—*"

Turning to his friend, the bodyguard murmured, "Elehar, please try, a little sip."

I could see he was most concerned for his partner, and it fit my wish as well as the serving-girl's character to help. I reached out to take the short one's other arm, and my fingers grazed the torc there, wound so tightly that I wondered his bones had not broken.

"Don't touch that!" The tall Bedou-uu was frantic, slapping my arm down to the waist and slopping the drink all over. Mumbling and weeping, he held the goblet to his friend's lip, and in Elehar I beheld the face of a man either unconscious or standing up dead.

"*—have my own ways, beware Red Cup.*"

"*Oh nonsense, you think I didn't know about your meeting with Salivaar? The hottest wind of all is only what comes from your mouth, Teretheny. My men are everywhere! Remember that, you holy amateur. I have already instructed Salivaar—no further elixir except directly to me.*"

A few drops of wine made it past Elehar's lips, and he coughed a bit, blinking weakly.

"That's it, well done!" his friend encouraged him like an older brother in a game.

"Is he sick, then?" I asked with wide eyes, trying not to look as panicked as I felt.

"Sick, yes, maybe. Is there any food?"

"A palaceful, I would say!" I threw in my best giggle, but it had no effect this time, and my heart dropped at what he would certainly ask next.

"*You dare! You grasping mountebank,*"

"Can you get him something? He might eat."

I thought fast while the harangue continued within.

"is everything reduced to a pile of coin with you? Paying off assassins—"

"Me? Well, of course, but what does he like? You could tell better, and I could—"

"Please, mistress," he cried, "sometimes, when the master is away, he can do better."

"buying rival items to further confusion, spreading your foul drugs across the city—"

There was no way I could miss this, so I gave my best giggle and patted the big fellow's arm.

"I'll watch over him like a mother hen, you can be back in a trice."

He bit his lip, swore and ran off the way I pointed.

Now Mias was talking and sounding pleased with himself.

"—prepare the rabble properly for the change in leadership. Everywhere in what they drink, smoke, wear, I have put a little, em, inducement to dull the senses and distract from purpose. And there has not been time enough yet, mystic. Another week."

From within the chamber Teretheny burst into foreign words, punctuated like curses. I looked again at Elehar in my arms, and whispered to him while pretending to arrange his outfit.

"What do you do? Why are you here?"

The little man's eyes seemed to roll like marbles in every direction, blinking heavily and unable to focus. With a little wine-drool from his mouth he began to mutter.

"wishes. whatever he wishes…"

"—week, for you to pursue that lovely flit in purple who has fooled you from the start. She knows, I tell you! She plans to stop us, and we must move at once."

The big fellow down the hall was grabbing food from several trays, nearly done. I had perhaps seconds.

"Wishes? But you can hardly stand!"

"fluxxx. wishes, band, band… master tells Sanhim, then he me, then band wish fluxxxx"

Clearly delirious. I smiled and patted his shoulder, brushing up again on the dark brown-grey torc about his arm. I felt a charge through my hand like a rainfall of sparks, and saw flashes of everything—treasures, crowds cheering, gorgeous women, men fighting, an enormous palace completely under the earth. Staggering back with a small scream, not nearly girlish enough for comfort, I almost missed the debate inside which was sprouting wings of real argument.

"—*will not await your petty schemes, red man! The stars declare its coming, and you will either help stoke the storm or be caught in it!*"

"*Enough, ratty-robed fanatic! I have told you how it will be, and your attempt to go behind my back has failed. I hold no ill will that you tried, or very little, but I will not allow you to panic over the visions of the Heaven's Eye—*"

There was clearly more but now Sanhim was back, filled with urgency.

"What did you say to him?"

"I? Nothing, sir," I batted my eyes and stepped back to give him room, taking the conversation within out of earshot. My entire right side still tingled with that light touch: as Sanhim broke off crumbs of bread, meat and sweets for his friend, I glanced down to catch a better view of the torc. Plain with a twisted flute, no gems, writing or other design that I could make out. Yet it struck me as terribly, horribly old. It was tight around Elehar's arm, almost a blessing he was not fully conscious or it would have been agony.

He took a few bits of food from his friend and a sip of wine from me. I could tell they were bound to each other, and my instinct told me these two were in a terrible fix. Feldspar snorted in disinterest, but I kicked a little. Jonn Simith had learned, a bit, to care about other people, not just patrons who could pay.

Carnad Mias could pay, and I knew I would never work for him.

"*What are you doing?*" The Red Cup's voice was rising with concern, but there were no sounds of struggle and the two Bedou-uu paid no heed.

Teretheny was speaking, low and controlled, and I thought I caught the words "*still useful to me*".

"*Enough now, leave me alone! Take your eyes, leave me now!*"

Sanhim stopped and listened with a face etched in horror and shoulders raised in expectation of a blow. Anyone seeing him would have done the same, so I did. Elehar canted up against the door, chewing quietly and almost looking rational.

"*Now, indeed you begin to suspect. Look further, Carnad Mias, see the approaching storm.*" There was a long pause in which I heard just a hint of whimpering. "*Now sleep, your guests will celebrate for a time without you.*"
106

His booted step was quick and Sanhim could not recover quickly enough. As the door opened Elehar fell in. I reached to catch him faster than a serving girl could have, and together we tumbled into the chest of the Devout Teretheny.

"Anayi belachtim!" the preacher shouted in surprise and anger. I managed to keep his erstwhile bodyguard off the floor, staggering most unladylike with my legs astride him and my head poking rather flirtingly into the monk's midriff. One chance to sell this- I decided I was drunk.

"Wheeee! This one's already out of steam, milord, perhaps you'd care to ride instead?"

"Away with you, trull!" He seized my dress and threw me to one side, tearing the sleeve and nearly forcing one breast more fully into view than I could afford. I rolled to my stomach, still giggling, and wiggled my hips as if the offer was still good.

"Better hurry, before I sober up."

"Sanhim, come at once."

"Master, may I not feed him a little more."

"Now, Sanhim. No further delay. The storm rises."

I kept giggling for a while longer, pretended to throw up a bit for good measure, until the trio of footsteps had faded completely beneath the sounds of the distant gala. Then I picked myself up and entered the private chamber, closing the door behind me.

There lay Carnad Mias sprawled across enough pillows and furniture to hold two people, head back, snoring louder than the ratchet of a crossbow-crank. Despite his heavy slumber, that face in sleep saw nightmares. I regarded him there for a moment, and thought about conspiracies and assassins, drugs and staggering wealth, fanatical allies and evil magic. And I thought, for a moment, how much better off the city of Cryssigens might be if this fat carker had one more line of thick red across his neck.

But there was no risk in that. And no time either, to get back out the way I had come. I saw a lovely window set with crimson panes and suffused with moonlight. By leaving that way undetected with a dead man behind me, the city would know Feldspar had been here: and I am no assassin. I'm a Stealthic.

I left the Red dress draped across Carnad's feet, just to raise his panic level closer to that of his erstwhile ally when he awoke. I unhooked the backpack from behind my legs, got into my working clothes, and climbed to the roof then toward the river.

I was probably headed for another cold swim, but there was no chance in all the hells of Despair I'd let Teretheny get away from me tonight.

⊕ ⊕ ⊕

Dawn came cold, bringing nothing with it besides pale light and a break in the fighting. The darkness leaked away as the hulking forms of the enemy shuffled back under cover of the black castle, leaving behind just a few corpses too badly chopped to animate. Only the distant portcullis creak, the taunting laughter of Perishune from within the gate, and the rising scream of the flying horrors as they flapped off to roost near the opposite towers spiced the silence. The survivors of Justin's company watched them go, those still alive in the chill of day leaning heavily on their shields or falling to their knees in exhaustion.

M'nesa Zetee looked around the tiny camp, resisting the urge to count the men again. At least seven of them were behind the gate now, numbered with the enemy, animate and cold. Tonight, no doubt they would lead the charge, that their former comrades could see them clearly, and think about their future fate at the moment of decision. One day left, perhaps, to consider devising an alternative.

"Five men to gather the bodies, and five more to guard them," he said, pointing with his sword. "Three to stand watch, and another ten to gather fuel: the pyre will be there at the back. The rest to sleep until mid-morning." M'nesa realized his arm ached from shoulder to wrist, because he was still clenching the weapon so hard. With an effort he managed to loosen his fingers, biting a lip at the pain of returning circulation and relaxed muscles.

Flexing his hand he moved back to the wagons, to look in on the children—still sleeping under the tarp, for a wonder—and asked the trumpet-boy to start the cookfires. Then M'nesa walked to the edge of the encampment and stared down into the ditch dug two days ago.

Tass was there, retrieving his sword from where it had fallen in the fight, and putting back his cestus for future use. The burly human

108

showed few ill-effects from the nightlong fighting, ignoring several seeping cuts on his back and legs as if he could feel them no more than see them. His boots as he walked plashed in a solid inch of blood pooled at the base of the ditch: M'nesa pondered how much pain it represented, and how most of that crimson fluid, now scumming over, was no colder than when it first left the bodies of the undead. Soon, there would be enough to drown in.

Tass grinned as he took M'nesa's hand up out of the ditch.

"That was entertainment not to be missed, Zetee!"

"So glad you were pleased, dekentar. More on tap tonight, or I fail in my guess."

"Aye," the human replied, "attendance mandatory, so long as we stay here."

"Captain's orders." M'nesa's shrug was gentle but firm and the human nodded without breaking eye contact. They were as different as any two beings in the Emperor's cadre, but M'nesa felt they understood one another.

A thought nudged as he saw the tall human take a deep breath and let out what might have been a tired sigh.

"Tass, would you do me a favor, and go on up to relieve our man scouting the castle?"

"Nothing to see up there, Zetee: Argens' Balls, we know what's coming."

"Nevertheless, I think the men need to know, we're always trying. He's just up where that brush provides a little cover. You can't see him, but he's there." M'nesa paused to let his words sink in with the mortal, and Tass's eyes flared as the hint took hold. Mortal Men needed sleep, but the dekentar was the only non-Elf in the company, and M'nesa knew what this ex-gladiator's reputation was worth. "I could send someone up around noon, say, to relieve you."

Tass made a wry face, hating to compromise on his legendary toughness, but clapped M'nesa's arm in comradery. "Aye, I suppose symbols are important. I'll, heh, make the sacrifice, for you Zetee."

"I'm in your debt."

Tass laughed aloud at this and stomped off up the hill to take his post. M'nesa knew he would sit and watch, at first, until sleep overtook him. But no soldier here would know for certain and that was all that mattered.

The gryphon stirred in its cage, angry as always to be confined but as tired as any of them after the all-night battle. M'nesa watched the trumpet-boy, formerly the wagon drover, toss it a slab of meat before returning to the cook-fires. More symbols: their beast had frightened the flying things somewhat, but could not be released to any effect without the Captain here. And soon they'd all be out of food, forced to either eat the beast or let it go. M'nesa looked at the sleepy children munching on bread and remembered Justin's final order, to care for them at all costs. But how?

The gryphon cawed angrily in its cage, and M'nesa thought how similar their situations were. Caged whether behind bars or a ditch, the only difference between the men and the monster was that the Emperor's company had chosen to remain within their prison as their fate approached. The gryphon's pen was just another symbol, in that regard.

Then M'nesa's thoughts led him somewhere he never expected. Striding through the rows of men who had just lain down, he quietly said "I need seven volunteers."

Just before noon, Tass returned down the steep slope to see the tiny camp crawling like ants. Not a single soldier lay sleeping. Four men stood to either side of the gryphon, which was beyond its bars and held down only with two large neck-chains anchored by iron staples directly into the rock of the mountainside. The children and drover sat on a supply wagon weaving ropes into a net shape. Everyone else not guarding the perimeter or keeping watch on the blazing pyre was sitting around munching rations and pointing, chatting and joking in high spirits as M'nesa conferred with the veteran dekentar hobbling around what remained of the gryphon's wagon-cage.

The wheels and base of the wagon were still there, but all the upper structure had been stripped away. The former cage bars were broken off, bent, and severed into too many shapes and piles to make much sense except to the designers. Near one end of the wagon floor, a large hole had been cut; M'nesa directed a team of men returning to camp with the only sizable sapling trunk in the area, stripped of branches and wrapped with rope around the base.

110

Tass arrived in time to help them raise and set the trunk into the hole, then turned to M'nesa with a wondering grin.

"An engine. Loins of the First, you intend to throw rocks at them."

M'nesa gave a slight nod and shrug. "It could serve to annoy them, perhaps."

"And the men," Tass returned, as they looked around to see high spirits in all directions. "You thought of that too didn't you, clever Elf."

"A symbol, as you said."

Tass stood arms akimbo, and suddenly ripped out with a meaty laugh that ran through the company and returned in a cheer.

"Well boys, we're a long way from our first throw, so let's hop to it!"

"Here's a bit of a problem," the veteran said as he hobbled over still using a stick to support his bad leg. "Hard to tell what size stone to gather until we know what distance we'll get on the throw."

Tass shook his head at once. "Large stones only. Big enough to hurt those walls."

"And if they fall short?" the veteran challenged, but Tass did not hesitate.

"That's why this witty fellow in charge of us left the wheels on. We'll roll it closer."

That brought the banter down, and M'nesa could see men watching Tass as he leaned against the former sapling without concern.

"How close, dekentar?" one of the men called out.

"Too close, if you want to live forever!" he spat back and the men all cheered.

More were needed now, to help set the metal poles and straps into place and bring the sapling-arm back steadily but not too quickly to position. The children brought over the rope-net, and men were sent in search of rocks no smaller than a man's torso. The gryphon, so close to free, occasionally hunched and launched into the air, choked back at once by the chain but never giving up or sleeping as was its former habit. Its struggles punctuated the race to finish the engine before nightfall and the next expected attack.

It was a race M'nesa ultimately lost, at his choice.

The manual had given lessons on how to construct such engines, the best options for each situation, but the cadre had had no time to engage in building one, just their use during a brief exercise in training. The veteran dekentar, who had seen some built during his early days as the Empire put down minor revolts, knew this and that, but M'nesa could see he was clearly guessing. The real problem was not to show one's hand too soon: firing a test rock would give away the game, and he feared watching their first salvo fall pathetically short. Whether it hurt the castle was secondary. The men, the symbol of their efforts, that was everything. And the more time they spent debating the tension, calculating the position of the piece, or whether the reinforcements were sufficient, the higher the stakes became.

The sun had already set by the time all was in readiness. After triple-checking his numbers and firing arrows to estimate the distance from their position, M'nesa ordered the men to pull the engine over the land-bridge and out of the camp, to a spot some fifty paces closer to the fortress gate which would be their target.

Men rolled stones and cut stakes to create a barricade around the firing position, large enough for the engine crew and a dekent more to guard them. Two dekents of cavalry stood by to protect the flanks. The company was not large enough to defend both camps at once: M'nesa left a half-dekent behind with the veteran and the children, and orders to flee if this position fell. That was all he could think of, the Captain's orders notwithstanding. M'nesa was committed to this mad venture now, putting everything he had into his Hope. He hoped that the engine would discomfit his enemies, just as he hoped his Captain and Kein were still alive.

But he no longer expected it.

The men sang as they braced the engine's wheels and cranked the sapling-pole back into place. Tass helped load a stone as wide as one arm's reach into the rope bag, and they gauged the angle of fire once again. They were aiming for the larger tower bracing the left side of the gate. As Tass had said out loud to the men, "Strength against strength; when we finally damage it, they will know there's no place we cannot bring down." And as he muttered privately to M'nesa "Plus, no reason for them to lose spirit when the first one does little."

M'nesa stood by the release and bowed his head in prayer. Son of the Sun, bring your light into dark places and look with favor on our efforts today. Let us acquit ourselves like men, if this be our last hour let us strike a blow as you would wish.

Then he let the weapon loose.

The entire wagon kicked and rocked as the enormous arm flipped up and around. Every man watched the boulder come away at the apogee and sail like a feathered thing across the space, twice as far as a bow could fly. M'nesa felt tears in his eyes even before it came down; his fears that the engine would fall apart on the first attempt proved groundless. But the aim...

The rock came down too soon, smashing against the base of the tower and shattering to flinders with no apparent damage to the massive castle. Yet the men cheered with abandon, and M'nesa reflected there was much cause for pride that the first shot had scored at all. He felt something surge up then, even as the stars came visible overhead and he heard the creak of the portcullis signaling their doom coming.

"Reload!" he cried. "Loosen the wheels men, and move her right to the front stakes here! Top-down, that's how you destroy a tower."

The men cheered again and hopped to the task, and M'nesa felt for the first time the same thrill that a captain of men should, to know an entire company obeyed the order given. Yet he earnestly hoped he would not have to feel this way again.

Perishune's heavy-armed men had cleared the gate now, parting to let gaunts wearing imperial uniforms through the ranks, and forming up to attack the engine-site. As the arm cranked back for a second throw, M'nesa gauged the distance and estimated the next— perhaps final—shot would strike somewhere more than halfway up the tower. That would be a fine blow, one perhaps his captain could have been proud of.

⊕ ⊕ ⊕

I saw the entire scheme in a glance. Behind me in the darkened alleyway lay Sanhim and Elehar unconscious, easy victims to my skill with the noun-chakas. Just around the corner I could make out the broad back of Carnad Mias—yes, the Red Cup himself in seeming—giving orders to a skulking shape in the shadows that could only be Salivaar, the Rat-King of Old Cryss. The voice of the crimson king-maker was perfect, his dress exactly the same as that of the original, no doubt still sleeping in his chambers where I left him not a half-hour ago. Watching Teretheny so perfectly mimic

113

his form made me nearly forget how soaked and cold I was, from another hasty river-crossing.

"I don't care what I told you before, listen to me now, vermin." It was the same tone, the accents of the city noble, down to the last assonant and diphthong. "You have done well not to give the Devout any more elixir, but I shall take charge of what you have now. At once."

"Of course, great Cup of Red," Salivaar replied, holding up a canteen that sloshed heavily in his hands, "it's just that I thought our original schedule was—"

"Never mind the schedule!" True, the monk's acting was very imperfect. He hurried, interrupted like a mortal Man; for all his dreams of power, Teretheny was not comfortable with command, he did not feel the part. I was sure I could do better, though I wasn't certain all the added body I needed would come off right. Feldspar curtly informed me this was a waste of thought, and I reluctantly agreed. I watched like a hawk as the imitation Red Cup took the canteen and waved dismissively at Salivaar.

"More, as soon as you can."

"Yes, great Cup of Red, and I assume the usual agreement applies? We shall have to procure further bodies in exchange for—"

"Of course, of course, whatever you need. Only send the message, when you are ready, to the Stargazer temple. I, ahm, I am having the monk watched every second now and, ah, you shall tell him to come a full day later than needed. That way I shall know to come at the proper hour."

"Yes, milord, as you say." Salivaar had probably never looked so puzzled in his life before, not that I felt any sympathy for the leader of such cutthroats.

Then he faded back into shadow, and I knew I had just seconds to act. But what was I going to do?

Justin knew, but no longer believed, that a week had not passed since Sordinay's visit. It only felt that way. He knew likewise that his last sip of elixir had probably only been a few hours ago. The weakness throughout his frame and constant thought of food or drink was just that, weakness, which he needed to counter with the force of his will. Talking in the darkness to Kein Trador brought some small comfort, but no better sense of time's movement; each word was dropped into a bottomless well and no echo or other return gave it measure or beat, to punctuate eternity. He sloshed his vial, to sense without sight or sound how much might be left. Save it, the young Baron had advised, but he could not have said how long.

No use thinking back anymore. Justin had already trod the steps he took then, when there was time, when making decisions and issuing orders consumed moments and regulated the hours ahead. He had bitterly recriminated himself for every mistake, countless scathing reviews of his conduct from the harshest critic he knew. Accepting the invitation. Not giving M'nesa permission to withdraw after some period of days (surely at least a week had gone by, his company doomed by that lack of foresight). Entering the keep without further assurances; but then, he weakly protested to himself, what guarantee would have sufficed from his host? The rules hardly applied to an immortal parasite, a necromancer wearing the robes of living office. No matter, he savagely concluded, there were warning signs enough. Even she had known…

Justin fell to thinking of her again, not for the pain of separation, nor the humiliation of his hopeless love for a woman so unattainable; or at least, not only for that. That was another occasion, he reflected, when time had seemed to stop. Interviewing her, at first with no understanding and then in a rush of vision and miracle: Justin had seen such intelligence, such a fierce fire of purpose in that smooth slender body as would have shaken a larger frame to pieces. How could he not love her? And how did that in any way distinguish him from all men with warm blood still in their veins?

Perhaps, he thought again, that was why he had impulsively designed to come here. The quest to win the Baron's vote was arduous and unlikely: but her fear at what he faced, more than anything, had determined his course. To impress her, to show her perhaps his worthiness, he had bound his life and that of his loyal men to destruction. A final critique to himself, and a blow he did not shirk to suffer. If he had come alone, Justin knew he would have thought the loss worth it.

And he knew he was hearing her voice again, there in the utter darkness, speaking of her city's plight as if to someone unknown. But

Justin could not believe it, any more than any of his grim imaginings, brewed down here in the world of his mind deep below the walls of the castle.

"But this is not to the point, Milord. Forces within the city are preparing to move, to launch a coup of some kind, well before the next vote, and perhaps within days."

How like her voice he was imagining her. The urgency, the intelligence radiating from every syllable. It even sounded as if she were addressing some kind of superior, perhaps Gaspar Heugen or—no, just as if she were delivering his message to Morinack the Emperor's Hand back in Argens. Justin smiled faintly, to think even now that his wishes were of the flag of mission, his orders to report. Pleasant to think she might have done just as he asked. He reached to turn the warm ax-ring on his hand as he indulged this harmless fantasy.

"I believe they can, milord."

Justin started; he had imagined a speech, not a conversation, yet W'starrah's voice was answering some unheard question.

"Or rather, one of them will draw off enough of the city's strength to allow the other…"

Now he began to imagine light, not flaring and fading spots as was usually the case down here, but something steady, faint yet carrying the promise of illumination. He could almost make out a form.

"W'starrah?" he croaked. Before he could feel embarrassed about speaking to no one, he heard an answer beyond his power of dreaming.

"Justin? My captain, where are you?"

Justin's heart leaped completely out of his dungeon to hear her speak of him possessively. Surely still a mirage? But he began, a little, to believe.

"W'starrah? I can see you, but there is no light here."

In another moment, the light grew larger, a lantern at the edge of a window within his cell that could not exist. And holding the lantern, her, not as clearly as he imagined but more real, more present to him in shadow than ever in darkness. He even caught a scent of jasmine, and when Justin recalled the sprig pinned to his chest it did not dismay him as it should have. At least, the perfume proved he could not have been here as long as he imagined.

116

Justin still did not believe there was much hope. But he knew now, there might be enough time.

See what you have created, cherished one. Even now, the intrepid Ferret strikes the Arbalest, lays him low, and peels back his current form. He gains the chance to rescue a crown from darkness, at your behest.

The Arbalest when he awakens, will panic. As will the Serpent and Dragon, once they have consulted in their confusion.

Trapped against the black cliffs, Fire Ants labor to free their captain, your beloved, and their fight now is one that can shake the darkness before them to its foundation. Nearby the Gryphon rages at its confinement, and soon will be free. These too play their parts at your direction: guided by my vision, you foresaw the needs of all, judging that they outweighed any personal desire.

Thanks to your words too, just a night ago, the Raccoon and Stone Oak have edged somewhat closer, and might survive what comes. Many more, of course, must burn, but your city and purpose will survive thanks to the wheels you, cherished one, have set in motion. Your enemies will strike too soon to access their full strength, while allies may yet avoid the destruction intended.

How you deserve to see this, beloved. The agony you suffer now, though not of my making, was so long foreseen that it feels my own fault. That too is pain, and that, at least, I kept from your visions. Soon, we will both share freedom from the body's weakness, and you may enjoy the knowledge that your love saved at least some of your city. For others, that you now love, the lightness of immortality among the stars will relieve you of that hurt. Come, cherished one, your reward awaits.

Awakening in the pitch black of his cell for what seemed like the hundredth time, Kein Trador returned at once to thoughts of his failure. He was unworthy to be in Justin's company, and it brought him close to tears as the growing throb of his wrist never could. What had he done except fail? Such thoughts flooded in immediately upon the return of consciousness, as the young dekentar ran through a familiar litany of shortcomings.

Not answering well enough to be chosen as one of Justin's dekentars, Kein had willingly stripped his badges and fought to become one of the soldiers, even among the infantry, just to be near his hero. But Tass had thoroughly beaten him, allowing Kein to join only from spite; a Man's joke to heap more insult and degradation on an Elf's back, which Kein willingly accepted in an effort to prove himself. Just two days later, after the fighting in the hills, his friend M'nesa had come with good news; their losses meant his promotion back to the rank of dekentar. But now Kein could see that this had been mere pity, a courtesy to Justin's favored second in command, not for any merit he had shown.

"Betrayed." The Captain was speaking now, perhaps praying to Argens: and Kein knew who Justin meant. "The Baron ignored my truce-flag. Took me prisoner. My men, cut off outside the keep."

Kein rolled to one side and rubbed his arm trying to ease the pain of that broken wrist. Here they both lay in durance and soon no doubt to suffer death, because of his final and most fatal error. Why did he bother awakening, just to rehearse such regrets and doubts?

"W'starrah, I... I have failed you."

Now Kein Trador felt a new flush of shame; the captain was thinking aloud of his love; and he deserved privacy, at least. But even there his worst soldier had failed him, by surviving to overhear.

After the force-march to Cryssigens, Justin had taken Kein along on patrols several times, and he had dared to hope. But now he could see, it was merely to keep a closer eye on a weak link in the chain of command. And what had he done, what brave deed did he perform to raise his grade in the eyes of his captain? Dallying with children and rummaging in an abandoned office; Kein felt a fool to think back on that day, seemingly so long ago.

Then the final failure, chosen to be Justin's adjutant when he entered the enemy's fortress with everything on the line; and what did Kein do? One harmless blow, no assistance, wounded and captured. And now a broken sack of meat, thrown here to await a feast featuring himself and the man who was his hero. Kein shook the empty vial, another weakness displayed, unable to reserve it as advised by Sordinay. The pain in his arm, his gnawing despair, had proven too great for him, just like every other test.

118

Justin's speech, most likely, was what had awakened Kein. He looked helplessly in the direction of his captain's voice and his febrile brain conjured the sight of him there, sitting straight at this moment and looking slightly up as if to the heavens in appeal. He fancied he could see him ever more clearly as time went by, and Kein knew his mind's failure was joining with that of his heart and body.

But the dekentar could never have imagined hearing a woman's voice in that chamber.

"Justin, my love, come back to me. May Argens bless you, and see you through all trials, and bring you back."

Now a liquid light poured into Justin's cell and clung to his captain, so that he became a kind of living lantern. Kein felt his hair stand on end: it was enough to see by dimly, he could measure distances, make out his own hands and clothing.

Suddenly the area shivered, the tremor of a quake, and Kein shouted in fear as bits of plaster and rock came down into his cell and elsewhere. The ancient construction of this dungeon, unattended for countless decades, would any moment collapse and entomb them far beneath the surface and air and light.

Except for Justin's light, shining as he stood and looked on himself in wonder.

"My captain," Kein stammered, "you are, I can see you."

"I saw, I spoke with someone," Justin answered and his voice carried beyond normal volume. He closed his eyes and laid hands on the bars of his cell. Kein could make out no strong effort, it was instead as if he prayed. But more bits of plaster fell from where the thick bars joined the ceiling, and Kein saw them bend outward slowly as if made of young wood instead of steel. They stayed in place when Justin released them and stepped through, staring at his hands.

"By the grace of the First—" he whispered.

At that moment the chamber rocked again, and now more stones fell along with enough dust to cloud the air. But Kein at last felt no fear, knowing what must happen.

"Captain, save yourself, the door!"

Justin looked at Kein and smiled; the young dekentar knew then he could die happy under such kind regard. But his heart plunged when Justin moved instead to his cell and seized the bars.

"No captain, please there is no time!"

"I believe there is," Justin replied and laughed at a private joke.

The same miracle repeated itself, and despite more falling plaster Kein Trador stumbled coughing from his cell. Justin seized one arm and Kein felt such strength there as even his monstrous opponent had not displayed. They were at the wooden door and through to a narrow hallway in moments. Several tunnels here, with a circular stair leading up to one side; Kein's memory jogged him, of that time he had been dragged down it.

"Partway up, captain, there is a chamber where they threw our weapons. Go on, sir, I can be of no use to you now, my wrist, I'm sorry."

The captain still glowed and it lent a heroic aura to every motion and word. His eyes seemed focused on the world above all this rock and darkness. "Your wrist? Let me see that." He smiled and touched it lightly, imbuing Kein's left side with a tingling warmth. Justin handed over his vial of elixir. "Drink this. For the moment I am feeling better than well."

Kein swallowed his fear and did as ordered. A small voice inside him suggested that he was here precisely because he already revered Justin. Perhaps he could still act, be of some use. The flush of the elixir felt as if it ran directly down his left arm, and Kein imagined that the throb in his wrist, while not precisely fading, became more manageable. He led the way up the stairs feeling somewhere between elated and dizzy.

After several flights and enough curves to run a full circle they came to a door, set with a heavy lock but not thrown closed. Pushing in, the men saw a heap of random weaponry, mostly swords and knives, lying wherever they had fallen or slid, many covered with dust. As Justin stepped fully into the chamber his light illumined a longer blade, half out of its sheath, made of something darker than steel and flecked with bright argent points throughout. He took it up with a face that said he had found what he knew would be there.

Kein saw his own sword near the front, but behind it, nearer the wall, a longish knife lay on a shelf and drew his attention. Stepping over and blowing it off, Kein felt its heft was beyond metal, the rough-hewn blade not polished or smooth but seemingly made of stone. And there in the corner was a stone mace, little more than a rounded rock half the size of his head, set onto a wooden pole nearly as thick as his arm. He took them both and followed Justin further up.

When the stairs ended in a tiny guardroom, Kein guessed they might be level with the ground, on the outer wall to judge by the two arrow-slits here. Justin stepped up to one, then turned back for one of the doors, while summarizing succinctly: "Night, fighting at the gates."

The portal rattled as if locked, but Justin flexed his arm and the entire keyplate came out of the wood in his hand. The captain and dekentar looked to each other a moment, then burst into fey laughter before running down the empty corridor ahead. Kein Trador again felt he would be quite content to die in his captain's presence, but this time he was becoming greedy. Perhaps to take one or two of the enemy with him...

At the end of a long corridor was another, larger door. Kein listened and heard shouts, distant clashes of metal and more. But Justin looked to his right as if directly through the stone, then gestured they should move through.

"Captain, let me go ahead; you will be ready for whatever is there."

Justin smiled, but shook his head. "I bear the mark of the First, dekentar. Let us trust him as long as I deserve it."

Kein grinned. "We all die eventually, sir."

Again Justin laughed without a care in the world, and opened the portal.

Kein charged behind his captain into the gatehouse, and everything seemed to happen at once. This room housed the portcullis mechanism, and an archway opposite led to the gate. Rows of slow-moving bodies were shuffling past on their way to reinforce the castle levy outside in battle with the company. Several of the Baron's men lay crushed beneath fallen stones, including Zogith, one of the two heavily armored nobles who had stood guard behind the throne.

The other, Bel't, turned with two-handed sword out, surprised and furious at the pace of events. He fell back a step snarling at the light from Justin's body, and Kein darted past the captain eager to strike the first blow. Dodging under the blade he lashed out blindly with the mace, not a weapon he was trained to though it seemed simple enough. His strike came just short of his opponent's skull, swiping the helm off and scraping the cheek with a dark bruise.

When the tall warrior returned his blade for a second sweep, Kein instinctively tried to parry as he would with a sword. He caught the blade on the haft of his mace and it nearly carried out of his hand, knocking him over. But Bel't screamed in pain, and from the floor Kein could see the welt on his face was only growing and deepening. A mere scratch, yet the fearsome healing abilities of this one's monstrous elder brother were not evident now. Kein rolled to his feet and hefted the mace again.

Justin meanwhile, had seized the opportunity without hesitation. Stepping behind Bel't to the mechanism, he chopped through the chains engaging the portcullis. Outside, thick metal bars plunged through flesh to crash wetly on stone, and Kein also heard shouts of dismay from those outside now cut off. Their foe whirled to face Justin and screeched at the deed. Kein's mace glanced off his armored back, but the captain ran him through and in the time it took Bel't to howl in agony his body crumbled to rancid bits inside his armor, falling beside his brother near the pile of stones.

"This way!" Justin shouted and they entered the gatehouse where several dozen gaunts stood packed against the portcullis, treading their former neighbors underfoot as they vainly tried to follow orders and join the fray outside. Kein caught just a flash of men on horseback lancing grounded foes, while monsters on leathery wings stooped to grab and rend, a vision of shouts and wrack and death, before they turned up the passage and ran into the castle tunnel, taking the same path they had long ago toward the main bailey.

Kein did not question his captain's decision though his every instinct was to join the fighting outside. Justin was clearly in the grip of a miracle and Kein was content to come along and do whatever good he was able. At the inner portal, closed and locked, Justin pounded with the hilt of his longsword.

"Sordinay! Milord Baron, open it is your friends."

There was silence except the distant riot of the battle, yet again Justin seemed to hear the presence on the inside of the keep.

"Those who love the light and warmth of Argens have come" he said distinctly, in the words of the prophecy the seventh son had told them.

Kein, feeling a stranger to himself, added "With your help, we shall make the Baron anew."

Another moment's delay, and a large key rattled in the lock before the portal opened to reveal Sordinay in the darkened empty chamber, standing back with jaw open at the sight of Justin still glowing with the miracle.

"Where is he?"

Sordinay stood carved in shock, not even breathing as he struggled inwardly to regain a nobleman's composure.

"Milord Baron, there may be only moments though we will essay the task whatever our outward protections. This is your time!"

"He rests," the son managed, "last night's assaults, two times he cast the ritual of raising, and with those unturned by earth, it was... he needed to restore his strength through blood, but was still afraid to use you before... I have hidden my mother in a kitchen barrel." Sordinay fell into a reverie and spoke as if only to himself. "I was so certain, he would use me at last... he drank two of the servants instead, and it is not yet enough."

"Milord Baron," Kein stepped forward and took Sordinay by the arm, only later realizing he was using his left hand. "Now is the moment to strike. I have found the weapon we need," and here he held up the abrasor knife.

Sordinay stared a moment, his face hardening into something terrible, and Kein had to steady his feet not to step back.

"He was once my father. That is all." Sordinay took the blade and looked to Justin. "His chambers." Leading the way down a side passage, the son practically ran and held the knife with mortal purpose.

Justin grinned like a wolf and followed. Down several turnings with rich but aging cloth décor, they stopped before double wooden doors emblazoned with the sign of disembodied wings.

"Mind you," Sordinay said quietly, "the eldest, Vol'tun, stands guard."

Justin cocked his head still grinning, "The one who is as loyal as he is ugly?"

Kein smiled back and hefted his mace. "Be serious captain. Who could possibly be that loyal?"

Sordinay threw open the chamber doors with the abrasor knife between his teeth.

M'nesa had tried everything, to keep the door to survival open. But finishing the engine had taken him too long, even with the men jumping to every task there were only so many at a time who could help. Night had fallen before the first rock: no shots taken during the day when the dekentar had hoped his enemy would be helpless. Only two volleys, and now the men were exhausted from no sleep and the constant mental battering of the undead-terror.

Too close to the castle, this engine palisade would prove indefensible against so many. His plan of the night before, to avoid the sacrifice of more lives, could not hold. The enemy was emerging, with horrors flying overhead, and retreat now could mean the loss of a third of his company. Those bodies would add to the numerical advantage the enemy already held.

M'nesa looked to Tass, commanding the infantry at the front of the engine pit where a few stakes made poor substitutes for the ditch they had enjoyed at the camp. Tass waved back with his grim grin, and M'nesa remembered that day when he interviewed to be in Justin's company. Not to live to see forty years, that was the mortal's fondest wish, now surely granted.

"It has been an honor, Tass," he called out, moving to mount his horse and lead a last charge.

"We're carked for sure, Zetee," the gladiator bellowed back, "but that's not on you. It was just the hand we were dealt." M'nesa thought it an uncommonly gracious gesture from his uncouth fellow officer. How different they both were, united only by service to perhaps the greatest leader M'nesa had ever known. Now that noble Elf was certainly dead, along with Kein Trador, his best friend. The door was closed, and all that remained was to make a good ending.

"Bowmen, provide what cover you can against those monsters." M'nesa eyed the armored escort emerging from the portcullis, and the ranks of the undead levy behind those of his former comrades shambling out like a vomit of sludge. Perishune at their head had visor up, laughing aloud at the prospect of catching his foe nearly in the open. Two flying forms overhead instead of three, one small blessing. "Cavalry to lance: we'll let them come a bit closer and then charge at will."

When the portcullis came ringing down atop the undead, M'nesa could not at first believe his eyes or ears. But as he heard Perishune cry out in surprise and rage to see the bulk of his cadre trapped within, M'nesa knew the truth.

One door was still open. Justin was alive, and perhaps Kein as well.

It meant nothing for his own chances; more than likely they all would die in the next hour. But it was at least possible that they might sacrifice those lives in the service of Hope.

"Now men! Take them in division while they are separated. The Emperor, and Argens!"

The Baron's bedroom was wide and deep enough to make the low ceiling especially claustrophobic. Kein saw only fragments of the darkly-gorgeous appointments, the Baron sitting up enraged but starkly and horridly older than before, and stunned by the fact that Justin's body gave off the only light in the room. Then Vol'tun emerged from his place by the bedpost, hissing and spreading his wings with talons outstretched.

Justin stood forth in full view, and both monsters cringed in the radiance. The Baron's skin began to shrivel and tear into creviced strips, and even his tongue split in mid-cry.

"No! The blohhd iss immourtahl!"

Sordinay ran to the bedside and Kein lost sight of him as he moved to intercept Vol'tun.

"Hello again!" he shouted in fey humor, "May we take a second pass?"

Vol'tun, desperate to reach the opposite bedside, ignored Kein, and the dekentar gritted his teeth at the unearthly movement, the enormous fleshy wings. Swinging with everything he had—and both hands—Kein placed the head of the mace directly into the ribs beneath one taloned arm. The creature convulsed onto the lower half of its father's body still sitting; Kein felt the keen kiss across his back from flailing claws, and stumbled forward half onto the gigantic silk-draped bed.

Vol'tun flapped and shrieked like some giant hawkish thing, while the Baron of Blood looked on his firstborn in horror. The wound Kein inflicted grew as a spill, chewing away the stone-grey flesh and form. The dekentar straightened up, mock-bowed to his host, and brought the mace down directly on the monster's head, crushing it into the mattress before shielding his face with both arms from the battering of the wings as it flailed in death-throes.

"Beware only the seventh generation," Justin said grimly as his light flared even higher and the Baron's eyes began to smoke.

Sordinay's face was hard and only his eyes seemed to move. "You gave me life," he rasped, "and for that my decades of service shall stand as payment. This is for my mother, and my people." He plunged the abrasor blade deep into the heart of what had once been Voev T'yr, and heard only a slight gasp, of utter astonishment, as the blinded beast turned in the direction of the blow and clutched with ever-feebler strength at Sordinay's tunic, before falling to pieces, then to bones, and finally to dust.

Kein and Justin stepped back and knelt then, before the new Baron of Tralmachia. In Justin's case it was completely voluntary. Kein tried not to let the bleeding from his ribs show as he clamped one arm over the wounds. It was enough, dying here would be a good end.

Justin's glow began to slowly fade, but Sordinay moved with decision to take up the end of the silversteel blade in Justin's hand. Striking it against his abrasor knife, he produced a shower of sparks that quickly caught on the silk of the bedding.

"Let all in this room burn," Baron Sordinay T'yr said, "there is much in this fortress in need of purifying flame." Kein had dared to think the seventh son as young as he. But now the mantle of rulership was already settling on the new Baron's shoulders. "Come, captain, and also you, brave dekentar; we shall free my mother and attend to other urgent matters as we see them."

"If it please you, milord," Kein said quietly, "leave me here to guard the flames. I will likely only hold you back and you must—"

"Not by my will," Sordinay said with force, "there are salves less than a hundred steps away, and who better than you to deserve them?

I shall root out the butler from wherever he has hidden and see to it at once." Sordinay leaned down and got Kein's blood on his hand raising him up. "It is not my will that you should die, dekentar. For one thing, many of my enemies are likely still alive. And it is in my head that my mother will need a protector."

Kein looked to his captain, now lit only by the flickering of the bed-pyre, and saw there a grin that did nothing to counter his confusion. But it was a proud grin, like that of a leader well satisfied. And Kein Trador started to believe, from that moment, that perhaps all was not lost for his reputation as an officer. The acidic pain in his side faded as if already salved, as the three men moved slowly from the red-lit chamber.

After the initial charge, all was confusion for a time. The enemy, caught unprepared by their separation, reacted slowly. M'nesa's company cantered in with lances lowering at just the right time to spear several of the armored retainers, while the flying things overhead shrank from interfering. M'nesa caught one footman straight through the neck, at the joint between armored helm and hauberk; his foe fumbled the halberd uselessly away and M'nesa yanked up hard on his lance, bearing the enemy completely off the ground where its weight tore the rotting flesh in two, dropping brain and body to the sward to lay unmoving while he wheeled and surveyed the scene.

Tass had also ordered the charge, and behind his infantry the archers crab-stepped closer scanning the skies. Discipline held nearly perfect, with the cadre of Castle T'yr still in disarray. The winged monsters finally stooped toward the cavalry in anger, and two men were dislodged to fall among the undead, where M'nesa saw them no more. Arrows flew but at too great a range, and M'nesa's heart fell to realize the enemy were still too many, too powerful. Yet a kind of fell humor was on him, most unusual, and he fancied he felt a bit as Tass did, ready to die if he could just make the foe remember him.

The human dekentar bore straight for Perishune as anyone could have guessed. The leader of the castle forces stepped behind his retainers, and Tass growled as he engaged one of the armored foes first. Thrusting his sword past the halberd's guard and into the enemy's hip below the plate, Tass left it there and suddenly seized his enemy's pole-weapon in both hands, ignoring a glancing blow from another quarter as he ripped it from his foe by sheer strength. In the time it took his enemy to clumsily regain balance, Tass took the polearm and broke the haft over his knee, coming away with a large battleax which he promptly used to sunder his opponent diagonally across the torso, through plate and chain and all. Howling with laughter, he stepped between the rendered meat to engage Perishune on equal terms.

M'nesa had no time for more as an unearthly screech from overhead warned him to duck low over his horse's neck. Wings battered his back as he just cantered from under the reach of one of the horrors; M'nesa had to drop his lance from the surprise. Clawing out his sword, he spurred into the fray again, hoping without much hope that proximity to the enemy as well as his bowmen could protect him.

It was filthy work. Hitting a foot soldier from horseback was generally a one-blow affair. Height and momentum converted nearly any hit into a disabling wound. But the undead felt nothing, thought of nothing, and hoped for even less. M'nesa needed one blow to stop, and two or four more to chop his enemies, before the bits that remained posed no threat. And always there were more foes, on all sides, panicking the mount and hardly calming him if truth be known. The battle cries of "The Emperor! For Justin! Ar Aralte!" came only from his men, which increased the sense of wrongness about the desperate fighting.

M'nesa still had his horse under him, a timeless time later, when he saw the end ahead. Tass, momentarily spun away from Perishune by the wrack of battle, had just finished another retainer with his ax and stooped forward a bit to clear blood from his eyes. Perishune rose behind him with ax in hand and a killing stroke in easy reach. M'nesa was too far to help, his voice too dry to carry in warning.

Suddenly the back of Perishune's helmet sprouted half an arrow, the shock of it causing him to turn and glare behind him in fury. There stood a soldier, less than twelve feet away, the one Tass had mockingly called Bullseye for loosing an arrow in fear. Now the human dekentar whirled back with a roar, leveling his makeshift ax completely through his foe's neck and toppling him in two with a huge clatter of metal and flesh. Over the body, Tass stared gape-jawed at Bullseye, who grinned and gestured to his holster, now empty of shafts.

Tass started to laugh full and long, and as he fell to his knees in helpless hilarity, M'nesa noticed the undead also beginning to fall. To pieces.

The retainers went down first, as flesh long dead crumbled inside the metal suits. The peasant levy and Justin's former soldiers, both on the field and within the gatehouse, folded more slowly but just as finally down to earth and stone. The flying things, screeching in agony, spiraled dizzily to the ground as their wings shredded first, claws and flesh also eroding as they landed a furlong or more off and stumbled away into the darkness; one reached the edge of the cleft that separated the valley from the outer walls, and fell in.

Habits died harder than soldiers, and M'nesa counted the men without thinking. Eleven more lost, just six dekents plus three surviving. Why so few, and how, he was too tired to ask even himself. But living so long was indeed worth a laugh, whether this constituted noble behavior or not.

$$\oplus \oplus \oplus$$

I stood in the alley over the unconscious body of the Devout Teretheny and thought about the problems that come with leaving bad people alive.

Carnad Mias, another splendid example, might just be stirring back in his palace across the river where this worthy monk had put him to sleep before coming here. Two fine fellows, who between them had tried to kill W'starrah Altieri at least once apiece. Both also dealing with a rodent—literally—like Salivaar, at whose orders little Keilee had been kidnapped and nearly eaten or who knows what at the hands of giant Bugs. And I had let each of them off with their lives within the past few days. Was I ever going to learn from my mistakes, or would I pass over a third one here now?

Fine, thought Feldspar at once, more risk for me. And I realized, it was someone very much like Jonn Simith, who was arguing to red-stripe Teretheny's neck. Was I defending my young friend, or perhaps just being tugged around by boyish ardor for my patron? Maybe it was all a lie, and Gaspar Heugen was playing me for a fool with a tale that Mias only seemed to affirm. In which case, should I return to the Crystal Palace and knock him unconscious before deciding?

This was getting me nowhere. Teretheny would soon rouse from the blow I had struck, I needed to kill him or admit I hadn't needed to even attack him. Maybe I just wanted to.

At that moment, I thought a ray of light from neither moon nor star lanced into the alleyway, falling on the gap between the monk's cowl and tunic, reflecting something golden there. A shot of energy passed through me and my brain cleared. Of course, that was why I had followed him, without even understanding it. This villain had too much power, and I was going to take it away.

I pulled the cowl up and there it sat, the Throat of the Spider. The sourceless glint illumined the spot perfectly; segmented golden legs, hard blue-black body the width of my palm and rimmed with gold, sporting platinum mandibles. All its eyes, all its joints, every fingernail's breadth of the thing glittering with gems of all hues. Even as I watched, those legs stirred a little of their own accord—couldn't be his breathing, they were independent of each other.

And every inch of my skin tried to crawl off to the end of the alley.

Elves can't ignore the repulsion they have for Bugs. Some of my acquaintances from theater days couldn't stand the normal sized things (one of them would stand and leave the room if we mentioned any type by name). I remembered the blind white Bug from the temple, and all his alien allies, what they might be doing with their human captives. Fighting fire with fire was just a motto people liked to say: I was willing to bet not a living soul in Cryssigens would willingly touch this trinket.

But I'm a Stealthic. The service of Hope beckoned me; I reached out and laid two fingers lightly on either side of its horrid, hard body.

My digits jumped back of their own accord, but the jeweled choker showed no new reaction, sprang no trap, made no sound. Feeling again, I noted a pair of studs at the widest point, and pressed them at the same time. With a click, the legs formerly clenched all the way around the unconscious villain's neck unclasped, and I pulled away a slowly wriggling, metallic, priceless abomination about the size of a child's ball. A ball with eight legs and teeth worth a knight's ransom. Feldspar calmly noted that I was probably holding five times the value of the commission I was being paid, and I felt a bit ill.

I knew it would bite me. I could not doubt that for a second. But I thought there was no better way to hide it on my person, and revulsion or no, I was never going to throw such a thing away. Sweating in the mid-night of late winter, I ripped up my own cowl and laid the thing against my neck.

It bit me. Of course.

But the pain was far from the worst I've had, and there was no follow-on rush of venom, not even any bleeding. No, the worst part was its eight legs wrapping themselves around my neck in a gem-edged embrace while I had all I could do not to throw up. I steadied my own legs, the two with blood in them, and tried to assess how different I felt. So far, nothing seemed out of the ordinary, except a small additional voice in my head, like an instinct whispering of possibilities.

I told the voice to take a seat while I argued with Feldspar about what to do. Next to Teretheny on the street was that canteen he'd received from Salivaar. I knew it was safe to handle, so I picked up and carefully sloshed it. Some liquid nearly as thick as pudding inside, perhaps with solid bits in it. I had no idea what it was or what it could be used for; leaving it with this bastard had little appeal but trying to use it seemed much worse. Feldspar casually remarked it might be some kind of incendiary fluid and that decided me. I set it back down next to his body; this dog's fangs were pulled now, without the Throat he would have to remain himself.

Should he stay ignorant of who had bested him, Feldspar asked. I set one of my marked gems into his half-open palm and stepped away satisfied. He would not know, but he would ask: my legend would do its work for me and perhaps he'd back away now.

The monk was beginning to stir and I moved off to reach the shadows. Back with his unconscious so-called bodyguards, I hesitated just a moment and wondered again what to do. Though I faulted them the company they kept, I hardly thought these two worthy of death. I wondered if perhaps I should take that tingling torc off Elehar's arm. Out of sympathy, Feldspar sneered; perhaps new shoes for the orphans home next. Teretheny coughed and my time was up. I jogged silently away, and circled around in the direction of the Eye of the World.

Inside the old theater again, I finished work on the contraption I could use to cross the Tepid without getting wet, and then sought out a dressing room with my bullseye lantern half shuttered. Under the stage, as usual, I found a row of them, though something here was rank beyond garbage and too sickly-sweet to be just ordure. Locating a room with a serviceable mirror, I stripped off my Feldspar blacks and faced my reflection as Jonn Simith.

I hadn't removed the Throat while working, afraid it might crawl off when I wasn't looking. Now I gawked, then felt my neck; neither seeing nor touching was believing.

The priceless, ornate gewgaw as thick as my forearm was gone from view; around my throat I saw only a small gemstone on a leather thong. Leaning in, I inspected the red-brown flecks and broke into a titter of laughter. It was an inch-long piece of feldspar. Yet with my hands I detected exactly the same artefact as I had seen on Teretheny; eight golden segmented legs, multiple eyes, fangs and body and crusted with gems. Only very slightly moving, just enough to remind me of its unearthly existence. Yet now I felt no automatic revulsion as I has been sure I would.

I redressed in black covering the Throat, and concentrated on the image of Salivaar, and instantly realized I would have to choose between his earthly and lycanthropic form. The latter, I realized, was much easier to conjure, so I brought up the image of him standing in the moonlight, dagger-nosed, protruding incisors, gleam and gait and wicked grin.

At first I was just standing there like a fool, imagining being someone other than Feldspar. The rush of energy flowing over my skin was prickly but cool, and I lost attention to look down before back up. There rippling into the mirror was the very image of the rat-king of Old Cryss, wriggling his nose whenever I did and looking at himself with razor-sharp attention. I even saw the end of a tail flicker into view over my shoulder; my cackle sounded just like Salivaar's.

I knew I would sound the same as well, but I threw myself into the part, just to keep in practice.

"Evening, boys, how's the crop of victims looking tonight? Bring me that crown, and hop to it. I've a meeting with our allies and I want an ace in the hole."

132

The Brow was as good as back in W'starrah's hands. And Feldspar could dispense with costumes and make-up forever. I meant to laugh in good humor, but only the sound of a man-rat echoed in my dressing room. Something still stank, a voice inside me insisted. And I knew that thought was Simith talking.

$$\oplus \oplus \oplus$$

Chaktha is hunting now, as he has not done since his youth. With the hide shield limbered and spear held forward, he stalks a jungle made of brick and paving stones, head swinging side to side in search of the monsters who run loose here at night.

Chaktha knows what the Elves do not, because he has seen the monsters' work, at the house of the jewel-man, the Orange one the priestess called Welles. His fingers have felt the ragged wounds and noted the collapsed empty skull, he scented their earthy, cloying presence, and knows his ears did not deceive him with the bony clicks he heard on his approach. For his eyes, Chaktha is content to wait. He is hunting them, the sight will come.

He paces quickly now back to the priestess, ignoring these Elves who build and cast magic and pretend not to sleep as he does; who always draw back from his path, even when Chaktha's spear is not out and ready for use. He does not blame them, or resent them, any more than he was angry as a child when monkeys scattered thus, while he hunted his first tiger. It is in the order of things, and Chaktha thinks now only of her safety, and how long he has been away.

The Heaven's Eye is not at her tower, nor the teacher her friend, nor even that half-naked priest whom Chaktha dislikes. His two guards stand by here, awaiting her return with urgent messages from him; they speak of others who have come to talk with her, such as the Fire Grip himself and later a grey-clad stranger.

She said she would stay when she ordered him to leave, but has broken her word. Or been taken despite it. Chaktha enters and these guards, two more monkeys, do not bar his path.

The chambers are empty, just the scent of her jasmine behind. The lantern lays on one side, its spent wick telling of hours, not minutes gone. No signs of violence, simply some papers on the floor, and Chaktha has never understood the symbols on them. Yet he feels as if the tiger is watching him now. The priestess thought she saw monsters here once, and later in the schoolhouse, then here again. Chaktha never saw them, but the sight often comes last in hunting. Now he has their scent. Behind the statue of her hero, Chaktha again bends down and sniffs. Just a trace of the same odor, somewhere behind this stone.

He fears then that they have taken her. His spear and fingers cannot affect these blocks of granite, and Chaktha becomes frantic. He bounds down the stairs and out of the tower now. He cannot track her by scent, the gardens bear her favorite flower. But the house of the Orange one; he can begin there. The monsters, like smaller insects, are probably of the same tribe, he thinks. Follow one, find them all.

The rest of the night brings Chaktha only a few blocks beyond the ravaged empty home of the jewel-man. Strong scents within quickly fade as he backtracks, and it seems to him that several traces crossed in the night, never leaving a visible sign. The Elves, they do not believe in the hunt, because sight for them comes always first. As daylight returns and the small ones stir from a sleep they do not need, Chaktha hunches on a street corner and waits, for quiet and clear paths and resumption of the search.

The people of this precinct steer well clear of the giant black Man sitting on a barrel with his cape around him, and Chaktha has plenty of time to think, between dozing and fending off the desire for food. Before he could become a man in his tribe, the Elves of the Empire raided and took him away, to be sold and trained for war in the Emperor's bodyguard. But Chaktha grew large even for his people, still too unruly for those who held only the power to kill him, not his loyalty. So Chaktha had been sold to a noble family from this city, who assigned him as guardian for their daughter.

She had looked all the way up at him, aged only seven then, and announced at once that he was free.

Her parents had laughed, while the servants of the household looked to each other uncertainly, but she kept staring up and smiling. That was the day, the first he knew the priestess (even before she took that station), the day that Chaktha became no longer a slave to chains, but to love. He could hold her aloft on one of his hands then, and she squealed with delight whenever he raised her up, a little closer to the stars. Even then she loved them, and made him stand with her

134

deep into the night as she recited their shapes and taught him the meanings used by the Elves. Chaktha had carried his mistress on his back, everywhere she went about the estate and even into the city; she called him her stallion then, though not in years since. To him the girl was always light to bear.

And of course Chaktha had carried her from the arena, that day her parents died in the dragon's fire, bringing her to the temple for the first time, where the Stargazers heard her speak in vision, recognized her true place. And his place as well, always by her side.

Chaktha rouses from slumber now, to see those stars returning, the steps of citizens fading away. He stands and resumes the hunt. He knows that deep within he hungers, and that this appetite is most likely not for food, but revenge.

His senses give him few clues, but over the next hours he is carried closer to the river, and finally to a district beneath the docks not far from the place he awaited her days ago. The priestess had left him to visit the healer, but returned by a different way and Chaktha asked no explanation. He wishes now he had spoken, but that is not his way. Down, under the docks, he steps toe-first with spear out along abandoned, twisted boards.

Her scream—filled with terror and pain she has never known, yet Chaktha recognizes her voice.

"Priestess!" there is no answer, but he runs ahead, and now he scents the enemy, the stench of earth and tight spaces. Stopping to listen, he hears distant shouts of those uninvolved, the lapping of the water, the breeze. Chaktha ignores them, hears more: perhaps a muffled cry, a single click of bone or wood, then something forged by Man, tak ting-tak.

And a slight scent, just a trace of jasmine, tainted with blood.

Chaktha bellows again, he brays in fury her name and words in his native tongue, but the echoes of his own voice do nothing to locate her. He moves at a gallop, seeking to get ever-lower, ever-darker, to places where such monstrous cowards would hide. His instincts tell him, whatever their outward form, he hunts scavengers.

There are no further signs of the priestess but the smell of them becomes stronger until he stands at a point on the wooden planks so close to the water that the boards are rotted, protesting with mortal splintering at every step of the giant ebony hunter. He stops when the smell begins to fade, turns back, looks down. Something approaches, not clicking but the boots of humankind and again that metallic drum-rhythm. Chaktha prepares to throw his spear, but waits to see.

Into the strips of under-dock starlight steps a man in grey, a mortal Man who seems both old and young, and holds a metal-clad staff of silvery light in both hands. The two regard each other a long, silent moment. Chaktha senses another hunter, like himself, and smiles as he seldom does around the Elves.

The grey one speaks, pointing to the brooch fastening Chaktha's cloak. "You are a member of the Stargazer temple. Do you seek the missing priestess, W'starrah Altieri?"

Chaktha nods, and the Man continues.

"I too, must find her. I owe a debt, if she has been harmed. I thought I heard a scream. Will you abide with me, then, that we may search together?"

Chaktha nods, and the Man laughs as if unused to the process.

"Sooth! And seldom have I borne so great a weight in conversation. Yet lead the way, and if we find the Lavender Lady in durance let her captors hear well the language we both can speak best, mayhap, with our weapons."

Chaktha trusts the little man; though he speaks like one of the nobles, he is hard and certain of what he wishes to do. Chaktha points to the boards at their feet and the other stoops down, then speaks a miracle.

"Luxar simis Aral." He is much like the priestess himself, then.

The small ball of blue light atop his staff shows that below the planks there is a hole, large enough for anyone but Chaktha to enter easily. They exchange a glance, then strike at the rotted boards with staff and spear, chopping through in moments, and lowering into the hole which smells of the scavengers.

The tunnel continues down steeply and soon the air is choking. There is never a place where Chaktha can stand up straight, and many where the Man must also stoop to proceed. The light shows smaller tunnels leading off, and soon the twists and turns are too many for Chaktha to remember.

136

When he hears the first Bugs approaching he stops, signaling the man in grey who covers the light with his cape. In shadows, ten or more Insectirs the size of mastiffs march across their path at the tunnel ahead, antennae flicking toward the light but not slowing their march. It has been far too long and Chaktha cannot sense the priestess any more in these cloying wet shafts. His partner pushes past him to the intersection, where he slowly uncovers his miracle-light and looks first after the Bugs, then back the way they came.

"Can you tell which way is best?" he asks, and Chaktha must shake his head.

"I would guess those things were ordered forth on some mission or other. Let us reverse their course then, for if the Myster Altieri has been taken it was surely to a leader, and in this way we may find a clue of her."

Again Chaktha nods, and the mortal Man grins, as if not accustomed. There is a look in his eye that reckons not much between whether he lives or dies, and Chaktha, who can no longer imagine the way back to air and life, understands it. He follows the Man bearing light, and fondly imagines carrying the priestess once more, up and away from here. If she is harmed before Chaktha can arrive, many will die.

In this way they progress, taking any tunnel which is larger or leads downward, and backtracking Insectirs whenever they see them. Three times, in this measureless darkness, the creatures appear directly ahead, and the two must retreat hastily to take a side-corridor for the Bugs to pass. Many are the large, hard-shelled ones with six legs of which two carry weapons; their eyes are like gems with many facets, and these monsters seem to have their own will. But other Insectirs are bulbous and glistening like enormous snails, with hundreds of legs or none, moving in orderly rows, or in masses, or alone.

As they rest near a three-way intersection, the man in grey pulls jerky from his pack and hands a piece over, followed by his canteen. Neither hunter has spoken for what seems like a day and a night; they are very deep underground now, beyond a long stretch of tunnel which dripped with sea-water. They chew and sip and look upon each other awhile by the soft blue light of the miracle.

"You are loyal to the priestess," he says, "In this city, it seems everyone has two masters, or more."

Chaktha sees no reason to nod, this fellow is speaking almost to himself.

"Heroes, guilds, Colors, noble houses; I have been here less than a fortnight and my head aches with the effort to straighten them." He looks steadily on Chaktha a long moment. "It is good to have a single purpose, whatever it—"

Out of the darkness behind the man in grey loom two of the warrior Bugs, shaded from the light by his body. One slashes with its weapon, and the Man ducks as Chaktha thrusts to stave back the second. But the man in grey is stabbed before he can gain room to use his staff, and gasps though keeping his footing.

Chaktha longs for room, to use his height and to have the option to throw his massive spear. This enclosed tunnel is a place for tight, small motions and his rage is too large for it. As the man in grey pokes and blocks, the two Insectirs chitter and scream in alarm and rage; surely if there are more behind them they will come. Shouting in his fury, Chaktha stabs his opponent hard directly in the eye and it reels back in writhing agony. Then he thrusts hard into the earthen roof above them, three times, five, and pulls his comrade back as the soggy clay collapses atop the other's dome. They flee and take several turns before stopping; there is no pursuit, but Chaktha feels as if there is heightened alertness everywhere, a tight, stinging aroma in the thick tunnel air.

The man in grey puts one hand over the wound in his thigh and utters strange words, "Intacta volar". In a moment, he straightens and looks around as if nothing had happened.

Chaktha stares at this miracle-worker by the blue light near his staff, while the mortal checks him over for injuries as well. The grey man looks both ways in the tunnel and continues speaking as calmly as if standing in a bedroom.

"I failed her. Your priestess. When I saw her near the river, I thought only of the moment, that she was in need of some small assistance for that hour. I did not consider... the circumstances that brought her near danger might be pressing, more permanent. I was proud, and did not inquire how I might serve... but I sense that she had a great destiny, beyond perhaps that of any single person to fulfill." A grimace crosses his face as he looks up at Chaktha. "You think to find her alive?"

Chaktha nods fiercely and moves forward in a fighting stance. The man in grey holds up one hand.

"As ye will, warrior. Sooth, I pray she is still well, but... you feel you have also failed her?"

Chaktha flushes with hot shame, looks down and pounds the butt of his spear into the sodden tunnel floor. At the Man's touch on his arm, he snaps back up to look him in the eye.

"Methinks yours was by far the lesser fault; sooth at the temple they told me, she had ordered you away, and in obedience there can be no great crime. But let us not compare, mighty one, and instead turn our thoughts and hearts to what may be done now."

"Certes, they shall spread the alarm; we tempt fate down here so great a time. If you would be counseled by me, bodyguard, we should run and try to reach a larger chamber. Let the heroes guide our path, and if it come to the worst, may we live long enough to do some good before the end."

Chaktha feels his whole frame quiver with excitement, as when near the end of the hunt. He grips his spear for answer, gesturing that the man in grey should select the path. They set off at a trot, constrained for speed only by the tunnel's height.

And this impediment lessens within a hundred paces, as a large crossing tunnel is tall enough even for Chaktha. He laughs and looks above him, where some kind of dim luminescence clings, enough to show the ceiling crammed with wriggling, entwining bodies. Each about the size of a kitten, they are multi-legged and all moving one way, for whatever purpose he cannot guess. Swallowing hard, he follows the man in grey at a full run in the opposite direction.

Suddenly the tunnel widens into a chamber, and Chaktha knows he has come to the quarry of his long hunt. The sight comes last, and what he sees Chaktha still does not believe.

A roughly circular chamber glowing as the tunnel, with three other exits and guard-Bugs at each. There is no furniture, or items such as warm blooded beings have, but the bumps and protrusions of the chamber are yet purposeful, hewing to an alien design.

In the center of the vault, near a giant beetle-thing bristling with talons and scythe-like claws, there is a rough altar of earth and on it lies the body of the priestess. Only the shreds of lavender gown, a few wisps of champagne hair, confirm the identity of a physical shell so horribly torn, so deeply gored and broken. The top half of this altar is stained near to crimson from what had been life-giving when that body was whole, and breathing and containing everything beautiful in Chaktha's short life.

Beyond the altar, a white ant the size of a pony stirs bubbling thick fluid in a kind of trough. No source of heat explains the motion of its contents, and the creature has no eyes to see its progress. From the trough to the altar there is a small channel, ending by the priestess' head. The beetle-thing is preparing to cut there.

Chaktha roars, and a red haze descends over his sight and memory. The great spear hurtles from his hand, taking the beetle-gore just below the maw and plowing out two feet from the back of its head. Drawing a long-bladed knife, Chaktha slams his shield into the reeling foe, shouting with joy as pincers and nails scrape his sides, thrusting hard into the thing's exposed belly and rolling it back onto the floor. It still struggles and slashes while trying to regain balance.

The white ant swivels its eyeless head back and forth, as the guardians close from all sides. The grey man engages one and now his staff is whirling with speed, blocking attacks and driving his foe back with a broken limb. Three others approach the altar area now. Chaktha at last finds a crevice in the central section of the beetle-gore and plunges his longknife through it and into the earth. Rising, he grasps the spear and wrenches it loose, tearing most of its head off and spattering gobs that smell of sour decay and feel cold on his chest. Turning back, Chaktha swings the spear like a scythe to keep the others at bay. His great arms and the added length of his shaft are beyond the multi-jointed reach of these Bugs, and they lack real courage, already bothered by the blue light this close.

The mortal blocks two more strikes and counters with an overhand blow that crushes his enemy's skull. It folds unevenly and falls half against the trough, and now he turns to face the bone-white ant, which even without eyes seems to sense him and scuttles back a four-footed pace.

Chaktha wonders at his partner's choice, to attack a helpless servant with several Bugs holding weapons behind him, but he has thrown his trust in with the mortal's light and will not stop now. He glances down, at the body of the priestess, and redoubles his sweeping attacks, stepping into the gore of the foe who slew her and laughing again with fierce joy, that he at least avenged his mistress.

The mortal raises his staff, then stops as the white ant faces him fully. The Man staggers, shakes his head, and then clenches his weapon anew, crying "Nay, demon, try not to control my spirit for lo, and I have resisted such foul magics before you."

As he raises his staff again, the white ant smoothly turns to face directly at Chaktha.

Suddenly the room is silent, completely empty except for the white Bug. The icy grip of fear is upon his heart now, and Chaktha hardly realizes that he has dropped his weapon. He screams as a cloud descends over his vision, or worse, he feels he has fallen asleep.

A shout of pain pulls him back to himself, and Chaktha discovers to his horror that he has seized his comrade from behind, hefting him off the ground and leaving him open to attack. The Bugs have closed in and slashed the Man twice across his middle with their claws, bringing blood and heat. Chaktha tries to let go, to turn and fight, but he is frozen, his limbs held in place by strings he cannot reach.

As the Bugs prepare to finish their victim, the man in grey cries out in a loud voice.

"Luxar! Luxar simis Solar!"

The blue light drowns in a large ball of white-yellow flame. After so much darkness, it hangs in the chamber like a permanent stroke of lightning. Chaktha is blinded, feels the strings on his limbs snap, and drops the Man to cover his own eyes. Squeals and chitters drown all other sounds; he drops to all fours and gropes through the ichor and body parts to find his spear again.

He forces his eyes open, and can make out only shapes, darker against the painful light, scores of limbs waving like a field of corn in a windstorm. The guardian Bugs, and several more who have arrived, lie curled in agony. Something grey and backed by flesh near the center of the light is struggling to stand, to use its staff against them while they are stunned. Chaktha howls in victory and joins in.

141

The earth of the chamber becomes a threshing floor as the two chop and smash, separating limbs from bodies, wiping away what splashes up to sting and stain them.

The man in grey leaks badly from both sides, and Chaktha's legs shout in pain from the death-dealt wounds of the beetle-gore. He spares a glance for the entrance by the trough and there the white ant is staggering back, not hurt directly yet fending with its arms as if the connections give it sight, and pain, and for once confusion. It is gone, and the others now sprawl in severed, flinching defeat.

Chaktha's companion looks about the chamber, leaning harder and harder on his staff until he slumps to sit with his back against the trough. The light of the sun dims and shrinks a bit, still bright but smaller and now eyes born to the air are used to it. The scavenger-cowards lie dead everywhere and the scent Chaktha had before is again subtly changed; when he sniffs deeply he gets an image of retreat, and thinks of the way jackals pull back when the lion has made a kill. For now.

"In-intacta v-volar." The Man's wounds close up a little, the bleeding stops, but Chaktha can see there is yellow-green around the scars, and with his hand he feels heat. The same from his calves and thighs, though the bleeding there has stopped of its own. Chaktha stands above the trough and contemplates its thick, bubbling stew without comprehension. Disgust decides him and he stabs low and hard on one side, puncturing the earthen cauldron and watching awhile as the chunky pale-dirt fluid leaks away into the floor of the chamber.

"I am sorry, my friend," the man in grey whispers, "I have failed your priestess again, and you in the bargain. We both, both made a good end of it I think." He swallows and leans back, his eyes steady through the pain. "Keep the light—long as you can—use it against— seek the air again."

He speaks no more and it is as if the Man has fallen asleep with eyes slightly open. The light of the sun dims a bit more, still better to see by. Chaktha stands alone in the grotesque chamber a long moment.

And he decides that this hunt is not yet over.

He carefully lays the man in grey upon his hide shield with his staff atop him still glowing, and removes the Man's cloak. Then Chaktha returns to the altar: something in his eyes makes it difficult to see, but he wipes in alternation as he carefully arranges her remaining hair around the priestess' face. The wounds there, at least, are less disfiguring, and Chaktha fancies he can see his mistress as she once was, perhaps still breathing in a sleep she never needed. And her skull is not violated, its contents no part of that evil brew now spilling away with some portion of her enemies' plans.

He covers her body thoroughly with the grey man's cloak and turns away. Lifting the shield with effort, he regards his comrade still lying there eyes half-open, barely moving in response. He is full-grown and the task of carrying him would have challenged Chaktha at the start of a good day, on steady clean streets. But he walks with him, wounded legs and rising fever and all, across the spattered gore of this earthen devil's chamber, not focused on making the entire journey, but simply the next ten steps. Ten steps he can do, and after that Chaktha will see.

Those ten steps bring him to the altar where he also takes up the priestess. She, at least, has never felt heavy to him, and now the stallion will bear her one last time. Ten more steps.

⊕ ⊕ ⊕

T he light draws you on, no longer held back by your body, and a single step is enough. Free now, your spirit bathes in illumination, stars and sun and all enter you undimmed by the chains of flesh. And I too am here with you.

In the Now.

To me you have always been here, but you see Now for the first time. The torn corpse left behind, the city at night, and again by day, every day at once, the light of all time suffusing you. Your spirit in mortal life took in only a portion of this, sifting and blocking and constraining light to see some as past, some as future (and most not seen at all). There you felt weariness and hunger and doubt, distractions without number requiring an order to time. But in the Now, you are free at last, and I am with you, my cherished one.

You turn to me, see me as you never had with mere eyes, and our embrace is joyous, welcoming, safe, eternal. I have always hugged you to me, as every father to each daughter. All time passes in that instant and still we embrace. Well done, faithful follower. Rest.

Yet you pull back a little, and a ripple of Next enters the Now.

"What has happened?"

"What always would happen, cherished one. What has always happened."

"I am dead now?"

"Your body is no longer with you. You see all. We are Now. I have always enjoyed this moment, and only briefly awaited it. Do you see?"

You nod, in wonder and joy, yet your brow also creases and another ripple moves us a little apart. This too you always were bound to do, and I know it as I always have. Yet there is sadness here, at what must be a while longer.

"But what of my people? Where is Kat, or Chaktha, Tanar'h will be—Lord of Light, my Captain!"

"Be at peace, cherished one. They still live in the body, in time. The world continues."

"But what will happen to them?"

"What will always happen."

"But, my part in them, is now over?"

"Why, cherished one, because you have died? Because you are here in the Now? When I crossed over, did I cease to play a part in your life?"

You turn and move away—how charming, the habits of the body still hold—and aside from me the light fills you, suffuses you as you gasp—still breathing!—with comprehension.

"Yes, I see. I see… so much, milord Stargazer, it is just as you…" You look back and the thought occurs, as it must, as it already has. "You knew, you foresaw that I would go mad, lose my way, fall prey to those Bugs…"

My embrace is still warm, comforting. "I asked so much of you, cherished one. By your passion the city may now be saved."

"But my friends! They are still in danger, I must help them." You are still so much with the earth, as I knew you would be. The pain I feel, to see you struggling thus, is familiar to me, for this moment like all moments has been Now.

"It cannot be undone. You are here."

Your beautiful gaze fires with passion and closes down. How many times have I seen this!

144

"I am sworn to help them. Let me see, Stargazer, let me see them all."

"All of them are yours, cherished one. But remember, nothing changes where you are. The Now is eternal."

Together then we look upon those most dangerous to you, their images falling dim and rising sharp as you require, wherever and whenever they are pursuing your destiny most nearly.

The Serpent Salivaar converses with his minion rats, moving about nervously with rubbing hands and awaiting word from his various masters. Soon will be another Now, where he leaves with rats in train, and the Ferret, changing to the Serpent's verminous form, may enter to retrieve the flaming crown.

Back in the night-lit city, the Dragon Carnad Mias rouses snorting from sleep and fears his treasures are stolen. He snaps orders and clambers off to seek the Fly on his own, to release it in advance of his former plan.

In the same wise, Teretheny the Arbalest, brown robes and bodyguards hiding his true character, has also become unnerved at things he does not understand. He approaches the center-city, past the wagons filled with sand and attended by guards from the desert. His canteen is smaller than his desire, but the cowardly mercenary who strikes from afar gambles that it may be enough to achieve his purpose.

"You see, cherished one? All these powerful evil men, thrown to confusion by your bright flame, panicked into acting too soon rather than await the fullness of Now to triumph more easily." I look fondly upon you, that you may realize the worth of your noble sacrifice. "Though it cost you the body and breath, yet now Hope may survive the coming storm."

"Yet the storm still comes, milord. I can see some of what they intend—ah, so many will die! The fire, it ravages everywhere, and sand and swords. Great Argens, can you not stop this?"

"Peace, cherished one." I wait as ripples of unquiet Next swirl and push on our spirits, and you try to regain calm. "You know my word, W'starrah, all the prophecy must come to pass."

Together we watch the vision again.

A hot swirling wind blows over Cryssigens by night... from the Dragon's breath leading the men of flaming livery to battle; while the Serpent's minions swarm across the river and tangle in the streets with fleeing citizens, as Bugs emerge from the shadows adding to the wrack; to the Arbalest's bolt that reaps a whirlwind and its harvest of spiders; we view it all and see those portions which came true when your body housed you, bright and etched in stone. For the rest, it is as if there are shadows among the brightness, certain things that it cannot illuminate. The light prisms past these moments, possibilities burgeon beyond even the ability of spirit-eyes to discern. Blue sea and red fire are everywhere at war, racked or raised by the howling wind...

You shiver in horror and empathy for those still in flesh, who cannot see what comes to them. My gift brings you little happiness.

The next-ripples fade and become still, before you speak again.

"So, the enemies of Hope may not succeed. And only some of the Children of Hope will die? Great Argens, will you suffer this to pass?"

"What I have suffered, cherished one, is not yet for you to know. Take what steps you can, but know this. When I have spoken to you in vision, these words create a kind of barrier to the light, for crafting the future darkens it. What I have shown you, cannot be changed. It happens. It has always been Now."

You nod, then fix your gaze on those dear to you.

The brave Ferret Feldspar watches and waits his chance, observing the Serpent by the cold temple walls and working in the lonely, abandoned theater as everywhere packs of human rats seek for him.

"He is mortally brave, your Ferret"

You smile but feel a pang at the object of his quest; for if he snatches the crown of fire from its prison among thieves and murderers, what then?

Your dearest friend Kat still teaches, still asks for word of you from all she sees, still prays for guidance—each word of prayer a little droplet of light falling on us, bringing contentment and allowing us to see still more. Tanar'h too prays, by the statue in the main chapel, but his soul is torn open with grief and fear, shedding little light in your direction but filling with a perilous resolve.

"They bear the mark of your light, cherished one, each carrying on in their own way. You saved your teacher and her students from death, and to my High Heart you brought back the sight of the rightful course, though he is pained to take it."

Through darkened ways far below the earth, a small light quavers but holds, and Chaktha treads heavily onward bearing two bodies on his back, ten steps at a time. He emerges to the air and stars, near the home of the Turtle, the healer Kama who takes them in and ministers to the grey one as the Stallion continues on with the second load of flesh.

"My poor Stallion," you murmur watching his stoic face as he marches through shadowed streets.

"Those two mortals are not my followers," I say to you carefully, "and I do not see them clearly. Your bodyguard has done well to recover your form, as without proper internment your spirit in the Now will always feel bound to the earth."

Your face holds shock, even dismay, as the light of this truth shines full.

"You mean, this is why I feel so much concern, Stargazer? And when my flesh is burned…"

"Then you will be fully free, cherished one. The second Man, that strange grey youth in the Turtle's care, he knows more of this than most."

"He rescued me, that night below the docks. Who is he, milord?"

"I cannot fully say. He is not one of us."

"Not a follower of Argens?"

"Not a Child of Hope, at least not by parentage. He is an alien from another land entirely, and his vision is strange to me. Yet he sees more… more than most in some ways. There is shadow around him."

"What does that mean, is he in Despair?"

"He hews closely to its sources, rather, in his effort to do good by his own lights. His own lights, yes… he puzzles me, that one, W'starrah. The future is not clear where he draws close. Yet he did well by you, as you say."

And there! As I knew you must, you look on a darkened near-empty fortress by dawn, as the Captain emerges from durance and his Fire Ants cheer like men gone mad. Now you catch the breath you no longer require and sob with pain you no longer need to feel.

"Ah see him, milord," you weep, "his men surround him and sing, your miracle accomplished this great deed."

"Your miracle, cherished one, as much as my own. Your love for the Captain, more than his need for my help, enabled me to work in the realm of time and life."

"And now—oh great lord, it is too much! He hurries, exchanges last orders, he will hasten back to the city as I urged him. He believes— oh Stargazer, this is too much, please you must, you cannot leave me here without him."

"You think me capable of rolling back death? Not for any of us, not even the greatest of the heroes has this power. The legions of Despair could only cast its warped, awful counterfeit in undeath. The power exists, aye, but it is as mysterious to me as to you. That grey youth, perhaps, suspects this and follows his own path. But I cannot see where it will lead him."

You cry in tears the Now does not normally endure, and the waves of Next are everywhere, pushing us apart, creating shadows in the light. Long have I seen this moment, but very little of what lies around it. Your spirit reaches to me for comfort, and I can only supply my regard for you. When you enter a course of Next, I cannot aid even you, cherished one.

"You will do nothing?" Your face, more lovely Now than ever it was on earth, is filled at first with confusion, then resolves into determination backed by the wit and spirit that make all who know you love you.

"Yet you also sent me a prophecy, milord," and your voice rings with a kind of fey joy as you chant the doom, roiling the Next into hardened columns and plinths that stand between the light though yet made of it, and casting shadows where none can see. A little space of the future exists here in the Now, a decision made that throws open the door to possibility, and events. And which chances failure.

"Recall what you told me, lord Stargazer, even when I was a child."

As the rule of men fails
A woman's spirit rises to lead them
Argens' Fire will not sear this soul

Nor wound and ruin impede her path

I stand back from you as I must, Now, and let this unknowable future take its course steered by your decision. I gaze upon you, mayhap for the last time, and I bow in respect of it without giving approval or shouting a denial.

You bow slowly in return, and move steadily around the edge of the Next you have chosen, a little closer to the world of mortality and time.

It may mean salvation for your city. It may mean I have looked my last upon you. This moment, where I know not the future, reminds me of life itself and how it must feel for those who follow me. Perhaps I envy them their lives, a little.

⊕ ⊕ ⊕

Justin emerged from the gatehouse with Kein Trador and the young Baron, blinking back tears caused by morning light after so much darkness. Surely. The bodies of the undead lay piled thick before the portcullis, fallen in place at the monster's destruction. Looking down Justin saw faces he knew, men who had followed him before their bodies were conscripted into the services of Despair. These, he could not save; Justin felt a sliver of emptiness across his middle.

As he crossed the drawbridge the men of his company cheered the sight of him, rushing over with no discipline whatsoever to pound his back and raise him overhead like the groom at a Rom wedding.

"You should have seen the charge, sir!"

"And then like a bolt it dropped from the sky on us, that thing—"

"Poor Taeba, he was right next to me, right there—"

"The village children, sir," M'nesa's gentle voice somehow carried through the careening words, "those you charged me with, quite safe, by the wagons."

"Captain, here's Bullseye," Tass roared, "You remember that last arrow I made him fetch? Now what do you suppose he did with it, but save his favorite officer's life!"

"Cark me, wish I'd shot myself instead."

Relief and adulation flowed into their Captain from all sides, helping to sustain him as the energy of Argens' miracle faded. He was starting to feel the wounds and aches of his long privation. But there was more work to do than ever. That empty slice in his gut had grown into an amorphous pang of desire amid the tumult, a strange longing that named itself "home".

"Enough! At attention, every man of you." The surviving company snapped into ranks on both sides, forming a rag-ended hallway around their commander. They too had fought for their lives with many injuries and no sleep. But in their eyes Justin could see devotion that erased all doubt.

"Men, I give you the Baron of Tralmachia, milord Sordinay T'yr."

"HAIL, BARON!" the men drew swords and saluted.

"By his hand, a monstrous evil has been destroyed, and this land given a chance to rebuild. The cost was high and the danger not yet past."

"Several of my brothers may still survive," the Baron spoke with quiet resolve. "You brave men have seen some of what they can do."

"And until his rule is on a safer footing, the Baron and his family will require protection." Justin looked around at the company, barely six complete dekents left, and assessed his needs. Horses by the camp, the awakened gryphon pulling petulantly at its twin chains, and a small engine sitting abandoned on the plain, like something out of nothing. He looked to M'nesa Zetee whose tiny grin held the promise of a marvelous tale. But a leader of soldiers made no small talk in public. Time for orders.

"All foot dekents will remain here with Kein Trador, to guard the Baron and follow his orders until such time as he can recruit your replacements." Justin exchanged a glance with Sordinay and saw there his relief, which he fully intended to invest for his benefit. "The rest of you," he let his voice hang a moment, "are supposed to have been horsemen, once upon a time. Now you will ride as never before."

The cheers of the men were thunderous, slapping around the vale rocks and cresting even the gryphon's caw as Justin motioned his dekentars toward the camp, and stepped to one side with Sordinay.

"Captain Thyme, I owe you my mother's life and that of my people."

"It was Argens who wrought the miracle, milord. But if you are minded to be grateful…"

"Name it."

"Your vote, milord." Justin gauged the effect of this request on the new Baron. "You must remain here, to secure your rule and restore faith to the people. Order my men as you will in this, I shall instruct Trador to obey you in all lawful things. But let the Mark know that Tralmachia's absence from affairs of state is ended."

"You wish me to vote you for the new Overlord?"

Justin smiled. "Vest me, rather with your vote, and make it known by seal that I speak for you in this matter. If you can trust me."

"With my life. Scribe!" Sordinay spun off to summon paper and seals, and Justin caught up to his subalterns near the camp as the gryphon fretted and yanked at its bonds. Something in that angry screech touched his own desire, and the closer he came the more he felt its tug without yet understanding its meaning.

"You must ride well, dekentar," he said to M'nesa without looking at him: all the subalterns knew the rank-order. "You will have a small surplus of horses, now, to serve as remounts. I need you in Cryssigens in a day."

"Yes sir," Zetee responded quietly, then noted, "They will likely be winded for a fight."

"No use to us anyway in the streets, unless we ignored the danger to common citizens, which we will not. Muster at the arena first, and if I am not there to greet you, quarter them and make for the Stargazer temple on foot. You must treat all armed men as if enemies until they declare otherwise by their deeds. But do not look to start a fight unless they attack you or bar the way."

Salutes from all the dekentars, this was at last a battle plan they understood.

"And me, Captain," Tass grunted. "Am I to serve under the Strategos there?" He pointed to Trador assisting Sordinay near the castle, grinning with the good nature of one who had dished it out and now stood ready to take his turn.

"Stay here, dekentar?" Justin affected surprise. "What, when the streets of your home city are like to run with blood, and dirty street fighting on foot beckons us?"

Tass smiled across his entire face to hear this, but his jaw dropped open at Justin's next word.

"You will take Furta yourself. See you treat her well."

151

"A horse!" he croaked, "But I don't ride."

"Then you may tie your neck to her tail and run, dekentar. I need every man in Cryssigens and I do not intend to await the pleasure of any sleep-drowning human in my company, do I make my intention plain?"

Tass' face crossed a bridge of distaste to recover its accustomed insolence. "You do indeed sir." He actually saluted, and Justin, not wishing to waste such a rare opportunity, returned it.

Gazing a moment around the vale Justin saw his men gathering bodies for internment, assisted by a few of the Baron's staff who had emerged from hiding in the depths of the castle. The men were still in high spirits, and wherever Kein Trador went it seemed a story was spreading. Faces looked in Justin's direction, jaws dropped, holy signs were made, heads and hands shook. Some of the subalterns with him had already heard. Justin's reputation was becoming larger than life; the light of Argens had fallen upon him, and the men in his company could never suffer defeat.

But could he?

Pointing to the chained beast he said only "Saddle it."

"Captain! No, it will kill you this time!" Several officers were shouting, and the handler too from behind them. At the noise, the gryphon tried to leap into the air, and pulled one chain several inches from the stone.

"Sir, it will be dangerous." M'nesa's voice was barely restrained. "Without its cage—sorry about that, Captain, we needed the wood— but that thing has been increasingly restless ever since."

Justin laid a hand on his subaltern's shoulder. "Your engine helped save the life of your friend, and this barony. Well done indeed. As for myself, I trust that Argens will keep me in his hand as he has before."

In his heart Justin felt nothing of the kind; the smart bet said that he was stretching his run of luck too far. But he retrieved the riding crop and straightened his helm to stand before the beast as if nothing could be of less concern. The gryphon was in no mood to be strapped and restrained; it never tried to bite Justin but kicked with its rear talons to keep the handlers from getting close to its side.

Justin knew this had to work. "Home", he realized with wonder, did not mean his family foef now resting in the hands of another

152

noble line. It did not mean the barracks of Argens nor any other place he had spent much time in a life still only decades old. Home, the spot he had to reach, was a place he had only been once before.

With her.

Driven by a desperate need to see the priestess again, Justin stepped in as the men gasped and swore. Right to the creature's beak, close enough that it could snap his head off his neck like a grape, Justin raised a free hand and touched the monster's feathered neck as it reared back in shock.

"One last time," he murmured to it quietly, just as he would a nervous horse though Justin had never tried to calm a mount that ate flesh. "You wish to be free, yes? I swear to you, bear me now and then fly where you will, mighty one. I must reach her, you understand? One last ride."

The gryphon stood frozen and tense, no longer cawing, hardly breathing, like a snake ready to strike. Justin stared the monster down, knowing this was the only way to see her again in time. What was death, compared to failure? After an awful frozen moment, he signaled with a finger for the handlers to approach, and in no time the beast was saddled.

Tossing it a slab of meat from the supply wagon, Justin clapped the young handler on the shoulder. "Well done, lad, I discharge you from service. Take these children into the castle and find them some food." A runner arrived with a thick parchment bearing the baronial seal and he stuffed it in his jacket without glancing. Let judges decide whether a vote could be cast by proxy. Justin saluted M'nesa Zetee and leaped up to strap himself in the saddle. Tass and another dekentar stood ready and at his signal they loosed the chains.

"Hai!" Justin kicked but the creature was already airborne. The men below went wild again with cheers and song as he turned south in the whistling breeze of morning, cold with a hint of coming spring. Justin urged the gryphon to its greatest speed and felt alternate waves of joy and anguish. Justin was returning to her with three votes in hand, as representative of the Emperor and of Tralmachia. If W'starrah had found the Brow, six more and what could Carnad Mias do to counter that. Justin remembered the vision they had shared, all the fire and wrack still to come, and knew that given the choice to fulfill some cold destiny or protect the woman who kept his heart in her hands, he would let all Cryssigens burn. But there must still be time, a chance to serve her and the flag of mission. The gryphon screamed to give a voice to his torment, and flew faster than ever before.

He might fail in courage or strategy, when the final battle came. But Justin knew all that mattered was to get there in time.

$$\oplus \oplus \oplus$$

The closer I got to the time, the less I could focus on anything but the stench. My preparations were complete and I had gone over every step, thought out all the possibilities I could. Aral the lower moon was full tonight, so my paths would be clear and the shadows easy to gauge, at least until midnight when Unal arose to chase it. Most of all, it was a day for Salivaar to leave the temple-camp. I had discovered by watching and overhearing, he visited his mysterious patron twice a week. First the bandit-king would exit, then "he" would come back; I could grab the Brow, and done.

But the awful stink, I knew it was partly my imagination as I waited in the theater, yet it seemed to grow and grow until I couldn't breathe without coughing. Nerves, Feldspar scoffed, always so confident. I had spent days over here now, so I probably noticed it more. But I knew—only my eyes could play tricks this well, not the nose.

The more time I had spent in the place, the less I felt like eating. Sometimes my vision blurred, brought a wave of weakness. That stubborn sneeze never quite left me either. The crossing-raft was completed and safely stored out of sight by the stone piers on the Old Cryss side. I found myself checking it again tonight, just to get some fresher air down by the river. I laughed to think sea air would ever smell so sweet. That's when I knew it must be something wrong and I had to determine what. Someday. I forced down a little dried fruit and water, and headed back toward the piazzo to do the deed.

Cutting crosswise through a few streets I hadn't used before, a little ways between theater and temple, I passed a narrow alley and felt a blast of frigid air laced with that awful odor. Between stiff breeze and stark bouquet I nearly fell down. That tore it, I needed to settle this or I wouldn't be able to concentrate. Someday was now. I tied a black rag previously soaked in soap around my lower face, and prowled down the darkened street.

154

In a space between two buildings a giant hole, a rent delving through the stony pavement beckoned like the maw of a leviathan. Solid stone, two feet thick and more lay scattered about and torn like cloth: the hole dropped a dozen feet into pitch blackness that defied even my lantern. The stench was becoming nearly a solid thing now, gripping me in nausea and suggesting, with no subtlety at all, that I panic. I coughed, but Feldspar laughed. I secured a climbing cord nearby and lowered myself in.

The walls were still worked stone here, a basement or perhaps parts of two cellars, monumental and straight like everything else in this abandoned city. But the floor was wracked by some quake or explosion, tilting down in several directions and slick with ancient slime. I played the narrow beam of the bullseye lantern in all directions, trying to put my finger on what unnerved me so much.

Walking carefully inward, the answer stole up gradually while the darkness took me into its grip. Just like above ground, it was the size of the place. Huge, empty underground chambers, archways between rooms strong enough to hold up a bridge, and nowhere a single fixture, nothing of wood or cloth I could clearly see to give the slightest hint why. For what earthly reason would our ancestors have built so many houses above with more room than they could use, buttressed by cellar chambers the same? People did not live here, that much I realized from exploring the streets. Alright, but what did they store down below, what unthinkable treasures required so much room, what colossal prisoners demanded internment? And where were they now?

The floors continued to cant and tilt in places, huge planes of stone thrown out of alignment by that mysterious convulsion. In the sixth chamber back from the hole, I saw something that made my heart drop even further, and stood there stunned to believe my eyes. Stairs, leading down. A wide flight of solid basalt treads. Another level? Yet more empty space beneath the city. Astor's Chance, why? Down we went.

My light was less than a drop in the ocean, the ebon stench-air to all sides crowded thick with monsters of the mind. The Throat of the Spider grew even colder around my neck, and I fancied I could hear its voice again, whispering of the Bug tunnels and the chance to find them. Time disappeared, but even Feldspar was too curious to care about our mission for now. All it needed was the slightest sound, I was sure, and my heart would stop.

There.

I stopped and waited for my heartbeat to resume.

It was a sound like a cat knocking over a box in the next chamber. But wetter.

Or the noise a fish makes flopping once in the bottom of a boat. But bigger.

Or the echo of a many-legged monster, carefully stepping on a slimy stone floor. But deeper.

Heartbeats started in again, faster than usual to make up for lost time. I felt a wave of dizziness, driven by that horrendous smell, and threw my arms out for balance while breathing deep.

Out of completely nowhere I sneezed, as loud as you would on purpose to frighten someone. The echoes slapped around the solid stone walls and I admitted that someone was indeed scared now.

I held my breath and waited, and after a count of ten heard the sound again. A little higher, a little closer, and a great deal more... mundane. There, a third one, this time almost too distant to hear, but squishier and longer than the first two. Not a single thing, then, or many of the same thing but happening in a larger space, large even by the standards of Old Cryss. I was close, whatever it was, and nothing in the world could stop me from finding out what, even if it meant my death.

Up ahead the floors began consistently tilting down, plates of stone atop earth that had collapsed beneath them. The walls in the direction of the sound had broken away in most places, hanging overhead with torn remnants below forming a barrier at my knees. I could see dimly now, there was a luminescent lichen or mold on all the earthy surfaces of the chamber ahead, like in the Bug tunnels.

A titanic underground space. If you cleared out all of center city back near the fountains, and ripped up the entire precinct to throw it down here, it would fit neatly into this unthinkable hard-earth cavern. My mind reeled at the sight, the shape indicated by glowing rippling plants on all the walls and ceiling, punctuated by hundreds of small holes, stretching away like dots to all sides. And below...

It took me several moments to stare at what lay before and beneath me, my eyes blinked and I coughed up bile and I think I cried out in pain but it didn't matter. I fell to my knees and tried to describe, or even believe, what I could see.

For the longest time it was a single thing, a massive, moldy wet pile that seemed to wriggle or flinch. The sounds continued every few moments, and I tried without success to follow them, to see a form or body a score of furlongs across, a lone shape. The stench was so powerful I could hardly line up my thoughts, or choke down my fear long enough to consider them.

Then something plopped down onto the pile within a few steps of where I huddled, and my eye flashed to the spot fast enough to see it.

Shit.

With a little urine, probably.

More plops, not often but every eight or twenty counts, from all across the cavern, adding to the mass I finally recognized. There was no holding it back any more, and I leaned over the crumbled wall to throw up what little food I had in me. The perfect place for it anyway. Right where everyone else in Cryssigens was putting theirs, without knowing.

These arrogant nobles of centuries ago, it seems there was nothing they didn't dare. Merging all the heroes in their temple, raising towers to the sky as if to step directly into heaven, then burying their bodies below ground to make it even more impossible. Binding demons, forging dangerous artefacts, and to trump all, creating or using this cavernous space as a dump for the trash and sewage of an entire city.

Every second down here I had felt the chill, but now I was heating up with fury. Never was particularly a religious man: Astor the Prince of Stealthics showed me a way to find adventure and meaning in my life, and I tried to imitate him as best I could. But who among the heroes ever asked for such crushing expenditure, dared followers to vie in pride and vanity, encouraged this level of heedless disregard for the good, or even the lives of the Children of Hope? And secrecy too; no doubt it was only a chosen few, with the power and lore and strut-proud ambition, who kept their plans to themselves without thought for the future impact. Hardly anyone knew where their bodies were buried, to quote the Despairing adage. But I knew, and right now I wanted to dig each of those privileged bastards up and slap their rotted jaws off.

I tried to chuckle but it ended in a racking cough. I had to get out of here.

I half-rose and moved to one side, still on the edge of this basement level and hoping to find another exit, one more direct to the surface. The glowing mold was everywhere, my vision nearly as good down here as it would have been under the stars. From the edges of my sight came a constant sense of movement—I suddenly realized it was no mirage. The mold itself was in motion, not just lights pulsing in waves across separate plants but portions of the glowing lichen crawling very slowly over ceilings, along the walls and on the surface of this massive sewer-pit. Once I knew what to look for, I spotted dozens of flat patches, making no faster progress than a spill of ink in sand, but ceaseless and horribly alive.

Some of the moldy glowing patches rested on thicker shapes. Taller, limbed and trudging forms. Wading and slowly floundering through the waste of centuries, skeletal bodies carried glowing mold around the cesspool, sometimes disappearing into its depths and at others clawing out to one side and making headway toward a hole or cavern. I guessed with a tingle that the mold might have an animating power. Bodies of men buried, or murdered, or just abandoned somehow wound up down here and now walked again, fueling legends of the gaunts and other undead that we all told of Old Cryss.

I came across a room where half a stairway hung in space overhead, probably within reach. Would it hold? I had never seen architecture made so completely of stone, and my common sense told me the thick rock treads shouldn't have lasted a day up there. Yet there they were, one run-leap-reach away and promising a return to the air and stars above. I measured the distance and picked out a path between the rubble at my feet, but froze when I heard a very different sound from the sewer-cavern behind me.

Clicking.

Of course I turned to look.

Far down the cavern to the right of my position, a line of Bugs marched in from a side tunnel and up to the edge of the muck. Eight of them were six-limbed, weapon carrying mantis-types like the ones that had attacked me in the Demonbender temple. But a dozen more, wriggling between their guards, were softer, worm-like centipedal forms the size of mastiffs with darker bumps on their sides. As they sidled up to the sea of excrement, their guardians delved into the bumpy parts—pouches, I realized—and withdrew white ovals the size of… well, it didn't take much reflection to determine what they were.

The guard Bugs scattered the small eggs into the muck, where they sank. Rejects, I wondered? But then they moved on a few yards along the sewage-beach, and began to dig directly into the pile. I choked on gorge to see them spreading and separating, but I could not tear my eyes away. Up to their abdomens they waded in filth; then one pulled up something smooth, and dripping with nameless grime, but showing bright white by the pulsing light of nearby mold.

An oval shaped something. Grown to the size of my head.

My mind could not move a thought forward at the enormity of what it had learned. We, ourselves, in total ignorance were creating the menace we feared, putting weapons into the hands of men like Salivaar, and Mias and Teretheny. A race of giant insects, undead creatures, disease and who knew what other horrors, while on the other side of the Tepid River our houses were clean and we celebrated twice a week. Only a few went missing, hardly to be noticed. Like Keilee had gone, before Feldspar rescued her. Maybe the greater good and the good one could see were not so different after all.

Damn this cold! Another sneeze before I could think to stifle it, and every Bug eye swiveled to face my direction. They were out of range for now, but it was without question time to leave this place. I had a moment to feel amazed, almost happy, from the way my memory of being torn open and poisoned by these Insectirs at the temple was now lending an extra jolt of energy to my thighs and groin. When I had measured the leap I judged I would be able to grab the lowest tread, perhaps the second, and hang on before kipping up. As it happened I got both feet on the stone in a single bound: though it was covered in slime I did not slip an inch, as indeed I had not done at any moment down here. Time for that mystery later. I fled up the stairs, trailed a hand along the massive walls and jogged through darkness, ever seeking the way up and out.

For the first time since coming to Old Cryss, I left a building by the front door, closing the enormous portal behind me and stepping down into the empty street as if I were the owner just locking up for the night. The chill of the hour before midnight was fresh and warm compared to the caverns; the air merely dank and foul hit like perfume, and I breathed deep, coughed and spat as if to rid my lungs of all traces of where they had been.

The smell, unfortunately, was another matter. Like smoke it clung to my outfit, though I had touched nothing my nose reported I had rolled in sewage. I looked around, a street not far from the piazzo as it happened. Salivaar generally left the temple for his patron-visits at this time, just before midnight. It would only take moments to retrieve the Brow, and if I chose not to proceed I would have to wait two more days. Not someday, now. As I pattered silently toward the piazzo I comforted myself with the notion that the rat-king I set out to imitate tonight was a frequent denizen of these tunnels himself, and an unlikely bather. Perhaps this aroma would work in my own favor.

I slipped over the low retaining wall and across the open space between the temple, kemetaria and the raised statue-park. The only eyes watching me were made of stone, and I had to hurry. I reached the temple and listened near a window for sounds of the bandits within. It was quieter than usual, no shouts or laughter, bad songs or desultory scuffles. I knew from past reconnaissance, that meant Salivaar was still within. Someone was speaking to the rat-king, and I recognized the gruff curse-laden tones of Barkarr as they moved down the center aisle toward the front door. I slid along and waited around the corner in the shadow of a buttress.

Barkarr spoke a lot, Salivaar only a word at a time. The dialogue was inaudible, but I could tell it was the bandit urging some course of action, and the leader demurring. I gently touched the Throat and caught myself tapping a foot. Over at the statues, I could see the eyes of one staring unblinking at me and had to shake my head to keep focus. The Exemplars, I knew vaguely from the stories, were forgotten names from centuries ago, each a perfect follower of this or that hero, who had done enough in their lifetime to have their effigy raised in stone more than eight feet high, while they still lived. Too proud to record their deeds there, and now anonymous to me.

But I bet myself one was likely a follower of Astor, a Stealthic like me. Maybe the one looking my way now. Maybe a good sign.

The same two voices now came from the front more clearly than the window. Salivaar and Barkarr alright, still deep in conversation as the guards came to attention. I crouched at the last corner and watched their backs down the entrance path, catching the last fragments of their speech.

"I swear to you, boss, that urchin brat is the key! Whoever this intruder is, he came to get her back."

"You seem certain. What was her precinct?"

"The Boards, boss. And strange things there, too…"

Suddenly, my mission seemed a little less simple. Focused on my grand, easy scheme to recover an ancient artefact, I had been too happy to sit and observe, tinker in my new theater hideout and explore the antechamber of hell beneath the old city. Meanwhile Barkarr, cark him, was putting two and two together faster than I had. He didn't have to know who I was to see who was dear to me.

To Jonn Simith, Feldspar impatiently quipped; let's get on with the job.

To me! I shouted back so savagely I shrank back against the wall on instinct, as if I had made noise.

Then hurry, Feldspar rejoined. And there I had to admit, he had me.

I retreated, crossed the low border fence again, and crouched near the entry gate to the temple path that my mark had taken on his way out. Forcing myself to wait five minutes before "returning" as Salivaar, I realized I hadn't ever tried the transformation without checking for success in a mirror. None of those nearby, how inconvenient; another complication. When I thought enough time had passed for my intended excuse, I concentrated on the rat-king's lycanthropic shape. I felt the familiar cool tingling I had before, and a few moments later saw my tail flick into view. One deep breath, I stood up and sauntered back to the front temple door without a care in the world. I even slipped the noun-chakas around to one side, pleased to see a rusty longsword at my waist to fit the part.

As the door guards saw me I grinned and held my hands out in resignation. "Too easily distracted, I guess fellows. Left without the most important thing!"

They chuckled nervously, as folks who know a joke has been made and don't want to be left out. Just as I passed the threshold one said, "Where's Barkarr, then sir?"

"Ah, him." I scrambled to cover while Feldspar tsked me for the oversight. "Talking my ear off, that was the problem. I ah, sent him on ahead."

Then I was in the temple, and within ten steps every eye was on me.

I knew what to do with center stage. Walking with complete confidence (but careful not to hurry), I nodded left and right and kept my eye mostly ahead, to the altar area where Salivaar's bodyguards lounged. I had already put myself in his mind. I had walked this path a thousand times. Everything in here was mine to command; I felt it, I let it show in the tilt of my grin and the occasional lash of my tail. Astor's Pride, this artefact was perfection; I swore to myself I could almost feel its support. This thing wanted to be used.

Prayer benches on both sides of the central aisle were shifted, broken up or pushed over to create little camps of followers, various gangs among the bandit crew. Plenty of torchlight and a couple campfires reflected back from the two-storey windows, reaching almost to the soaring ceiling space overhead, where rents and broken panes let in the stars in places. But none of that merited more than a moment's glance, I was no tourist but master of the house. I ignored a hundred blades, wondering if this was how a man like Carnad Mias or Gaspar Heugen felt all the time.

To the right I saw again the cages, perhaps a dozen stacked two-high made of wooden struts and tied with rope. Keilee had been dragged from one of those, less than a fortnight ago, to be served up to the Insectirs for food of some kind. The torchlight was too dim over there to see how many were occupied. Someday, I said to myself. Nearer the altar the left-hand nave opened into the former pleasure-garden, now being used to hold female prisoners, chained near the benches for the fortunate few. I had to order my hand to unclench and keep on my path ahead. Another someday, Feldspar assured me—this mission had gotten leagues away from simple.

Now I was on the lowest altar-step, close enough to touch the spot where Farley burned to a cinder, with the altar before me and the swarthy, pocked shapes of my personal guard gathered nearby. They looked at me curiously as I approached the height of the gambit. So far, no one had raised a flicker of suspicion that their king had returned so soon after leaving. The trick was not to keep those misgivings at zero, because that was impossible. But do nothing to fan the flames, and let events take their course.

I nodded to the one who had carried it out before. "Bring me the crown, I'm taking it to the meeting."

His jaw went slack, as I expected: surely Salivaar had never done this before. I waited a beat, then tilted my head slightly to show my impatience and wriggled my nose at him for emphasis. Jaw clapped shut, he bowed and hustled back to the covered compartment while fumbling his key to hand.

My heart soared as he returned with a plate covered by a damask cloth and something destiny-shaped beneath it. I controlled my movements to snatch it off without trembling, holding it to my side while fingering the three woven metal bands, one sharp crown point in my palm and a gem the size of my largest knuckle set there. I started to turn away with a forgivable grin.

"You want us to come with you, boss?"

"No!" I shouted too quickly, and again Feldspar chided my lack of foresight. "I mean, I have this well in hand, you boys stay here and I'll be back—acheww!—within the hour."

Cark me with a rasp.

"Boss, are you alright?"

"I'm fine."

"But what about the black intruder? You said he could still be out there, half of us looking for him."

"And a fine job you've all done finding him!" I thundered my improvisation. "But that bouncing jackanapes is no threat to the lord of Old Cryss." I let the scolding sit in the air awhile as my disease-ridden bodyguard looked properly abashed. I realized, if I left my bodyguard dressed-down before the others, many would suspect something was off. I screamed inwardly against where the character pulled, but a role is a role.

I shrugged theatrically, saying "Nevertheless your loyalty is touching. Alright, you two with me now." And I snapped around at a quickened pace to cut off further protest. Now I had them behind me to deal with, and I wasn't sure what it would take to outpace or subdue them. I recalled a distant day when some idiot thought this would be an easy job.

But I didn't know the half of it, until I was almost to the front door and heard one of the sentries exclaim in surprise.

"Boss! Cark, how did you get back out here so fast?"

No time for indecision. I thrust one arm through the Brow until it rested over my shoulder, hoping the ancients who made it understood I wasn't trying to wear the thing. Dashing ahead through the door I saw two forms and immediately dove at the one shaped like a were-rat, tackling him to the ground and making sure to roll over at least twice with him in my grip.

Flat-footed surprised, Salivaar still snarled and tried to bite me on the neck. But his teeth hit the legs of my jeweled choker, and when we smashed into the pavement his breath left him and he went slack a moment. Rising up, I half-lifted and threw him another spin away from me in the temple shadows and clutched my side as if wounded.

"An imposter! Help, he's trying to kill me."

Barkarr, the bodyguards and the door wardens all looked back and forth as I took another few steps back and prepared to run. Almost as one their faces clouded over in doubt.

"Wounded? That doesn't—"

"Hey, he sneezed before!"

"Idiots," rasped Salivaar catching his breath. "He's stealing the Brow, get him!"

Before the end of "Idiots" I had turned and fled, vaulting the retaining wall and out of the piazzo. Behind me the tumult grew and over everything I heard a gravel-voice cursing that turned my heart to stone inside me.

"Carking black-man! I know where to look for you! And we'll start with that tasty morsel you took last time!"

"Take your men," Salivaar cried, "burn it down but find him!"

Complicated had become a weak word to describe the mission now. Feldspar snorted that I was getting mixed up again, and I told him to shut the cark up in terms so clear I almost heard his jaw snap shut inside my mind. But he was right about one thing; the immediate issue was escape.

I am fairly fleet of foot and keep myself in top condition. I took four random turns, including one that moved back toward the temple, and then again onto Scapegrace Street, running diagonally along part of the piazzo and straight off into the northwestern quadrant of Old Cryss, closer to the Tepid where it empties into the sea. After another four or five furlongs, I slowed and started to keep a weather-eye out for patrols, since Salivaar had so thoughtfully put them to looking for me after my first visit. I kept walking, but aside from one group spotted two blocks away and easily avoided, I had no trouble and the pursuit was nowhere in sound. Not even a carking sneeze could get me in trouble now.

I took the Brow off my arm and placed it atop the damask cloth. Even by Aral's light the gems sparkled as large as eyes, and the workmanship of the gold, silver and orichalc bands was magnificent. I thought about what would most likely happen if I transferred it just a few inches further and placed it on my head; I nearly wet my breeks.

I had to get this to W'starrah Altieri at once. Slipping it into my backpack, I turned directly toward the waterfront and began to assess the best way across.

I was too far west now, closer to the sea than either the tunnel I had used or the crossing I set up for myself. I tried thinking about the routes I could take, but kept losing my mental way within seconds. I could pick a course across—the crank-raft, or the dock pilings—but when my mind reached the shore and tried to make center-city or the Stargazer compound it stalled. Was I weak from exertion? No, I realized with growing anger at Feldspar who had been smoothly guiding the thoughts. I was heading the wrong way.

We are not going to The Boards, he hissed, once exposed in my mind.

Yes. Oh yes, we very much are. I ran straight to the water now and while my argument raged I laughed.

Coward! Feldspar spat. Getting across the city undetected will be dangerous risky work. Our kind of work. For all you know the fighting could have started already. Your patron may be in trouble, in desperate need of the Brow. And you will instead run to save a child, one life when the city—

I, you say I am the one afraid? Listen to you, Feldspar. A half-hour's delay, to perhaps save a girl and a neighborhood, and practically no hope of keeping Jonn Simith alive whatever happens. If we go your way, the girl dies and my secret stays safe.

I let it sink in while I rounded the final corner near the riverside, still too far west to see The Boards. Then I hit him with everything I had.

You craven bouncing ape. You fear losing Simith, because then you'd have no company. No one you could blame when Astor forbid, I try to do a decent thing.

But don't you worry Feldspar. If you stop whining and move your clumsy feet with speed for once, we can still save everyone.

Spurred by the insult to myself, I sped down a stone pier and leaped again, arrow-arms ahead into the chilly Tepid. All that work to keep dry. Kicking faster than a gull's wings I knifed the water and headed toward the lower boardwalk, the path that led to the gaol.

I couldn't give myself more than a few moments to summon character, and was still quite soggy when I rapped on the door. Beryl could not have been more astonished to see me, and the feeling was nearly mutual.

"Milord Fire Grip!"

"Dekentar, summon two squads and proceed to The Boards district immediately." I could not get used to the sound of my own voice under the glamor of The Throat of the Spider. I hung back from the doorway to avoid the light, because I did not care to explain how this gorgeous blue tunic and sash got so wet. "My agents inform me the ruffians who have been kidnapping citizens will strike there tonight. Hurry, this could be a marvelous opportunity for advancement."

"At once Milord Heugen." I turned away and ran as soon as I heard the alarm bell ringing. Saving The Boards was not enough, I had to find Keilee. And for that I needed to be Jonn Simith. I ran at top speed near center-city, heedless who might question the Fire Grip's haste. Crowds were everywhere tonight, and I could feel the agitation even as I turned down the less-used alleys. I slipped into
166

my changing-shed, dropped the spell, and got into my plain clothes. It never occurred to me to use the Throat. Too many risks.

As Feldspar stewed with the delay, I donned a side pouch to hold the Brow and ran back to The Boards. Still a bit before midnight, but far too long since Barkarr uttered his vile threat. The streetlamps were off, and the lower moon should not have provided so much light in a working-class neighborhood. Heat too. From blocks away I could make out the pulsing radiance of the flames.

People ran in every direction, several houses facing the river were on fire. I saw guards ahead, some giving battle and others giving chase, as darker forms scattered with shouts and cries of pain. Barkarr's men had come here indeed, and met with an unexpected response from the city guard. Beryl might make Captain if he could keep his mouth shut when Heugen denied visiting him. And of course, Feldspar sighed, then he'll have more resources to pursue us. Never mind that now: I slipped back several blocks from the riverside fires that drew everyone's attention, and cut across to my street.

Before I made the corner, right where I had been mugged on my first night here, I heard a child's scream. I couldn't feel the stones beneath my sandals as I flew into view. Keilee ran down the street, behind her a hulking sword-armed figure backlit by the flames roared and staggered, slightly wounded, after her. With no alternatives to her mind, Keilee ran up my stoop, pulled out the key I had given her and threw herself inside. So, I thought, things could hardly be worse.

Barkarr hurled his body against the jamb and I heard a loud crack. She had locked it but doors in this city were not built to withstand fighting men with murder in their souls.

"I'll roust you out, little morsel!" he bellowed, "and after you've told me where he is, we'll have a celebration." Again against the door, as I flinched out of my stupor and ran toward him. "Then it's the Bugs for you, but you don't have to be alive when it happens." Another shoulder-thrust and he was through.

That tore it. I already had no objection to Barkarr's death, but I was the only person with the right to destroy things in my house. It was time for another masterful performance.

Keilee had tried to bar the door with her body, which meant no chance to hide. Barkarr had her by the hair struggling there in the

167

antechamber. I slowed my last three steps and walked in, the innocent home-owner with my jaw open at this act of vandalism.

"What, er that is, what in all the Lands?"

"Stay out of this, carker!" Barkarr turned in my direction for a moment, stopped and narrowed his eyes. "You!" he rasped, "I should have—aaagh!"

His inattention had given Keilee the chance she was seeking. Gripping his forearm she raised herself off the ground and sank her teeth into his wrist.

"Bitch!" He flung her off like a raindrop, two feet into the wall; Keilee cried out and slumped to the floor, breathing but stunned or even unconscious.

"Help! Guards!" I squeaked, dodging a backhand and swiveling past his barrel-frame to run upstairs, away from the girl. Barkarr would not want to leave any witnesses. Sure enough, he followed me up. Out of sight I would have no hesitation killing this animal.

At the top of the stairs the first sight of Barkarr's ugly mug received the hard-swung end of a chair broken over his head. Served them both right: any chair set in an upstairs hallway was asking for trouble. He staggered back, spit out a tooth, and roared in with his sword thrusting. I planned to evade him, break the wrist and then end him any one of several painful ways right there on the landing.

But cark me, Keilee staggered into view on the bottom step, holding her head and crying "Mr. Simith, look out!" Just one more complication.

I swerved past the blade and grabbed his wrist, thinking then that I had likely never felt so alive in all my years. Irrelevantly I heard the first bell of the hour and all my senses came awake at once.

Midnight. Full lower moon. The marvelous sanitation system and where things led from there.

Shrieking and falling backward, I rolled with both feet tucked in tight and pulled Barkarr down on top of me. As our heads hit I kipped up and pushed off with both legs as hard as I could. Ignorant of my design and probably still dazed by the chair, he brought all his bulk forward without resistance. Heavy as he was, I flipped him like a playing card, straight over my head and behind me.

Hard into the bathroom door, knocking it open and then banging closed behind him.

The scream I heard then was beyond description, my sweat chilled to ice all over and I listened to him fading, falling, fading. Barkarr was where he belonged.

I sat up hugging myself, and there was Keilee looking around with eyes the size of palms.

"What happened? Where is he?"

"I, that is, I cannot actually say. I heard guard whistles and some shouting, but... say, are you alright little one?"

"I'm fine, but the big man he was up here!" Keilee shook her head hard to clear it, and I smiled with a helpless shrug. Against all odds, Jonn Simith might survive the night.

"I must say, I was knocked over a little winded, er, or stunned, and then I don't know exactly what happened. Perhaps he decided to run off, lucky for us." I smiled as I sat on the top step and patted her shoulder; when Keilee threw herself into my arms it took me completely by surprise. She clung like a barnacle and I was sure she was sobbing. Feldspar, of course, absented himself immediately, and I was left alone to deal with the moment.

"There now, you've had a close call little one. But your parents, where are they? And is your house alright?"

"My house!" She jumped back with a face of alarm and took the stairs three at a time back down. "Good night Mister Simith, I'm sorry about your door." Gone in a wink. I had no earthly idea how I felt, but the tracks on my cheeks gave a clue.

So much left to do, yet I just sat there on my top step with the fragments of another broken chair all around me. Have to get my door fixed, no question. It would arouse suspicion even if someone didn't wander in and find my secret panels. Yes, I agreed with a yawn, fix the front door. Someday. I leaned back and rested my head just for a moment, felt the waves of expended energy echoing over me. In my pouch the hard shape of the ancient artefact was still safe. First, I had the city to save, my commission to fulfill and a fortune to earn. I patted the crown and continued lying there, just another moment. With twenty thousand silver pieces I could fix my door in metal, and buy half the other houses on my block. But surely the first thing was getting up and delivering the Brow, not resting. I could sleep someday soon, for hours on end if I wanted. I lay there and thought about what had to happen first, and before I knew it someday became now.

⊕ ⊕ ⊕

ou return from Now to the Next, closer to the world and all its people, desperate to help though unable to imagine how.

Your first thought is of the Captain, where he might be and how to aid him. But you flow instead to the temple; of course, even as a spirit your habits are strong. There at the foot of my statue is Tanar'h, kneeling and shaking as he fears the worst for you and the city. How long have you been missing? You shed tears for him as you never did in life, to see your rival this way. His devotion to me, and love for you loom rather larger, his pride and intemperance shrink from across the divide of death. Or has he changed somehow in a scatter of hours since he saw you last? You slapped him, just over there at the steps, and parted angry; yet here he kneels and prays for your welfare first, the city's second, and his own not at all.

You reach to touch his shoulder as if you still had a hand. "Oh dear Tanar'h," you whisper, "how ill I used you, forgive me. I have always loved you as a brother, I see that now. Too jealous, not sincere enough. I crave your pardon."

He does not reply, though his shaking subsides into long sighs. Back in the pews you see his wives, sitting together and holding hands as they stare at their husband. They whisper how changed, how dramatically affected he has become at your estrangement and the pang runs through you to realize, they do not know your fate.

To the other side there is Kat, quietly walking up to him at the statue, and again you forget what you are.

"Kat! Dear Kat!" you cry out and rush to her, then stop with a sob as the tiny woman walks straight through the spot you occupy. Denied the hug you knew for years brings a fresh grief. You turn to see her lay a hand, a real hand on Tanar'h's head. He looks up to her from his knees and reverently kisses it.

"Teacher," he says in unaccustomed gentleness. "Teach me again. Who is my brother? To whom do I owe forgiveness, and of whom should I beg it?"

How strange! That his thoughts should march so closely with what you tried to say.

Kat smiles at her former student, his head barely lower than hers though he kneels. "You worry for W'starrah, as I do. She has been gone far too long, and Chaktha too though he was sent away before."

"We parted in anger, and I lectured her again. I bitterly regret my haste and pride."

Kat beams at him now, as if at a perfect answer, and cups his face in her hand without bending down.

"Do you remember a day when I read the tale of the Hawk and the Serpent? And I could not give the moral because one of my students complained, louder than all objections, that I had not told it correctly!"

You have never heard this tale before, and it cheers you amid all this grief to see the High Heart blush.

"I remember, teacher. I insisted—I was cross, and young." He smiles at last, briefly, and Kat giggles in good fun. "But I thought it a disgrace that the mighty Hawk should find himself bested by such a foul creature."

"Like the Hawk, Tanar'h, you have always been proud and brave, rather than patient. And this is how the church needs you."

"But I have allowed a serpent, indeed, into this church. A man who is my—who had a claim on me, and I hesitated until perhaps too late."

Kat frowns a bit. "Do you mean, the holy man from Sinter, Teretheny?"

Without words, Tanar'h returns a gaze filled with pain as the tears stream down. Unbidden, his wives leap up and rush to embrace him, all three seemingly needed to keep him from throwing his body prostrate on the marble steps.

"I became entangled… in the branches, I could not fight him."

"There, now," Kat says encouragingly. "You must not let your mind walk such dark paths."

"But he is out in the city!" Tanar'h cries, and you feel the sting of fear along with him. "His strength renewed, plans laid, among the doves he will wreak his havoc unchecked."

No one knows what the High Heart can mean by this; Kat kneels into the circle of arms around him and considers before speaking.

"You asked me about family, and forgiveness Tanar'h. Would you hear my answer now?"

He nods.

"You spend much time and energy showing how you care for those around you. Your wives, teachers, the Stargazer and your fellow preachers like W'starrah. You love us with passion, a shouted love that does not much bend nor await an answer. I do not say this to shame you, Tanar'h, it is what makes you precious to us. Now, this monk I do not know. But if you would determine where your obligations lie, consider this. Who are they who care for you, regardless of your notice?"

Tanar'h slowly nods and thinks.

"Truly, I thought only how to express my love, and not enough how to let others—teacher, I thank you."

He rises now and moves toward the front exit with purpose.

"Where are you going?" Kat calls after him.

"In search of the Serpent. It is not too late, perhaps, for this Hawk to give combat."

At this, his wives cry out in dismay, but Tanar'h, turning back at the door, firmly gestures them to remain.

"Tanar'h," Kat warns, "the Hawk lost his life in that fight."

"Aye," Tanar'h returns levelly, "but his mate lived on."

As the women all moan in anguish, he is gone. You think of Devout Teretheny, with his strange elixir and foreign bodyguards, and how he raised that fatal storm of death and maiming at the Glass Parade. Tanar'h against such force would be a straw in the wind. Though you have no idea how to reach him, you follow resolved to try.

But the eddies of Next push your spirit as the wind moves smoke, and carry you across the city in a direction contrary to your wish.

Where is the Captain? What will become of Tanar'h? Not for the first time, you struggle against the odds, to stay near the lights of center city where some menacing evil gathers. It is like a dark fire, or a hot wind of the ethereal world, and you do not doubt who stands at its center. But still new to this spiritual existence, the Next draws you by means of strings you cannot yet sense. West, into a darkened precinct with looming empty buildings in the shadow of the Crystal Palace, with a small foundation hole and a tiny shed. The Turtle sits next to his cot where lies another guest, the Man in Grey who saved you beneath the Boards just two nights ago.

He lies still and hardly breathes as the little man ministers to his flesh, murmuring phrases in the Ancient tongue as the small gem on his necklace flickers. Wounds across the warrior's body close into tight scars, though the awful tinge beneath the flesh remains. The youth's breathing deepens but is still ragged; understanding nothing of this art, you watch in horror as the healer puts both hands on the victim's body and gasps with exertion to speak again.

You reach out with your hands and hope to the healer, helpless yet driven to act. "Let this miracle-worker know your comfort, great Argens. He is not of your faith, but most worthy. Help him, that he may help others."

Your effort is without immediate effect, and the healer sags against the prone warrior's body, whispering as if dying of thirst and barely able to keep his eyes open. He does not notice that a soft steady glow has returned to the gem about his neck.

Without preamble, the grey youth's eyes snap open, and he half-rises, gritting his teeth against the weakness still coursing through him, to take the healer by the shoulders and hold him up.

"Be at peace, holy sir; I am much restored by your arts and would incur no further... no further debt to you." The two men lean heavily on each other a moment.

"But the poison," Kama gasps, "it must be drawn from you, and soon. Your friend, the Nubian, his wounds were severe... I am too weak, it seems, to..."

"Is it healing?" the youth asks, "I have some small ability—"

The healer shakes his head. "You must, must draw the poison. But the Ancient tongue—"

The youth nods once, asking "Thusly?" he places a hand on his own chest and says "Trahari vituprandor".

You can feel the surge of power even from the spirit plane, as a cloud of something dark, deadly and no longer material moves out of the Man in Grey's body, dissolving on contact with the air while the glow of his hand slowly fades. The healer looks on in astonishment beyond his exhaustion, then smiles and puts a friendly hand on the Man in Grey's shoulder. The latter shakes his head once and chuffs out a hard breath as if to clear the last droplets of venom from his system. Then he stands and turns to place the healer on the cot in his place.

"How did you learn this ability, young man?"

"From you, holy sir."

"What, this instant! Do you mean no one ever taught you lore?"

The Man in Grey shrugs as he brings a bowl of broth to the new patient.

"My teacher, long ago, gave me what was needful then."

"The words, perhaps," Kama replies, too fascinated to eat. "But where did you acquire the faith, lad? And how can you, that is, pardon me but you are a man of war if ever I saw one. How also a healer?"

The grey youth does not answer, merely assembling his staff and hat, shrugging shoulders as if trying to feel the absent cape about him.

"Sooth, I have endeavored to learn what I could."

Kama chuckles at this modest evasion. "I must say, a quick study, young man. Let me put it another way, if you don't mind my prying. Upon whom do you call? Which of the heroes do you follow?"

The Man in Grey looks down upon the little man in the cot for several long moments before answering. "Which of them is needful?"

"What!"

"For healing, certes I think on Telhol and his great courage. To destroy revenants or divers spawn of undeath, Areghel seemeth most meet."

"But you could hardly imagine two of our ancestors less in agreement!"

The Man in Grey answers only with a shrug. "Each had his gifts, a part of the whole I would say, though mine scholarship be sadly lacking in so many respects." He stands awhile looking down and then more quietly adds, "Sooth, and most often I think upon mine own father when I attempt such lore."

"Your father?"

"The man who bore me hence, aye, these seven years gone. I remember his face."

"You think of a man. A mortal." Kama speaks in wonder.

"As do you, holy sir. Telhol was first born of all the heroes in this country."

"Assuredly, it's just… well, we each have come to think of our heroes as something more, if you take my meaning. I have, and all my former companions did in their separate measure, to Araluntir, and Ma-Eldar, Areghel. As did Astor hold reverence from the Stealthic Feldspar, who lay on my cot here just a few nights past."

You feel a flush of shame and hilarity then; the Ferret was wounded in your service and when you visited the Turtle you thought him entertaining a lover!

The Man in Grey nods, his lips a straight line. "As do I for my sire." He turns to leave, but stops, and faces the healer again reluctantly. "A'times, mine deepest thought bears me to consider, in sooth, that the race of the Heroes, too, must have had a father of sorts."

"How do you mean?"

"Not simply a sire for so many races, but a kind of same One, certes, a hero unto these Heroes. Else to whom did they pray, when they taught their descendants to do the same?"

Kama leans back now with an open jaw. "You take our religion into a place I had never considered young man." He sits up, as if the talk itself restored a part of his strength. "I have heard tell of a preacher here now, one Devout Teretheny, who speaks in this vein."

"No!" you shout in anger and terror, still heedless than you cannot be heard by the living. "Do not hear that Serpent's words, don't be taken in!"

The Man in Grey looks to Kama with interest now. "Sooth, he preaches of a source to all faith?"

"So I have heard, though I paid it little heed. I note the glow of center-city herein, some large gathering though it seemed to me a kind of menacing light. Will you hear him?"

The grey-haired youth shrugs. "Twas that way mine companion the bodyguard went, with the body of the priestess. I would see to his welfare now as we were companions in peril together. If this preacher be there, mayhap I will hear him."

"And if there is more danger, further violence?"

The grey youth holds a hand out to one side. "I would retrieve my cloak."

With a laugh, Kama levers himself up from his cot then, and the Man in Grey tarries to lend him an arm as they make their way out of the shed and toward the central plaza.

You must follow them, find a way to reach their minds and warn them of the danger. But Next is merciless and instead you skirt again the orange glow from center-city, slewing around to darkened ways between the palace and river, where a squadron of red-liveried guards listens to their leader, Carnad Mias give instructions for revolution.

"Muster at your ordained positions and follow my orders to attack as soon as any kind of storm hits. That lunatic Devout wants to move early, he will find me ready to counter him."

"Targets, great Cup?"

"Seize the Stargazer Temple, the Mason's Guild, South Gate and docks. Let Teretheny's fanatics have the center city and the residential precincts until you see the second sign."

"You mean, the Shard Demon?"

"Aye, I cannot say where I will send him first, nor how long it will take to break his bonds." Mias licks his lips with the effort to seem confident. "Hours, certainly, perhaps by morning. But I will try the Crystal Palace. Once he's loose, you can turn on the desert dwellers with no fear. Step off now, I'm for the monster's chamber."

With that, Mias sets out alone for the under-boards, while his men watch him go, exchange glances and then trot off opposite. You must stop him, warn Gaspar Heugen; yet once again your efforts to follow are whelmed in a kind of spirit-tide; flailing and screaming at your failure, you find yourself wafting high above the center-city.

Among the many bright lights of lamppost, mansion and carriage there lies a kind of radiant blackness, to one side of the open plaza where thousands mill. Others, you sense, see nothing of this, only the robed man at its center who stands between his guards and harangues them with words of promised unity and destruction. Another way from the temple comes Tanar'h also with his guards, his face set in a mask of pain and fists clenched. From a third direction you make out a black-robed shadow, your Ferret with something bright and perilous shedding gleams within his pack. Down another street comes Chaktha, holding your body under a cloak of grey. Before you can

176

wonder, you are distracted by the Gryphon's cry and the rush of approaching wings.

It is your Captain, flying on a level with your spirit-form and noticing as you had the tumultuous crowd below. For another instant you are heedless of this new state of being, and throw your arms wide only to feel the same crushing sense of loss as he flies straight through you. Shouting with madness, you keep up with him now as he circles above: some in the crowd have noticed the monster and are pointing, or turning to flee.

Can you communicate with him by any means? The pain of separation keenly slices your middle like a dagger drenched in acid.

"My Captain! Return to your men, and go back home again. My city's fate is sealed and I can hold you no longer."

He is clearly exhausted, his mount also, and shakes his head to clear vision while looking down on the square. Something has arisen there, a maelstrom of evil glints circling in the opposite direction. Fire and smoke are in it. Wagons tightly covered break open and add their lethal fuel to the whirling wrack. Teretheny was standing beneath its eye when last you marked him.

The storm of spiders has begun.

Coming as close to his ear as you can imagine, you shout "Home! My Captain, go home, save yourself!"

He slumps forward, as if losing consciousness, but only to grasp the neck feathers of the Gryphon and murmur against the rising cyclone just beneath you.

"Come, fellow," he urges, "home now. A promise is a promise."

Relief cleanses you, though it shears your heart to think you will never see him again. The Captain will be safe, at least, his honor and upright nature preserved for some future day. An expert tug on the reins and a little kick takes man and monster away from you, and now the destruction below draws all your attention. Screaming, wind, the sound of fighting, sharp points of light lancing from glassy bits in the air. What can you do, why did you ever leave the comfort of the Now to suffer as the living can without sharing that life?

The Next is drawing you down, through the funnel of the sandstorm to the plaza where your family is bleeding. You are content.

Mayhap you can direct the brunt of the Arbalest's bolt on yourself, or guide a loved one to safety.

Then you realize, the Captain's course was west.

North and east, to his men. South back to Argens. But he said "home", before flying west. To the temple.

That is the moment, cherished one, when you surprise even me.

You ponder the meaning of his sacrifice, look to the plaza below, the manful struggle already taking place, and think of he who threatens your family unopposed. You set your entire mind and spirit to the task, and with clenched fist and inaudible scream you will yourself away.

The Next yields, though you gasp with the effort to move even a body-length. You head toward the sea, the darkness, the lair of the Shard Demon.

Justin saw the wrack below him and knew the conspiracy had launched. Carnad Mias, probably, with whatever allies he had assembled evidently including those with sorcerous power. People might be dying in the center-city now but he hewed the reins over and headed straight for the Temple of the Stargazers. So close now, he felt his strength ebbing after fourteen straight hours in the air. He had to reach his home. The grounds swept beneath him, preachers and guards pointing up at the ominous sign in the sky. Only the gryphon's scream kept him conscious as he angled for the tower on the right-hand side.

The landing was not up to form. Justin fought off a wave of exhaustion and nearly missed the final stall, then heaved the bridle too hard and almost came up short of the battlements. The creature's foreleg nicked a crenelment on the near side, and lurched onto the roof at a stumbling angle.

Justin's body spat from the saddle and skidded helmet-first into the retaining wall; his last view of the Arbalest and Dragon overhead blurred to meaningless sparks and went black.

I came back from that black someday, and sat up with a cry, as it suddenly became now again. One leg was draped over the top of the stair, my spine hurt from sprawling across the broken remains of a chair that had clearly wandered into a bad neighborhood; suddenly the memory came back to me.

Home. Barkarr. Keilee. The Brow.

I ran outside—still dark, but it must have been a full day—and saw the fires of the neighborhood were well under control, though the damage was bad and some would be homeless. That put a sour taste in my gut; my simple plan had caused this. Some, maybe, Feldspar insisted but I was in no mood to slice it. Finish the mission. I slipped back through my ruined door and got into working clothes before heading back toward the temple.

There were enough steps along the way for me to wonder briefly, if I did the right thing by taking this lethal artefact to W'starrah Altieri. The largest commission I had ever been offered never crossed my mind, but I decided whatever reservations a fellow like Kama had placed in my head, it was my job to complete the task. I had a reputation to keep up, which immediately struck me as the weakest witticism I'd ever told myself.

Then I heard the clamor near the central plaza and all my other thoughts drained away.

Still blocks away I could hear the deep drone of thousands chanting, punctuated by a single voice that carried to me clearly.

"The One Wind comes, my children!"

"Let the Wind come, may it pass by me and cleanse."

It only seemed like the entire city was there. But crowded was a mild word to describe the serried rows of packed flesh that crammed the enormous central space. I perched on a low roof at one edge and scanned near the opposite side for what was drawing the attention of a score-thousand people so late at night.

I heard the hard, uncaring voice before I pinpointed the angular form between his two guards, standing on a speaking platform north of the fountain. Teretheny, of course. I felt the cold tingle at my neck and grinned to think him stripped of that power at least. Everyone would know him now.

But as I heard him speak, I realized the brown-robed fanatic had no fear of being seen. This mob was already in his hand by some arcane means.

"The storm will erase all division!"

"For who can stand against the One Wind?"

He called them all to unity, a single purpose that enjoyed freedom from choice and the satisfaction of obedience to fate itself. He warned of a powerful wind, driving fire that would cleanse men to their souls and sweep away the chaff of any who did not see the truth.

"Come, children, away from the confusion and division of your separate, blind faiths and churches."

"We take refuge from the One Wind"

"Set it at your back and thrive!"

"While unbelievers are swept from view."

I caught myself chanting along and felt my middle go cold. He was making a kind of sense, I reflected crouching on my shadowed rooftop overlooking the bright-lit plaza. I looked among the smiling eager faces, Colors and guilds and rival religions rubbing elbows without rancor. How many feuds had their source in squabbles for status among the various sects? And wasn't all Hope really the same thing? What made the difference between Argens and Conar, or Helmon worth dying for? How did Astor—

Then it hit me so hard I nearly fell from the roof in shock. Teretheny was getting into my brain, speaking to me. I looked again across the square and saw those thousands of people, all heights and ranks and shades, nodding inanely to each other as he railed on about how equally unimportant they all were. There was comfort there, a freedom from the need to be someone. His words, just a layer of smoke before the eyes to cover the thrust he made, the real magic, as he put his sorcerous voice inside their heads.

And that, praise Astor, is where he lost me. I know about voices in my head: Feldspar, Simith, Chay, the beggar, I even had an artefact inviting me to change my outward shape, and hinting I could walk down this wall using only my bare feet. There was no confusion Devout Teretheny could add to the joyous fractious hubbub I embraced every day. I leaped down into an alley and watched a merchant who was moving clockwise across the plaza, trying for a better view. I quickly focused on the details of his appearance, and felt the cool tingle of the Throat's glamor copying it. Then I moved counter-clockwise through the crowd, looking to get behind the fanatic and do something perilous.

I shouldered my way between throngs of people, all shuffling slowly closer to hear the orator as I circled toward his side of the enormous central fountain. There were more than a dozen tightly-covered wagons taking up space on the flagstones, channeling people around them and their turbaned guardians. This late the pumps were off and the reflections of a thousand lights mirrored from the surface of the pool, helping make it almost as bright as morning across the plaza. Teretheny spoke on, and I had to admit his voice was marvelous, echoing off the buildings in every direction and reaching all the people at once. He raised his fist in emphasis, and they nodded and cheered; no word to their fellows to seek agreement or make a joke. I was perhaps thirty feet from him now on his side of the fountain, but there were four hundred bodies between us and Teretheny was facing out toward them. To sneak up I would need to be in the water at his back, too far below for the deed I contemplated.

"Only this way, on this path alone, may you survive the wrack which awaits you, which has already beset you, and—"

"Traitor!" the shout was strong yet ragged, from across the swell of flesh on the opposite side of the plaza. I scampered to the fountain's edge and hopped up, as the parting crowds revealed the Stargazer preacher, Tanar'h, his face twisted in fury and trailing two guards of his own. When I'd seen him before I thought this preacher a poser, plenty of oil and muscles and hot air; dressed as the fencing bravo I had felt no concern that he could have harmed me. Now I noted his eyes, flaming with rage and pain, and thought it was just as well to have the fountain pool between us.

"Hail, brother," Teretheny called out in an arrogant humor. "Come to join me at last?"

The gathered crowd kept their eyes on the monk as he disputed with Tanar'h: only the wagon guards turned to look angrily on the newcomer. I noted they all bore crossed scimitars on their backs. Men of no Color, not the city guard, more than a score of them here in center city.

"A brother!" Tanar'h cried, fists clenching, "very well Teretheny, I shall give you my confession. Let everyone hear it." He pitched his voice to carry and turned to all sides with the ease of a practiced speaker. "This man and I share a father's seed. It is my greatest shame, and he is no family to me, I swear before the Stargazer."

"Family has nothing to do with blood, except when spilled for another," Teretheny spat, his face finally showing some anger and throwing out one hand to forestall the turbaned guards lunging for Tanar'h. "You sheltered with these pampered roof-dwellers and their false hero so long, you've forgotten the need to risk, to struggle for the greater cause. Temples and jewelry, thousands to elevate your spirit and tell you how marvelous you are. All an illusion, you fool! The One Wind brings the true reality. You will join with it, become a part of its force, or fate will scour your flesh to the bone."

"You think I care to live?" Tanar'h shrieked. "What has happened to W'starrah Altieri, Teretheny, what have you and your foul allies done with her?"

My knees almost failed, when I heard my patron was missing. It was all I could manage, not to fall into the pool. Most of me had no idea what to do, or where to go now. All my efforts, to retrieve this artefact from the clutch of villains, and for what? Simith was completely lost; wallowing in dismay and confusion, he would have given up.

But the part of me that worked in black knew this was my time. Slipping down from the fountain edge, I wriggled through the staring, sighing masses to get closer to Teretheny and behind him as he shouted at Tanar'h. The Brow in my pack banged gently against the spine: let us just see, I thought, if he is worthy.

Some few in the crowd were looking to Tanar'h now, as if sleepy and not sure what they heard.

"She is missing!" Tanar'h shouted pointing at Teretheny. "She preached of love and family, of facing trouble together. I of all people should have listened to her. Not this merciless, grinding wheel of fate you rant about. W'starrah Altieri stood in your way and now she's gone. What have you done to her?"

"I? Tis the One Wind, brother, that acts here. Do not seek to blame me when your mistress whirls off to practice her licentious devilry on another lover."

Tanar'h was choking on his words and ready to throw himself across the space at the fanatic. I could see the guards waiting for orders, knew he had no chance to reach Teretheny; whatever miraculous lore he held, even if he thought to use it, would not suffice. I was gauging the distance to the Devout's back, perhaps four more steps and his guards too distracted to be a factor. But over his shoulder up in the sky, I saw the Gryphon and cried out in alarm despite myself.

"Look! Up there!"

The crowd followed my arm. Screams and panic broke out across the plaza at the sight of the circling winged monster. I couldn't hold my place against the tide of bodies as people fell back from the center, and some at the edges turned to flee. If only I could have kept my mouth shut another few seconds.

"See!" cried Tanar'h, "the emblem of senseless destruction, an omen of the future you bring, Teretheny."

I could see the monk turn to the taller guard and snap an order. The Bedou-uu pleaded as before, and Teretheny slapped him hard, drawing a dagger to place against the chest of the other. The smaller man, barely standing on his own, seemed insensible to the threat, but his partner raised hands in surrender, and seemed to repeat after his master a short phrase into the little man's ear. Teretheny meanwhile drew up his canteen—the one I had left him with in the Old City— and drank deeply, quickly, dribs of white fluid and a few chunks of something spilling down his face in his greedy haste to consume.

The little man spoke, as the ancient torc on his arm glowed and seemed to tighten even further. Teretheny raised both arms overhead and a cyclone appeared a bowshot above the plaza, gaining speed and thickness each second. Some evil sorcery was Teretheny's to command, and his hypnotic charisma allowed him to draw it from the artefact using the Bedou-uu as his dupes, to avoid the penalty.

And I had left them there, in the alley when I had all three at my mercy. Everything that happened now lay on me.

The Gryphon overhead shot away to the west, and Teretheny cried out to the crowd with a voice that carried even above the rising wind.

"See indeed! The Gryphon flies to your temple, brother, toward your lover and to the destruction of her immoral, ignorant vision. Now comes the One Wind! Obey or be destroyed!"

Thousands still huddled in the plaza, and almost all of them cried out to Teretheny, declaring their loyalty, falling to their knees huddling a few inches further from the descending cone of the storm, which grew only stronger as it fed on their cries. Tanar'h stood bathed in tears, tendons standing out across his body with the strain of his helplessness.

Through it all, I could still see the Nubian when he entered the square. Gradually everyone else saw him too.

He stood in the torchlight imposing and massive, carrying something under a cloak whose shape turned my heart to ash inside me. The furious dignity etched on his face left no doubt, and despite their fear at the storm overhead the people pulled back to give him a clear path. Chaktha walked a few steps at a time, stopping between to gather strength, and the crowds closed in behind him. Teretheny kept talking, but no one was listening any more, his spell of words completely broken and all else forgotten. The storm seemed to quiet a little.

Ten steps at a time Chaktha carried his burden across the plaza, to the foot of the speaking platform where Tanar'h stood. The preacher, his face filled with horror, gave way and Chaktha climbed into his spot before laying down his load with gentle care, as if not to awaken her. Then he limbered his shield and spear standing to attention, at guard behind her form.

Tanar'h knelt by the platform and reached out with a shaking hand to lift one edge of the cloak. I saw his face writhe with disgust and lapse into sorrow. When he stood and turned to face the crowd, thousands cried out just from what they witnessed there.

"Now we see the proof!" Teretheny cried, his voice cracking in mad triumph. "Lust and pride struck down, your final warning before the advent of the unifying wind that will scour this city. Choose obedience or to share her fate."

Many looked to Teretheny on this, with faces of pain and fear, and a few glanced up at the circling storm above them. But when Tanar'h spoke he had everyone's attention united, focused on the grief as well as the truth in his speech.

"Proof indeed," he shouted above the wind, "here lies the best evidence of the love W'starrah Altieri bore for her city. A love to which I once aspired, in my blindness and need. But she showed me, showed all of us, what it should mean to be a family. She preached it, as many of you here heard that day, and while we all thought her vain, or silly, she went forth to defend us. An orphan as a child, she took each of us as her family, and sacrificed her reputation, to scout out our enemies as we slept. Walking arm in arm with conspirators, she sought only to defy any power that threatened us, to provide comfort and shelter that others here despise."

"Striving against monstrous evil," he turned to face Teretheny now as his voice rose higher, "against sorcerous threats to all we held dear. And the Heaven's Eye has given us her proofs, in the end, paying with her life. The Bolt of the Arbalest flew straight into the heart of this city, and taken her from us." Tanarh's' glare left no doubt as to which man he held responsible. The crowd was his, won back to Hope by his eulogy; the man's grief defied any doubt.

"We are left to carry on," he continued more quietly, "and each must choose whether to be a formless, numberless boot-licker to a monster without a heart, or to find an echo of the love W'starrah Altieri held for all of us, in imitation of her courage, and the decision to face the fire."

My heart surged with a storm of emotions at Tanar'h's words. I remembered the admiration of her beauty which I shared with the preacher, with all men. I felt again the flame of her spirit when she brought me into her plan for this city, and I staggered under the responsibility of what to do now she was gone. I saw across the plaza everyone moved nearer the platform where she lay, as a line of people filed closer, knelt and prayed a few moments before rising to grasp arms with Tanar'h. Others brought gifts hastily produced or summoned to lay on the informal bier: jewels and silks removed and set at her feet, small bundles of aromatic wood and jars of funeral oil. I recognized a young couple dressed in purple, the noble sage J'seff'n who had assisted my researches, with his wife who wept profusely as they knelt, and produced a large violet covering-cloth. Chaktha stood there like a statue, stirring only to lower his spear whenever someone too young moved to raise the cloth, and otherwise letting the act speak for itself. The enormous circle-storm boiled ten fathoms overhead but moved no closer yet.

Teretheny tried to talk on, but his voice petered away with only his mysterious guards for audience. He scowled with rage, and I realized he needed the worship of the crowd to whip his storm to its fullest strength. Without it, he hesitated and I bet that was a mistake. The little one behind him had fallen into his partner's arms and seemed unconscious or worse. I had a clear path to execute my plan and crown the monk with the Brow.

But I felt a prompting within, and for once my voices were in agreement. Feldspar sniffed that it was not, after all, a very perilous thing for me to attempt. Simith hemmed a bit and admitted that W'starrah would not want to be associated with an assassination, however worthy the target. And I also realized something else. That Gryphon, the same as I saw at the arena two weeks ago, had a rider. Headed for the temple. I remembered the Captain and thought he should know the truth.

Before I could leave the area, I saw two more figures enter the square. One was Kama, the other a staff-bearing warrior dressed all in grey that I had never seen before. Yet there was something about him; I pride myself on the ability to act instantly, and I had several options open to me now. Attack the monk while he was distracted, or overbear the small guard, try to get that torc off his arm. I could bring the Brow to Tanar'h, or to Gaspar Heugen. How about simply getting a league or so away from the storm overhead, that had certain advantages, though none I cared for.

But in the end, I watched the grey warrior. A voice in my head, a new one I'm sure and I think it might have been Astor himself, whispered "that fellow looks like a man to draw peril. Might be fun to stand nearby."

He walked slowly through the crowd toward W'starrah's bier, sidestepping the line of mourners and meeting Tanar'h's challenging gaze without flinching. After a long moment, the grey man stepped past the preacher and knelt by the covered figure. First he prayed, intently; I wondered to whom. He did not lift the covering, but reached gently within to remove the cloak, flipping it over his shoulders as he rose. Looking up at Chaktha a long moment, he nodded once and slowly. Turning back to Tanar'h he offered him an arm to clasp. As he stepped back, Tanar'h, his face bathed in tears, held both arms over the bier and prayed with upturned palms.

186

That voice I thought of as Astor's said, "Here now, watch my companion give a gift."

Out of the heavens, from a place between the stars and the storm came a flume of sunfire. As the crowd cried out in wonder it fell directly between Tanar'h's arms and ignited the bier in a fingersnap. By the glare of a day-bright bonfire I saw his face still shining with grief despite the inferno. The most potent public miracle I'd ever seen or heard tell of. I reckoned this preacher was no poser, at least not anymore.

The body and all the offerings disappeared in the consuming flame. In moments, a reverse-rain of bright embers took flight, where the whirling storm above the rooftops took them spinning up and out in all directions. It was a second panoply of stars, fiery orange, white and tints of every hue. To me they seemed shards of light, each a tiny gemstone of a great woman's soul spreading her final benediction over the city she loved so well.

Folks were pointing at the man in grey, a wholesome sign if not good news for the stranger. Near me they murmured "He was there, he must have killed her." I doubted anyone as loyal as Chaktha would hesitate to attack her murderer, but people's opinions are easy to sway.

And sometimes the flow of rumor is up. Teretheny, choking with hatred at the frustration of his desire for a following, pointed and screamed, "See! He was there, stands now with her blood on his hands! And the body of your beloved leader now scatters on the One Wind. Abandon your heretic faiths, reject the heroes and follow me or be destroyed."

The warrior turned to face the monk, unconcerned though surrounded by hostility, as a man who is accustomed.

"Aye, I bear the blame for this fair woman's death. Think what ye wish of that effort. And sooth there be a single cause, a sole mover, behind all the many faiths of our land. How could there be else? But the gardener nursing many fruits does not despise their varied beauty. Any man who preaches a unity that destroys our differences, which makes us equal only in how far down it can grind—"

The warrior stopped suddenly, pointing to the dribbling canteen near Teretheny's foot. From behind the monk I saw the grey man's gaze go from laconic to volcanic.

"Yet see thee there, yon white elixir, distilled from the very minds of human victims. Near a vat of such brew is where we found the priestess, and from the clutches of monstrous alchemists we recovered her body before it could be so horrible violated." He looked up to the monk in stony fury and raised his accusing arm. "Before such as thee could make use of it, to what foul ends I know not."

Drawing a breath, he boomed "I call upon Conar to detect Despair!"

Before all the crowd, an aura of bright red flared over Teretheny's form, and another from the left arm of the shorter of his guards.

For the space of a single gasp, the rising wind was all the sound in that crowded plaza. Then a second storm rose, as the crowd united in outrage and shouted at the monk. For his part, Teretheny signaled with a dropped arm to the wagon guards. They turned as one to chop loose the tight canvas coverings and reveal tons of sparkling sand.

"Fools! Die then under the storm that punishes unbelief. Now, my dervijaye, purify this place!"

With a clawing gesture Teretheny tugged down the swirling storm at last, until it nearly touched the plaza stones. People were thrown screaming and grabbing at neighbors, and the wagons vibrated off the axles as they spat up their loads of lethal silt into the gyring gale. At once, some of the sand began to ignite and explode, increasing the destructive power of the storm. I threw both arms before my face and hunched for cover, while the howling wind tried to bore a shaft through me at the ears. A thousand sewing-needles of pain struck my flesh, even through the cloth, and I began to panic at the sheer helplessness of this cataclysm.

That voice chuckled through all the noise, and spoke to me again. "Yes, waiting is often hard. But soon, I think we shall have an opportunity here."

The pin-stabs crested and began to fade, though I was sure I bled from every pore. Peeking out, I could see the wind was strong as ever, but its load of flaming sand was circling further out and away, thank the heroes. The calmer eye centered on Teretheny, and I was close enough to benefit. The cyclone was so powerful that even the waters of the fountain were drawn up into it, along with wheels, a lamppost, every common article that pocket or pack could hold, and I'm fairly certain at least one bloody arm.

People lay dead or bleeding to all sides, as if the plaza floor had been strewn with petals of flesh. My brain could not estimate that quickly, but it seemed possible that hundreds, perhaps half the people had fled the plaza before the center of the storm hit. Yet hundreds more were down. Tanar'h lay half-into the empty fountain, breathing but not moving. The man in grey, gone flat to the ground, now struggled to his feet and looked around for Teretheny.

The turbaned guards, none the worse for wear, all drew their scimitars and began to hack those unbelievers still moving. I could see an eerie skein of dark energy from each of them leading back to the monk who still focused his attention on the storm, guiding it further out to engulf the rest of the city.

I saw Kama, who had hung back at the edge of the plaza from the beginning, now advanced into the wrack with his eyes always on the monk. One of the dervijaye assailed him with crab-stepping feet and two curved blades whirling. He seemed to have as many limbs as a spider and a blood-curdling scream to boot; yet Kama calmly ducked him with an economy of motion that made a virtue of his small size. Gently touching his foe with one hand, he murmured something and the swordsman abruptly dropped his weapons and sat down.

The grey warrior had no such subtlety to employ. Whirling his staff with flourishes and feints, he wove ahead and struck down three, then four of the fanatics before they could properly swing. His quick decision and the reach of his weapon were surprisingly effective, and by his dodges I could tell he was a seasoned combatant. His path met Kama's and the quarterstaff provided some protection for the little man as they turned toward the monk. With a roar and a mighty leap, Chaktha joined them and speared one desert foe into another, killing both. Teretheny for his part seemed glued to his spot, the storm taking all his concentration to direct. But a dozen fanatics were converging on the three of them now, and the grey warrior had to stop more than twenty feet short to defend on two sides.

Kama spoke urgently to the grey man as he fought, and the latter nodded sharply, perhaps in permission. As I took up my station again behind Teretheny, I watched while the healer knelt and clasped his hands. The others plied staff and spear in all directions, even over the little man's head to ward off the flickering blades, but it couldn't last long.

The voice again, so close to me I jumped. "Now would be a good time."

I looked at the monk, his guards, the torc, that web of evil energy, the storm still raging and growing. And maybe Astor kept helping me, I don't think I'll ever decide.

But I knew what had to be done.

And I knew who had to do it.

A growing heat on Justin's hand drew him up from the depths into pain, and breath and points of light everywhere. His head rang like a gong and he felt a trickle of blood from scalp to jaw. He pushed up from the stone floor of the tower battlement, and coughed at the rank stench of eaten meat behind him. The gryphon stood not four feet away, panting hard and watching him as a cat does a beetle, for any movement so sudden as to signal a resumption of the game.

The heat from his hand, from the ring, became quite intense. Looking down he saw a bright ember resting on the ax-symbol like a jewel, just now cooling and dimming in a way that filled him with sadness despite all the distraction and peril. Justin stared at the glowing bit and wondered why the tears came to him now, of all moments. No time to figure it out.

Keeping his eyes on the gryphon Justin carefully stood and stepped back two paces, then turned to look out over the crenelments at a city on fire. The storm he saw rising at center city now spread to every precinct, carrying with it glittery glimmers of something deadly, as well as ten thousand cinders like the one that landed on him, floating and glowing in all colors between the rooftops and the stars in heaven. From his time unconscious, then, he might be too late by now; certainly this part of the vision was already coming true. The storm bringing fire and water to the streets. But if the bolt of the Arbalest had flown, who was its victim?

And there would be fighting, in this tower, Fire Ants and Spiders.

Justin pivoted to face the gryphon again and stared at the beast. Sidling slowly around its head, he gently drew his knife as the creature watched, and reached out to slice the billet and cinch straps. As the saddle slipped off the other side, Justin reached to catch the reins, and walking back before the monster he held its unblinking gaze and opened his own mouth wide. The gryphon did the same and Justin neatly tugged the bit from its maw, where it clanged musically on the stones.

"Promise kept," he said, "well done. You are free."

He dropped the reins and stepped back, and still the creature stared as if unbelieving. Justin gestured with both arms, yelling "Hai!"; the monster crouched low, then screamed with fierce and utter joy before leaping up into the storm, whirling and cartwheeling either out of control or completely heedless of its course. Justin felt a surge of loneliness as he watched the creature celebrating freedom from all care and orders. Might it land nearby and wreak havoc on the helpless? Justin doubted that, but his promise meant something. Get below and prevent worse.

On the stairway down Justin became aware he was fussing. Helmet off, a hand clawed through his hair, gauntlets tucked into his belt, then put on, then tucked away again. Dusting his breeks, rubbing each boot against his calves. At the final turn he stopped and realized his breathing had quickened. For a long moment he stood there, unable to remember anything about votes or undead destroyed, of Argens' miracle or the words of love he had heard. Only her stunning beauty mattered, the impossible height between them. Justin felt fully grounded now, no longer able to ascend those heavens he imagined her proper place. Barking angrily at himself, he pulled his tunic straight and marched down, following his own orders to complete his mission.

He saw her chamber-door ajar, and felt the first sting of panic. With a soldier's eye he noted the recent strong repairs and remembered the fighting in vision he had seen happening here. Too late again? Justin charged in, not knowing how he achieved a sword drawn and shield limbered.

Empty, dark and still. He saw the expended lantern tipped on the floor and another jerk of dread tightened on his chest. In the inner chamber, the light of star and storm outside revealed an empty bed, disorder, papers on the floor. Back in the main room, Justin turned to the statue of Argens, his spirits drowning in the uncertainty that for the soldier is worse than fear, and knelt to pray. But his love for the priestess turned every plea to a selfish demand; unable to order his thoughts he instead became distracted by the enormous jewel on the statue's belt. Its obvious wealth was not what pulled him, he was sure. Perhaps…

The sound of voices from below snapped him to readiness and Justin stood with weapons in hand to face the door. Absurdly, he expected giant insects to breach the portal, but his ears told him there were just two men, one in a strong voice, the other impossibly deep.

They shouldered through the portal glaring at each other, white and black, tall and gigantic, practically naked to the waist. Justin could have achieved complete surprise, had he chosen to attack. But that they would both simply enter without asking dealt his heart another stab of fear.

"Where is she" he growled as they jumped to confront him.

"Intruder!" the leather-belted preacher shouted, "you have no right to trespass this holy space."

"Where" Justin ground out taking a step toward the men.

"Imperial dog!" the giant black cried, leveling his great spear.

Shaking with rage, Justin threw his sword sideways at the bodyguard's feet and stepped into the tip of the weapon. "Where is she!"

Both men stepped back and looked to each other. But the answer came in a husky whisper, from the inner room.

"Dead, Captain. Murdered."

I staggered from the central plaza, where behind me everything was still a human ruin. In my wildest dreams I had not expected to cause an explosion. The flash in my eyes tinted the fighting Colors on all sides to the same hue, and I heard nothing but a dull ring in my ears: perhaps I had gone deaf for good. But that evil torc was destroyed, and Teretheny too as a bonus. Too bad about the others, but the death-count had nearly included me.

The dervijaye were filtering in everywhere, and the desert men with twin scimitars were very selective about which men they engaged. They attacked the Blue by preference, whether on the city guard or not, and also citizens without arms if they came within reach. I saw them set two wagons on fire to panic the animals and spread flames down crowded shop streets and trample the unsuspecting caught by the storm. I set my teeth and turned aside from them, making my way to the temple of the Stargazers.

Voices inside my head were chuckling with satisfaction anyway, no tug from them to seek further peril for now. I still could hardly believe I had pulled it off, earlier at the fountain. Moving so quickly, changing appearance in just a few moments, stepping behind Teretheny while his attention was focused on the storm. And the result: I might be injured for life, my left shoulder joint was on fire and the inner voices were all I could hear anymore. Teretheny was gone, I was sure of it, destroyed in the blast. The man in grey, most likely too had died, brave fellow, and some of the dervijaye nearby. Time to sort out the blame later, for now I had to keep moving.

No guards at the outer wall, of course, discipline was never a strong point for the Stargazers. I easily kipped over and ran to the tower, climbing up to the darkened window by her inner chamber. Papers on the floor, perhaps a clue. Easing over the sill, I made out voices again, and realized my hearing had returned.

"Where," said a voice filled with a keen and dreadful purpose, and then again, "Where is she!" I recognized the unseen man W'starrah had spoken to on that fateful night she hired me. The mysterious agent I had thought an assassin, but now through the chamber door I beheld the Captain, the man I had come to see, standing against Tanar'h and Chaktha, holding his own and demanding to know the truth.

So I told him.

Justin whirled to see a man in tight black clothing and dark leather mask, who had certainly come through the window and held papers in his hand. Justin staggered back from the blow of those words, impossible yet confirming his worst fears, and didn't stop until he felt furniture behind him which he knocked to the floor. W'starrah, dead. The miracle, the quest, his desperate flight—was this all for nothing?

He heard a distant voice, as if the preacher spoke from down the stairs.

"You are the Captain of the Emperor's men? There is fighting now in the streets... are you listening?"

Justin tried without success to put a name to his pain. It was not sharp or narrow, he had been stabbed before a half-dozen times. Twice at Tor Perite, before he was unhorsed and taken prisoner by the Emperor's men. But after the battle, when he learned his father had not survived... this was akin to that, a stunning ache across his entire frame, knocking his mind from his limbs, murdering time and reason, hollowing him.

"Emperor's man," a deep voice, "Yellow and Red fight everywhere together, and desert men. Your soldiers too, they fight."

Justin shook his head hard enough to knock tears from his face, but the stubborn fog around his future refused to clear. Staring at the preacher, he saw a mirror of his own pain, and his instincts stirred.

"You loved her. You loved her too."

"I did" he admitted, and Justin saw truth in the flush of his face better than his words.

"And you," he said, turning to the Nubian, "you guarded her, for years I suspect." The black giant stood straight without bothering to respond, yet the signs in his breathing and neck and in his eyes were still there. Stepping forward, Justin retrieved and sheathed his sword before nodding up at the man. Turning to the third, Justin knew it was useless to seek truth behind the mask. But they nodded once to each other and it was enough.

"So we have all lost her then. And none of us did enough to save her life. That's the truth of it. But blame can await the morning; this city is still in peril, and we may yet rescue her desire."

When Justin turned again to face the man in black, he still felt a ruin inside, no idea what to do. But as he held his hand out for the papers, part of him realized, he was back in command.

Scanning the longer letter first, Justin saw a barely-legible scrabble of words, an attempted warning of some kind from a mind owned by fear. He looked up at the Nubian and asked, "Who is this fellow Welles?"

"Dead." the warrior replied. "Insectirs slew him in his home," he pointed to the statue, "after making that."

194

Justin considered the gem a moment with suspicion. This raving letter, if not from the hand of a dead man, would have seemed worthless. Yet when he prayed, before these men came in…

He turned back to the preacher and forced the words from his mouth. "W'starrah Altieri was alive two nights ago. What happened to her?"

"She, she had been missing, almost a day and a night. Some secret scheme, or so I thought, and then too, Chaktha here is always with her."

"She sent me away!" the other cried. For a moment the pair looked ready to resume their feud. Justin's reaction was instantaneous.

"Enough!" He glared until he took in both their faces in turn. "Regrets tomorrow, I won't say it again. She sent you, to seek this Welles perhaps? And you found him murdered? What then?"

"I sought the priestess, and together with another we found her, among monsters in tunnels far beneath the ground. Already slain." The great warrior shook then with emotion and Justin laid one hand on his shoulder.

"He brought her back," the preacher said, "to the central plaza, where I, we conducted her funeral and confronted the author of this evil storm, a mad monk named Teretheny."

"And this Eye mentioned in the letter, what is that?" Shrugs all around. "Or the Blind King, who could—"

"Yes!" Chaktha shouted, "In the tunnels, the leader was white and blind, no eye."

Justin turned to the man in black. "You look a handy sort. A Stealthic perhaps?"

The masked man nodded and Justin continued.

"She hired you?" Another nod.

"Do you think you could get that gem free, without touching it?"

The slender fellow drew a thin knife and moved to the statue.

"But there is fighting in the streets, your men—"

"My men have their orders, Reverend Myster. By the time they arrive I need to know what to do here."

"You ordered your men to these grounds?"

"I saw, with her, we had a vision. I don't know why but it is vital that we hold this tower. Tell me about Teretheny, who can summon such a storm."

"An evil man. And my half-brother, I should have—but he has a power to conquer one's will, to draw them in, and by some sorcery he can change his shape, and other miracles."

"No more," the man in black whispered, setting the gem down on the table between them. "That Serpent, his fangs are drawn."

"You mean he's dead?" Justin demanded.

"Aye," said Chaktha. "I saw them both."

"Both!"

"The grey warrior, and the healer, they fought the desert men. I ran to join them, and make a good ending, now that the Priestess is gone."

Justin felt a stab at this, fresh pain but nodded for him to continue.

"The healer knelt and I saw the circle of white power flow from him as a ripple in the quiet river. It passed over the grey man and his foes and myself, and across the plaza. And wherever it went, the storm faded, the desert men staggered and fell, and the monk... was struck dumb." Chaktha shrugged, wasting no time on things beyond his knowledge. "And then, in an instant there was another monk standing there, behind the first and unawares."

"What did he do?" Justin asked.

"The first monk," Chaktha declaimed "leaped from the stand and tried to attack the healer, but the grey man interposed and struck him down. The twin turned to one of the guards and spoke to him, holding out his hand, and the desert man took off his arm-wrapping and gave it up."

"Aye, I saw that," Tanar'h said, "I had lost my senses but came to just as the monk, the one with the torc, cried out and tossed it to the feet of the grey warrior. It still glowed bright red, evil, and Teretheny shouted in fear, lunging after it. But the grey warrior did not hesitate. With a great cry, he brought down his staff, glowing silver. And there was an enormous explosion."

Silence for a moment, then Chaktha continued. "The monk was dead, the grey warrior gone and the arm-jewel lay in small pieces everywhere. The twin likewise was missing."

"We left then, both of us," Tanar'h added, "to see to the safety of the temple. And whether that gryphon, if there was any damage here."

Justin took in this report with a nod. "So at least one of her foes is beyond the reach of the law now." He shuffled up the second paper, and the scent of jasmine knocked him askew again. Leaning against the back of a chair, he drew a deep breath and hammered back the tears, forcing his eyes to do service upon what seemed a list of sorts, in her handwriting:

-Warn the Raccoon of the Arbalest's bolt

-Tell Morinack of the Red Dragon's plan to release the Shard Demon

"Well then, that bolt has already flown," Justin said to himself as the others stared. "If she had time, she must have done so herself."

He looked at Tanar'h. "Can Carnad Mias release the Shard Demon?"

The preacher was surprised and shook his head in uncertainty. "If money can purchase the means, nothing is beyond the Red Cup. He was a devotee of the Demonbender temple before it was outlawed by your Emperor. Since then of course he," and Tanar'h checked whatever he was going to say next. "But to release the Demon?"

"Where is its prison located?"

Again Tanar'h shook his head. "Legends say beneath the Crystal Palace."

Justin considered that a moment. "No, or at least, not yet. I must defend this tower first and foremost. And Morinack in Argens can do nothing to help us in time. What about this item: '-Take the Spider's Throat from Teretheny'?"

"Done." The Stealthic's husky voice was not loud, but certain.

"As you say, then. Here's the rest: '-Find the Stone Oak's new mate'."

"I'm sorry Captain, there again she speaks in riddles."

"There's more here," Justin said, showing the note to the preacher.

-Save Tanar'h from himself

Tanar'h swallowed hard and squeezed tears from the sides of his eyes, then nodded fiercely and said "Also done."

Justin's eye fell to the last line on the note, and an enormous hand squeezed his heart too hard for it to beat.

-Love the Captain all your days, and beyond.

You press on through the Next, every few yards an effort harder than herding smoke as you leave the temple district and enter the Underboards. Still tied to the body's habits, you gasp and feel winded though there is no more to breathe. Your people run past in panic and agitation: behind and above, the Boards are aflame, and guards' whistles and shouted orders dimly come to you. Some of these few unhomed folk down here, agitated by the dead-night tumult, are unnerved and pull down their own rough-hewn structures, barriers between the walkways and the water, and knocking over small firepits, which spread their flames to all the nearby wood.

Should you stay? What help could you lend, even to calming the minds of these few unnoticed, unhinged members of your family? Carnad Mias is already so far ahead. Flames lick the walls and boards in every direction, most still small but joining as regiments of an unearthly army to overwhelm the district.

From the hilltop palace comes the sound of a deep horn, one you have never heard before but feel certain was told you, in school. Something about a warning, a need to leave the area. And even these desperate denizens snap around to look, then flee with rare purpose on their faces. Away from resisting, or plunder or helping the flames, away and up to the city above.

The grinding sound of wheels and levers not used in many years presages a deluge from the upper levels. Reserves of water, pumped in from the Tepid and held in red-brick pipes, release down upon the Underboards, quenching flames and carrying off most of the ramshackle structures there.

… *blue sea and red fire are everywhere at war, racked or raised by the howling wind.* You notice that storm now, as a wave of air slams into the area from the direction of center-city. Scores of glowing embers ride the gale; as they pass through you, there is a sense of a snapping chain, freedom of movement returned.

You are free, cherished one. Free to return to the Now, to my arms, to perfect sight of future days with me. I see you, but not the Next, for your willful spirit still desires things I cannot see. I must wait, in ignorance and anticipation as all mortals do, for the future.

You see the crisis here averted, turn your eyes to the heavens again, feel my presence and strong regard for you. But the clicking turns you away.

At first, a sound too strong and sharp to be real, a false percussive rhythm made in some way by human hands. Then the real thing, as an Insectir responds with its throat and tongue. Back and forth, and before you know it you are following, the decision of a lifetime already made.

Carnad Mias stands in a half-foot of water holding a small crank-box and conversing with a group of six-legged warrior Bugs at the entrance to a tunnel. Your mind reaches into those around you and words you never could have understood become plain. A demon freed, an eye returned, the bargain struck. Four of the enormous armored monsters follow Mias into the tunnel here at the base of the palace cliff. The others move off, agitated and nervous but under orders from the Blind King. You follow the Red Cup more freely now. With your body destroyed you should have ascended the heavens, but the choice is made. My sadness burns like a cold flame at this parting, but it drowns and is extinguished at my pride for your choice, cherished one. Go, do what you can. I have a new future to contemplate, now I see it clearly and will wonder at its coming.

$\oplus$

Hearing such snap and vigor in the Captain's voice, I was reminded of the last time I heard it, here in this tower when I thought W'starrah spoke to an assassin. There was the same certainty, a kind of devotion in the tone which carried over into his every move. I am no soldier myself, and generally made a joke of guardsmen wherever I found them. But this man, I thought, I could follow.

It was completely unlike the spell that Teretheny had tried to cast over us. At the center of the monk's call had been himself, and whatever form he took with the artefact that was now mine, his motives remained bent to his own profit. His followers were all the same.

But this Captain, supposedly the tool of an Emperor any right-thinking citizen would despise, he pushed always to some noble purpose outside himself. Trying to save a city that hated him, for a lost love who had wanted it saved. Devotion like that, I realized, was missing from most lives, including any of mine. Except when

199

Feldspar had a mission, none of my personas served a purpose in that way. I wondered if they could.

He read and discussed the first letter with Tanar'h and Chaktha, and I smiled inside my mask as they described the riddle of Teretheny's twin. I had no idea what might happen when I had thrown the torc, only that it was pulling at me to put it on with a force I had never encountered. Even if it hadn't glowed crimson, I would have wanted nothing to do with it. All my strength would not have lasted another ten beats—I threw it off the same way I would have a poisonous snake. I never thought someone might die, not even the monk though I would shed no tears on his account. Praise Astor, Kama was shielded from that mystic blast by the grey warrior. I couldn't see him or anyone else for a long time, so I had run from the plaza to preserve any chance of discovery.

I saw the Captain read the last item on the second note without speaking, and for a few moments he sagged as if he might fall. But he recovered, carefully folded the paper and put it inside his jacket to the left. I suddenly felt as if I had intruded on a private prayer, and turned away to look again out the open window.

There I saw the shape of things to come. And it was as unpleasant as it was close.

Good thing I had a Captain of men with me.

Justin read that last line forty times in three breaths, and managed to hold his hands still as he carefully placed it over his heart. The center of his chest was filled with iron now, and he knew he had little time left. The need to grieve, and perhaps to choose his Moment, was only a small space of hours ahead. Here in the chapel of the Stargazers, he thought he might be granted sight of that future more clearly. I beg you, Argens lord of the heavens, how much longer must I bear this weight for my beloved? Is the battle coming soon, will I be permitted to lay down my life here, where she lived, and will that satisfy your augury?

Justin held his breath and waited for an answer. It came in a whisper, too husky for heaven.

"Captain," the man in black hissed from the window, "you will want to see this."

Together with the preacher and the bodyguard, he stepped to the window of the outer chamber, overlooking the grounds and a section of the precinct wall.

I had never seen such an unwelcome sight. The temple guards buzzing back and forth on the low parapet, clumping together at the center and shouting at each other in confusion, while outside the gates stood a double-row of men with the Sun blazon of the Empire ready to march in. Beyond the wall, streams of Yellow and Red filtering from the streets and approaching the largely unguarded wall. I could already see hands above the battlements as they clambered up and over. The fight not yet started, and already the temple wall had fallen.

Worse yet, to the far right, the hands I saw were not human. The armor there shone darkly, but would not come off its wearers. They were few but their arms were many. Scattered guards in that direction already fled leaving shields and spears in their wake, from that same repugnance all Elves feel at the sight of Bugs.

I tore my eyes away to regard the Captain, and beneath my mask the jaw dropped open. To see him smiling.

Justin scanned the parapets where the Stealthic was pointing, and felt the pain in his center begin to ease. To their left, men of the Red and Yellow houses evidently worked in concert to scale the temple walls: several times the Stargazer cohort, they clearly outnumbered even the half-dozen dekents of his own men still outside the gate. Plus they were maneuvering along a coordinated plan of attack, whereas some on his own side did not yet realize who would lead them. To the right, Justin felt his guts jump, shattering the iron ingot around his heart with the prospect of facing the legendary Insectirs. The Stargazer guards in that quarter had already routed at their first approach, and would take too long to rally now. Further behind this tumult came a wave of desert men, each with a pair of curved swords and showing none of the fear that Elves feel at the sight of the Bugs. The storm winds blew across the grounds, making communication by mouth next to impossible.

What could be better.

Justin spun to face the others, knowing in his heart that this was his time. To use all his wiles, create havoc among the enemy, hold this tower for as long as mortal strength could manage, plus an hour, and then let the heroes have the result along with his final breath. The knight's son he had been a half-year ago would have said he was far from home now. But Justin knew at last where he belonged.

He looked to Tanar'h, whose face was brimming with dread at this invasion.

"Can you rally your guards, get them to you somehow?"

"Me, can I, you mean—"

"Reverend Myster, I mean to fight to preserve this temple, this tower, and I need to know what I can count on. For Argens, and for her."

Tanar'h gulped and nodded, saying "I will bring them," as he turned to go.

"Wait, one moment. Open the gate to my men, then bring your soldiers to M'nesa Zetee, my subaltern. Place your men under his command, and tell him to pull the Colors away from the temple by any trick or tactic."

"You mean, to leave you here alone?"

"Tell him to send Tass and one dekent here. The rest with him. He must draw the men of Red and Yellow away."

Tanar'h nodded grimly, then his face lit with emotion. "I know how. If I hurry, I can do it." He ran for the door and down the stairs.

Justin looked up at Chaktha.

"Will you fight with me to hold this place?"

The Nubian's eyes were fierce and he smiled, lightly hefting his enormous spear.

"Good. Bar the door below to all except my men."

As the bodyguard descended, Justin looked back out across the grounds to assess the situation. Tanar'h ran toward the gate waving his arms, as the House men on the left took their time to assemble having won the wall. A mistake, but only training could see it. He forced himself to look at the Insectirs again, and held his gorge as they came on relentlessly in a loose column, no hesitation and direct toward the tower itself.

"Stealthic, I don't think you should stay—" Justin realized no one was with him at the window. The man in black crouched near the small alcove behind the statue, empty and just large enough for a single man to stand.

"What is it?"

"There's a draft here, from the floor. And this stone..." the Stealthic passed his hands over the area, lightly touching the statue pedestal, the base of the curved wall. "Some kind of door."

At these words, Justin had a flash of the vision, fighting in this room and on the stair below, Spiders and Fire Ants. Then a crown ablaze and a Fly with merging legs, shattering glass, in a place dark and deep. His chest stirred again, and he reacted on instinct.

"I intend to hold this room as long as I am able. Can you open that door?"

The Stealthic cocked his head in masked mockery. "I presume sooner would be better?"

Justin grinned. "It would indeed."

He vaulted down the stair to Chaktha in the lower chamber, with the growing sounds of violence beyond the portal. He nodded to the Nubian, who opened quickly and gave Justin a clear view of the wrack outside at ground level. Down the paved way from the gate, ten of his men jogged with Tass to the side casually swinging a two-bladed ax in one hand. His grin was infectious, and when clicking from the right caused the Elves to start and look aside in terror, the former gladiator laughed and cursed them to move more quickly. As they filed past Justin and into the chamber, he looked left and saw order slowly emerging through the tumult of bodies, as men fell and lines drew sharper.

M'nesa had his unit in convex crescent, bowmen in the second rank taking down several House men as they recoiled and turned aside in response to the attack. They had to, missile troops on a flank could hardly be ignored. But the plan was working, temporarily.

Tanar'h stood with drawn dagger in the front rank at risk from rival weapons, but calling back and pointing behind the group to the lower ground, down the path to an ivy walled garden. Justin's heart fell at this. The preacher, no doubt ignorant of sound tactics, was taking them to a place of disadvantage, perhaps relying on the hedge to serve as protection but sacrificing high ground against a foe already superior in numbers. It couldn't last—Justin wondered briefly how M'nesa could be so taken in, but the dekentar nodded and called out, reinforcing some hasty plan.

No time to worry about that now. Glancing at the oncoming Bugs, Justin stepped back and Chaktha barred the door. He looked to his men, panting in a rough semicircle and gawking at the gorgeous purple appointments.

"We hold this tower," Justin said, "against all who come." Almost as one, his men swallowed, and nodded. "Our opponents are unusual," he continued, taking in their gaze, "but for us, this is nothing new." That worked, as they smiled and chuckled. "You can do nothing about the unsettling instinct you feel when you face these monsters. But realize that your enemy is outside you, not within. Take fewer swings, and make each one count."

The sounds of rising wind forced him to shout as the storm enveloped the grounds outside. There came bumping against the door, hard but not heavy, as if a child used a shield to knock. Light, solid things hit the tower walls, and as they listened Justin recognized a pattern among the patter, stony clicks that started out on the ground, and seemed to rise along the outer wall to head level, then higher.

"They are climbing," he announced, and his men all looked to the ceiling uselessly. He needed a solution fast. "Chaktha, to the roof, can you stave them off?"

The Nubian smiled again, as if something he did rarely, and bounded up the stairs. He was a Man, and not as nervous in the presence of the Insectirs as Justin and his Elves, plus the reach of his spear and coverage of his shield should prove a formidable barrier.

"You four, bows and the bottom steps," Justin said, pointing to the stairs leading up. "On my command, fire to cover our retreat."

Outside the door, scraping sounds gave way to a kind of deep hiss and the smell of burning. Though the bumping of hard-shell bodies seemed too light to matter, yet the wooden portal started to crack and give way. The men cried out at the sorcery, but Tass shouldered through them with an oath and stood to the hinge-side with his axe. The first monster to break through lost both his forelegs and fell back chittering into his fellows as the severed limbs flinched and rolled

204

on the floor. Another, larger hole and Tass yelled out swinging hard, beheading a second Bug in a spatter of ichor and flailing legs while its writhing body momentarily clogged the breach.

Justin noted, even as his heart tried to flee through his throat, that the Bugs recoiled briefly, clicking and seeming to spasm more than usual, only after a few moments reaching to pull the corpse from the hole and clear it to one side. The smell of the thing's fluids was sharper than vinegar and not half as healthy. Perhaps they had to fight an instinct at that aroma. He forced himself forward to thrust his sword at the first replacement, even as the rest of the portal tore away in charred strips. His point scored a crack in the monster's carapace, and he blocked the counter strikes from two limbs while stepping back. Two other men lurched up to plug the gap between Justin and Tass, faces grey as the stone but stabbing with their spears fast enough to matter. Justin realized he was clenching his jaw so hard there was powder between his teeth. His sword was too short to avoid their reach, but its weight was more effective than the thrusting motion of the spears. Tass cut diagonally through another Bug with his axe, leaving two limbs and a head on the floor and causing the wave to fall back again.

But now the monsters in the second rank began to spit at the men inside. Justin's shield-block stopped a gob of something hot and hissing, and he felt his arm heating up through the metal. One of the men with a larger, wooden shield cried out and fell back shaking off the burning pieces. Tass was grazed in the hip by a near-miss and had to step away to tear his tunic off. More men stumbled up to fill the gap but now the Insectirs were slowly making way into the chamber. Worse, Justin could see the desert men coming on as well, working their way between the ranks as one of their number stood in the back working a small box with a crank that emitted a clicking rhythm over and over.

The circular chamber was a poor place to meet superior numbers. Justin looked to Tass, naked above the waist and flexing his arms, ignoring the dark red patch of bubbling Bug-toxin on his ribs. He nodded to Justin and waded back in, swinging wide to create room and force his opponents back a half-step.

"To the stairs, now!" Justin cried, and his men retreated as their Captain and subaltern wove a momentary net of steel to cover them. Justin met a desert fighter swinging his scimitars in alternation, feinted, and then bashed with his shield to knock the man over. Turning with Tass, he charged back to the stairs bent over at the waist as the four bowmen fired above his head. The six of them charged up together, filing between the remaining soldiers at the first curve who returned their spears to level and thrust hard and down.

This was more like it. The tread of the staircase could allow three men holding pole weapons to stand abreast, while their attackers with swinging edges could afford no more than two. For a few moments it was desperately quiet in the tower, as men thrust and recovered, missed and ducked, gasped and chuffed in the frantic business of dealing and avoiding wounds. The Bedou-uu warriors had been quicker up the tread, but their fanaticism was a poor substitute for reach and discipline. Two of them fell either dead or seriously wounded, and their inhuman allies stepped on their bodies to stab high with blade or claw. Clicking, coughs of effort, and the occasional cry of a hit went on for some time.

"Check on Chaktha," Justin said to Tass; but before the human could take a step up, Justin saw through the ruined portal of the lower door a flailing body land on its back and snap awkwardly into multiple pieces. A hearty laugh and curse from above apprised them the Nubian was holding his own.

"Keep them here," he revised, "and be mindful of their poison. Also fire, there will be flames here soon." Tass eyed him sidelong and shrugged. Justin leaped two treads at a time to the upper chamber, to check on the Stealthic's progress.

His heart dropped when he saw the empty room, and realized the churl must have fled.

I tingled with nerves at the sounds of combat below, the telltale clicks on the outside wall, the storm-rattling shutters at my back. Concentration eluded me, there might be only seconds left. And if I succeeded in opening this trap door, Astor only knew what monsters lay in wait on the other side for me alone. But only a rascal would have left this Captain in the lurch.

Stripping off my gloves, I felt the stones again. Everything seemed completely solid, yet the sensation of moving air and a slight smell of deep earth persisted. Think, try not to be an idiot, I told myself. The masonry was that ancient style, every stone a unique size, fit together in mosaic pattern. No hint of mortar showed between their perfect matching intersections; typically these were laid on a bed of cement to hold them still. None of the flagging pieces stood out for color, or type, or... wait, by the wall, that was the only one large enough. I felt around every edge and confirmed the draft with another jangle in my gut.

Through the open door I could hear the sounds of men dying, and knew my time was short. Despite the emergency my mind was drawn to those marvelous acting days, rehearsing fight scenes and moments of wounding, of dramatic last lines and thunderous applause. Part of me realized, I was distracted because I was being critical of their performance. All the shouting, groans of agony wasted because no one waited their turn to declaim. Amateurs. Give me a wooden sword and my blood bag, I would show them.

I slapped my own face so fast I couldn't dodge the blow, stinging myself back to reality. Men were truly dying out there, not all of them evil or monstrous. This was not a rehearsal, unless all of life was a performance. I drew a deep breath, reached out again to the stone on the floor and thought about it. No hinge, there was no room. No handle, no concealed button or lever on the wall.

A pivot, then.

I laid my hands flat and started to work the stone left, right, diagonally. On the fifth or sixth attempt, I felt it move the width of a fingernail. Astor's voice in my head: Ah yes, I remember this one. My hands moved of their own accord, working in concert, left, toward me, away, left again, right.

The stone flagging pivoted in the middle, back half up in the air, front half down into darkness. My legs were in the hole before I could think; part of me wondered if there was an endless drop below, or a trap. Another voice murmured quietly to put my feet against the wall, and all would be well. I placed them both there and slithered down and in.

The stone was lightly spring-loaded; I laid my gloves over the lip with perhaps the fingertips showing and let it close behind me. I stood with just my booted feet against a vertical wall, as the Throat of the Spider emanated cool energy across my body and I felt the elation of defying gravity. In total darkness I drew my lantern from its belt-pouch and lit it. Just six or seven feet down the shaft the floor was shaped like rough steps, curving inside the wall of the tower and descending into the deep earth out of sight below.

I decided to scout before bothering the Captain, who sounded as if he had his hands full. Three steps down the wall, my feet as secure as if already on the ground but my body reporting falling every second until I stepped on the treads leading into the lower levels. Sound was almost completely masked here, and I didn't think it was merely stone. I descended more than three complete circles lower; the steps ended in a rough-cut rock chamber with a tunnel sloping down further into the earth. I had lost orientation, no idea what direction I was facing. But I knew what Insectir smelled like, and there was plenty of that ahead of me.

I walked on, my nerves tussling between the obvious need for caution and an unexplained impulse to hurry. I tried to inspect all my thoughts, knowing that albino ant might be nearby. One thing for certain, I did not feel in the least like sleeping. Turning my bullseye lantern to all sides as I walked, I noted the usual tunnels from every angle, perhaps one every twenty steps or so. There might be a hundred more Bugs creeping up behind me, or ahead for that matter. No sense worrying about could be.

After several tense minutes of continuing descent, I felt the walls and air getting wetter, and wondered if the Tepid could be nearby. I came to a level intersection of four paths, and heard scrabbling both left and right. I had no time to think. Shuttering the lantern I walked up the walls before remembering that no man should be able to do that. Without my light I realized there was a dim illumination now from that same phosphorescence I had seen in the tunnels of Old Cryss. The twin processions of bearer-Bugs lumbered across the intersection, one loaded with wrapped bundles and stone containers, the other empty of all but their backstraps. At the end of each line was a warrior, the giant mantis-type with two of its four forearms holding jagged weapons. I held perfectly still, and discovered that Insectirs are much like their human enemies in one respect. They hardly ever look up. As the lines receded into the distance I noted that I also felt none of the instinctive disquiet I had in previous encounters. My neck-piece was still coolly tingling, and I heard the slightest suggestion I could even take their form if I wished. I did not, but marveled at this artefact all the same. The dear departed Devout probably hadn't bothered to figure out all its powers.

Continuing ahead I soon felt a deep cold descend, not driven by wind or added depth and thus all the more sinister. I slowed and came to the edge of an enormous chamber, not lit by the glow-lichen but bearing several points of light near the opposite end. Before a thick glass wall running the width of the chamber's end stood Carnad Mias with a half-dozen Insectirs armed and plated. He had just finished using a small box to make clicking sounds, and now turned to kneel before the wall with several metal items, which he laid at its base out of my sight before starting to chant.

And behind the wall the torchlight revealed something that turned my bones to grease inside me. Standing nearly eight feet tall was a three-legged monster made entirely of glints and panes that reflected the torchlight and turned it blood red. It moved before I could conclude it was a statue, sending bright ruby sparks in all directions to bounce off the stone walls behind it and the glass barrier before. There was something else in the chamber too, something I would have taken for a mist had it not been so small and held its shape so well. I couldn't make out any details, but the mist, the monsters and Mias all became bigger in my vision, and I realized that was due to the fact that I was charging into the chamber.

I threw a handful of sharpened stars from some distance, because there was no sense denying my desperation now. Two bounced from Bug plate, two others stuck resulting in awful squeals, and one more pinged off the glass wall with no effect. But the last one sliced Carnad Mias in the shoulder, making him cry out and interrupting his chant. Everyone turned in my direction, and the demon-thing started up, with another shower of crimson sparks arcing over the wall and bouncing from the stone floor before dying.

I had no plan to fight so many foes, but I knew that running was out of the question if it gave Carnad Mias a chance to resume whatever foul sorcery he was attempting. As the Bugs charged me, I took out another flash-gem and threw it down. Here in the darkened cavern, the effect was even greater than it had been in the shadowy temple where I rescued Keilee. All the guard Bugs fell back or down, flailing and chittering in obvious pain. But Mias had shielded his eyes from the worst of it, and now seized his small wooden box to vigorously crank out a message whose meaning was sadly easy to guess.

There were too many limbs between me and the Red Cup to risk charging through, or throwing something else. As I started to back away, I comforted myself that at least I wasn't feeling the panic Elves usually suffered in similar circumstances. Cold comfort if I didn't survive to stop him. And Prince of Peril, how cold it was already here. If I didn't have an urgent need to run up the walls of this cavern, I swear I might have dropped down for a nap right there. But now the Bugs were recovering—the albino ant entered from one side as my heart fell, and its warriors came blindly on in a loose semi-circle to engage with me, no doubt guided by their leader's mind. Carnad Mias was back to his chanting and I had failed. The Shard Demon would soon be free, the city ruined, all plans to delay it doomed.

When the mist near me spoke, I couldn't for my life answer. But fortunately someone else did.

You move with less effort in the Next, near the world and the people you gave your life to save. After Carnad Mias into the tunnel, down into the frozen subearth on the trail of his inhuman guards and into the cavern where his lantern reflects a sight to blast your soul.

The legends did not lie, a monster made of bloody crystal behind a pane that seems too flimsy to hold under its own weight, much less to restrain the horror behind it. The Shard Demon hunkers down, a misshapen razor-edged Fly with its six legs melded into three, as the Dragon crouches before its prison and lays out sorcerous treasures to essay its freedom. The wurm does not notice you, nor the Insectirs arrayed behind him, but the trapped Demon swivels its head in a spray of sparks to gaze directly on your ghostly shape. Its gem-eyes

210

glitter with fiery amusement; a tremor lightly rocks the cavern as the Dragon begins to chant in the voice of Carnad Mias.

You must stop him, but how? Drifting closer you shout to him, pleading, begging him to return to the family of Hope. Almost he seems to see something, but the mind is closed to your thoughts, and the head snaps back to his business. Desire is raging in you now, a need close to fury that ransacks every corner of your spirit looking for something it can use. Downcast, you notice there is a bit of substance where you are, like a mist...

The Ferret! Silvery stars bounce into and through the enemy, and the Dragon is grazed, destroying the cadence of his incantation. Your heart swells with both hope and fear, that he would be so loyal to come here now, but that he is all alone and they are many. Clever fellow, he drops something from his hand and a flash like lightning pulses the room, distressing the Bugs and drawing a roar and shift from the demon that sprays the room with momentary fire. One cinder passes directly through you and by an echo of its heat you realize the cavern is icy cold.

And that you can feel cold again, as you did in life.

The Ferret looks around for help or escape, and his eyes cross yours, noticing but not recognizing you. He seeks to defend himself as the giant Bugs recover, and Mias returns to chanting. The soprano snap of glass signals that a web of cracks is spreading, from where the Dragon chants across the lower end of the wall. It is too late, you are here yet there is not enough of you present to matter.

But hearing a manly shout, you realize the rest of you has arrived.

M'nesa wished he had the rest of the men, but there was little to be gained from desires. Down the garden path he led them, one dekent stopping to fire a volley up at the advancing foe while the others fell back through the ranks. An orderly retreat, and the men of Red and Yellow had no missile weapons to respond. Without their superior numbers, the enemy would not have been able to press this advantage. But the Imperial troops were indeed outnumbered, more than three to one.

"Hurry!" Tanar'h shouted, pointing the way back to the garden entrance.

M'nesa gauged the distance and held up a restraining hand. From their hurried consultation, he knew the chance of success was slim indeed. Timing would be everything.

And now their time had run out. Still seventy paces from the garden entrance, some of the Yellow House drew flasks from their belts and lobbed them downhill at the Imperial ranks. They shattered with no apparent result, but men in the front rank began to choke and fall.

"Back! Double-time back!" The ranks waited their turns before fleeing downhill. Most went directly through the hedge-gate in a double-row, and from there followed Tanar'h's hand signals directing them further in along the center path. None of the troop deployed to the hedge, to beat back the assault, though one dekent drifted left and right before the entrance, seemingly fleeing in bad order around the outside of the enclosure. M'nesa watched them run and felt his heart swell with pride as he turned with three of his volunteers and Tanar'h to stand just outside the aperture.

"Getting away!" "Death to the Empire!" "Hurry!" the House men broke into full pursuit, covering their faces as they ran over the bodies of collapsed Imperials downed by the poison gas. M'nesa watched them come and briefly wondered, if the remarkable story Tanar'h had conveyed could possibly be true. He would never have trusted the word of a local coming to him on his own, with death on the line. But the Captain had sent this preacher, and trust was all a soldier could live by.

"On my word, gentlemen," he said calmly, "run, but not too quickly."

"After me," Tanar'h said nodding, "do not stray. Trust in the Stargazer."

When M'nesa could make out the eagerness in his enemies' faces, he barked the word, "Back!" and turned to run through the maze of pleasure benches and cobbled paths after Tanar'h in the lead. Not twelve paces behind came a wave of crimson-blonde anger, yelling for their blood outside the gate, strangely quiet within. He looked down at the sword in his hand, and realized in wonder he could not form the intent to raise it against them. And his heart surged with Hope, to know that the miracle the preacher spoke of was real.

At the outer gate M'nesa turned and slammed the iron bars in place without two seconds to spare. The House men hit the barrier and stood there, with faces fading from hatred to astonishment. To both sides of the entrance, Imperial soldiers stood just above the hedge-line with weapons and smiles, waiting further orders. Tanar'h had not hesitated but immediately cut and run around the outside of the garden, looping back to the front gate and the outside men who had rallied back to block it.

Throughout the entire lawn, scores of Red and Yellow retainers ran back and forth in increasing confusion, eager to fight, then simply desperate to escape, but cowed by the deep layers of enchantment laying over the Stargazer grounds, unable to use their weapons or bodies to attack their scattered guards on all sides.

"No fighting!" M'nesa called, "let these men surrender and exit without weapons. Whenever, that is, they are ready."

"Or they may stay at their pleasure," shouted Tanar'h, "to contemplate the error of a violent existence, and turn instead to thoughts of prayer and love."

The soldiers sent up a mighty cheer and M'nesa saw their enemies trapped within the peaceful garden looking to all sides in disbelief. Their paltry foe, so recently running in apparent panic, now surrounded them and from outside the garden could still strike blows to anyone trying to leave under arms. They cursed with great invention, but without much passion, and from various quarters began to drop their weapons.

He ordered some of the men to oversee the internment, others to tend to those struck down by weapons or poison. M'nesa looked to the priestesses' tower, the front door a ruin and giant Bugs swarming up the sides, and prayed earnestly to Argens to deliver his Captain a proper reward for his courage.

⊕

Justin stood alone in the room where he had last seen his lover, listening to the sounds of combat above and below and hoping for death as a reward for his pain. He had thought he sensed something in the masked Stealthic, a kind of comradery that welcomed peril for differing reasons. But obviously Justin had misjudged yet another situation. He picked up the orange gem and stowed it in a belt pouch, drew his sword again and moved to the landing for the final phase of the battle.

The Bugs below were throwing their acid again, heedless of whether they hit allies or enemies on the crowded stairs; the screams of pain sounded very much alike. Dropped torches gave flickering tribute to the scene of desperate death-dealing, but he could see at least three of his men were already down. It was sufficient, they had cost the invaders four times that number already. Perhaps a score of foes left, a half-dozen of his own.

"Chaktha! Down here now!"

"Bugs at the windows, Emperor-man!"

"To me, Chaktha, we'll take them together from inside."

"Aye, I come. Together we shall kill them."

The enormous fighter came bounding down taking the treads four at a time, paying no more heed to the red streaks across his chest and forehead than if he had used paint. Flashing three fingers at Justin, he grinned and charged within to where the shutters were rattling from something harder than storm wind.

"Now men, back! Into the chamber."

Justin flattened against the wall at the last turn as his men ran up, the final man staggering by weaponless on Tass' arm. The swarming steps of the enemy were on their heels and shadows made all shapes inhuman. Lunging out, Justin screamed and slashed, taking the foreclaw of an Insectir at the start of the sweep and gashing the shoulder of a desert fighter at the end. The two spurted and fell together, blocking the way another moment, and he seized the chance to fall back through the portal as Tass slammed it shut.

Tass, Chaktha and four men looked back at their Captain by the light of the relit lantern, the wounded one lying on the couch with one hand pressed atop his leaking thigh. Justin nodded to Chaktha, pointing to the window; stepping through the room, he closed the door to the bed chamber. He caught a scent of jasmine and nearly burst into tears, but mastered himself before turning back to address them over the rattling of weapons on wood at both sides.

"Soldiers of the Empire do not measure their worth in the length of days, but in the quality of their discipline and adherence to the given order. I can hardly imagine… nay, it is not possible that any

214

men could have been more perfect in their loyalty than you have here tonight." Justin saw the flush of grim pleasure from all. "To hold this chamber was your mission, and we cannot wish to be in any other place in all of Argens for that purpose. We should see the end of this contest soon; meantime, that portal will hold a while. There should be wine in the cabinet."

Tass laughed by the door with his ax, as eager hands passed entire bottles to each man. "To the finest Captain gold can buy!" He bellowed with his flask in salute and the men all echoed it. He drained a third of it in one pull and exclaimed, "Cark me, but how we slew them."

Justin cut a swath from the purple curtain and pulled it tight around the wounded man's leg, hard enough to make him cry out. Two long swigs from his bottle later, he grinned saying "Reckon I could stand on it now, sir."

Justin put an arm on his shoulder, saying, "Rest a while yet." He pressed a dropped dagger into his hand. "Time enough when they come through."

The shouts of the desert men mingled with the horrid hissing of that acid being used on the thick outer door. Tass stood to one side again, hefting the ax and smiling like a child holding a Darksebb gift. With a deep shout, Chaktha stabbed through the weakening shutters with his spear, answered by a screeching chittering squeal and a brief view of too many limbs flailing through the hole he made. Bracing one foot against the wall, the Nubian pulled back clearing the weapon and the scream descended. Turning back, he signaled with four fingers and everyone laughed.

Breaking wood from the inner chamber, sharp blades punching through at the shutters and the doorway now. Justin's men ran to their places without orders, and he stood ready to assist wherever the enemy pushed in first. The din of battle became deafening; Tass leading the men in their favorite song, Chaktha calling out in his native tongue, chitters and desert cries and the clash of metal. Yet Justin swore he could hear her voice, calling his name from a great distance.

He looked to the statue of Argens, and began to form a prayer, that he might die well now at the end and earn whatever reward a soldier of Hope could expect. But his thoughts were distracted by the memory of her call, and his eyes could not focus on Argens' face, or his missing belt-gem, but instead to a spot on the floor behind him where something small and black poked through the flagging.

The wave of elation made Justin cry out, though it went unheeded in the wrack of fighting. He stepped behind the statue and pressed his boot against the spot, making the stone flag pivot down. His last view of the room showed his men holding their own on three fronts, and to the wounded man on the couch it probably appeared as if his Captain melded into the statue of Argens itself. The bite of regret was strong but brief; his men were used to their Captain going on ahead. And they had held the tower long enough.

He dropped to the stone steps a man-length below and immediately started running. Dim illumination gave only a hint of where he was headed but Justin felt guided by a steady trace. It could not be, none of this should happen in any sane, awakened life, but he threw himself down the corridor and deeper into the earth and cold. His only thought was that the Stealthic had come this way. And did Justin dare believe…

The unearthly illumination never grew strong but the tunnel surface was fairly smooth, turning from earth to stone and back. Images of other paths, large insectoid shapes drawing back from him, perhaps even a weapon or two all flashed by in instants as Justin ran faster than he had in his life. When he saw a cavern open ahead, it was again her voice that drew him, echoing from the walls exactly as if she were there, just a few steps away.

"Do not do this! Stay your hand!" Dim and faint, but it was her voice, Justin could not doubt it. The world might be insane but that was his heart speaking.

"W'starrah? How can this be?" it was the voice of the fat man from the arena, the Cup of Red. Justin skidded into the chamber to see the Stealthic distracting a cadre of Insectirs, and beyond them a tableau of blood red, pale mist, cracked glass and a horror beyond words.

"Great Cup of Red, I beg you, there is still time!" The Bugs before him made Justin's nerves jump as always, but he saw in the coalescing mist a familiar form that cored his breast and settled his mind.

"Too much time, spirit of the air," the kneeling man replied, still weaving his arms and holding metal wands of some kind in each hand.
216

"An immortal life, nothing left to grasp in earthly wealth or pleasure. Power remains the only object worth my attention. Thank you for your help, and your bartered affections when in the flesh, wanton girl; now hence to the spirit world where you belong."

With that, Justin's course came clear, as his noble training reared up to tell him what to do.

"Ho there, fat man!" Every being in the chamber, even the one without eyes, turned then to behold the intruder. Justin brandished his sword in one hand while the other drew forth the orange gem. "The lady does as she wishes."

He felt a strong immediate urge, to hand over the gem that another might see. And Justin knew it for what it was, the instruction of an enemy.

He dropped the gem and stomped it beneath his boot.

The faceted crystal burst to chips, and the white ant-thing recoiled as if from a mighty blow, squalling from no mouth as the voice in Justin's head cut off. After thrashing the head hard enough to snap the neck-joint, its top segment burst open splattering buckets of milky-grey pieces in all directions as it fell. The remaining Insectirs also roiled and began to swing stupidly in all directions. The Stealthic, laughing, pulled forth an odd weapon like two linked staves and attacked, and Justin was pleased to join him hacking a path toward the Red Cup through limbs and mandibles to both sides.

Carnad Mias, shouting in fear, spun back to face the wall and tapped it rapidly with the metal hammers, not hard, but as if ringing a chime, in a sequence impossible to follow. With each blow the web of cracks across the glassy barrier grew deeper and longer. The Red Cup positioned himself inside a small circle of metal parts just as the last blow touched, and the entire crystalline wall came down with a deep thunderous crash and rush of wind. A tremor passed through the chamber bringing down showers of deep earth and stone; distantly there sounded crashing from the world above.

The Shard Demon stood up with a shrieking, grinding noise like heavy claws on slate, and the cavern was fully illuminated by the sparks that accompanied its movement. With each step, the tremors continued; a tunnel other than the one Justin came in collapsed in a roar of broken rock.

"You are unset, beast! Obey me by the ancient strictures of the Demonbenders, destroy my enemies and fulfill my wish ere I return you to hell and freedom."

Justin stared up at the colossal statue of moving crystal, just making out a toothy maw and the sharp facets of its many edges. The Bugs were down or fled, but what could they do against this monstrosity?

"Too late, lackey of the Emperor! No strength of arms or lore from this age can restrain the Shard Demon."

Justin felt forced to agree. Neither the ring nor the flag he inherited on this mission would be well served by his failure. But then he had not sought this fight in order to live through it. He looked to the ghostly form, and her expression brimmed with love and regret. Even in life she had never been more beautiful, and Justin longed more than anything to join her. But as she turned to face Carnad Mias, Justin saw a change in her that turned his resolve to water.

I thought I couldn't be happier, to see the Captain join me, though I wondered at his speed in arriving. Then when he crushed the Eye and the Blind King died, I remembered how Keilee had been in such danger and my joy notched up a bit higher. Without their leader the Bugs were not difficult to engage: I knew better how to avoid the double-blows of their twin weapons and they fought as if still blinded. The Captain too was a whirlwind, hacking and feinting with remarkable skill. I was glad the city guard didn't have that level of training or my work would be even more difficult.

But we couldn't reach Carnad Mias in time, and as the wall came down I wondered how to make a good ending after all that had happened. Fight here, run away, what difference? All my various disguises, secret caches and tricks amounted to nothing here. I would fence the reputation of every role I'd ever played, to have even a desperate gamble I could try.

But the ghostly form of W'starrah Altieri seemed to have other ideas.

You hear his insults, and see the valiant effort of your Fire Ant and Ferret, and instinctively you know what to do. As you move before the Dragon, you think of your last moments alive, and show to him that body.

Mias cringes in shock and utter horror, at the blood, the hanging flaps of skin and broken bones exposed.

"Stay back! No, I wasn't, keep away from me!"

"You longed for my embrace, Carnad Mias. Come to me now, enjoy what you have created."

As he screams, you can see signs of aging appear on his face, in his hair and skin. Both of you sense, Carnad Mias has been driven by his terror beyond the body-age of his Moment, and into that period when a righteous Elf should choose to die.

And in a way, he does. Shouting and begging in unaccustomed fear, the Red Cup staggers two steps back, placing one boot across the line of the metal circle from which he summoned the Shard Demon.

Before he can think, the creature reaches out and draws him by that leg into a perilous embrace indeed. As Mias screams and chokes and stares at you, the Shard Demon hugs him close, rubbing tender meaty flesh across its many planes of razor sharp glass and slicing him to a half-dozen shanks, bathing itself in dark garnet blood. Mias' torso and head fall to the ground with still a little air to finish a gasping scream, and thus the Dragon dies.

Now remains the Fly, free of its web and ready to rain destruction on your city.

⊕

I gagged at the dismemberment, and a part of me wondered if even such an evil man deserved that death. But more pressing now was the question of this eight-foot glass monster broken free. I ransacked my brain for something to try, and that voice, the one I thought of as Astor himself, had a suggestion.

Why not complete the mission?

I drew out the Brow of the Ecclesiast and ran to where W'starrah floated just a foot above the cavern floor. I couldn't look on the wounds but held it out and said "I believe you asked me to find this."

I could tell she was smiling and when I dared to look she was once again the most beautiful woman I had ever seen. But now the rain of sparks from the monster's advance was driving me back, half-blinded and rolling on the floor just to survive.

Justin saw the Stealthic run forward and followed on, to be what help he could. Perhaps the joints, made of glass, would be weaker; if he could only wound the monster.

W'starrah's ghostly hands took a crown, now glowing, from the man in black and raised it to her head. Immediately she was drenched in flame from head to toe. But Argens' fire did not sear her soul, and as she turned to face the Shard Demon it bellowed in fury, with a shower of cinders and sparks that passed harmlessly through her form.

The fiery ghost spread her arms and floated higher. The temperature of the cavern moved from frozen to furnace, icy water boiling to mist in seconds. Before his eyes, Justin saw the broken slices of thick crystal begin to reform, reflecting the illumination of holy fire and demon spark as they floated into place. Everywhere he saw shards of light, as in moments the barrier reformed. The Shard Demon threw itself against the glass pounding down with barrel-sized fists. A dull deep ringing sound and the cascade of ricocheting sparks were the only results. The cracks began to seal, if anything the barrier looked twice as thick as before. After one crackling roar of fury laced with anguish, the prisoner settled slowly back to earth, reaching down to snatch up a few gobbets of flesh that had once been the Red Cup of Cryssigens, a meal to last the centuries as it spat out sparks and returned to waiting.

The flames faded when she lifted the crown from her head and returned it to me. Once again she resembled the dazzling light of the world, untorn and joyous, still floating above the ground but filled with happy purpose. I bowed to her before receiving the Brow, its glow gone and cool to the touch.

"Dear brave, clever Ferret, you have served me well beyond all imagining. May your reward exceed payment, but be sure to apply for what we contracted when all is well above. I entrust this crown to you, for safekeeping."

"Thank you, milady," I whispered, thinking hard. "I believe I know just where to put it."

She turned to the Captain then, and the look on her face was unmistakable. It was time to make myself scarce, and fortunately for me that is one of my best things.

⊕

Justin looked up at the floating form of the most beautiful woman he had ever known, dropping his sword and frantically wiping at his face, no doubt from the reforming condensation of the chamber.

"My Captain, my heart, how I have ill-used you." Justin fancied he could see her outline more clearly now that she had passed through the flames. Unable to restrain old habits he reached to kiss her hand. Though his fingers felt nothing, he thought his lips just brushed a warmth, a softness, and the eternal scent of jasmine.

"Hearing of your death, W'starrah, I sought out my own. But nothing I plan seems to go as it should."

Her laughter was as misty as her form, yet warm and alive. "This feeling is among many we share, my love. Though the sight of the future was Argens' gift to me I, could never have foreseen the way his vision would be enacted. All had a part to play, even our enemies."

Justin could not think clearly engaged in such eerie banter. His longing cut through him more deeply than any wound sustained in battle. He fought again to keep the tears from his face, and could not imagine how to spend the next hour.

His love saw him and reached to caress his face with ghostly hands that he must have imagined were tingling across his skin. "Dear Captain, I am sorry our games, my pride and ambition, have brought us here. But I have sworn to love you all my life and beyond. This is all I can offer now."

With those words Justin saw a tiny crack of light into a future world, and felt the stirrings of ambition to widen it. "The choice is simple, milady. I may endure this life with you, or any other without you. I am content to abide where my heart has lain since I first saw your face and heard your voice. If Argens should grant that we speak in future, rest assured I shall be at your disposal then, as I had hoped to be of service to you in the past."

"And if not," he tried to continue but the words stuck. W'starrah's ghost rushed close to him then, her arms comprising a feathery embrace and her words like a whisper in his ear.

"I shall always be with you, my Captain. Whatever you come to love, wherever you assign your service, there I shall be also."

Justin closed his eyes for a long moment, and when he looked again into the cavern, to judge only by earthly vision, he was alone.

⊕ ⊕ ⊕

Epilogue

𝕸 'nesa Zetee knocked at the temple-tower door and brushed down his new uniform to look its best. The weather had warmed more than expected in the short week since he had earned this doublet and sash. While the badge over his heart declared his new employer, the dekentar's double-bars on his shoulder seemed to him a matching accent and a resume`. Others would notice them, and remember who they were dealing with.

The portal opened and M'nesa bowed before the elegantly beautiful elderly preacher within. "Heaven's Eye Ekaterinye, I am sent to inquire—"

"Please, good guardsman," she interrupted with a hand on his arm, "call me Kat. I am not used to my new title."

M'nesa smiled. "Not an uncommon problem, Reverend Myster. My commander sends to know if repairs are proceeding well on your tower and the temple grounds."

"Very well indeed, won't you come in sir."

"With regret, I have many rounds to make. But the Cliff Grip has instructed me to say that you need only inquire."

"He has been most kind, I assure you. May we expect you at service this evening, dekentar?"

"I believe we are assigned a rotation, Reverend Myster. To avoid the imputation of favoritism."

The lady's laughter was musical and most engaging, M'nesa thought, not unlike his grandmother who passed when he was still a boy.

From the garden path came Tanar'h with his guards, carrying tools and a sack of seed.

"The dekentar will always be welcome here, when his orders allow." The two men gripped arms and M'nesa felt again the thrill of their shared risk, just a few nights ago. He looked up at the tower shutters still shattered, and across the grounds to places where things broken and burned were being rebuilt and replanted.

M'nesa nodded to Tanar'h's guards while the two preachers discussed the preaching schedule. Tamess and Jal'i seemed a bit subdued now, though they'd gotten to know this guardsman well from his previous visits. M'nesa looked closely and realized they each lacked the bright Yellow braid they'd worn before their city shivered and cracked. Some House Colors had suffered more than just the loss of men and treasure that night.

Just then Tanar'h brought the subject of riches into his own conversation.

"I cannot say I approve, h-Heaven's Eye," he stumbled a moment, "this level of expenditure without account. Twenty thousand silver pieces?"

"I did not fully understand her purpose," the teacher responded gently, "though it had to do with the search for the Brow of the Ecclesiast."

"Which remains missing, to judge from your face, Kat,"

Ekaterinye shrugged with a small smile. "That may not have been the commission, High Heart. But it was her final wish expressed to me. I believe we were compelled to honor it."

"Yes, well of course, I agree we should always bear tribute to her memory." He fretted a moment, then burst out, "Never mind what, but to whom! This ridiculous business of a mysterious messenger, letters of credit, several banks in other sections of the city."

Tanar'h stopped when Kat's laughter interrupted him, glared a moment, then remembered M'nesa standing there and broke into a grin.

"Our Hawk still has his talons," she rallied with a hand on his shoulder, "let all who threaten the nest beware!"

Tanar'h laughed then, bowed to his peer and gripped arms with M'nesa before leaving.

"My thanks once again, dekentar, for the help you and your captain provided this temple."

"It was your stratagem, Reverend Myster, which won the night. All the city speaks of it, and of your prodigious miracle."

"Nonsense, a trick that can never work a second time. As for her funeral," he paused and still did not mention the lady's name, "I was happy to serve, even so late."

"It is never too late to serve," M'nesa agreed before saluting and stepping off. There were plenty more doors to knock on today, before the new recruits arrived to be vetted. No sense letting Tass have all the fun.

⊕

I no longer jumped when someone knocked at my door. I was so absorbed, in fact—in paperwork, of all things—they had to knock again before I noticed. My idle thought about actually selling stone to customers had blossomed marvelously, in the week since a tenth of the city's buildings came down around folks' ears. Jonn Simith had more work than he knew what to do with: Feldspar, relegated to the background for days on end, had sulked off to a distant corner of my mind. As I rose from my desk and walked through the antechamber, I heard Keilee bustling in my kitchen, and realized it must be later than I expected.

I opened the door, and the Stealthic came rushing back to the front in an instant. There stood Kama.

"You!" I shouted, "What are, that is, em, hello."

Kama cocked his head slightly, taken aback. "Have we met sir?"

"Why no, or I should say, I em, I saw you, Reverend Myster, in the plaza, that night, I was there. At the, em funeral as it were?"

He nodded but took in my eyes a moment and I wondered if he knew.

"I have been directed here with a question. You are citizen Simith?"

"Won't you come in, that is, won't you all come in." I only now noticed that my savior and nemesis was not alone. Two men dressed in desert garb, one tall and the other short, stood at his shoulders looking rather haggard but on the whole much healthier and happier than they had been that night.

"Right this way, won't you take a—oh no, not that one, still broken, here try this chair sir. Gentlemen, will you not sit? I have plenty of seats as you can see."

The two men shook their heads and Kama sighed.

"This is Elehar and this Sanhim, once of the Bedou-uu. They have conceived themselves obligated to me, in the way of their people, and now insist on serving as my guards."

I shook hands with them both and noted how the smaller man still favored his left arm. But his gaze was clear and while he hardly seemed well rested, sleep looked like it was a possibility again for him.

Sitting at my desk, I turned again to Kama and began the dance.

"So then, holy sir, you said you had, em, a question for me?"

"It is this, citizen Simith. I have received a donation of building supplies for my chapel. Really quite a staggering one, in fact, a dozen large pallets and mortar. Together with a crew of laborers and a mason to oversee them. All paid for through the season, the man tells me, and no one seems to know the slightest thing about where it all comes from."

"Ah. Ah. So it is, in fact, anonymous?" Playing dumb was second nature to me, I enjoyed it more than I should have.

"Precisely. I was hoping to discover and properly thank the benefactor, yet when I inquired I was stupefied by the maze of arrangements that had been made. I have visited four banks and credit houses, consulted with the Mason's Guild, and asked everyone I know for a lead, coming no closer to a clue than when I started. But your name came up several times, as someone knowledgeable about such supplies. I was hoping you might have an answer for me."

"Such an interesting puzzle! I wish, that is I tell you honestly sir, I have been paid by no person to arrange such a substantial order." I gestured at the papers on my desk. "Business has certainly been brisk, but I feel certain I should have remembered."

Kama nodded and looked down in disappointment. This was better than gifting at Darksebb, I had to tone down my smile to something less wicked.

"Is it, em, a complete order then? Nothing missing, that is, your crew able to work well?"

"The chapel grows at frightening speed, I have never seen anything like it." Kama sounded sincere but I saw in his face something almost sad. He probably hated to feel obligated.

"I am deeply disappointed to be of so little use to you. Ah but here is some tea, thank you Keilee." I was just as pleased as surprised when she tottered in with a tray of mugs, and took a cup with a nod like the lord of the manor as she moved around concentrating on the job.

"You are too kind sir, thank you."

"Oh nonsense, Reverend Myster, I'm sure it is I who hold a debt to you. I was after all there when you cast that miraculous circle of light, which em, that cut off that lunatic's spell." It was harder to make up speeches that came close to the truth like this but I felt strangely impelled to try and cheer him up. "Indeed, there is most likely the source of your mystery. Why, there could not have been less than five thousand persons in the great plaza that night, and one of them a nobleman, who wishes to show his appreciation."

"Anonymously?"

"Yes, yes of course anonymously. You are new to our great city, sir, that is, or so I understand. From what people have said. You will find it a web, Reverend Myster, a veritable maze of obligations and ties, alliances and what not. You represent a new religion, indeed? And those with great power… with resources, as it were, they are already, ahm, already constrained and must sometimes act in secret."

At this, Kama's face rose and brightened. "You mean, someone who needs to hide his face."

I felt stabbed in the groin and choked on my tea. "Why yes, rather a nice way to put it."

"Of course," he mused half to himself. "That's why the one stone… why did I not guess." I was sure I knew what he meant and had to order my lips to stay down at the ends.

Kama rose and extended his arm. "I thank you, citizen Simith, for helping me see the solution here."

"At all events," I replied rising to show the way out, "you needn't question such largesse, sir. A favor given in secret need trigger no obligation. Indeed, I would guess the patron feels he, as it were, is discharging a debt."

"No doubt," Kama nodded. "If you will excuse me, I must return to the mason and issue some instructions now. Thank you again for your time, citizen, and I hope we may see you at service once the chapel is complete."

"I thank you, Reverend. From what I hear, sir, you will have no shortage of visitors." I turned to his two guardsmen as they shouldered past. "All fortune to you as well, em, sirs."

The tall one turned quickly back to me at that.

"Wish me no fortune, sir! Elehar and I would have done with great luck, for the one kind has led us only to the other for almost a year now."

I was amazed at the lyric language the fellow used, then stunned when his companion joined in.

"First our band of brothers," the short one muttered, "mighty and hale, destroyed in a trice, by those accursed adventurers."

"Aye, we alone survive and nearly starve, only to find that horrid torc! We thought our luck had turned up then, eh Elehar?"

"We should have been forewarned, Sanhim, since the corpse where we found it was clearly one of those same adventurers, a Stealthic no less."

"Ah, a Stealthic!" I was chilled but intrigued. "Nothing good to come from such men, I'm sure."

His friend in response could only whisper. "And when it transpired that the cursed thing could grant our wishes…"

His tall partner continued, "We believed, fools both, that we would be lords among men. But it only dragged us down, the cursed relic. Then we came across the monk. And since then, our lives were indeed a misery until a week ago. I longed for death, by my sire it is true."

I had always known there was more to their story, and felt sure there was much more indeed to tell.

"And now," Elehar said, rubbing his arm, "we are fortunate beyond all men, to live, and to have found healing with this great man. Our deaths before his harm, as long as we live."

"And may we have no further 'fortune' until our days have ended." Sanhim concluded fervently.

I looked to Kama who shrugged eloquently, smiled, and turned to leave with his new bodyguard in tow. I was very happy to see that, for indeed the little man needed protection in a nest of rats like Cryssigens. He knew, I guessed, how much he would be protecting us all in the future, by keeping our little secret. Almost I regretted keeping my part of that secret from him. But things being what they were, Feldspar would likely visit the chapel of Telhol again someday, and perhaps even incur a new debt.

As a Stealthic I only did favors for others, with wealth and fame as my rewards. All Feldspar's deeds were in the end anonymous, his praise coming in song, not in person. But real people, they formed ties. The owed each other, they kept in touch, they made sure. Feldspar was afraid of no knife or trap, but he still wanted me away from such dangerous notions. Let him be afraid, that would keep him sharp. Jonn Simith was coming to like being alive.

From inside Keilee shouted "Dinner!"

"Ah excellent, Keilee, you are saving me from a horrid death. By, em, paperwork. I am in your debt."

$$\oplus$$

"Quit!" Hansen roared. "You can't just up and leave the Imperial Cadre, you carking traitor!"

Justin felt the ring buzzing cool on his finger, while a shimmering window inside the Fire Grip's office showed him Morinack the Emperor's Hand as well as Hansen his former boss.

"I have not left Argens, Commander," he replied with an effort to keep the emotion from his voice. "For indeed as you ordered on my mission, the North Mark is not, in fact, in rebellion. May I have the honor to present milord Gaspar Heugen, regent of Cryssigens and the man voted to become next Overlord of the Mark." Justin half-turned and bowed to indicate Heugen, standing in his dress Blue uniform and badge-sash of office, who nodded curtly.

"Milord Heugen," Morinack said mildly, "I am pleased to make your personal acquaintance."

"Meaning, you have sent other spies before this one, to scout out my life and position."

"Certainly," Morinack returned with a grin, "probably thousands."

This brought a tight smile and nod from Heugen.

"We congratulate you on achieving your position and look forward to your visit, to make the customary show of fealty to the Emperor Yula."

"I am co-ruler only, Emperor's Hand," Heugen replied with a raised palm, "My marriage to Kitari Creel, by our agreement, will seal the pact voted jointly by the nobles and people of the North. We shall rule this Mark in concert in all matters."

"We would be delighted to host you both, of course."

"Of course. Tell the dwarf I shall marry, and then ascend, and then pay my visit to Argens. As I find the time."

The Halfling nodded his full understanding. "No doubt, milord, there is much to do." Justin saw in Morinack's grin that they anticipated no visit from Cryssigens ever.

"Never mind this nonsense!" Hansen cracked, "You can't take my officer from me, I need him. Justin, I order you back to the capital at once."

This was the moment Justin dreaded. Squaring up with his helmet under one arm he adjusted his new sash of office and faced his superior officer.

"Commander, it is my duty to report that the mission you entrusted to me is now completed. I have milord Heugen's assurance that he plans no rebellion against the throne of Argens—"

"Under current circumstances," Heugen put in.

"—and thus I submit my resignation from the Imperial Cadre, effective immediately."

"Cark me!" Hansen thundered and Justin was taken aback at the implied compliment. "First I hear from Morinack here, some gorgeous woman pleading for help, says your life is in danger. Before I can even get the cavalry together, we see you standing here quitting on us. I knew you were good, Justin, but who shall I send to the Far Mark now, I need to—"

The Halfling raised one hand and the strapping human Commander cut off in mid word. "We shall not trouble to inquire too closely of your motives, Captain. I thank you for your previous service to the Empire and am glad to see you well."

"Probably bedding down that woman the moment we stop talking," Hansen muttered. Justin felt a pang at that but held his face still. No need to respond if the only stakes were his reputation. Honor mattered. Resigning mattered.

After a moment, Hansen shook his head and looked up with a grin. "I'm glad you're still alive. Keep the helmet. And the ring—don't worry, Overlord, its magic ends with this third use."

"Perhaps," Morinack said quietly with his face intent, "we shall meet again after all." With a slight bow, he removed his ax-ring and the window disappeared.

Justin spun to salute his new superior, who returned it but looked askance at the matching ring.

"How am I to trust that this sorcery is ended now?"

Justin tried to face the thought of taking it off and something within him stiffened. "I have their word, milord. And you have mine. The ring I shall keep, as a memento."

Without waiting for a response he strode to the window overlooking the city's temple district. He saw a crew of workmen at the Telholian chapel already raising the walls around the first floor, with the foundation pit filled and tiles being laid. A small man, the preacher he believed, was at work on the inside while the others labored beyond the wall. The distance should have prevented him noticing, but Justin felt a feathery touch at his chin, caressing and directing him to watch closely. He saw with interest that one column-stone had a niche carved in it, and the preacher was carefully placing something circular wrapped in cloth within, before troweling facing-plaster across the hole. Secrets everywhere, he mused: at least he had heard good things about this fellow's character.

"With the Shard Demon again contained," Heugen spoke from his desk still covered with reports, "the city's rebuilding is progressing well. I need my City Grip to keep order and tolerate no nonsense among the guilds and Cups, holding up deliveries or extorting unfair prices at such a time." Heugen looked up. "Fortunate for me, to have a man I can trust, without House ties for such a job."

"You may rely on me, milord. And my request for new recruits?"

"Of course, whichever you need up to eight dekents. I've taken the liberty of bringing in a few men we can trust."

Justin's inner sense rose up at that, and he crossed the room to look down on the inner courtyard where his surviving company and officers drilled in their new uniforms, while a crowd of onlooking soldiers stood by.

"With thanks, milord, I have developed methods for testing admission to my company."

Heugen's face hardened at this. "I won't tolerate disloyalty under my command, City Grip."

It was a statement intended to cow and isolate, but the new Mark of Cryssigens saw only that Justin smiled, putting his ring-hand to his shoulder as if someone else were comforting him there.

"I'm pleased you approve the concept, milord Mark. Neither will I, you see."

He waited a moment while Heugen registered surprise, and then a grudging nod of respect.

"You may review your estate and holdings after the city is in order."

"Estate?"

Heugen looked surprised. "Of course, Commander, city offices are part of the noble order. You have the use of a manor in the eastern quarter, and lands beyond the plateau tithe to you for the usual upkeep." He smiled like a cat. "Or did you simply take the job for the work it entails? You are a nobleman again, Commander Thyme."

Justin's head whirled as if he flew again at a great height. A foef! And a house in the city, it was too much to take in. Hundreds of miles from the Imperial Domain and the lands of his departed father, he had indeed found a new home, in the city of his love. Departed? Not in any way that mattered.

"May I congratulate you on your impending wedding, milord Mark."

"An extraordinary woman," Heugen said almost to himself. "All these years I avoided having to write that damnable poem! And now…" He looked at Justin squarely, sharing a man's thoughts. "She will rule beside me, we've discussed the matter and nothing else makes sense. Every day she will push for policies that put me further in trouble—wants to bring back the Demonbender worship for one thing. They'll surely be happy with that in Argens! Fully expect to fight with her every single day. About how to rule, that is." His face softened, for the first time in Justin's acquaintance. "I would not have said this a month ago, Justin, but I hope you find such a partner to guide you. To challenge you."

Justin swallowed and bowed, saying only "I have, milord," before striding out and down to the parade grounds with his heart too full for further words. He wore the ring for good reason.

On the level stone of the courtyard he saw Kein Trador, recently returned from Tralmachia, speaking to a man dressed all in grey, while Chaktha loomed nearby. The stranger nodded, offered his arm to the dekentar, then looked up to the gallows by the wall. After a single moment, he donned his hat and spun to leave the palace, followed by the giant black. Trador hustled up to report, while Tass ambled over with his usual lack of concern and jaunty grin.

"Who was that fellow, Trador?"

"A traveler, Commander, he asked me to confirm the rumors that the undead walked in Tralmachia. He says now he has work to do."

"You left the Baron secure, so whatever that man intends he'll be Sordinay T'yr's problem. Alright, Tass, let's recruit."

Walking before his own men at attention, Justin nodded to them, nearly threescore hardened veterans of Imperial training who had been through horrors unknown in recent history. Every story they told, in the inns off duty or to women they courted, would add to the legend of the Emperor's men who defeated all odds and ate monsters for breakfast. Beyond their ranks he approached a gang of hundreds more, waiting for him to select some of their number. They came to attention as he arrived with Tass and Kein at his shoulders.

"The City Guard is recruiting two dekents to join my company for special detail work. I doubt very seriously if five in ten of you will qualify." Justin looked to Tass, who grinned and held up two fingers. "Probably less," he amended.

"Those who try and fail lose no honor in my eyes. But any soldier under my command who disobeys orders, who uses his uniform or weapons to harm the innocent or to cover his cowardice, will wind up in the same place as those two rapists and thieves up there." Everyone looked to the gallows to see the very real effect of justice done: Justin had only read the report of men who had threatened W'starrah Altieri, and belatedly recalled the grey man whose testimony had led to their doom. Perhaps if that one came back to Cryssigens he could thank him. He thought he would love to have Chaktha in his company if he returned. Perhaps someday.

"You will fall out to be tested by my dekentar here. Prepare for disappointment, most of you, and bruises the rest."

"Commander," one yelled out, "what about Colors then?"

Justin spotted flashes of Blue, some Orange and even one or two of Purple among the candidates. He knew the City Guard had leaned toward Gaspar Heugen's Color till now, and it was time to nip this problem aborning.

"The only color I care about," he roared loud enough for the city to hear, "is white. The same shade of the flag waved by anyone who defies the City Guard of Cryssigens!"

The palace echoed with a cheer nearly strong enough to break glass. Justin thought about one crystal barrier in particular, far below his feet, and the deathless beauty who put it there. From nowhere at all a breeze brought him the scent of jasmine, and Justin settled in to watch Tass bouting the recruits, and to dream yet again of the orders not yet given.

The End

GLOSSARY

Altair Way	street	main thoroughfare of Cryssigens
Ancient	language	tongue of heroes, dragons and beings of power; mortals may not lie when using it
Areghel	hero	first king of the Percentalion, hero of martial wizards
Argens	city	capital city of the Southern Empire, on the central western coast, named for its hero
Argens Demonbender		hero-aspect, major form of devotion to Argens, currently outlawed, emphasizing sorcerous lore and mastery of demons
Argens Hopeforger		hero-aspect, major form of devotion to Argens, emphasizing courage, light and leadership
Argens Stargazer		hero-aspect, major form of devotion to Argens, emphasizing foresight and love
Argensian Empire		aka the Southlands, vast Elven Empire established by Argens, capital city also named Argens
Astor	hero	Perilsgroom, hero of Stealthics from ancient days
Bald Top	mountain	small loaf-shaped mountain the border hills
Battle of Broken Chains		Dolphin 2001 ADR, first victory of the rebellion over Loyalist forces of the North Mark
Battle of the Razor		pivotal battle of ancient times, Despair was ejected from the Lands forever in the year 0 ADR
Battle of Tor Perite		site of decisive battle (Serpent, 2001 ADR) that defeated Viridian XXVII and put Yula I on the throne of Argens
Bedou-uu	race	desert dwelling nomads of the Shimmering Mindsea
bought badge	phrase	insulting term for an officer who purchased a commission he could not earn
Brow of the Ecclesiast		artefact, mystic crown with fabulous powers, burns the unworthy wearer

centar		unit of soldiers, ten dekents = 100 men
Cesmir	barony	southern barony of the North Mark
cestus	weapon	spiked metal glove used by gladiators
Charnel Testing		an attempt to wear the Brow of the Ecclesiast, which results in death by burning for the unworthy
Conar	city	capital of the kingdom of Men, named for its hero
Cryssians	sect	devotees of Cryss Altair
Cryssigens	city	capital city of the North Mark, wealthy and Color-ful
Dagnaluviran	song	heroic tale of love between Dagnar and Elosira
dekent		unit of soldiers, one dekent equals ten men (led by a dekentar)
dekentar		junior officer's rank in the army or guards
Devouting Sinter		monastery of holy men in Gaden, bordering the Shimmering Mindsea
Earthcut River		runs through Gaden and Cesmir to the Western Sea
Ekhonon	hero	second son of Conar, judgement and architecture
Exemplars	hero	minor heroes of ancient times
Far Mark		recently recolonized duchy of the Argensian Empire, next to the Swords of Stone
Fire Grip	title	City Commander of Cryssigens, regent of the Mark in the absence of the Overlord
Flame of the First		mild oath, reference to Argens who caught a slice of the Sun in his hand
Gaden	barony	east-central barony of the North Mark
Gelvorging Deep		thick forested area, unsettled and hiding bandits or monsters
glassteel		clear substance harder than metal
Grog's Lees	tavern	modest, in The Boards neighborhood of Cryssigens
Highforge	title	rank given to the Preacher worthy of the Brow of the Ecclesiast
Horn of the Serpent		relic of those devoted to Khoirah the Betrayer, stolen by Trekelny and now lost (*see Three Minutes to Midnight*)

House Cups	title	heads of various Colors in Cryssigens, wielding great wealth and influence
Ides of the Dolphin		date, mid-point of the 2nd month, 15th
Imperial Domain		barony, gorgeous settled lands adjacent to Argens and direct vassalage to the Emperor
Insectir	monster	giant bug creatures, repugnant to Elves
intakta volar	language	in Ancient: I wish for healing
kemetaria	feature	burial ground, a Despairing practice to put bodies under the earth instead of cremation
Khoirah	anti-hero	the Betrayer, third son of Conar who treated with Despair in ancient times
lith	drug	performance enhancing, addictive, poisonous
Ma-Eldar	hero	Hopelord of Elves, father of Argens
Master of Horse		leader of all Imperial cavalry
North Mark		northern duchy of Argens, with a history of rebellion; capital city Cryssigens
noun-chakas	weapon	two wooden hafts connected by a few links of chain
Nubian	race	tall black Men living in the Southern jungle, fearsome warriors
odd as three feet		phrase, reference to demonic creatures, meaning something is very strange or unexpected
Old City		northeastern quarter of Cryssigens, once wealthy but long since abandoned
Overlord	title	aka North Mark, title of the ruler of that duchy
Palace o. t. Sun	castle	Emperor's dwelling in Argens' capital
Patriarch	title	church leader in a nation or great city
pentadek		unit of soldiers, five dekents = 50 men
piazzo		center of abandoned Old Cryss, open paved area with temples and more
Ring of Peace	miracle	Telholian invocation creating a no-magic, no-violence zone
Salva Way		bordering the piazzo in Old Cryss
Scapegrace Street		bordering the piazzo in Old Cryss
Shard Demon	monster	held prisoner beneath the palace in Cryssigens

Shimmering Mindsea		large sandy desert between Argens and the Swords of Stone
silversteel		magical metal, unbreakable and rare
somnos	drug	induces sleep
Son of the Sun	title	honorific title for the Emperor, successor to Argens
strategos	title	senior officer's rank in the army or guard
Sun Throne		Emperor's throne in Argens, also a reference to the Emperor's rank
Tamar	city	small trading city about a day's journey from Cryssigens
Telhol	hero	fourth son of Conar, hero of peace and healing
Tepid River		separates Cryssigens from the Old City on its way to the Western Sea
The Boards		poor neighborhood in Cryssigens bordering the River Cryss
Tralmachia	barony	northernmost barony of the North Mark, mountainous and isolated
Viper	sect	secret police under Viridian, now outlawed

Shards of Light I: The Ring and the Flag

A Sword and Sorcery novel from the Lands of Hope.

In 2002 ADR, the jewel of the southern empire is the city of Cryssigens, where life is an unending carnival of display, while intrigue brews beneath the surface. Nobles, guilds and House Cups scheme with and against each other, even in the best of times. But civil war stripped the city of its Overlord, and now factions emerge daring all in a bid to succeed to the throne.

Newly-graduated imperial officer Justin is convinced he has no future, and hearing the details of the secret mission he's assigned for the Emperor won't change his mind. Civil War threatens the North Mark. Justin must race against time to form a company, and lead his men into the center of the web; but what happens when his loyalty to the Empire means the death of those who follow him?

available as eBook and in print
ISBN 978-3-95681-094-7

SHARDS OF LIGHT II: FENCING REPUTATION

A Sword and Sorcery novel from the Lands of Hope.

When the elven lords, preachers and merchants of Cryssigens need wrongs righted without clues, they look for the stealthic Feldspar to solve their problems. But the legend without a face is hard to find: and when Feldspar takes a commission from the most famous, and beautiful, priestess in the city, he finds problems of his own piling up, and is forced to choose between Hope and safety.

available as eBook and in print
ISBN 978-3-95681-095-4

SHARDS OF LIGHT III: PERILOUS EMBRACES

A Sword and Sorcery novel from the Lands of Hope.

One of the leading lights of Cryssigensian society is W'starrah Altieri, the Lavender Lady, high-ranking priestess of the sect of Argens Stargazer; while others see only her dazzling beauty her eyes are filled with foreknowledge of the future. She willingly risks life and reputation to save her city, but juggling visions, rivals, suitors and the occasional assassin pushes the real world further from her grasp. Who could expect that in the midst of this she would meet the promised love of her life, or foresee that he too is doomed?

available as eBook and in print
ISBN 978-3-95681-096-1

THE PLANE OF DREAMS

A standalone novel from the Lands of Hope

In the southern empire of Argens just roiled by the rebellion of Yula, a band of adventurers returns from the Shimmering Mindsea bearing enormous treasure and minus one of its members. The Tributarians, unaware of the growing threat to the waking world, embark on separate plans. But the spirit of the hero lives on in all of them, as their good deeds have consequences beyond their original intention. Will it be enough to avert the peril they have unwittingly brought about?

This first epic-length tale set in the Lands of Hope features a complex world and intelligent, dedicated characters whose actions entwine over distances and beyond their own comprehension. Like any world worth living in, the Lands have humor, mystery, horror and action to delight and entertain the reader.

available as eBook and in print
ISBN 978-3-95681-066-4

Judgement's Tale
The Full Omnibus

Two millenia of peace are coming to an end.

For twenty centuries the Lands of Hope prospered from their Heroes' peace, but suffer now from their absence. Chaos grows in the central kingdom of the Lands of Hope known as the Percentalion. Even the bravest adventurers seem unable to travel in or out safely. The sundered populations are trapped there, beyond communication and without hope.

Worse yet, the liche Wolga Vrule plots escape from his extra-worldly prison to unleash a tide of undeath, and enlists the Earth Demon Kog, who ruled the Percentalion millennia ago, as an uneasy ally.

On the western coast of the Lands of Hope, Solemn Judgement comes ashore, having journeyed with his father across the ocean. Solemn arrives both a stranger and and orphan, driven to complete the lore his father died to give him. Will he discover Wolga Vrule's plan in time to prevent the return of Despair?

available as eBook and in print
ISBN 978-3-95681-066-4

THE EYE OF KOG
A Sequel to Judgement's Tale

A standalone novel from the Lands of Hope

A Force of Ancient Despair Stirs Again and twenty centuries of peace in the Lands of Hope are shattered. But in the chaotic Percentalion, evil's return goes unnoticed by all but a few. The grim young scholar Solemn Judgement, sails and walks a circuit of the northern kingdoms, in search of lore to fend off the plague of undeath. Meanwhile, the Woodsman Treaman struggles to guide his adventuring party to safety, but instead encounters deep loss and inherits a quest to pit all of their lives against desperate odds.

The demon Kog, formerly ruler of these lands, searches for his lost Eye which will render him again invincible. His uneasy ally, the liche Wolga Vrule, schemes to expand his undead army and overwhelm the unsuspecting kingdoms in his own bid for power. What part can a discovered scepter or a missing crown, a dwindling holy order of knights, a ghoul-guarded tomb, or an ancient prophecy play in the chance to ward off such threats?

The quest begun in Judgement's Tale reaches its climax

available as eBook and in print
ISBN 978-3-95681-082-4